PARAHUMAN...

Humanity is changing…

HANNAH HOARE

A Wild Wolf Publication

Published by Wild Wolf Publishing in 2023
Copyright © 2023 Hannah Hoare

All rights reserved. No part of this book may be reproduced, stored in a retrieval system or transmitted in any form or by any means without the prior written permission of the publishers, except by a reviewer who may quote brief passages in a review to be printed by a newspaper, magazine or journal.

First print

ISBN: 9798385944996
Also available as an E-book

www.wildwolfpublishing.com

"I look about me at my fellow men. And I go in fear. I see faces keen and bright, others dull or dangerous, others unsteady, insincere; none that have the calm authority of a reasonable soul. I feel as though the animal was surging up through them…"
~ H. G. Wells, *The Island of Doctor Moreau*

"We wanted to replace God, but how can we know what is best for mankind when we are no more than men ourselves?"
~ Doctor Jean-Luc Tati, *Confession*

To my grandmother, Judy Cawthorn: for her support, encouragement, and for letting me turn her spare room into a writing studio for the creation of this novel.

PART ONE: THE CIVILISED WORLD

It's evening when I arrive at the cabins, but the sunlight still lingers. I can trace the desert all the way to the horizon.

Having only experienced the westerly side of the mountain before, I'm not sure what I expected to find on the other side. Certainly not this: miles and miles of untouched, unsullied sand, stretching out like a blank canvas from here to a distant line where the sky meets the land. The only signs of human life: two wooden cabins (evidently built by quite a craftsman, I might add – I could not have done much better myself), about a mile or so from the mountain's base. One is the size of a very small cottage. The other, smaller still, faces it, and was perhaps once a workroom or storage for whoever inhabited the larger building. Or even a guesthouse. Yes: the way it is set up – makeshift kitchenette in the corner by the door, desk gently sagging beneath the tiny single window, sun-stained refrigerator peeking from under a bookshelf - someone could easily live here.

Both buildings are equally dead. No lights on in the windows, no sounds coming from within. After lengthy consideration... I take the smaller building.

The door whines gratefully open when I nudge it. As I step over the threshold, clouds of captive dust mob me. Cling to my eyes. Flood my throat. I choke and claw it away. As my eyes clear, I take in the space: somehow bigger and brighter than it had appeared through the grimy window, the furniture touched with gold from the setting sun. Eight staggering strides take me from the door to the desk – that makes it eighteen feet across, I think, assuming my stride has remained the same length. Good. I don't think I could stand another cage.

I unpack alone. It crosses my mind as I do this that, even though I have been lonely before, this is the first time in my life that I will ever be properly **alone**. What happens to Katrina when she is alone? It is bound to affect my mind somehow. Perhaps a stronger, smarter new me will rise, unrestrained, out of the chaos and confusion? That's something to look forward to.

I loosen the straps and detach the Portable CryoBag from my back. My shoulders ache from the weight, but I manage to lower the bulky synthetic cube softly to the floor, then push it gently into the shadiest corner. Its whirring seems louder now, in the silence of the cabin: an infant's cry.

I put the rusty little chain across the splintering front door. Draw the curtains across the small single window. I line up my test tubes – twenty-six of them, all fresh out of the packet - along the dusty wooden desk. This will be my work station.

I find items in my lab-coat pockets which I can't remember taking. I remove them one-by-one and line them up on the desk. Three pens, ten half-melted Hershey's Kisses which I must have nabbed from the laboratory kitchen, and an old-style cassette tape. I peer at the name scribbled in ballpoint on the label.

It is Alexander Bai's.

I throw it across the room where it shatters against the wall, the film lolling from the plastic like a dead animal's tongue. I hiss at the pieces.

Food far from my mind, I investigate the kitchenette with logical detachment. It consists of an old solar-powered Eco-Kettle, a jar of instant coffee, and a little fridge-freezer: broken. But I think I can fix it-

Of course I can fix it! There are five days of power left in the CryoBag. This will be plenty until I can get the proper freezer working again. It will.

I close my eyes and think the words, just in case Alexander Bai can hear me telepathically. I have to let him know that wherever he is, no matter how hard he tries to stop me, I have things under cont-

The dead cassette. Its film sticking out. Mocking me.

I shrug off my lab-coat, throw it over the cassette, and let the dying sunlight warm my naked body for a moment. Then I make myself a cup of instant coffee (the Eco-Kettle had a little stale water and some power left in it) and take it over to the corner of the room where I sit against the wall with my legs bunched up to my chest. Focus on strong thoughts.

Any emotions I am feeling now – they're wrong. All my misery has been left on the other side of the mountain. A new, stronger animal is leaning against the wall of this cabin, head against the boards and eyes on the ceiling, waiting in the dark for the sun to rise.

CHAPTER ONE
TWO YEARS BEFORE

A dream, or perhaps a memory, comes to me as I lie on the cabin floor, drifting between sleep and consciousness...

Somewhere in the Pacific Ocean, under a clear blue sky and with the calm blue water rocking and swaying all around her, back and forth, back and forth, beautifully, mindlessly – stands a girl on a raft.

Look. Can you see her?

The raft is an oddity. A Frankenstein's monster of logs, twigs, clay, reeds – things you could find anywhere on an island, in a forest or by a beach, say – and parts of what looks like a cannibalized boat: a board here, a rope there, an oar resting along the back of the raft for balance, ready to use should the wind stop blowing. It looks as if it has been pieced together in a hurry, but not in a frenzy. Patchworked and unsymmetrical though it may be, it has clearly been assembled by somebody with a sufficient level of structural expertise, a good eye for mechanics - and a great deal of intelligence.

A mast from the cannibalized boat sticks out from the body of the raft at only a very slight tilt. The girl is gripping this with one small, sun-darkened, leathery hand, fingers stiff and curled. She holds her right arm out for balance. Her legs are apart. Her arms swing back slightly with the forward momentum of the vessel; other than this, she barely moves at all. Even her face is static, frozen in an unreadable, dead expression. But to me, her thoughts are obvious: this raft is in a delicate state of balance. Any movement, even of the facial muscles, and it could capsize. She does not want to die. Not now she has come so far.

Her clothes are unusual. Well, by your standards. A long dress which was clearly supposed to be ankle-length on somebody much taller than herself. It pools around her feet, so she has tied it at the back to stop it from getting wet and dragging her underwater. It is a mix of yellow, pale grey, and the subtlest touch of moss-green. It could have once been white.

On its own, the neck of the dress would have been immodestly low, but the girl has had sense enough to pin it at the top with the only other piece of manmade adornment on her body: a brooch of plain, tarnished metal, in the shape of a crucifix. The head of the crucifix is pointing down, towards the sea. It was the easiest position to pin it.

Other than this, nothing. No shoes, no jacket. Just a small leather bag, aged, pungent and damp, strapped across her body below the bust of the dress with the buckle sealed. The thinning material of the bag conforms to the shape of the object within: a journal, thick.

Her hair is red. Her face is tanned. Her eyes are emerald-green, and those eyes are fixed straight ahead, on her destination.

There.

Shining in the not-too-distant distance. A golden beach with white houses beyond, set against towering hills. A pier stretches from the beach, reaching out towards the girl like an arm, beckoning her in to that epic land mass. 'California'. The third most populous territory of the most powerful country in all the Civilised World. Populated by people like her; a place where she will finally find acceptance.

Just like Father promised her.

The girl leans forward ever-so-slightly, carefully, ignoring the splinters in her fingers and squinting against the sunlight which bounces blindingly back at her from those impossibly white beachside houses. She clicks her tongue. Waits. Strains her ears to listen. Keeps her eyes focused ahead.

Silence.

Then a wind picks up. Suddenly, unexpectedly, it blows down from the hills, snakes through the houses, rushes over the beach and across the sea. It whips the girl in the face, forcing her back. She is prepared, though. She keeps her body tense, her head pointed forward. Stays streamlined. The wind rakes through her hair, fingers clawing her scalp.

Fingers in her hair. Fingers against her skin. Fingers trying to penetrate her flesh, to tear hair from scalp, to drag her down! A voice from her memory, a rasping male voice, screams at her: *Run, before they get you too!*

A change comes over the girl. A tear forms in the corner of one eye. It crystallizes, prepares to drop. She swipes it away.

Unfortunately, this movement is just enough to upset the oh-so-delicate balance of the raft. It tilts. A section of the girl's trailing dress falls into the water. It becomes soaked. It starts, slowly, to pull her in.

She yanks it back with a determined, loathing hiss, and with some teetering she manages to regain her balance. She stares furiously ahead again, towards the beach, the houses, the people. The Civilised World. Her destination.

This girl, approximately seventeen years old, is someone I barely recognise anymore. But deep inside, I know her. I know her name is Katrina. Somehow, years ago, this was me.

California, here I come.

#

Perhaps an hour after the incident in the ocean, I was standing on the beach, rocking backwards and forwards, trying to convince my feet they were no longer at sea. They refused to believe me, but I kept at it.

My raft lay further down the beach, sagging on the sand. Most people – adults, anyway – who had seen me arrive on the beach and step awkwardly onto the land, fall over, pick myself up and plant myself in position beneath the sun, had by now apparently blocked the logical discrepancy from their minds and drifted back to their activities. Only a few children remained interested, tapping at the raft with soft bare feet; with their dextrous, babyish hands.

What amazing people these were.

I can distinctly recall the first thing that struck me about California. Moreso than the feel of the sand beneath my blistered feet - smooth, compact, pebbleless - the breeze coming pleasantly off the ocean, the sharp flavour-scent of roasting meat, or the way the sun seemed to stretch its rays out triumphantly across the cloudless sky. It was the sheer overwhelming multi-coloured volume of *humanity* which populated the Civilized World. Mostly young like me, they spread out across the beach, mingling and drifting; dark skin, pale skin, hair of all lengths and textures. Half were virtually naked; the other half wore green-and-white shirts, shorts, no footwear. They moved amongst the other beachgoers, offering green sheets of paper and wide, white, fearless smiles.

"Friends of Ferdinand Mann, thank you for a great day for democracy!"

I almost fled.

Glancing around, I traced the electronic shout to a male in a green shirt, a white plastic cone held to his lips. A stretch of fabric rippled behind him, green and white, and he called again into the cone. *"Please clear the beach, and take your trash!"*

A girl walked past me up the beach, caught my eye. I remember her hair was down to her thighs, blonde, glossy, and that she was wearing a pink floral outfit tight around her body – a 'bathing suit'. She moved as if in slow motion, with a fearlessness and a pride in herself that I had never seen before. She saw me – looked at me with bright, baby-blue eyes – and smiled. "Thanks for coming out."

"You're welcome," I said.

"Vote for Ferdinand Mann."

"Okay," I said. "Excuse me…"

But the girl continued up the beach. After a few seconds a dark male became apparent, moving down the beach towards her. Excitement bloomed in the girl when she saw him. Her pace quickened until she broke into a run which ended in a clash, a kiss, an embrace. He ran his hand through her hair, she did the same with his.

I rocked back and forth on the sand determinedly. Licked my lips.

A young man who was sunning himself in the arms of a girl stood up and sauntered lazily up the beach to where several other young people were passing a small white object between them from foot to foot. (Seemingly some sort of playful activity, rather than a cause for concern as I had first thought.) As the young man approached, the players rearranged themselves wordlessly to incorporate him into their game. The young man who had the white object kicked it to the new player, and the game resumed.

Another electronic shout: *"The rally is over, folks! Please clear the beach!"*

Still further down the beach, two young men with their arms around each other's waists accepted a girl into their joint embrace. Two children braided each other's hair in the sun. An older couple, apparently fearless of death, baked side-by-side beneath it.

Was this how I had imagined the Civilised World? Perhaps. The films in the Edu-Centre had been accurate, to an extent, but they hadn't prepared me for the warmth and the colour. The confident, frenzied excitement, bubbling through the flesh of these intelligent young creatures.

"Friends of Ferdinand Mann, thank you for a great day for democracy!"

My eyes flitted to where the white-cone-man was walking, past my raft. The children were still there, tapping at the vessel; one with a driftwood stick, the others with their slender little human paws. They saw me looking and stared back. Why? If this had been home, I would have read it as a challenge – but this was the Civilised World. I couldn't read their expressions.

The boy with the stick stood on tiptoe, still looking at me. Then he dropped his stick and reached up towards the mast.

I stared back. Wouldn't drop my gaze.

Still, when I heard that 'snap' of the mast being broken in two, I couldn't help but close my eyes for a moment. I gripped my bag tightly and crushed it to my chest. I heard a laugh, echoed by the other boys.

When I opened my eyes again, I saw that the rest of the group had taken this as their queue to tear my raft apart: judging by their laughter, just for the fun of it. It was what I had been waiting for, what I wanted to happen. The destruction of the only link to my old life. But it was still difficult to watch.

"Thank you for a great day for democracy."

I turned and was looking into the eyes of a young, white male. He was pressing a shiny paper into my hand, presenting rows of white teeth. "There'll be another rally next week. Tell your friends. Vote for Ferdinand Mann."

"How?" I asked.

But he was already gone, leaving me with the paper, green and white. Indiscernible scribbles on one side. Their writing. It wasn't the same as the writing in my journal, but it matched the text in the Edu-Centre books. I glanced around, looking for someone to translate, but nobody met my eye. I flipped the paper over: on the other side, two still images. Still images always intrigued me, even more so than the Edu-Centre films back on the Island. A single moment in life, frozen on a page. Father could never explain how these were made.

The top image showed an older male with no hair on his head, dark hair on his chin, a smile and a suit. The image below displayed two men – one small and stout and pale, one willowy and dark - and a woman, bunched together over a table, in long white coats and thick glasses. The woman had an animal, perhaps a 'monkey', pinned to the table like prey. A red line had been drawn through the lower image, bloodily bisecting the three figures.

"Can we all clear the beach, folks? Clear the beach, take your trash. The rally is now over. Vote for Ferdinand Mann. Thank you for a great day for democracy!"

With a final glance back at the ruins of my raft, I tucked the paper into my bag beside my journal, then turned and headed up the beach. My carefully rationed stash of nuts and fruits had been sufficient for my time at sea, but now I needed to find more sustenance.

#

The houses which lined the beach were bleached white, each surrounded by a low wooden barrier enclosing an identical yard. In one of these yards was an orange tree.

I would have preferred meat. Still, a guest on foreign soil must take what is offered. Only polite.

I jumped the barrier and landed on my hands and feet in the yard, then picked myself up, remembering – and I was proud that I had remembered this – to rearrange my skirt in a way that would seem socially acceptable to the people of the Civilised World. When I had done this, I reached up, plucked an orange from the tree, and sank my little yellow teeth into the skin.

The sweet taste of nourishment filling my mouth was extremely welcome but short-lived.

"Hey! What in the Hell do you think you're doing?"

I stopped eating and turned. A large woman in an apron was standing in the doorway of the house, bristling as if she wanted to attack me. I took a few steps back but kept the orange in my hand.

"You think that belongs to you?" She pointed a stubby finger at the orange. "Huh?"

My hand froze into a clamp around the orange and wouldn't let it go.

The woman stepped forward. "Get out!" She looked over my shoulder. "The rest of you, too. Go!"

I looked behind me. A small group of young people, all long hair and dirty, colourful clothes, had assembled behind the barrier to watch this exchange.

"You'd better watch out." The woman turned back to me. "You dirty little tree-hugger! The police might have no power these days but come here again, eat my fruit again and so help me God I'll-"

"Hey! You should lay off her, lady," one of the people behind me – a girl, in a rolled-up green T-shirt and shorts – interrupted. "Seems she just wanted to get some fruit. Fruit belongs to everyone."

"No," the lady corrected her. "Fruit does not belong to everyone. That fruit is off that tree – that tree belongs to *me*!"

I turned again to see the group recoil in horror at this assertion, as if sacrilege had been committed. The girl who had spoken, in particular, appeared genuinely upset. Her mouth was open.

The lady continued. "What is it with you people, anyway? You've had your party, wrecked the beach, ruined the neighbourhood, now you're leading the polls, isn't that enough?" Anger was building within her. She let it out in one final burst. "I will not be dictated to in my own front yard by a pack of self-righteous little bastards young enough to be my goddamn grandchildren!"

There were two boys in the group as well as the girl. One of them put an arm around her naked waist. "Harsh," he said. With that, the group drifted away, disappearing into a gap between two houses.

The lady called after them. "Goddamn kids! Think everything belongs to you, just because the government's gone far-out senile? My God, this country's going to go to Hell with the likes of you in charge of it! And you," she said, turning back to me. "What do you have to say for yourself?"

I did not know what the question meant, so I didn't answer. Then a thought came to me. I began to understand where I had gone wrong. "Oh," I said. "Is this your territory?"

"What?" The lady gawked, open-mouthed. "Yeah. This is my garden. What, you thought it was a public park or something?"

"You haven't marked it clearly," I explained.

The lady pointed a trembling finger at the low, white, wooden barrier. "What do you think that fence is for?"

"I don't know." Some of the videos in the Edu-Centre were damaged, concepts lost, words missing from my vocabulary. Then it came to me. "Oh, you put that there?" I nodded to show my understanding. "I assumed it was growing."

As the lady continued to stare, I bent down, placed the half-mauled orange on the grass before her and, maintaining eye-contact throughout, backed off at a slow and respectful pace. I hopped over the fence and carried on my way past the houses.

Posts sprouted from the middles of lawns and coloured cards winked in windows, blue, red, green. Those houses marked as red or blue were often tainted somehow, with broken glass or black paint dashed across the grass. The green-card houses remained unscathed.

As my legs began to tire, I found myself standing on the outside of another fence, staring into another garden. This garden was different. A tangled mess of foliage. Somebody had painted designs over the walls and a hole the size of a fist gaped in one of the windows. An image had been burnt into the grass, a circle, a triangle within.

Movement and heat beside me. People. Without looking, I could tell there were several. I stiffened, forced myself to remain in place.

"Creepy, isn't it?" A female voice.

I flinched, then swallowed, ran my tongue over my lips. *Creepy*. It was different, wild, and, yes, a little unsettling. The marks in the grass, on the walls. The chaos of the space within the fence. But then, everything I had seen today was different.

"It was Helen Monroe's place." A male voice. "You know that?"

The inflection made it sound like a question, but the phrasing was a statement. I didn't know whether or not to reply so I tried to change the subject. "Why did she make it look like that?"

"Oh, no." The girl gave a light, tinkling laugh. "We did that!" From the corner of my eye, I could see her raise a hand, gesturing towards the window, the cracks spreading across the murky glass. "That was where they found her body all those years ago, in there, see? No-one's lived in the house since."

I squinted. Couldn't see anything through the glass.

"Wait a second," the girl said. She stepped back, looked me up and down. "It's you – the orange girl. Are you alright?" Her voice was like pleasant, scented smoke, and her breath matched it.

I turned away. I had no idea what to say in response to this.

The girl followed, walked around me, and positioned herself where she could see my face. "Hey - are you *okay*?"

Again, I wasn't sure how to respond to this but, seeing as my path was obstructed, I stopped and had a go. "Yes," I said. "I am okay."

The girl smiled at this. "That lady back there was so mean," she said. "I mean, you can't, like - *own* a tree!"

"Really?" This concept intrigued me. "Not even if it's on your territory?"

Somebody laughed: one of the boys - he was wearing jeans with a scarf tied around the waist and no top; his healthy, muscular body baked a light brown by the sun. "Are you for real?"

"Yeah, I mean – you can't really *own* anything, right?" The other boy – blond, bearded - stepped up beside them. The girl nodded. "I mean, you were hungry, right? You were just following your natural instincts. And then – *pow*!" He slapped his hands together. I jumped back in alarm. "She came along with all her pent-up hate and *stopped* you, and I bet she wasn't even going to eat the orange herself." He shook his head. "So not cool."

It was hard to pick out meaning through the dialect, but I thought I understood. They were sympathizing with me.

They stood watching me silently for a while, these three colourful young Californians who were beautiful beyond anything I could have imagined; watching me with fearless, misty-yet-inquisitive eyes, as I stood expectantly before them and forced myself to hold their gaze. The topless boy's eyes travelled down my body and focused on something at my midriff. He stared for a while. Then, without a change in expression, he whispered to the girl. She followed his gaze to my midriff, then looked up at my face again. All the while the blond boy watched motionlessly, blue eyes glazed and lips apart in a dopey smile.

"Hey - you got anything you could share with us in there?" That was the girl.

For a moment I was completely lost – then I realized that she was referring to my bag. I grabbed it and clutched it tightly to me. "*No*!"

The girl cocked her head to one side, regarding me. Then she came closer and stretched out her hand. My muscles went rigid. I stepped back.

Her hand came closer – and closed lightly over mine. "Hey, that's cool," she said, and laughed. "Don't freak out about it!" She flashed me a smile. Behind her, the boys started to chuckle.

"Must be some pretty good stuff you got in there," said the blond boy. His dopey smile remained. "So – you want to do something, go somewhere?"

Somehow, I became a member of their group for the rest of the afternoon. We ambled aimlessly past the beachside houses for a while, and I listened with interest to their wonderfully peculiar manner of speaking. It was all so new to me.

"What do they call you?"

"Katrina."

"You come far?"

"Yes."

"Where you come from, then?"

I didn't answer.

"Were your parents cool with you coming here?"

I didn't answer.

An image had been pasted to the side of a house, the image from the paper nestled in my bag: short pale man, tall dark man, a woman, a pinioned monkey, a red slash across it. The girl pointed to the picture of the woman. "Helen Monroe," she said. She jabbed a finger at the topless boy. "She's watching you! She knows you messed up her house: she's mad at you!" She whooped.

I wanted to ask if she could read. I wanted to show her the paper, maybe my journal too. Perhaps I could trust her? But then she ran off, beckoning us to follow, and the moment was gone.

There came a point where the houses ran out, so we turned up the little street between the final two buildings and ended up at a big, busy road: a 'highway'. We all ran across it, the young people going on ahead, me following. The heat from the unobstructed sun grilled my shoulders and evaporated a lot of my common sense. The rush of the vehicles travelling past us, sometimes inches from my body, and the warm, ghostly glow of the streetlamps which had started to light made me feel as if I was drifting through a dream-world. I noticed things, like the way our shadows seemed to stretch out forever in the reddening sunlight, and the way the skin on my new friends' backs seemed smoother and softer than my own, even though they had grown up in a similar climate and walked barefoot, like me, with no trouble at all.

I noticed a man with thick facial hair, dressed in rags, sitting before a smoking metal cylinder, waving his hands in front of it as the smoke rose up, up, up into the crimson sky. And I noticed the smell, the beautiful scent of herbs and petals, which drifted back to me from the pores of the three fantastical creatures which ran ahead of me, laughing and chattering: fearless, uninhibited, free.

We reached the other side of the highway. Here, another smell gripped me. Something appetizing and warm.

I turned and followed the scent at a quick, loping pace. The young people, apparently curious, followed behind. I didn't look back at them, I was absorbed by my pursuit, but I could sense their excitement as they trailed me. They didn't seem to have any notion whatsoever of what I was doing or where I was going; they followed because they wanted to find out. Their blind innocence, their naivety, was touching.

The scent led me to a large white building, through a garden of chairs and tables. The smell grew stronger into a tongue-prickling flavour-scent as I rounded the corner of the building, my pace quickening, to where a pile of waste was pouring from a burst plastic sack. There I stopped.

Two animals stood on top of the sack, bristling at me. Dogs. Hungry and mindlessly territorial. However, today they were outnumbered.

I looked the pile over, once, twice. Selected my prize.

My group had assembled behind me. I glanced over my shoulder to check – there they were, staring blankly like children – and gave them what I hoped was a meaningful look, before turning back to the dogs. One of the group (the girl, most likely) said something. I blocked her out, hearing the sound, not the words.

With quick, stiff steps and my head up, I advanced towards the pile.

The dogs saw me. Also advanced.

But I was too quick for them. I plunged elbow-deep into the pile, clamped onto the foodstuff I wanted and within seconds was out again, baring my teeth in defiance, clutching my prize. The dogs stood their ground and snarled back, but it was all for nothing. I had won.

Victory. An unusual feeling. I savoured it.

The food I had salvaged smelled peculiar: smelled of chemicals, treatments, spices. All the smells of my new home. I held it up to my face and breathed them all in.

I was ravenous. Still, I wanted to share the fruits of my efforts with my new friends. Trying my best to imitate their smiles, I turned around and held my food out to where they had been – but I found that I was alone. Completely.

How very strange.

So I ate the piece of raw steak myself, taking note of the unusual under-tastes of citrus and preserving chemicals which mingled with the familiar flavours of blood and flesh. I memorized this difference, filing it away in my cabinet of experiences to refer to at a later date.

The Civilised World was sure to be full of fascinating new experiences. I looked forward to what was to come.

#

Now, imagine. You are four years old - or so Father estimates. A tiny thing.

Your home is the Edu-Centre. A little cabin, forty-three of your baby-strides across. It has been home for almost a year: ever since you started making word-like sounds; since Father deemed it too dangerous for you to be outside with the others.

The air inside the Edu-Centre is thick with heat and dust this evening: those impossibly flat wooden slabs which make up the cabin, so unlike the rough logs and fallen branches everywhere else on the Island, trap warmth. Beyond these walls is the Island. You don't often see it except when the Edu-Centre's door opens. But you can hear it, always, all around you.

As much as you try to shut it out, you can hear them barking, growling. It's the forest-dogs, you tell yourself; just the forest-dogs…

Something – a tree branch outside, maybe, hopefully – scrapes like claws.

You jump at the sound.

Father holds you tighter in his lap, arms folded snuggly across your body. His thick-furred chest, the comforting huff of his breath in your hair, soothes you. Brother Rawg – a few years older than your four, limbs rangy – stares at Father. Father stares back. You know something passes between them: silent communication you will never understand. Their minds are different: like their stocky, bristled bodies, their bottomless black eyes. Whenever the television's power dies and the screen becomes blank and reflective, you are reminded just how different: you see yourself, a little white hairless ghost, sitting between their earthy, solid forms.

The wall you all face is stacked with endless boxes of books, video tapes, papers; mysterious other items, whose names you do not yet know. Nestled among the boxes is that magical cube: the television. The power pack latched onto its casing pulses green.

On the bulging eyeball of the screen is Lorna Lane, her long white dress pinched up at her neck, glossy yellow hair hanging loose. Her strange figure: wide at the chest and hips, narrow at the waist. Various colourful images are conjured beside her. She points to each in turn. "T-shirt. Shirt. Jacket. Shorts. Pants. Skirt. Dress." She turns to you, lips stretched and curved upwards. "Now you try."

Now you try...

You screw up your face; Father nuzzles your hair. "T-surt," you try. Your lips don't want to form the words properly. "Surt..."

"Good job!" Lorna Lane claps. Lorna Lane is an idiot, but happy. "In America, we wear clothes. We wear clothes to cover our bodies when in public, because..." The screen flickers, black, blue, white, then Lorna Lane appears again. "In America, we live in houses. Inside the houses are lots of different rooms. Shall we see if we can name all the different rooms in the house?" Lorna Lane disappears and an image of something like the Edu-Centre, but bigger, replaces her.

"Yard-kitchen-living room-dining room-bedroom-bathroom-office-attic," Rawg says so fast he sounds like he's swallowing his tongue. Your brother shouldn't be so good at this. He turns to you and Father, wipes drool from his lips.

Father growls low in his throat.

He is not growling at Rawg, you see as you tilt your head up: he is facing left, the door. Father shifts you from his lap to the hard Edu-Centre floor. As he lumbers to the door, he catches Rawg's eye, holds it, telling him – what? Your mind whimpers: *Why can't I understand?*

Father opens the door just wide enough for him to pass through and slips out into the red evening light. On the other side of the door is what the video 'Our Wonderful Planet' would call their 'territory'. Father's territory, Rawg's territory. A vast stretch of the Island, thick forests and stony beaches, where you cannot go.

Before he closes the door, you see your cousins. Dozens of bottomless black eyes staring into the Edu-Centre.

Staring at you.

"Katrina!" Rawg flaps an arm to get your attention. He is putting on a new video.

On the television, Larry Larson is waiting as Lorna Lane's car stops outside his house. He opens the door to let her out. "Good morning, Miss Lane."

Lorna Lane arranges her long white dress around her and then offers her hand; he clasps and shakes it. "Saying Miss for an unmarried woman, Missus for married, and Mister for a man before their name is a sign of respect," Lorna explains. She shows her teeth: this is a smile, a good thing. "Try using it when you greet your instructor."

Rawg pushes the button to make the video freeze, then scoots closer to you. You shuffle back. You don't want him to grab you, even playfully: only Father knows how to hold you – your back to his chest, arms crossed around you - without it being painful.

Rawg seems to understand. He stops. "Good morning, Miss Katrina."

He's being like Larry Larson. You force yourself to try, "Goo-"

From outside the Edu-Centre comes the sound of Father snarling; the answering whimpers and huffs of what sounds like five, maybe more, of your cousins.

Rawg stiffens. Then he sticks out a hand towards you: curled, furred, stubby fingers retracting as far as possible to resemble Larry and Lorna's. He bares his long yellow teeth in an almost-smile. "Good morning, Miss Katrina."

You take a breath. You can do this…

"Good… mornin… Rawg."

Your flexible, long-fingered hand wraps around his fist.

CHAPTER TWO

California. With or without my new friends, I was here, and there was still so much to see. I stepped back out onto the highway, alone, and began my journey inland.

The sun, for all its beauty, was starting to burn my bare shoulders now, and my skirts got caught around my feet which made walking difficult. The sun in particular was coming as a bit of a shock. I had seen pictures, knew that there were few trees in urban California, but, stupidly enough, had not connected this with a lack of shade. I was so used to looking out at the sun from the protection of thick foliage - it surprised me that something so picturesque and desirable could, when unobstructed, sear your flesh and make you blister and bleed.

After twenty minutes of my following it, the highway started to curve inland. I glanced back over my shoulder at the disappearing beach. Stopped and stared, pain forgotten. Just visible between the buildings was the ocean, stretched-out and sparkling in a way I had never seen it sparkle before, under the reddening sky. Free, eternal, beautiful.

The world Father wanted for me.

I had intended to travel further on foot, but when a 'truck' pulled up beside me and the driver leaned out to ask if I wanted a ride to wherever I was going - "Back to college, maybe?" – the feel of the cool air seeping through his open window proved too much for my roasting skin to resist.

"Yes," I said.

The driver smiled.

I ran to him eagerly and he helped me to scramble up into the seat beside him. I stiffened when he leaned across me; but it was only to pull the door closed using the little handle. "So, the university?" he asked again, drawing back.

I had absolutely no idea what he was talking about. "The university. Yes." What did I have to lose? I settled back into the passenger seat, put my bag on my lap, and got ready to enjoy the ride.

I understood the concept of travelling in a vehicle. I had seen it done many times - in photographs, diagrams, drawings in books. The

'American Culture' video tapes that Father used to have playing in the Edu-Centre for me to learn from: they often showed people travelling by road. One video even named the different vehicle-types and explained components like 'steering wheel' and 'gearshift'. Nevertheless, the actual sensation was alien to me. Surely the seat wasn't supposed to vibrate so much? From what I had seen, I had imagined a sort of smooth, gliding sensation. Forcing these concerns to the back of my mind, I tried to concentrate on seeming as normal as possible so as not to alarm my driver and to focus on what he was saying.

"I knew you were a student," my driver murmured. He glanced at me, then turned his attention back to the road. "You've got a nice tan. And you clearly work out. I bet you've got membership with one of those pricey Westwood gyms, a personal trainer and everything. Funny, isn't it? How different groups of people have a… a sort of 'look' about them, which ties them all together?"

I kept my eyes on him, tried to concentrate, to really *understand* rather than just act as if I did.

My driver went on. "Take the hippies," he said. "You can tell by looking, can't you? Which are the new converts, the kids who dress in tie-dye because it's the in-thing, and which are the originals, the Ferdinand Mann fanatics. The ones who preach peace and love but wouldn't hesitate to stab you in the back if you dared go against their dogma. All the religionists look the same, too. And of course, there's the EcoTech employees: they're all melting into the same wall-eyed, hunch-backed, barely-human sub-species. Students have a look, too. A sort of - expensive look. Attractive, don't get me wrong. Expensive-attractive."

"I agree," I said. I wanted to ask him to go back and explain everything he had told me but managed to restrict myself to another attempted smile, another nod. The people of the Civilized World were welcoming to outsiders - the videos in the Edu-Centre had promised me that - but they might become offended if I undermined their social conventions by asking too many questions at once.

My driver glanced at me again. This time, he followed it with a longer, more penetrating look. "But – no," he said. "You're not wearing make-up. Not that you need any, of course – you're a pretty girl. And that dress of yours almost looks preacher-ish… except for the upside-down crucifix. You have a sense of humour about religion.

How refreshing!" He sniggered. "No, actually I was wrong. You don't look like you belong to any sort of group. Cling on to that. In times like these, being an individual is one of the bravest things you can do. I like a girl who can think for herself."

I did not respond because, yet again, I didn't know what to say. I think my unresponsiveness unsettled my driver, because he stopped talking. We travelled on in silence for a while before he attempted another conversation. "So," he said. "What are you studying?"

"Nothing," I replied truthfully.

"Oh? You're not a student?" My driver was quiet for a moment, then he said, "You know what? Good! I feel I can talk to you properly now." He chuckled. "I respect any of you young people who don't go to college. So many rich parents keep pushing their kids to go but there's no academic merit in it anymore, is there? Not since the Change in the Law. It's become more of a status thing, a money thing, you know?"

"No."

"What do you mean, 'no'?"

Now, here was my opportunity to request clarification. I took a moment to plan my response. "I didn't know there had been a change in the law," I said slowly. "I'll need that explaining to me."

My driver was silent for a moment. Then he began to laugh. "God, I almost thought you were being serious then!"

The truck stopped at a red light. By the roadside to our right another man was sitting by another smoking metal cylinder. I had seen several others like him on our journey so far but, as we had now stopped, I could wriggle up close to the window and get a good look at this one. He looked exactly like the one I had seen at the beach, right down to the bags under his eyes and the almost-animal facial hair. I would have thought it was the same man who had relocated, but he couldn't have walked this far in so short a time and he didn't seem to have a vehicle.

My driver peered out of my window. He honked his horn. (My pulse jumped.) The man with the facial hair looked up. My driver made a gesture at him with his thumbs, and the man smiled.

"You see a homeless person nowadays," my driver said, "and you can bet anything they used to be some kind of scientist."

The red light went out. The green one came on.

Minutes later we were climbing higher, moving further inland. Ahead of us now was an open stretch of road. On either side of it: vast areas of bare land, scourged barren as if a forest fire had spread, sparsely populated by a few large, cuboid buildings with square expanses of grey before them. On these grey expanses resided dozens of multi-coloured cars and trucks, some circling or manoeuvring, some stationary, some vibrating in readiness.

On each truck was a symbol: a triangle within a circle, white on green.

We accelerated along this road. I pushed my face up against the window and stared, fascinated, at every new building sprouting from the wasteland. I hadn't even seen pictures of these before.

My driver saw me staring. In the window, I caught a glimpse of his face. His expression morphed into a scowl so deep I turned and raised an elbow to block - I thought he was going to hit me.

"Goddamn EcoTech," he snarled. "That's the only part of this job I hate, you know? Hauling all the plastic and wiring and crap for those EcoTech traitor-scientists to play with, so they can pretend they're still making a difference. Makes me sick."

He was not going to hit me. In fact, he seemed to have forgotten my presence altogether. His mouth set in straight line; his knuckles whitened on the steering wheel. "I wouldn't join them. Never. I don't care what they say about EcoTech giving the scientists a purpose in life now the new law's fucked their careers up. You know, I don't even believe this new technology they keep churning out is eco-friendly. Fricking Ferdinand Mann is the only one profiting from this crap."

"What is EcoTech?" I enquired.

My driver sighed deeply. "No. I could never join EcoTech. Much better to live out your days in a job that lets you sit and dream of a better life. No scientist should plug themselves into a corporate machine that drains you of all your brainpower and pumps it into one pointless, disposable product after another… until there's nothing left up here!" He took one hand off the steering wheel and tapped violently on his temple.

I considered another question. "Why…?"

"*Why*? Because science used to be a noble profession! Because, despite everything the liberal media says about them, those poor bastards are the reason we don't get smallpox or flu anymore. They're the reason kids like you will never meet a person with a deformity or a serious mental problem."

I didn't know what smallpox was, but flu could kill people: they covered that in the Edu-Centre video, 'Let's Wash Our Hands: Health and Hygiene'. I considered. "If the scientists stopped sickness, why don't people like them?"

"Why? Because of what they caught Bai, Tati and Monroe doing! Have you been living under a rock?"

"No." Perhaps this was essential knowledge. I silently cursed those damaged videos. "I meant, what is your opinion on the subject?" I rephrased.

"Oh." My driver paused. "Well, the public is fickle. They took what they wanted from science, then they turned their backs. And nobody even found out what Bai, Tati and Monroe were trying to achieve with that chimpanzee's brain: it could have been something important. I mean, Tati did himself no favours babbling about human-animal Frankenstein plots, but it couldn't have been as bad as all that. You ask me, the guy was a paranoid schizophrenic. But the public buy it, a few publicity-hungry politicians start yacking about the 'evils of science'. And - boom! The human race reverts back to savage witch-hunters and sets about wiping out the so-called 'wicked'. Rioting, burning down labs; messing with some of the female researchers, poor girls…"

My hands flew to my ears to block them. *No.* This wasn't right. Those beautiful young people who had defended me and walked alongside me – they *weren't* savages. They couldn't have been. They were calm, civilized, *perfect* people, just as the video tapes in the Edu-Centre had described. I suddenly had a strong impulse to get out of the vehicle and escape this sacrilege - but I couldn't, so I didn't.

"Hypocrites." My driver shook his head. "Why, I remember a time when every other show on television was either a science documentary or a sci-fi flick."

"Television?" My hands dropped from my ears and rested on my lap. "Did you say 'television'?"

My driver ignored me. "Yep," he said. "People idolized science. Nobody will admit to it now, of course, but scientists created a stronger, healthier human race with no end of potential. And so many young people were set to join them."

We drove on in silence again. During this time, my driver calmed. After a while he glanced at me again, lingeringly; then he turned back to the road. "I'll tell you a secret," he said. "You seem the open-minded type, the kind who won't leap for my throat if I speak the truth."

"What is it?"

A small smile began to quiver at the corners of my driver's mouth. "Well," he said. "I went to college. That's right. My family had no money, my dad sold sponges door to door, for Christ's sake. But from the age of thirteen on, I saved up every cent I earned because I wanted to do what every human being on this planet should have the right to do: to use their brain. To help humanity move forward. You want to know what I studied? Huh? *Neuroscience.*"

He said the word with bared-teeth venom: as if he was admitting to a murder, albeit one he was particularly proud of. I didn't respond, but my driver nodded as if I had. "Yes - *neuroscience*. And that was just before the Change in the Law, so I bore the brunt of all those protests. But did that stop me from graduating top of my class? You bet your ass it didn't."

"What is neuroscience?" I asked, although I knew that I probably wasn't going to get a response.

My driver's fingers flexed on the steering wheel. His pale blue eyes had become glazed. "Yep. *Neuroscience*. The day of my graduation was a Saturday," he murmured, smiling. "I remember it clearly. We all went out for pizza then called it a night. Nobody dared switch on the TV or pick up a newspaper. The following Monday was when they changed the law. Science was almost completely illegalized and, unless you were a goddamn eco-technologist or a doctor, your career was in the can!" He paused. "And now – here I am, driving trucks. When the smart people are beaten down and the stupid and delusional take control… that is when society really starts to crumble. And they call this new world of ours a 'Utopia'. Ha!"

That final exclamation was short and sharp and violent. It made me flinch again.

We passed the last of the big buildings. Up ahead, a forest of tall towers, houses and lights swam into focus. We drove on steadily towards it.

"So," my driver said, "visiting a student friend of yours, are you?"

It seemed safer to agree. "Yes."

My driver nodded. "Expecting you at any particular time? She won't worry if you're a little late, will she?"

"No." She definitely wouldn't. She didn't exist.

My driver nodded again. "Good," he said. "Good, good. It's just – rush hour, you know? We might get held up. With the traffic."

But 'traffic' didn't seem to be a problem. A short while later we turned off the highway, onto a road which soon diverged into several smaller roads. We followed one of these out of the EcoTech wastelands and into a new California: one of tall buildings, glass, neat little spaces of grass and foliage where people sat and talked, smart little houses – or maybe 'stores' or 'shops'. My driver pointed to a complex of red-brick buildings set amongst perfectly green, immaculate gardens, where small clusters of people my own age were catching the last rays of sun as the sky darkened. "The university. Authentic-looking, isn't it? Seeing as it's a downsized rebuild of the original."

"Yes, authentic-looking," I agreed, deciding to ask someone to define 'authentic' later.

We drove on past the complex.

A little further down the road my driver flicked the indicator on and pulled into a small, dark side-road. Here, he stopped the truck and cut the engine. All the lights went off.

"Thank you," I said. I leaned towards the door.

"You know…" my driver began. His calloused hand gripped my arm and pulled me back into my seat.

I let out a squeal, prized the hand off. Curled around my bag. A shiver went down my spine. *Danger.*

No, not danger, I reassured myself. I was merely experiencing a new social norm that had not yet been explained to me. The videos in the Edu-Centre hadn't covered everything about the Civilized World - that much had been obvious from my first few minutes on Californian soil. I sat back in my seat, somewhat frustrated, but no longer scared. The man obviously wanted me to stay and talk.

"Most drivers would expect payment for a ride like that," he said in a peculiarly low, slow voice. "I've driven pretty far off my usual route for you. I have to be in Nevada by tomorrow."

"Yes. Thank you," I repeated. I gave what I hoped was, to him, an understanding nod. I wanted to get out.

My driver started to speak again. "You know... I get incredibly lonely sometimes. My wife ran off with this asshole eco-technologist last year. She said I was getting too crazy about the past. That I should give up the fight and earn some real money. I refused to turn traitor and slave away in the EcoTech factories, so she told me I'd had my chance, and up and left! She was my world. I haven't had a decent conversation with a woman since. Not before you. You understand me, you know?"

He leaned closer to me.

"You're such a pretty girl."

Laid a hand on my leg.

I didn't want to appear rude, but the physical contact was too much. I decided to make a break for it.

I slammed my palms against the door; then I remembered, and yanked at the handle. As the door swung open, I clutched my bag to my chest and jumped, landing hard on the concrete below. The man yelled something at me. I couldn't tell what. I felt bad; I could imagine Father snarling at me for disobeying the social conventions. Befriending these people was essential. I would have stayed to talk, but the feel of his hands on my skin - it was too much, too soon.

I ran down the road, aware that he was following me but only for a little way. He gave up when I approached the mouth of the street and I heard him go back to his vehicle. The engine growled. I ducked quickly out of the street; kept still as the immense truck rumbled and shuddered past me, inches from my face. On its side, twice my height in diameter, was that symbol, white on green: the same symbol I had seen branded on the vehicles in the EcoTech wastelands. A circle, a triangle within. I waited awhile, watching my driver get on his way, until the truck turned between two tall buildings and disappeared.

As I made my way back to the university, it struck me how lucky I was that my driver hadn't asked me for money. According to the videos in the Edu-Centre, when travelling in a stranger's vehicle in America, you were often expected upon arrival at your destination to give money (which, of course, I didn't have) in exchange for the transportation. And yet my driver hadn't requested payment. Not at all. What a nice man. In fact, so far, everyone I had come across seemed nice. Just as Father promised me.

There was no fence around the university gardens, which meant they didn't belong to anyone. As I stepped onto the grass, I looked up.

Evening was turning rapidly into night. I decided to put my plans to explore on hold and set about searching for a place to sleep.

I skulked around the complex in the twilight, out of sight, until I found somewhere suitable to lie: a low wall by a set of steps. Ordinarily I would have looked for somewhere less conspicuous: a wooded area, perhaps, or a crevasse between some stones but there was nowhere. Even the grass had been cut short. Camouflage was clearly neither desired nor required here.

I decided to risk it.

I curled my body around my bag and closed my eyes.

It felt... not uncomfortable, just odd, to lie down on the docked grass. Those peculiar little stubs, cut down to miniature-size, scratched at my legs and my elbows and my cheeks as I drifted to sleep.

#

Six years old. You are being dragged by the leg from the tall-tall grass, into the clearing where everyone sleeps – was sleeping.

Sharp, sharp fingers dig into your skin.

You're wailing. You can't help it.

They're standing over you now. Your cousins. Dozens of bottomless black eyes crowding you, blocking the moon and stars, boring into your mind. You struggle to your feet; they flinch back. You hold your sheet around your body like Lorna Lane tells you to in public places. Search the crowd desperately for a familiar face – "Father!"

Your voice sends them scattering, whimpering.

Father scrambles with surprising speed down from the big rock where the Leader sleeps. He scoops you up, the sheet falling, his arms tightening just the right amount to soothe your shaking body. He moves briskly, watching the cousins over his shoulder until you are deep in the forest, out of sight.

"Why can't I sleep with you?" you ask.

"Hush."

You can't get inside his mind like Rawg can, but you can feel Father's tension, his pulsing anger – at them, or at you? As he carries you back along the forest track, the rustle of his footfall in the undergrowth slows, the quick rise and fall of his chest evens out. The forest grows thicker, darker, quieter. No deer, no birds, no forest-dogs are out tonight. You listen to the little clicks Father makes with his tongue, silence as he waits for the answering echo, then another click, another echo: the forest calling back to him, guiding you both home.

In the Edu-Centre, Father lowers you to the floor. He finds the off-white dress – your favourite - in the box which holds soft materials, and wraps your naked body warm. He takes a video tape from one of the containers, slides it into the television's open mouth below the bulging screen. Touches your shoulder gently before he leaves.

In the quiet before the video starts, you hear the crunch of leaves as Father settles his heavy body in front of the Edu-Centre door.

The screen flickers. Lorna Lane appears, yellow hair pulled back into a white scarf. She sees you, and her lips twist into a happy smile. "Today, friends, we will talk about community. About how you – yes, you – will soon be welcomed into a very special, very loving community! A community under Jesus."

CHAPTER THREE

I cannot remember at what time I awoke but it couldn't have been particularly early because plenty of people were out – 'students'.

If the young people I had met on the beach were beautiful, these creatures were almost otherworldly by comparison. Seamlessly tanned. Most of them slim, blond, and long-legged. Their smooth, sleek hair had an artificial-looking sheen. They were dressed in cream and bronze-colours, unlike the colourful hippies but, like the hippies, many had woven symbols and ribbons of colourful silk into their otherwise understated outfits.

I was still wearing my yellowy dress with upside-down crucifix adornment.

Understandably, the students were keeping their distance from me this morning. I was new on their territory after all, and certainly wasn't dressed to fit in. I lay on the grass and watched them for a while. My head was propped up by my bag: I had moved it there during the night, where despite the solid journal within, it made a passable pillow. This was good practice for when I would get a bed of my own, I told myself.

Looking around, I noticed one person had taken an interest in me. She was a woman of late-childbearing age with dark skin, hair brushed back into a plain black scarf, and a golden talisman around her neck in the shape of my crucifix broach (except hers was pointing upwards). We made eye contact. Her eyes, dark pupils and yellowy whites, glistened for a moment in the sun. Then she approached, and was soon standing just a few feet away from me, looking down into my face with curiosity. It appeared that she expected a conversation.

I decided to take advantage of the opportunity. "Hello," I began.

"Hello, child," the woman said. She drew her lips back from her large, yellow-white teeth in a smile.

Not wanting to be rude, I levered myself up off the grass into a crouching position. The woman remained standing. "What a lovely day we're having," I said. That sentence was one of several socially-acceptable stock-phrases I had committed to memory back home, with the aid of a video called 'Polite Society' from the Edu-Centre.

"It is glorious day," beamed the woman. "One to be thankful for."

I searched the recesses of my mind for a response. 'Polite Society' didn't cover the concept of being thankful for good weather. There had also been a 'Polite Society II' and 'III' in the unpacked boxes of learning aids stashed in the corner of the Edu-Centre, but these were among the many that my cousins had doused in water and ripped apart. Through the same miracle that had left the 'English for Beginners' tapes unscathed, 'Polite Society I' had survived. My father would often look upon the piles of mangled rejects and lament the holes these would leave in my education.

Still, he had assured me I would get by. It would be as if one of his own people had arrived on the Island with an encyclopaedic knowledge of the former Leaders, but without the skills to hunt. How fortunate, he had said, that my people - these 'Americans' - appeared to be a passive, friendly race who would help me to fill in the blanks. I would just have to be polite and patient with them.

I wanted to be polite, I wanted to be patient but, more than anything, I wanted to converse. I fumbled a little longer. Then the woman surprised me by not only continuing to speak, but going off-script. "Tell me something, dear - how long have you been sleeping on the streets?"

"I have never slept on the streets," I replied, truthfully. "It seemed too dangerous to sleep on the streets. A vehicle might have injured me. I slept here on the grass last night."

The woman continued to stare and to smile. I understood both behaviours to be common in social interaction between Americans but this woman seemed to be taking these conventions to the extreme. The way she showed her teeth – those large, yellow, tombstone teeth - was almost frightening.

"Have you been drinking?" the woman said. I tried to recall but, with barely a pause, she continued. "Now, it'll do you no good to lie. I'll know. I've seen too many good young girls led astray. I'll bet you were drinking last night, weren't you?"

"Yes." I remembered now that I had taken a sip of tepid water from a bottle I had discovered under my seat in the truck.

The woman shook her head. "Poor, poor child. And drugs? Have you taken any drugs?"

What were drugs? I had no idea. "No," I guessed.

"But you have been drinking and sleeping rough," she acknowledged to herself, I think, more than to me. "Drugs are the next step. It's a slippery slope, it can only lead to one thing: destruction of the soul." She bent down over me. "I can tell you're unhappy, child. You are, deep down, a lost and a sad young girl. And you know what? I have no doubt that something terrible must have happened in your life. Am I right?"

I didn't answer.

"Am I right, child?"

I knew it was rude, but I didn't want to tell her.

There was a strange, tight feeling in my chest. An image was stirring in the back of my brain, a tiny hurricane gaining momentum and, for a moment, I had to look down at the grass and focus on counting the blades between my fingers. Still the hurricane grew. A bloody hand reached through the vortex towards me and a rasping, clumsy, painfully familiar voice started to burble: *Run, before they get you too...*

I reached out, grabbed my bag. Ran the leather strap soothingly through my hand.

"You don't have to answer." The woman finally gave up the interrogation and stood straight again. "But I know. You're trying to bury it now, of course. But, heed my words, one day it will come out."

I looked up at her. "How can you know that?"

The woman winked at me. "I have a special link with Jesus, child. Jesus knows everything."

'Jesus'. I knew that name.

Suddenly the woman crouched down on the grass before me and shuffled closer. "But there is hope! There can be salvation. Anybody, anybody in this world, can be saved from the mistakes they've made, from the misery of their past."

I felt her hot, rancid breath on my face, and moved back. "How?"

"Oh, I'll tell you, child," said the woman. "It really is the simplest thing in the world to do. And I can help you achieve it."

I was interested now. I wanted to hear what she had to say. Not sure what to expect - a revelation, or a helpful hint - I leaned closer.

But the woman never finished explaining. Because at that moment she saw my chest, and her eyes widened.

"You little bitch!"

Suddenly and for no discernible reason at all I was being called a 'wicked, wicked girl' and a 'child of Satan' and a colourful mix of other assorted insults, while having a stubby, righteous finger waved threateningly close to my face as if the woman wanted to stab me in the eyes. I crossed both arms over my bag and cowered behind it, then peered at her tremulously over my arm-barrier, blank with fear and confusion.

It was only after the torrent of words had dried up that she started pointing at my crucifix broach, and I realized the problem: I was wearing my jewellery the wrong way up. This was, apparently, terrible.

Hastily I fumbled with my broach, trying to turn it around while at the same time keeping the neck of my dress closed around the parts of the female body that I knew shouldn't be shown in public. Hard as I tried, I was unsuccessful.

The woman rose to her full height. Her weighty body trembled like an erupting volcano. "Wicked girl!" she spat. "Those who wear the mark of the Devil – wear it as a *fashion accessory*, no less – will be punished for their foolishness! One day you will feel an agony greater than any you ever thought possible. Your flesh will be stripped from your body! You will burn in a hellish pit for all eternity! Your soul will fall into the hands of the demon you so freely gave it to, and he will…"

At that moment, a man dressed in a sweater, tan jacket and long, trailing coat came skipping lightly over the grass from the path to my rescue. "Now, now!" he called. He stopped before the woman. "I think that's enough, don't you? The girl isn't interested. You can leave now."

The woman stared at him. Meanwhile, I seized my moment and crawled behind the man's long coat.

The woman had stopped speaking. She tried to look over the man's shoulder at where I was crouching but he repositioned himself to block me. I attempted a smile for him.

"Now, be a good girl and go back to wherever it is you're sleeping these days," the man said to the woman, softly. "Before I call the cops on you. You don't want to have that happen again." He took a step closer to her. "Do you?"

Amused now, I watched as the woman backed away. But before she left, she threw one last comment back in my direction: "This devil's child will bring Hell upon herself and no mistake!"

"Hey, hey!" my protector warned, and the woman hurried away.

My protector and I watched as she bustled down the campus path. She was stared at and sniggered at by a few of the students she passed, until finally she disappeared from view.

"Oh dear. Preachers," my protector muttered, gazing after the woman. "Don't take it personally. She's been in this area before. Attacked several students last year."

"Attacked?"

"Well, verbally," he said. "But people like that do get aggressive. Like that ex-nun who shot all those people on the New York subway, remember? Honestly – and it's not that I condone what the scientists did, but at least *they* tried to find useful employment with EcoTech and the like instead of... wow." He had turned to face me. He looked me up and down. "Now, that *is* an interesting get-up. Were you at a party last night?"

"A party?" I tried to recall the meaning of the word. "No. I don't think so – doesn't a party involve 'cake' and 'balloons'?"

The man laughed. "Okay, okay. Where were you last night, then?"

"Out here."

The man frowned. "Excuse me?"

I didn't know where the confusion lay, so I spoke louder. "Out *here*!" I pointed to the grass. "I slept out *here*!"

The man nodded. "Okay," he said quietly, perhaps to himself. "Wherever you were last night, you must have had a heck of a good time." Then he bent down towards me. I shuffled back as he plucked the piece of green paper which had slipped from my bag in the commotion. "Aha, that makes sense - the Ferdinand Mann rally! Not sure I support the owner of the biggest business in the country running things. Still, he has more of an opinion on the scientists than anyone else - which I guess is why he'll win, right?" He flipped the paper over, examined the images on the back. "I always wonder who took that photo, you know? You've got Doctors Tati, Bai and Monroe pictured together, and as far as I know they worked unassisted. If I didn't know better, I'd say it was doctored."

"The doctors were doctored," I experimented verbally.

The man quirked his lips as if I had said something amusing. Then he flipped the paper over. His eyes moved down the back. "Ferdinand Mann, founder of EcoTech, is the natural choice for leadership of our great nation and…"

It took me a moment, but then I realised - "You're reading it!"

"Well, I'm interested. I'm not *anti*-Ferdinand Mann per se…"

"You know what the writing says!" This was it. An educated man, and evidently kind. He would be my teacher. Perhaps he could translate the writing in my journal, too: clever people here could probably read all sorts of languages. "Keep going! Read some more, please?"

My protector stared at me a moment in silence, as if considering. "Look, why don't you come back to my apartment?" It appeared that he had surprised himself with the invitation because he laughed. "Don't worry, don't worry - I'm not a predator. I'm married. In fact, I have a daughter about your age. But my apartment's on-campus, and I can get you some strong coffee to sober you up. I don't like the idea of a girl in your vulnerable state laying about outside."

"Are you a student?" I asked.

He smiled softly and shook his head. "I teach here," he said. "Come on."

He reached down towards me and, steeling myself, I let him take my hand and pull me up. He had a firm grip but a soft and gentle hand, long dextrous fingers. A hand like mine. When I was on my feet, he put an arm around my waist to steady me. I tried another smile for him and pulled out of his grasp.

"I'm in the Professors' Accommodation Building," he explained as he directed me forward. "Now, don't feel sorry for me – sure it's cheap, but it's actually quite comfortable. You should be able to walk to your next lecture quite easily from there. Or your dorm, if you're on-campus."

"Do you know that woman?" I asked.

He glanced back over his shoulder as if he expected to see her again. "Yes," he said. "She's Petunia, the preacher who was skulking around campus last year – you won't remember if you're a freshman. She was… shall we say, a little too vocal? Security called the police, and she went away. Now it appears something's brought her back here."

"Why was she calling me a devil's child?" I asked.

The man shook his head. "God knows," he said. And then he laughed. "'God knows' - bad choice of phrasing, Michael!"

It was only a short walk to the 'Professors' Accommodation Building', during which time the man introduced himself as the 'Professor of the History of Biochemistry and Genetics' at 'yoo-see-elle-ay' which I came to understand was what the locals called the university. It also came up at some point during this conversation that his name was Professor Michael Salvador; but because the name was long, I just called him 'Professor'. He never corrected me on it.

#

The Professors' Accommodation Building was one of the taller, narrower, greyer buildings on the campus, and the Professor's apartment was on the second floor.

It consisted primarily of one main room: windowless, but well-lit by panels in the ceiling which could be made brighter or dimmer depending on which way you turned the plastic dial by the front door. The end of the room nearest the door was taken up by a small, compact kitchen and a glossy wooden table with a single chair. At the other end was a low bed with blankets in a heap, a shiny white wardrobe and, in one corner, a collection of brightly-coloured chairs and sofas clustered around a small white cube of a television set.

"Would you like some coffee?" the Professor asked, shutting the door behind me. He pointed out a jug on the kitchen counter, filled with a dark, strong-smelling liquid.

"No," I decided instantly.

The Professor paused midway through shrugging off his coat. "No?" He looked confused for a moment. Then he said, "Well, you'll probably want to get cleaned up, then. You can use the bathroom if you like?" He gestured to a door leading to a smaller, adjoining room.

It would be impolite to decline too many offers from the man who would protect me and teach me to read. "Yes. I will have a bath. Thank you."

"You want to use the actual *bath*?" Strangely, the Professor seemed taken aback that I had accepted his offer. "Well... okay. Yes. I suppose it might do you good." He discarded his coat over the table and disappeared into the smaller room. "It's one of those new Eco-Baths," he called back to me. "So it will take a while to run. Meantime, you make yourself at home. Oh - there's a bathrobe, here." He reached back behind the bathroom door and pointed to the pastel-blue robe which was hanging there.

I had just noticed the television. "Yes," I murmured. "There is."

As soon as the Professor finished speaking I went to the television, knelt down before it. My eager fingers quickly found and pressed the 'on' button. The television made a noise. A picture began to appear. Slowly I rose to my feet and stepped backwards until I felt the cool slippery texture of the orange sofa pressing against my legs; then I sat down to watch.

"So," the Professor called to me from the bathroom, over the sound of trickling water. "What are you studying here? Wait, don't tell me – let me guess. Modern art, perhaps? Film? No, actually I believe you are a - Twentieth Century Pop Culture major. Am I right?"

"No," I said. "I'm not studying anything."

"Really?" There was a pause. "You're not a student, then?"

I didn't respond to this.

Another pause. Then the Professor asked, "So, where's home for you?"

"I don't have a home," I replied shortly. The television was showing me something I hadn't seen on the one in the Edu-Centre: a series of short films explaining the benefits of buying different lotions for my hair and skin, gadgets for a car I didn't own, and various tantalizing food products. The final one was a long, abstract piece explaining why a forgettable man in a suit should be 'Re-elected for President' because he had supported the Change in the Law before Ferdinand Mann and was, therefore, a hero. I found the remote, turned up the volume. "*...a free America cannot prosper under a President who founded EcoTech, the single largest employer of educated men over forty...*"

Across the room, the bathroom door opened. The Professor looked out at me, his brow furrowed. "How long have you been homeless?" he asked.

We had come back to this again.

However, this time the Professor wasn't smiling when he asked me the question, and his voice was less sickly-sweet than that of the woman who had later accused me of being a 'devil's child', so I felt more inclined to answer. "Twenty-two nights," I replied.

"Really?" Another pause. "So... did you have troubles at home?"

"Yes." I did not want to be rude, but when I turned and gave him a warning look he seemed to get the message. He withdrew into the bathroom. As the door closed the image on the television switched to a still. It was the same as the image on the piece of paper from the beach: a woman and two men, crowded around a monkey on a table. Up close, I could see that the tall, dark man was not merely thin but skeletal, with tired eyes, a drooping mouth, and dangling limbs. He stood behind the other two. The second man, short and pale, leaned in to the woman who held the monkey down. The monkey appeared to be screaming. A voice, low and crackly and strange-sounding, spoke over the picture: *"I am sorry. Science is sorry. We wanted a better world, but no utopia is worth the destruction of animal life, nor of its people..."*

"Excuse me," I called to the Professor.

He poked his head around the bathroom door. "Yes?"

"Why is that man speaking like that?"

Silence. "You mean his accent? Doctor Tati was French."

"Oh." French means 'comes from France'. France is on the other side of the world. The image disappeared, the screen exploded into green and white, and a different voice started to instruct me, *"Don't let America repeat the mistakes of the past. Vote for restrictions on science, and freedom for all. Vote for Ferdinand Mann."*

I watched for another ten minutes, through a string of consecutive short films explaining why I should be using three different products in tubes to protect my hair's colour. Another short film showed how I could make it a different colour altogether: this would apparently make me more attractive and socially acceptable.

Eventually, my eyes started to wander elsewhere. They finally fell upon a framed photograph on top of the television. The image was of a girl about my age, with red hair in a bright blue bandana, pink glossy lips, and dark paint around her eyes. Once I had noticed this picture, I found it difficult to ignore. I shuffled to the other end of the sofa, but the eyes followed me. It seemed this girl wanted me to leave.

"I don't know what we're going to do about clean clothes for you, but there's a bathrobe on the back of the door," the Professor called out from the bathroom. "Did I show you?"

"Yes."

"Good," the Professor said. "It should fit you. It's my daughter's. She's living with her mother now, out of State - but I still keep it out for her, in case she ever visits. I know that must sound sad, right?"

"Yes." A daughter separated from her father. It sounded horribly sad.

The noise of running water stopped. Moments later, the Professor called that the bath was ready. "You have a nice wash, get all that street dirt off your body," he said. "Then we can talk about where you're going to sleep tonight."

"Okay." Accordingly, I stripped.

The Professor emerged. "I don't have any classes this morning, so I'll be here for as long as you – oh, Jesus! I am so sorry!" He clapped a hand to his eyes and whipped around to face the wall. "I didn't realize! Not right here, I meant... I did show you the bathrobe, didn't I?"

His reaction to seeing me standing in the pool of my discarded clothes was like that of a man who has been struck in the face by a venomous snake. Why, I didn't know. Clothes should always be worn in public, but I was no longer in public.

"Yes," I said. "It was nice. I liked the colour. Should I go in here?" Without waiting for an answer, I started towards the bathroom.

The Professor laughed uneasily. "I meant to say... you can *borrow* it... if you like?"

"Oh," I said. "No, thank you."

As soon as I had entered the bathroom, he closed the door behind me. I wanted to be able to hear if the Professor called me from outside, so I opened it again, a crack. Then, one foot at a time, I stepped into the bath. The temperature caught me by surprise. "It's warm!" I yelped.

From somewhere outside the bathroom, the Professor laughed. "All the conveniences of the modern age here. What, do they only bathe in cold water where you come from?"

"Yes." Bracing myself, I slithered down into the bath.

The effect was instantaneous. The steaming water immediately started loosening my muscles and clearing away the dirt. I noticed an array of lotions in tubes along the side of the bath to my left and, remembering the instructions from the television, I drenched myself in all of them.

Time blurred. The heat of the bath and the smells of the lotions combined and played with my mind in a wonderful way. After a few minutes or hours or days, from somewhere far away, I heard the Professor ask, "So, what's your name?"

"Katrina," I murmured.

"Katrina." He paused. "And if I may ask, Katrina... why did you leave home with nowhere else to go?"

Why did I leave home with nowhere else to go?

I think it must have been the heat of the bath, or the intoxicating smell of the lotions. Or maybe a combination of both. Normally I would never have answered him. Never.

But...

"My father is dead," I said. "My cousins killed him. And if I go back, they'll kill me too. So I had to leave."

#

Seven years old. You are sitting before the Edu-Centre television with Rawg, and Lorna Lane is telling you about families. About how the mother and father have sons and daughters, and live in houses away from the other blood-relatives: the uncles, the aunts, the cousins...

But that's not all.

"Because you are not only children of your mothers and fathers," Lorna Lane beams. "You are children of God!"

"How does that work?" you ask.

Rawg does that thing he does when he doesn't understand but wants to - he grits his teeth, furrows his brow, lets out a long, throaty rumble as he stares at the television. "Maybe," he says at last, "when you go back there – and find a family – it will be explained."

A sudden chill. The idea of 'going back', meeting your own kind – you know it's why you're doing this now, watching the videos again and again, getting ready; but it's never really spoken about. You have the urge to ask, Why can't I stay with you? But you know why.

"We may be different from one another," says Lorna Lane. "We may have different skin tones, languages, and abilities, which we get from our parents. But because we are all God's children, we are all the same. We are all equal in his eyes!"

The door opens with force. It hits the wooden wall hard.

You stiffen. Rawg scrambles to his feet.

Father stumbles into the Edu-Centre. His right shoulder sags; blood, torn flesh, mauled meat. This was the work of teeth.

You're on your feet too now, running to him with Rawg. When Father slumps to the floor, wincing, you both hold back at a respectful distance. "Who hurt you, Father?" you ask.

Father's eyes seem vacant, his breath panting and quick. He looks at you, and his eyes grow warmer, more alive. Then he turns to Rawg: they stare at one another for a beat, two, three... Silently communicating. Speech you cannot understand.

You stamp your foot. "Who hurt you, Father?"

Father turns to you with a snarl. Then his expression softens. He makes a noise, an almost-unintelligible growl, a close approximation of 'Rool': the Under-Leader.

If Father dies, his place will be assumed by Rool, one of the taller and stronger young males. But for anybody to challenge a man like Father, a male in his physical prime: it is unthinkable!

"Why did Rool hurt you?" you ask.

Father doesn't answer, maybe because he can't: with his unsuited jaw and none of the early speech practice you and Rawg had, words come with more difficulty to him. You look to Rawg for an answer, but his eyes flit away.

"Is he coming here?" you press. "Will he follow you?"

"He's dead," says Rawg. Father growls at him, fixes him with a glare. Whatever they are saying to each other now, with deep black eyes boring into each other, you will never know.

But you do know about healing. Father taught you the basics alongside Rawg, and you've seen the video 'Health and Hygiene' dozens of times. You run to the box of soft fabrics, retrieve a pale blue skirt. Father lets you take his thick, furred arm in your little pale hands and watches, breath slowing, as you wrap the fabric once, twice, over and over, up the arm, to the shoulder.

When you are finished, Father takes you in his unbound arm. Rawg, watching quietly from a few feet away, comes to nestle against Father's side.

You are all watching Lorna Lane talk about miles and kilometres, weights and numbers when there is a tap at the door. Another, louder, and then the door swings open.

Araga-Mawg, the Healer, is filling the doorway with their bulky form.

Araga-Mawg doesn't sleep or hunt with the other cousins. Araga-Mawg keeps to their den deep in the forest. Their blood-painted skin, their artfully scarred brow, their ambiguous sex concealed by a skirt of grey forest-dog skin: these mark the Healer as something different and special. But when you catch yourself staring you can't look away, because Araga-Mawg's eyes are locked on yours. Their lips curl back; you see crooked yellow teeth. Sharp as flint.

You see, in your mind, Father's ripped-open flesh.

Finally, Rawg takes your hand – you flinch at the touch - and gently pulls you away, off Father's lap, to the corner of the room.

Together, you watch Father stand stiffly and move to the door. As he approaches Araga, the Healer's eyes finally go to their injured Leader. Araga takes a quick double-step back. Crosses their arms across their thick-furred, rounded chest.

Father pauses. Then he slowly unwinds the pale blue skirt, now marked brown and crimson, from his arm, and lays it on the floor before following.

CHAPTER FOUR

I emerged from the Professor's bathroom in a cloud of steam. My hair had become inhumanly shiny and I smelt like honey and sugary fruit: rather pleasant, and, I thought, distinctly Californian.

I was wearing the bathrobe; the Professor had taken it from its hook and slipped it through the gap in the door while I was otherwise occupied and, noticing it on the floor as I scanned the room for the towel (which I knew, from Edu-Centre videos like 'The American Home', must have been in the bathroom somewhere), I finally took the hint and put it on. Admittedly, it did feel nice and soft: comfortably swaddling, without being too restricting. My bag-strap fit snuggly across the robe, keeping it closed.

The steam from the bathroom cleared. There was the Professor, sitting with his back to me at the wooden table near the kitchen. Aromas of all things edible filled the air: fresh vegetables, salts and sharp citrus flavours. Meat. Cooked meat. My senses flooded with the flavour-scent; my salivary glands whirred to life.

The Professor must have heard the bathroom door open but he did not immediately turn around. First he asked, "Are you wearing the bathrobe?"

"Yes." I searched for the source of the smells and found my attention drawn to the section of table the Professor's head was blocking.

The Professor turned in his seat. He stared at my hair in silence for a while, wide-eyed. His nostrils flared as he inhaled. Then he smiled widely and seemed to stifle a laugh. "Well, I guess I can't blame you for going a little overboard. You can't have had much of a chance to use shampoo lately, can you?"

"No," I said.

His eyes remained fixed on my hair. "My wife used to joke that I had more pampering products than her and our daughter combined," he murmured. "Actually, 'joked' probably isn't the right word…"

"And now you have none." I lingered in the bathroom doorway and watched him, waiting for instructions. Polite conversation was fine but now I wanted to be invited to eat. The Professor continued to smile at me infuriatingly. I inched closer.

"There's a pile of clothes that might fit you, down there," he said, pointing to my feet. I looked down. There was indeed a small, multi-coloured fabric pile by my feet.

"Put them on," said the Professor. "Then you can have some food." He turned away again.

Apparently, the 'cover your body' rule did not just apply to being in public. This was fine; I could adjust. But the clothes the Professor wanted me to wear were skin-tight and pointless. Instead of masking the naked body, as I had been led to believe clothes are supposed to do, these conformed to every curve and indent in my figure and did little more than add colour and pattern to my legs and torso. I now had a bright blue lower half, a red-and-white striped upper half, and was highly uncomfortable. I told the Professor this.

"Those clothes are designer. Expensive," was all he said. He turned to me again and inspected me. His eyebrows twitched a little; his eyes widened. "Yes," he said, slowly. "You look very nice in those."

I would have argued my point further but as the man clearly had a penchant for being evasive as well as indirect, I doubted it would get me anywhere. Besides, I was intrigued to see what sort of food had been laid out for me.

Restricting myself to a slow, cautious pace, holding my bag close to my side, I walked around the edge of the table clockwise. As I completed my slow, careful semi-circuit around the table, I entered the Professor's field of vision. He followed me with his eyes, frowning a little, until I stopped at the place that had evidentially been laid out for me - facing him. In front of me was a plate of something meaty, layered with vegetables and some pale flat sheets. I didn't quite see the point of them. They got in the way of the meat and tasted of nothing.

I had also been given a glass. When I reached my seat, the Professor leaned across and filled it from a bottle with something red. "Please," he said as he withdrew. "Sit down."

Slowly, keeping my eyes on the Professor at all times, I sank down into my seat. My first sit-down meal was about to commence. I settled my bag on my lap, feeling the comforting weight of the journal within, and waited.

"It's only a microwave lasagna, I'm afraid," said the Professor. "I usually have my main meal in the evening and obviously I wasn't expecting company, so I was going to get something on the way back from my lecture. But on the 'plus' side - it hasn't expired yet." He sniggered; fell silent. "Those clothes suit you, you know," he said, after a pause. "I'm glad. I thought they would." He was staring at me now in a slightly doped, detached way, as if I was producing some sort of intoxicating scent.

Then he gave a sudden, sharp shake of his head. "My daughter left those clothes behind, last time she came to stay," he said. "It was a surprise visit. Her mother dropped her here on her way to a business meeting in New York; well, what she *claimed* was a business meeting. The twenty-year-old surfer-boy at the wheel of her new Cadillac suggested otherwise. But, oh - it was so wonderful to have my little girl to myself again! You have no idea. She got up for breakfast with me every morning, sat in on all my lectures. Let me tutor her on Watson and Crick, Bai and Tati and Monroe in the evenings. That weekend I must have taken her to all the fashion stores in LA." He shook his head again and, in the absence of whatever intoxicating distraction he had succumbed to earlier, looked lost.

My eyes flitted from the Professor's face to his hands, to his cutlery then back up to his face again. He seemed to be taking a long time to get around to eating whatever he had prepared. I began to wonder if this meal was not for eating at all but a part of some masochistic ritual which the video tapes in the Edu-Centre had neglected to mention.

The Professor frowned. "Is there something wrong with the food?"

I glowered back at him with added intensity. "You tell me."

He took up his cutlery and sampled the meal. "It tastes absolutely fine to me," he said.

"Good."

I began to eat, still keeping one eye on the Professor– or rather, on his cutlery. Regardless of their primary purpose, and of how many times I reminded myself of the peaceful nature of those inhabiting the Civilised World, these little silver devices were potential weapons. They seemed strange design choices for eating utensils.

"Yes, my Aleshia's no academic, but she certainly has an excellent taste in fashion," said the Professor in an unprovoked attempt to turn his earlier comments into a conversation. "And really there's more of a future in that, the way the world's going. I expect she'll go to college in Hawaii. That's where she lives now, with her mother. She hasn't been back to visit me since she was fifteen." He gave a smile and looked down at his plate.

So many questions presented themselves. Where was Hawaii? How could this Aleshia *taste* fashion? How exactly was the world going and did this have anything to do with what the truck driver had described, this so-called 'Change in the Law'?

But before I could ask, the Professor started speaking again. "I was hoping she'd come over in the spring for her seventeenth," he continued. "But Celia – that's my wife, well, ex – threw some party together at the last minute. I think a new car was involved, too. So she stayed." He took a sip of the red liquid in his glass. Sighed. "I mean, I would have gone out to see her, of course - but for the expense."

"You don't have enough money to see your daughter?" I tried to work this out in my mind. In the Edu-Centre videos, mothers and fathers saw their children all the time, without having to offer payment. My father would never have had to trade his personal possessions for a visit with me. "Why?"

The Professor shook his head. "Flights and hotel prices skyrocket over spring break. And the History of Science department pays surprisingly little, despite those horrendous tuition fees. I don't know how they can justify them: a college degree doesn't count for anything anymore. Then again, the only students we get now have parents pulling in six-figure salaries, so I suppose the college can charge what it likes. And I have a pretty good idea of where that money goes." He did not elaborate. Just drank again, deeply, from his glass of red. "The head of the History of Science department just bought his wife a new convertible. An electric one. With an EcoTech price tag, no doubt."

These words meant nothing to me - a fact which bothered me little, as I was having considerable trouble with my cutlery and was considering resorting to fingers and palms. I knew of course that this was incorrect but I was prepared to sacrifice etiquette if it meant getting some food inside me.

"I was meaning to mention this earlier," the Professor said abruptly. I looked up. "There has been... a *weird smell* in here for a while. I didn't mention it before because it might have been, well... but you've had a bath now. Now I think it might be - *that*."

He nodded at my bag.

I crushed it to my chest.

"It looks ancient," the Professor said. "You know, I have a spare satchel of Aleshia's somewhere. Whatever you've got in there, we could..." He started reaching forward.

"No!"

I surged forward, knife in hand.

The Professor looked down at the fresh scratch across his knuckles, oozing blood. Then he looked at me.

Something primal overrode the embarrassment I knew I should feel for this outburst. I put my knife down slowly. Clutched my bag tighter.

"No," I said again, staring at the Professor.

"Okay," he said.

We continued to eat in silence.

After a while, the Professor's gaze shifted to the television set. "That's Aleshia," he said. "On top of the TV, where she can keep an eye on her old dad. Fifteen years old in that photograph. Doesn't she look stunning?"

I kept my mouth shut and nodded at him, pretending to be interested.

"Just like her mother." He drank half of the remaining red liquid in his glass, set it down on the table again, and gazed at it. Then he gripped it by the neck and took another swig. I tried to copy him but could barely manage more than a sip of mine: it tasted like poison.

"I don't know why... why she *left* me," the Professor continued, now with more difficulty. He sounded a little like Father did whenever he tried to speak. "I mean, I went through a bit of a rough patch after the Change in the Law, I'll admit. I'd lost all the funding for my research – I'd lost my *career*."

"Were you a scientist?" I asked.

The Professor nodded limply. "Zoology. When they shut down the labs, I didn't know *what* I was going to do with myself. But I was getting over that... I was looking into *teaching* jobs. And still – she *left* me. I don't know why! Yes... I do." He drained his glass of red; poured himself another. "It was that man – that damn *food technologist*. He said he'd found a way of making food with the exact

49

flavour and con... con*sistency* of a salmon fillet, but for vegetarians. Well, I was in the veggie aisle in the supermarket last week, and I didn't see any food with *his* name on it. Imagine – my beautiful Celia, in bed with that *swine!*"

I tried to imagine. "Is a swine a pig?" I asked.

"Yeah... that's right."

I took a few seconds to consider. "Isn't that called 'bestiality'?"

The Professor looked at me. "You really are a *fascinating* creature," he said. Then he smiled. "But I'm being rude. Sorry. Why don't you tell me about your family? I mean, I'm sorry, I know you lost your dad – but your mom, what about her? Where is she?"

Stiffly, I put my cutlery down (I had persevered with some success) and finished my mouthful. "Nowhere," I said. "I don't have a mother. I only had a father."

I tried to eat a little more food but for some reason it tasted bland. The Professor pushed his remaining mess around his plate for a long time, not saying anything. Slowly he sipped his second glass of red, then sipped it again, and again, until the glass was empty and he was reduced to chasing the final little drops around the bottom with his finger, seemingly oblivious to my presence. I tried my red drink again; still couldn't see the appeal.

Finally, the Professor spoke. "It's tragic," he said. "What happened to your father, I mean. It's... *heart-breaking*! And he left behind a daughter to fend for herself, with no family she could trust... I assume your cousins are in jail now?"

"No."

"What? Katrina, they should be punished!"

"That's not how things work where I'm from. If you're different, you die. If you try to protect someone who's different, you die."

And now the Professor shot me a fierce look, a little bit of sticky red staining his quivering lips. "Not *here*. You're safe here. I can promise you that."

Father had promised me, too. Here in the Civilised World, amongst my own people, I would be free of the tyranny he had tried to protect me from. That was why I had to find acceptance here: I owed it to Father. I felt my muscles loosen at the Professor's comment; I leaned back in my chair a little more.

"If I may ask," said the Professor. "Don't answer this if you don't want to, but... why *did* they want to kill him? Was it a gang thing, or...?" He leaned forward slightly in his chair, his red-stained lips making a pout, and clasped his hands before him.

"They didn't want to kill him," I said. "They loved my father. They wanted to kill me, and he was always in their way."

"Kill *you*?" Through the thick haze which had fallen over him after that second glass of red drink, the Professor was now looking at me with something close to alarm. "Why? I mean, what did you *do*?"

"I didn't do anything," I said. "It's just - I'm different. My family don't like difference. They see it as a bad omen."

"A bad *omen*?"

"Yes. They don't believe in 'love thy neighbour' and 'do unto others as you would have them do unto you' like your people do. They're uncivilised. They think all anomalies should be destroyed."

"What are you talking about? Katrina, where are you *from*?"

I bared my teeth at him. "I'm from here!"

The Professor frowned. He was trying to make sense of all this, I suppose, and failing. Finally - perhaps to refuel his mind, or perhaps to escape from it - he went to the kitchen and poured himself a third glass of red from another bottle he had waiting on the countertop.

My muscles had tensed again. I couldn't eat any more, so I stood up. "I'm going to sleep," I told the Professor. "You can wake me if you want me to leave." Although I hoped, after all I had confided, that the man would let me stay. I didn't have the energy to search for another protector, another educator.

The Professor made a couple of grunting noises, signalling his vague comprehension of what I had said. He did not look at me anymore but kept his eyes on the red liquid: his escape from my world of madness.

I carried my bag over to the sofas and lay down on the orange one, directly facing the television. Put the bag under my head. Closed my eyes. I was on the brink of sleep when the sound of the Professor's voice roused me. "Hey – Katrina? *Katrina?*"

My eyes opened a fraction. I peered across the room at him. "Yes?"

The Professor swallowed another gulp of red liquid, and then asked, "Your cousins... they won't try to find you *here*, will they?"

Behind him, I saw that there was a chain across the front door that hadn't been there before.

"They will try to find me," I said tiredly. "But not here."

"Yes," said the Professor. "*Yes* - but how can you be *sure*?"

"Because they haven't got a raft," I said. "And they can't swim."

Somehow, somewhere deep within that mind swimming in red liquid, this must have made sense to the Professor. He shut up for a bit; and I, stiff but warm and smelling of flowers, curled up against the back of the sofa, and waited for sleep to take me somewhere pleasant.

#

A few hours later, I woke to find that I had been moved across the room. I was now lying on the Professor's bed with various pieces of material draped over me. Panicked, I tussled them off the bed and into a mound on the floor.

The Professor was sitting at the table again, leaning over something. His face was turned away from me. He didn't look up; not even when I made my bed-linen-removal commotion. I thought he might have been asleep.

Relieved to find that my bag had been tucked next to me, I checked to make sure the journal was still inside – it was – and strung it across my body.

As I padded over to the Professor, he started to speak. "I called the police, about what you told me earlier. They said nothing of that kind had been reported. Seems like the sort of thing someone would report around here, right? A killing based on omens and folklore. They said you were messing with me. You know what I think, though?"

"No." Did he think I was lying?

"I think you're a girl who's just lost her dad, and needs to make up a heroic story to come to terms with the loss. And you're young, and scared, and clearly – well, *unusual*, psychologically. Someone's been filling your head with nonsense. You need someone to look out for you and a safe place to stay. Am I right?"

Too many points. I responded to the last one. "Yes."

"The officer I spoke to said I could bring you in, and he'd try to trace your family. But if you're telling the truth, and there's nobody left for you – and if they come to certain *conclusions* about your mind – well, I hate to think where you'd end up. The world's not a friendly place for people like you right now. So I've made a decision. You can stay with me."

"Thank you." The fact that most of his words made little sense was irrelevant: I only cared about the last bit. Relieved, I moved closer. Perhaps asking for an education would be appropriate now...

"You're most welcome," said the Professor. "As a parent and a teacher, it's my duty to look out for the welfare of young people. Especially people with your... *background*." His voice became low and soft. "Most people would have told Petunia to go away, but you were cowering like a beaten dog."

"Who is Petunia?"

The Professor did not respond, seemingly focused on something on the table before him. Standing close behind him now, I peered over his shoulder to see what was absorbing his attention. It was a book: an old, thick book, open at a creased double-page spread showing a diagram of a machine. The machine was full of human blood. Evidently it was supposed to create a vortex to separate the different components of the blood, so that the denser material could be harvested. Why anybody would want to do this I hadn't a clue, but it was an interesting little idea nonetheless.

I leaned over the Professor to study it in more detail; accidentally brushed his shoulder. The Professor started then turned to me. "Oh!" he said. "Sorry. Yes. Petunia, you remember, the preacher who harassed you this morning. I was thinking about how she must have reminded you of... well, whatever it is you've been through. People can get so aggressive over religion! I have this theory that, the more ludicrous a person's belief is, the more aggressive they'll become to defend it. It's just a distraction technique, really - to keep them from admitting to themselves that it's all a load of crap." He turned the page. "Anyway, you shouldn't pay her any attention. Most of the religious nuts around here are disillusioned Christians and Mormons, bitter over what's been happening in Utah."

"I don't know what's been happening in Utah," I said.

The Professor smiled and shook his head. "No, of course you don't. Anyway, the bottom line is - they're harmless. Completely mad, but wouldn't hurt a fly. Those people are pacifists."

I nodded but my attention was now completely absorbed by the diagram in the Professor's book. "That's interesting," I remarked, pointing.

"Oh," said the Professor. "Yes. That's called a centrifuge. I have to teach a class of thirty-five about it in..." He checked his watch. "Twenty minutes – lordy!" He clapped a hand to his forehead and shook his head. "Never drink at lunch, Michael, never drink at lunch..."

While the Professor berated himself, I reached over his shoulder and started to turn the page, revealing a new cross-sectional diagram of a machine that looked even more intriguing. But before I could begin to figure out how it worked or what it might have been used for, the Professor removed my hand, marked the page with the centrifuge on it, and shut the book. "Sorry," he said. "I'm going to need this today. As a reference. Because my brain's turned to mush." He snorted. "It's all that wine you made me drink at lunch. I never do, normally. You should have drunk a little more; then I wouldn't have had to finish your glass."

There was a mug of something black by the Professor's hand. He took a deep sip from it, wrinkling up his nose as if he was taking an unpleasant medicine, and stood up. "Maybe I'll explain the centrifuge to you when I get back. In the meantime..." He hurried over to a shelf of books by the front door, scanned titles, selected one, and carried it over, flicking through the pages as he did so.

"I can't read the writing," I protested. I looked up at him hopefully.

The Professor paused. "Well, then look at the pictures." He brought it down on the table before me and pushed it closer, open at a page showing the metamorphosis of a caterpillar into a moth. "Pretty butterflies," he said. "You can look at that, and when I get back, we'll discuss what we're going to do about your living situation. I should be back in about two hours. I only have one lecture, but there's a Q and A session afterwards and the students never miss a chance to tear my mangled brain to pieces. Help yourself to anything you want from the fridge, and... I'll see you in a couple of hours, okay? Bye-bye."

He left quickly, taking his coat. "Stay where you are. You'll be safe." I heard something click in the door behind me, followed by the sound of retreating footsteps.

Five minutes passed. I became bored with the moth.

Flicking through the book, I finally settled on a considerably more interesting page on dogs. In particular, their mating habits.

Of course, I knew it all anyway. My father was always open about such things with me, and I was, after all, seventeen. But it was nice to have something familiar to focus on, especially while on a stranger's territory.

#

Nine years old. The television casts a dull blue light across the cabin. The energy pack latched to its casing flickers orange, desperate to be energised by the sun. You couldn't take it to the beach today: the Dead-Talkers were using the space where the moon will shine brightest to prepare for tonight.

Now their voices, howls and cries, travel up from the beach over the struggling muted voice of Lorna Lane.

"What are they saying?" you wonder.

Rawg lies behind you, close enough for warmth, not quite touching. You can feel him tense. "Nonsense things," he says. "Pointless words."

"You're lying."

"Focus!"

The video is one you've seen countless times before. Peeking out from amongst the boxes, Lorna Lane's distorted face arcs towards you on the bubble-screen. Her voice is deep and dragging; sometimes it jumps, stutters. "There... is room... for all of you... in G-God's family... As J-Jesus says..."

"Rawg..."

"The Dead-Talkers feel the spirits inside them. They think the spirits come through the moon, not from Heaven. They think the spirits talk to them... Stupid! They don't know what your people know."

"What are the spirits saying?"

"Nonsense things," says Rawg. Then, "They are talking about the devil. Casting out the devil."

And Lorna Lane says, "...Accept... J-Jesus... into your hearts... and you will be... s-saved..."

"Do they think I am the 'devil'?"

Rawg hesitates. You sense him move behind you, perhaps craning his neck to look over your head at Lorna Lane: her slender female figure holds more interest for him lately. "Father will protect you until you're old enough to find your own people."

"Why do they think I'm a devil?" Your chest is tight. Your eyes are starting to water, like Jesus's eyes do on the video when he looks

skywards and hears the voice of God; but you hear nothing, not even Father's voice. You struggle and shudder against the water dripping down your burning cheeks. "Rawg, why?"

Lorna Lane says, "...Heaven awaits... all of you... no matter race... colour... creed..."

"Because they are stupid! They don't understand." Rawg gestures to the television's eye. "Not like them."

As if enchanted by Rawg's words, Lorna Lane wavers. The screen becomes black, blue, white, and then dies. The television is blind.

You lie in dead, quiet darkness. The voices of the Dead-Talkers travel up from the beach, through the trees, through the thin flat boards which make up the Edu-Centre's walls. Your body stills. The water cools on your cheeks.

You feel Rawg move behind you. Chill air as he leaves your side. You scramble to your knees, squinting against the darkness for him. Hear the clicks of his tongue as he navigates his way across the Edu-Centre floor. He opens the door, just a crack, letting in the howls and wails but also the silver light of the full moon. Rawg's silhouette against the glow is tall and broad-shouldered, like Father's

"We can't go to the beach now," you warn him. It is easier in the moonlight to find the television. You locate the energy pack by its now-red pulsing light, detach it. Heavy and hot in your hands. "We can go tomorrow."

Rawg comes over to you, sure-footed in the moonlight. He clamps a box from above the television between his stubby, curled hands, lowers it to the ground, and then tips it over with his foot. Into the sliver of moonlight spill the items Father deems impossible to understand: water-damaged books, video tapes and shiny discs smashed by fists and scratched by claws. Rawg kneels in amongst them, and you stand watching your brother as he sifts through: books with diagrams, smudged images; a big black book – it looks like Lorna Lane's prayer journal, with thin pages and tiny words in scrawling ink; images of the Edu-Centre as it appears from outside. Rawg scoops up a torn piece of paper. "Hold."

The paper is now in your hands, dry and wrinkled and delicate against your skin. But your eyes remain on Rawg.

He kneels before the television, closes his eyes. Clicks his tongue. Then he takes a piece of flint from the floor and hacks into the *boards, a line here, a line there, building, building a picture. He goes back to the television, places his hands on its screen, clicks. Moves back to the floor. This goes on and on, until finally Rawg rises.*

"Inside the television," he proclaims. He points to the picture he has created in the wood. "Show me the paper. Is it the same?"

Now you look at the paper. The image is similar to the one Rawg has created on the floorboards, except for one detail... you point to the arrow-shapes on the picture. "These aren't on yours."

"Those aren't solid. They show the energy, passing through," Rawg explains. "The energy makes it work. Lets faraway people speak to us. For real."

"How..."

The cries from the beach rise. So similar to the howls of the forest-dogs. Almost identical. Rawg turns to the door, and his lips lift at the sound.

"What are they saying now?"

"Doesn't matter." Rawg's voice comes out as a snarl. He stabs a stubby finger at the paper. "This is why your people are better! They don't need spirits and the moon: they're not animal-beings. They understand how things really are, and they create." He looks at me, wide black eyes deeper than the night sky. "It's like Lorna Lane says. Your people are descended from God."

CHAPTER FIVE

When the Professor returned sometime in the late afternoon I was sitting at the table, the Professor's bookshelf empty, his books strewn across the floor and three volumes open before me, looking from one to the other studiously between sips of something fizzy I had found in his refrigerator.

I heard him close the door and drift across the room. He said nothing.

Finally, his silence made me curious. I glanced up to see that he was replacing the books on the shelf. I moved my arm defensively around the three books I was currently working on, and continued to examine them, pausing occasionally to suck more sugary fuel from a can with a luminous-green thunderbolt on it.

When I next looked up, the Professor had both hands on the table and was staring at me.

I tried to smile but I don't think I succeeded. It felt like more of a grimace. "Hello," I said.

"Hello." The Professor reached across the table and nudged one of the books closer to him. He examined the page. "'Digestive Problems in Dogs'. What happened to the book I gave you?"

"I looked at it," I said. "I finished it. I put it on the floor, by the oven." I gestured to where I had left it lying on its crumpled pages, spine-up.

Wordlessly, the Professor left the table and went over to it. I pulled the book he had moved back towards me and continued my studies.

After half an hour, most of the books had been found and put back on the bookshelf. The Professor wandered to the table through the graveyard of scattered remainders. I watched him. I sipped my drink.

He was carrying the thick volume that he had originally given me, fingering its pages. When he reached me, he put it down heavily before me again. "You said you couldn't read."

"I can't," I said. "I'm working out the meaning from the pictures."

"Sounds difficult," the Professor said. "You know, if you were trying to look something up, you could have asked me."

"Oh," I said. "Would you have known the answer?"

He smiled. "Well," he said. "I am a professor of science."

"Of the *History* of Biochemistry and Genetics," I corrected.

The Professor did not comment on this. He glanced over the three books I had in front of me. All were open at different diagrams. "'The MRI Machine: A History'," he read. "'Doctor Abraham Willis and the Cure for Cancer'. 'Common Illnesses in Domestic Dogs'." He looked at me. "What's the connection?"

"They're the only three books I haven't looked at yet," I said.

The Professor nodded slowly. He leaned in closer, putting a hand on my shoulder (I shrugged it off), and focused on the book to my left, 'Common Illnesses in Domestic Dogs'. "Do you understand this?" he asked, pointing to a diagram of a dog's intestine.

I looked closer at the picture, making sure that it was what I thought it was. There could be little doubt. "Yes, of course I do," I said defensively. "Don't you?"

The Professor didn't answer. He moved in closer still. "Why don't you explain it to me?" he suggested.

I didn't know whether this was a test or whether he genuinely didn't understand the workings of the digestive system. I failed to see how anyone could get along in life without having at least a basic understanding of what went on inside their own body. The dog's digestive system is not so different from that of a human, I knew. Still, I decided to play along.

"The food has been broken up into little bits. Tiny bits," I explained, pointing to the relevant section of the diagram. "That all happens higher up in the body. And the bits aren't the same size as they are in this picture, you see. They're much smaller. When the bits reach this part of the body – the tubing, down here. Look." I demonstrated by placing my hands on my abdomen. "They drift out through the lining of the tubes, into the blood, where there aren't so many of the little bits. Then the blood carries the bits away and new blood with no bits in it comes along, and the process repeats. That's how the useful parts of food get to different parts of the body." I frowned at him. "Don't people here know that? I thought everyone knew that."

The Professor didn't answer. "And the MRI machine?" he said. "Can you explain that to me?"

"What's an Em Arr Eye machine?"

"An MRI machine – that." He tapped on the book in front of me.

"Oh." I looked it over again to refresh my memory. "It seems to work," I said, "based on the fact that if you project enough energy-waves at a body, you get a signal back, and you can see what it looks like on the inside. Like when you can't see something properly - you make a clicking noise and the echo comes back to you and builds up a picture inside your head." I clicked my tongue a few times in case he didn't know what I meant.

"Like echolocation in some mammals?" The Professor paused. "Now, that is an… *interesting* comparison."

"Yes. Except these waves are different from the ones you'd make clicking to find a tree in the dark. You use this machine to trigger the waves. And the image appears on a screen instead of inside your head," I continued. "Which is pointless and indirect."

"I'd hardly call it pointless," the Professor said. "Before the cure for cancer was discovered, machines like those were extremely useful for detecting and monitoring the spread of tumours inside the body. Which brings us to this one." He slid 'The MRI Machine: A History' away and pushed the final book in front of me. "Can you explain this, Katrina?"

I squinted at the image. I had been having trouble with this one. Instead of being a three-dimensional cross-section, as the others were, this image was made up of straight lines and was surrounded by clouds of tiny, unintelligible text. "No," I admitted finally. "I don't know what it's for." I looked up at the Professor, hoping for an explanation.

The Professor gave me a smile. "Now, *that*," he said slowly, "was one of the earliest stages in the development of the machine which replaced chemotherapy in the treatment of cancer. It was the last treatment to be used before the pill was brought in."

"Oh," I said. "What is 'cancer'?"

The Professor's smile faltered. "Your father didn't teach you that? Seriously, this is why they need to abolish home-schooling. Well, cancer is… it used to be quite a common disease. Let me see – how to explain it?" He was silent for a long time, frowning. It seemed he was trying to deconstruct everything he knew about 'cancer' and piece it back together in its simplest possible form. "It consisted," he began, hesitantly, "of... masses. Cells growing out of control, blocking up parts of the body."

"Oh. Masses," I said. "Yes, of course I know about *that*. My brother had one in his left testicle. I just didn't know you called it 'cancer'."

The Professor opened his mouth. No sound emerged.

"Anyway," I continued. "It was simple enough to treat. All you need to do is project sound at the mass, and pitch it so the vibrations don't damage any other parts of the body too badly. Vibrations destroy the masses. Like when you blow on a spider's web and it breaks."

I looked up at the Professor again. He was nodding, slowly. "That was exactly the premise behind Willis's machine," he said. "I have spent an entire term trying to explain that to my students. And some of them still don't get it."

"Maybe they have subnormal intelligence," I suggested. "Anyway, you don't need a machine to make the vibrations."

But the Professor wasn't listening anymore. He looked down at the remaining books on the floor, then across at the ones he had replaced on the shelf. "So, you can understand complex concepts, but not simple ones. You're confused, no social skills, you make up stories, and for some reason your dad decided to raise you away from mainstream society. But you're intelligent. Katrina, where did you learn to understand these things?"

"Back home. Father taught me what he knew, and there were books and video tapes."

"And where are you from? Really?"

"Here." It seemed he was trying to figure something out, but I couldn't tell what. I had told him all he needed to know about my background.

"Okay. Answer me honestly. Your father: did he try to keep you hidden from the world because of the way your mind works? Because you're... *different*?"

"Yes."

"Fascinating." The Professor stared at the wall for a while. During this time he was mostly silent; the only sound to escape his lips was the whistle of his steady breathing, in and out, in and out. Then he ran to the door.

"Where are you going?" I asked. I thought that maybe I had offended him, although I couldn't see how.

The Professor was at the door now, shrugging on his long coat. He snatched his keys from the kitchen counter. "Wait here one moment." He left the apartment and closed the door behind him, the click sounding again – the key turning in the lock, I recognised. I listened to his footsteps clatter down the staircase.

He had trapped me inside. But I was safe here, I reminded myself: I was alone.

When I could hear him no longer, I turned back to the cancer book, took another sip of the sugary drink from the lightning-bolt can and, after wiping droplets of luminous-green saliva from its pages, scanned the volume over again.

Sometime later, the Professor returned. I didn't look up when the front door opened, as I was once again engrossed. Detachedly, I listened to him lock the door and slip the keys into one of his pockets. "Right," he said. "Now we can have a *real* study session."

This did make me look up. The Professor was standing at the table, clutching a mysterious brown paper bag. He lowered it to the floor and from it removed a large blue tub which he held up for me to see. I watched as he carried it to the kitchen and placed it on the counter. "Every student knows that junk food is key to a successful study session," the Professor said, removing the lid of the tub. Inside, there was something cold and white and sweet-smelling.

"You're not a student," I reminded him absently, my eyes on the tub.

The Professor brought the tub, along with two impractically large spoons, back to the table. One of the spoons was forced into my hand. Then the Professor took a seat opposite me and stared straight into my eyes with a fierce intensity. "Okay," he said. "Let's get started. Katrina – show me how your mind works."

The contents of the tub smelled of nothing. My first bite of the white substance sent a wild, coursing pain up through my teeth to my skull; my second, encouraged by the Professor, proved addictively sweet.

Together, we worked our way through the tub's contents as we devoured the knowledge in the science books, starting with the ones on the floor, and then moving to the ones on the shelves, becoming increasingly high and restless on sweeter-than-sweet chemicals as we progressed. 'Diabetes: The Discovery of Insulin'; 'Diabetes: Cured'; 'Cancer, and Doctor Willis's Miracle Cure'; 'Monroe's Science of Brain Reconstruction'; 'The Removal of Mental Illness from Society: an Achievable Dream'. Obviously, we didn't read every book in its entirety. But we made a pretty good attempt at flicking to all the most weird and wonderful diagrams, and working out how the machines and animal body parts they represented were supposed to function.

Or rather, *I* worked them out. I would then explain them to the Professor, who absorbed the information eagerly while making mumbling noises which seemed to indicate fascination. Sometimes he would contribute a sentence or two, half-remembered from his student days. "Ah, I remember – it's to do with the pressure and the rate at which it oscillates – spins, I mean – isn't it?" I would nod, humouring him. He was an educator who had grown up in this world, and yet somehow, it seemed he was learning from me.

The contents of the tub rapidly disappeared. Within twenty minutes, we were on to the soda reserves stowed at the back of the Professor's fridge, which he claimed to be saving for when his daughter next came to visit.

After the entire tub of sweet, cold dessert had been eaten, six servings of soda had been swallowed, and twenty-five diagrams had been explained, the Professor left the table and took to walking around it in circles, clenching and unclenching his fists, his eyes wide and his lips white with synthetic sugar substance. He had started behaving less like a civilised human being, and more like a forest-dog let loose on a carcass after being deprived of food for a long time.

I found this behaviour unsettling. All the more so since I had also left my chair, and was now sitting cross-legged on the table, shivering like a possessed Dead-Talker. Perhaps the food was poisonous?

If so, it was too late to do anything about it now. I swallowed another soda. "Alright," I said with a gasp. "Ask me another question!"

The Professor halted, whirled around, and fixed me with a maniacal grin. A droplet of white drool seeped from the corner of his mouth, which was still slightly red-stained from the lunchtime drink. "Turn to chapter five of 'Early Twenty-First Century Medicine', my dear!" he said dramatically. "I want to test you on stroke reversal therapies."

I caught all his questions mid-air and responded to them with immediate answers, some of which I knew to be true, some of which were purely guesswork. He snatched each answer eagerly; threw me another question, to which I would respond by hurling back another answer. My brain had never had this much exercise before. It was a game.

"I cannot *believe* this!" the Professor enthused, suddenly breaking off from the flow of the game and sending my brain reeling, disoriented. "You're incredible! The way your brain processes things, the speed... it's like you're not *human*."

"I *am* human," I responded tersely.

Silence. The Professor looked at me, head tilted.

I locked him in a level stare. "I am human."

"Yes, yes." The Professor was beaming at me scarily now - hungrily, even. He clenched and unclenched his fists again and swayed as he tried to remain stationary in my line of sight. "But – your brain – it's beautiful! There are no people like you *left* in the world anymore."

"What do you mean, people like me?"

The Professor had stopped his swaying now, and had started to bounce. Up and down, up and down on the spot, in front of me. He was making me nauseous.

"Stop it!" I said.

But the bouncing continued. "You know, if you said you had fallen from space, or from Heaven, I would have believed you," he said. "That is how *insane* you make me!"

"I make you insane?" 'Insane' meant unable to reason; Godless. His enthusiasm for feeding on my knowledge had bubbled over into such an intense mania that I feared this assertion was apt. He was overdosing on my intelligence. It was welling up in his bulging eyes; dripping through his teeth as heavy, white animal-saliva.

"You are like a creature from another world, Katrina! A mythical creature, unheard of for years – all mine," the Professor burbled on. "Your brain. Your beautiful brain. You *are* beautiful. Brains and beauty!" He stopped bouncing now and grinned at me stupidly, like a puppy. "God... you're *beautiful*!"

I slipped off the table and quietly walked towards the door. Then I remembered that it was locked. I paused. Tried to think. I turned and walked at a quicker pace the other way, towards the bathroom. But as I passed the Professor, his arm shot out suddenly like a striking snake and he grabbed my hand and spun me around.

We were back-to-chest. The Professor's hands were on my waist. He spun me around again, slowly this time, so I was facing him. He stared down at me, wild with a dozen or more emotions that I couldn't begin to understand.

"Get off," I shrieked.

The Professor lunged for my face.

I tried to wriggle free.

His lips pressed against mine.

'Kissing' is something people do at the end of a marriage ceremony to seal their union - 'you may now kiss the bride'. 'Kissing' was invented by the ancient Romans as a way of detecting alcohol on their wives' lips. Both of these facts were on one of the videotapes, 'Bible Studies Three: Marriage, Sex and Sin'. The knowledge flooded my mind, but even with the explanation, it felt wrong. Very wrong.

"Get off!"

As suddenly as he had lunged for me, he withdrew. It was as if an invisible presence had slapped him across the face. He retreated backwards several steps, trying very hard not to look at me. If I was confused at this point, the Professor seemed more so. I ventured towards him, still intrigued, but now also a little concerned. "What are you doing?" I asked. Then, trying a gentler tone, "Is this behaviour normal for you?"

The Professor closed his eyes and shook his head. "No."

"No?"

"I just... I don't know what gets into me sometimes. You're young. Very young." He opened his eyes. Offered a smile. "I'll go slow with you, okay Katrina? I won't do anything you're uncomfortable with."

I didn't know what he meant. But when I looked into his eyes, the insanity seemed to have gone.

#

We started off in the same bed that night. He invited me, promising to keep from touching me, explaining that he was lonely, that he shared a bed with his daughter whenever she stayed - I could even keep my bag with me, as long as it stayed on my side. I accepted. I didn't want to seem rude.

Lying awake, I listened to the pattern of his breathing, keeping myself at a distance from his body, waiting. When I was certain that he was fully asleep, I left the bed and went to lie down on the orange sofa.

My bag became a pillow again. The thick smell of the leather was comforting, and I could feel the solidity of the journal within: the Professor could teach me to read its contents. It was a good thing I was staying with him. Very good.

I noticed the photograph of Aleshia out of the corner of my eye and looked up at her apologetically: I hadn't meant to take her place by her father. I felt confused but calm. Or maybe not calm. Just drained. Intellectually, emotionally and physically drained.

As I drifted, I found myself wondering vaguely what my brother might have been doing. Twenty-two nights had gone by since Father's death. No doubt my brother would have argued for him to be buried as a former Leader should be buried: anointed by Araga-Mawg, carried deep into the forest to the heart of the graveyard, placed in the ground to the broken howls of the women and the children. Rawg should have been Leader himself now. Maybe tonight he was lying in the same position as I was, looking up at a star-embroidered sky just as I was looking at the Professor's white ceiling. Thinking… of what? Of me?

Of *anything*?

No. He was still breathing. Of course he was still thinking.

The thought lingered for a minute or two then gradually faded as my mind drifted away to sleep.

#

You are still sitting on the floor of the Edu-Centre with Rawg as the sunlight comes in through the cracked door and warms the room. Around you are books, open to pages showing images: of machinery, buildings, organs. Folded in your arms is the journal, heavy and solid and so like Lorna Lane's prayer journal: full of interesting new script unlike anything in the other books. It seems special.

"Inside the body." Rawg points at a diagram, and then presses his hands to his chest. "Not just a picture. It shows the blood, moving about. The arrows – look."

Shifting the journal under your arm, you trace the arrows on the image.

The shaft of sunlight darkens. You look up to see Father standing in the doorway. "Open," he says. He points to the door.

"We needed light," you explain. "The television..." But Father has turned from you to Rawg. They are saying something; silent communication.

Why can't you understand? If you're descended from God and can make televisions and draw pictures of blood in the body with your freakish bendy fingers - why can't you understand their talking?

"I'm going to the beach." You pick up the energy pack, and head towards the door.

Father grips your shoulder and forces you back into the room. Slams the door as you scream. He knows. He knows not to touch you like that.

You drop the energy pack and curl around the journal. Shut your eyes. Water on your hot cheeks.

"Sorry." Father's voice. You curl tighter.

"Trina... sorry." His chest presses against your back, and he waits a breath before crossing his arms around you, pulling you in to him. The pressure slows your heartrate.

"What happened?" you ask. Water on your eyes, your cheeks. You sniff, trying to fight it away. Nobody else does this. Not even Lorna Lane. "What happened on the beach?"

You hear something drop to the ground before you. Open your eyes to see Rawg, crouched. He says, "The Dead-Talkers say..." Father huffs. Rawg stiffens, hesitates. "You will be safe," he says. "They won't try to hurt you until you reach adulthood. Wouldn't kill a child; even they believe that is unforgivable."

"But you're Leader." You turn to Father. "You can make them stay away..."

"Father is no longer Leader."

"But..."

"Bad now, better soon," Father tries in his rasping, thick-tongued voice. He leans his cheek against your hair, his scent thick, breath warm. You uncurl. Gently, he takes the journal from your hands and holds it before you. Turns its pages, his thick fingers impossibly gentle.

"We're going to get you off the Island," Rawg says. "We have lots of time."

"Years and years." Father stops turning pages. The spread he lands on has been decorated with pictures. Around the edge of the strange text are tiny, beautiful flowers, leaves, little birds. Father's big *rough hand covers yours, and he moves it to trace the design, so intricate, so otherworldly. "Years and years. Have to keep going, girl. Have to keep going."*

CHAPTER SIX

When I awoke the next morning (thankfully, this time I had been left to sleep on the sofa), the apartment was full of warm, edible smells again. The Professor was busy doing something in the kitchen. At first I could see only his blond-brown hair above the countertop, Then he started to rise up carefully and I could see his eyes, his freshly shaven chin, his arms, which cradled a stack of glossy black plates with a swirly gold design. He set them down delicately on the countertop. When he saw that I was awake and looking at him, he grinned hugely at me. "I found some more of Aleshia's clothes this morning," he said. "So you can have a change."

Drowsy, I slipped off the sofa and gravitated towards the kitchen, strapping my bag securely across my body.

"No, no, no," said the Professor, ushering me away with a wafting gesture. "You sit down at the table. I'll bring the food to *you*."

Unnecessary as this seemed, I chose not to fight civilised convention. I sat down and waited.

"I've decided what I'm going to do with you," said the Professor. The smells of cooking became stronger as he lifted a frying pan from the top of the oven and dislodged its charred contents with a fork. "I'm going to take you to my lectures today. What do you think of that, Katrina? You'll be my student. Free of charge, of course."

He came over to the table and put a plate of something involving burnt eggs and carbohydrates in front of me. Then he returned to the kitchen to scrub the pan. "I think we have a lot to offer each other," he spoke over his shoulder. "Your brain is amazing; you can help me understand more than the dry old brains of science historians ever could. And I can offer you food, education, and somewhere to sleep. Pretty girls living on the streets are one thing, but a girl with a brain like yours – well, you're bound to attract some creeps."

"I want you to teach me how to read," I said. I fingered the opening of my bag before picking up my cutlery.

"I was getting to that," the Professor said. "Although why your dad didn't teach you to read, I have no idea."

"And I want you not to touch me again," I added. "Please."

The Professor's lips turned downwards. He frowned. "Fine. If that's what you want right now," he said. "Eat up."

As I feasted on the charcoal, I was distantly aware that the Professor had put down his frying pan and was staring at me in silence, elbows on the countertop, his newly-shaven chin resting in his palms. It was disconcerting. I had to force the image to the back of my mind before I could continue my meal.

"Then, when you've eaten, you can get changed," the Professor said. I said nothing back; his voice was so low and murmuring, he seemed to be talking to himself. "Classes start in an hour. I can't wait to show you where I work, Katrina."

#

Inside one of the larger red-brick campus buildings, the Professor led me down a corridor, green-carpeted and empty. He strode ahead while I followed behind, examining the carpet, trying to downplay my disappointment. How anyone could do anything productive in such a narrow, uninspiring room was beyond me.

Suddenly, I was beckoned to the left and through a door. We emerged into what at first seemed to be a room of regular height – although considerably larger and grander than any room I had been in before. Four immaculate, white-painted walls and a vast ceiling of light-panels enclosed this manmade cavern, which was furnished in dark, old wood, and rows of leathery seats.

Following those ceiling lights with my eyes all the way to the back, I was shocked to discover that the far wall was at least three or four times the height of the wall behind me. The rows of seats sloped down, like in the Roman amphitheatres where nobles drooled over humiliated slaves before Christianity civilized the world (according to the Edu-Centre video, 'Bible History One'). Mounted on this wall was an immense black board; beneath this was a wooden stage.

"Better find a seat before anybody else gets here," the Professor whispered, his breath hot and close to my ear. "Don't want to look too conspicuous." He shepherded me down a set of steps into the belly of the amphitheatre. I moved quickly. Already I could sense the vibrations of approaching footsteps, hear the restless chatter of young people.

As the first cluster of students entered the room, the Professor took up position on the stage, where he was dwarfed by the immense board. He smiled and clasped his hands together as he watched his audience assemble: a sparse scattering of thirty-five young people, all wearing the uniform deep Californian tan and nonchalant expression, with pieces of coloured silk and feathers woven into their otherwise identical cream-and-bronze outfits - skirts and tight blouses, short pants and shirts.

I was wearing another pair of pointless skin-tight pants (in indigo, this time), and a striped, sleeveless sweater with a baggy neck that rolled over on itself. The result: my body from waist to chin was too hot, and my arms were exposed to the elements. I fail to understand clothing.

Initially I was seated at the front of the theatre, where the Professor had positioned me. However, as the room filled with students, I crept to the back. I don't like feeling people's eyes on the back of my neck. I made sure I was next to the central staircase, too, which would make things easier if it became necessary to leave quickly.

As the final few latecomers took their places, the collective whirr of the audience's voices started to die down. The show was about to begin. Sensing this, I leaned in expectantly towards the stage.

I knew about events like this, of course, in which a single entertainer would perform before a crowd. I knew the basic code of behaviour: sit still, stay silent, watch and enjoy. Yet I had never seen performances on such a scale as this before, or in such a place - and never because I had been *invited*. Most of what I had seen before consisted of dancing, talking to the spirits or demonstrations of magic: displays which I had occasionally hidden in the beachside foliage with Rawg to watch. I did not know quite what to expect from this performance, but I was positive that the Professor was no Dead-Talker. The only skill he seemed to possess was the ability to absorb knowledge, *my* knowledge, and I failed to see how such a skill could be adapted into a stage performance.

"Settle down, please. Settle," the Professor said. The vocal whirr died away into silence.

The Professor scanned the front row. He frowned, seemingly concerned for a moment. Then he looked up and saw me watching him from the back row. He beamed, and began: "At the end of the twentieth century..."

I watched him gesticulate with his hands like an enthusiastic conjurer. I followed him with my eyes as he paced the stage, soliloquizing. I guessed at who he was going to select from the audience to answer one of his many questions. (I didn't understand this practice at first, as the questions he asked were clearly ones he already knew the answers to, having mentioned them earlier in his monologue; however, I quickly gathered that this was his way of checking that the audience was still listening – it gave him something of an ego boost, I suspect.) I breathed a sigh of relief every time he didn't select me. I watched him draw little symbols and diagrams on the black board; appreciated them for their art, even though I didn't understand their significance; tried to guess what they might mean. But the actual *words* the Professor spoke meant little to me.

The students seemed to share this viewpoint, watching the Professor with dull eyes and vacant expressions, heads in hands, fingers playing with hair, not quite awake.

Nevertheless, the Professor continued to act the perfect showman. He performed with such passion that he did not seem to notice that at least half of his audience was completely oblivious to what he was talking about. "Chromosomal abnormalities... embryo screening... genetic engineering..." These were all phrases the Professor used; phrases I did not understand.

What a performer, though! He became so immersed in the character he was portraying - the Messiah, imparting divine knowledge to the flock - that he actually adopted the self-confidence and magnetism of the role and, lost in the moment, seemed to forget what he really was: a wifeless, childless reject of society. It was fascinating to watch the transformation.

After half an hour, I became aware that the behaviour of the audience was changing. They were becoming more attentive. As I surfaced from my contemplations, something interesting must have been said, because all the students shuffled forward eagerly with their eyes focused on the stage.

"Now, before I reveal the surprise," the Professor was saying, "I'm going to say a few words to put it into context. The device I am about to show you was designed by Doctor Helen Monroe." The Professor did something with his hand and a now-familiar image flashed onto the board: three people in white coats, a tall dark man, a squat pale man, a woman. The screaming monkey pinned to the table had not been captured in this version of the image. The Professor indicated the woman. "I'm sure you will all recognise this image, and also the name 'Helen Monroe' from her only lasting legacy, the Monroe Pill - which today is given to expectant mothers in early pregnancy to reduce the risk of a baby born with defects. But for decades before the Pill, and for many subsequent years, Monroe was working on advances in the field of neuroscience. Advances which it would be inappropriate for me to discuss here, on the grounds of ethics… and taste."

A girl sitting on the bench below me whispered something to her neighbour about the Change in the Law. The neighbouring girl nodded and hastily scribbled on a piece of paper.

"You may be familiar with some of her associates. Steinberg and Steinberg, for example, the husband-and-wife neurobiologist team responsible for the Alzheimer's cure. Hans Peterson, who discovered the schizophrenia gene. Doctor Tati and Doctor Bai, of course…" He pointed again to the image, first to the tall man, then to the short. "In fact, there is a passage about Monroe, describing her as 'a woman who, through her efforts to cleanse our species of neurological abnormalities, may well have laid the foundations for a stronger human race', in the book 'Humanity and Parahumanity' by James Bai and Jean-Luc Tati."

"Sick bastard!" somebody suddenly hollered from amongst the audience.

"Perverted freak!" a girl shouted. "Bestialist!"

"Sodomite!" I offered. Somebody turned around and gave me an unpleasant look, but I knew that 'sodomy' was on a par with 'bestiality' in the Bible. It said so in the video 'Bible Studies Three: Marriage, Sex and Sin'.

"Alright, alright," said the Professor. He flashed his teeth at the audience, but there was something contradictorily weak and forced about this smile. "I know, I know. Settle down. Now, Doctor Monroe was a member of 'Homo-SuperiUS'."

The professor wrote the ridiculous word on the board as I would soon be taught to spell it: a blending of the scientific name for 'human', the word 'superior', and the 'US' capitalised like it is for the United States.

"Homo-SuperiUS," the Professor repeated. "The group of US scientists who believed that they could use their respective talents to create a stronger human race. These were the people who, years ago, backed the proposed law which would have allowed scientists the freedom to perform any experiment, without necessarily adhering to a legal or ethical code, so long as their intent was to benefit humanity…"

"Yeah, right," said one of the students, and another called out, "Those sickos deserved everything they got, and more!"

I wanted to ask them what they meant but the Professor continued, "It has never been proven that Homo-SuperiUS as a whole was complicit in what Doctor Tati confessed to. In fact, Tati only named Doctors Bai and Monroe as accomplices when he went to the authorities to confess to unethical experimentation on humans and animals. Others have suggested that Doctor Tati's perception of reality was altered, that he was suffering from schizophrenia…"

"Which Monroe cured!" someone called from the back.

"Not exactly," said the Professor. "Monroe lowered the number of schizotypal children being born…"

"So it's a bullshit excuse!"

"And the chimp!"

I flinched as the girl next to me squealed.

"They found the chimp, with bits of other animals stuck to its brain! It would've been people next, like he said!"

"That's not exactly what he… yes, well…" said the Professor. "Perhaps it is a sign of guilt that all members of Homo-SuperiUS either committed suicide or disappeared after the Change in the Law. Other than Peterson, that is - who was, up until his recent death, a fairly successful product designer for EcoTech." He smiled again at this, I think. Or perhaps he was baring his teeth. "Uh - Helen Monroe was one of the ones who committed suicide."

An excited murmur arose from the audience.

"The machine I'm about to show you," the Professor resumed, "was found in Doctor Monroe's cellar shortly after her antidepressant overdose. It was built several years before the discovery of Doctor Tati's chimp-brain experiment, during that five-year period of intense scientific productivity preceding the Change in the Law – after which, as we know, public opinion of science changed somewhat. After Monroe's death, the machine was left in the hands of her daughter who, when she moved to Florida, left some of her mother's old possessions to the University – thus, I am very pleased to say, it has ended up with us."

With this, he gave the audience a grin and ducked behind a curtain at the far left of the stage. After a few seconds' delay, he emerged wheeling the machine in question. It was a large metal box, half his height again, with a refrigerator-like door at the front and a small screen at the top.

"This machine, according to Monroe's daughter, was created to help sufferers of neurological abnormalities by restructuring the brain," the Professor said. "All Monroe's instructions and diagrams were burned prior to her death – and, as the Pill is now used to control abnormal births, neurological restructuring clearly failed as a cure for disability. We are left to speculate how it was supposed to work. Would anyone like to venture a hypothesis?" A girl put her hand up. The Professor pointed at her. "Yes!" he said eagerly. "Go on?"

The fragments of pseudo-science which came spewing from this girl's mouth were rendered incomprehensible by frequent slang and unnecessary repetitions of 'well', 'like' and 'erm'. All I gathered from the bits I could understand was that she was completely and utterly wrong.

The Professor nodded enthusiastically. "Yes, I can see why you said that – but, no. Actually, that would go against several of Doctor Monroe's most important findings... and at least one of Newton's. Anyone else? Ah – yes! Girl at the back?"

"You know my name is Katrina," I said, lowering my hand. "I told it to you in the bath yesterday."

Some students gave each other looks, and there were one or two whistles from the audience. A girl sitting a few seats away looked at me then whispered to the girl next to her; about the Professor being 'at it again'. They giggled.

"Yes, of course." The Professor's face flushed red. "From the... *study session*. I let you use the bath afterwards. Yes. So, how do you suppose this machine works?"

Clearly the man thought I was superhuman. "I won't know until I examine it. May I approach the machine, please?"

The Professor hesitated. Apparently he hadn't expected anyone to take such an active interest in his teaching. "Well – I suppose. Yes, why not?" he said. "If you like."

So I slipped from my chair and went to the stage. The students were watching me, I knew, and the spider-like sensation of their collective gaze made me want to turn back; but if by using my mind I could make these people accept me, as the Professor had, I had to keep going. I forced myself onwards. The Professor followed me with his eyes. He stared as I walked around the machine in one slow, wide circle, stopping before its screen. I reached out to touch it.

"No!" the Professor shouted. He stepped towards me. "No touching the machine, please." I tilted my head to show confusion, but he didn't explain.

Slowly, I dropped to my knees before the machine, watching the screen rise high above me as I dropped lower, lower - until my eyes were level with the handle on its refrigerator-door. I shut them lightly. My fingers found my ears, brushed the hair away. I breathed. Focused.

Then I clicked my tongue.

The image that formed in my mind was a lot more complicated than I had expected. Inside, the machine contained hundreds upon hundreds of fiddly little interconnected wires, enabling electrical currents to flow all over the place. Doctor Monroe had clearly been the type to over-think and overcomplicate: traits I have since discovered in most people, not just the science-and-technology clique.

Still, I would have worked it out. I'm certain. Only, after a ridiculously brief period of mere seconds, the Professor interrupted me. "Sorry Katrina, but… your time's up."

Slowly, I drew back from the machine and opened my eyes.

It took a while for the blurriness to clear. When it did, I saw the Professor staring at me with wide eyes and a small, tense mouth. His face was even redder than when I had mentioned the bath. I remained kneeling, waiting patiently for him to regain the gift of speech.

"Return to your seat?" he suggested finally.

This seemed a strange request. Looking over my shoulder, I saw that the piercing eyes of thirty-five students were on me and the request seemed less strange. Still, even as I left the stage and made my way back to my seat, the students continued to follow me with their eyes. Some turned to leer at me after I had reached my seat. Being on stage had clearly given me an incredible magnetism which stayed with me, even after I had returned to my former status of 'audience member'. I remained still and silent and tense, waiting for the strangeness to be over.

Sure enough, once the Professor resumed his lecture, the audience's attention did divert, bit by bit, back to him. The performance continued. The Professor spoke some more, smiled, gesticulated. After a few minutes he drew more pictures on the board, explained them in terms I failed to understand, and told everyone to copy them down onto paper.

I had not been provided with paper. I saw the other students rummaging in their bags, bringing out notebooks in various colours, sizes and materials. They flicked to clean pages, took out pens and pencils, and began to draw.

I watched this. Then I looked at the Professor, who was smiling approvingly at the sight of thirty-five students doing what he had commanded them to do. He was completely ignoring me.

I realised that I had no alternative.

I rummaged in my own bag, and brought out my thick, leather-bound journal. It smelled faintly of the sea but mostly of the musty interior of the bag. There was another smell, too, one which reminded me of the Island - but I tried to block this out. I turned carefully to the first page, which I knew would be blank. Then I took a pencil which the girl next to me had allowed to roll across to my portion of the table, and began to copy down what the Professor had drawn on the board. But all the time thinking, thinking about Doctor Monroe's machine.

The Professor rounded the lecture off by asking if anyone had any questions. Nobody did. It seemed that this was normal, because the Professor only paused briefly before stepping in with another query: did anybody have any observations to share, or any comments to make?

I put my hand up.

The Professor saw my arm in the air. He jolted. Then he looked around wildly at the other students, but it appeared that nobody else had anything to say. In fact, most seemed more interested in me than anything else: thirty-five pairs of inquisitive eyes were on me again, thirty-five mouths smiling eagerly. I tried not to panic at this. Smiles are positive, I told myself: these people like me. I will not be torn to pieces.

"I have an observation to make," I called.

The Professor stopped midway through scanning the front row of students, most of whom had their backs to him. I think I heard him sigh. Slowly, he forced himself to look up at me. "Yes, Katrina?" He smiled. At least, I assumed it was a smile. It looked more like he was baring his teeth, showing me the fangs which would tear the flesh from my bones if I continued to displease him - but, according to the Edu-

Centre video tapes, people don't tend to do that. "What observation would you like to make?"

"I was thinking about that machine," I said.

"Doctor Monroe's machine?"

"Yes," I said. "I've figured out how it works."

The Professor sighed again; it was definitely a sigh, this time. He did not seem as eager as before to learn about the workings of 'Doctor Monroe's Machine'. But I was not prepared to let this matter go. I had to prove myself.

"Listen to me, please," I said, in as commanding a voice as I could muster. "I am going to explain."

The Professor looked frantically down the rows of students, taking in thirty-five backs of heads, until the rows ran out and he was staring at his own feet. He gave a small nod. "Okay. Have another go."

So I explained, in the simplest of terms, how that machine of his worked. And while I cannot remember the specifics, I do know this: my explanation was logical, and *correct*.

As I explained, many of the students turned away, apparently disappointed. The Professor, however, stared at me as if he was watching the resurrection of a dead body or a fire being conjured out of nowhere. His eyes bulged as I spoke.

After I had given my explanation, and the students had collected their notebooks and pens and filed out noisily, I was left alone in the silent lecture theatre with the Professor. As soon as the final student had pulled the door closed behind him, the Professor came up the aisle to where I was sitting and pressed his chalk into my hand.

I examined the little white stick. On the Island, children used to pick them up every day – you would find discarded ones left in the dirt near the rock faces they had been decorating. "Thank you," I said, looking back up at him.

He was smiling eagerly; hungrily, even. His eyes were shining. "I want you," he said, "to *show* me how it works."

I glanced at the chalk, then back at him. It took me a while to understand what he wanted, but eventually I worked it out. "Oh. Alright."

Once we were both on the stage, I turned to him and gave him back the chalk. He looked at it, then at me.

"Find me a clean piece of the black wall to draw on," I told him. "I didn't have enough time before to build up a good enough picture in my head. Don't disturb me this time."

The Professor nodded. He went over to the wall, picked up a large eraser and started to wipe away his strange drawings. I dropped to my knees behind him. The sound of him cleaning the board stopped, and I felt that stare penetrating the back of my skull. I opened my eyes and faced him. "That's distracting," I said. "Don't do that."

"Oh. Sorry." With obvious difficulty, he forced his attention back to the board.

I turned away and closed my eyes again, pulling down that familiar black shroud. My canvas. I put my tongue to the roof of my mouth. Clicked. Listened. Clicked again.

An echo came back.

I clicked some more. Even though it didn't seem to be part of the typical human repertoire, I silently thanked my brother for teaching me this skill.

Images began to collect on the shroud. The images multiplied, grew clearer, connected. Became a working diagram.

For all its unnecessary complications and pretensions, what Doctor Monroe had managed to create was, I had to admit, an admirable machine.

I opened my eyes, got up off the floor. "Right," I said.

"Right?" The Professor stopped scrubbing. The board was almost completely clean now - another blank canvas. "Are you ready now?" He wasn't smiling but he didn't seem angry or upset either. I don't think he knew how to feel. He stared at me with wide, watery, wondering eyes. "I've cleaned the board, Katrina. Come on. Show me how it works."

I took the chalk dangling from the Professor's limp hand. Again I closed my eyes, just for a moment, to see that image with perfect clarity one final time. There it was, on the black screen behind my eyelids: Doctor Monroe's machine.

I put the chalk to the board, opened my eyes, and began to draw.

The Professor looked on, brow furrowed, hand stroking chin. He made noises as he watched - grunts and 'uh-huh's. I tuned them out.

When I had finished I looked at the Professor for a response. He approached the board. Peered at it for a long time.

"Well?" I prompted.

The Professor shook his head. "I'm sorry, Katrina," he said. "I just don't see it."

How could he not? I had drawn it *very* clearly. What I had put on the board was exactly what Doctor Monroe's machine looked like on the inside. I had finished it with different patterns and shading to show how the energy flowed and the movements of the gears - what was there not to see?

"Oh – wait a minute. Unless…" The Professor made a gesture at me which I didn't understand. Then he grabbed the chalk from my hand and turned his back on me.

He drew a line on the board. Looked at my diagram. Drew another. He repeated this process again and again until he had created, in his own bizarre, linear style, with no shading or curvature or shape, an abstract picture of something I barely recognised. He was finished within a minute, and turned back to me. "That's it, isn't it?" he said. "Doctor Monroe's machine. That's what happens inside."

I studied the picture. "Not really."

The Professor frowned. "What did I get wrong?"

"The machine isn't two-dimensional."

The Professor's intense frown cracked into a grin. He laughed. I wasn't sure I liked that laugh. "Alright," he said. "Yours gets an A-plus from the art department. But, as far as the working of the machine goes?"

"You've got the basics right, I suppose," I said. "It's like the cancer machine. Except these vibrations are special. They can be focused on any part of the brain. One burst and the entire surface of that area of brain will be destroyed."

"A clean slate, ready to be moulded into a healthier shape." The Professor nodded. "Typical Monroe."

"Is there a lot of demand for machines that do that here?" I asked. The Professor didn't answer.

Within the machine, I had detected little metal loops in all of the four corners. I pointed to each in turn on my picture. "Do you know what these are for?" I wasn't testing him; I genuinely didn't know.

"Oh." The Professor came out of his stupor. "Those. They'll be clamps for the arms and legs." He seemed distracted. "Years of mystery, nobody knowing how it worked. It was going to be lost to history. But now somebody knows - no, *two* people." His hands fidgeted excitedly. "This is incredible! If I didn't know better, Katrina, I'd say you were some sort of magical being."

I took a step back. "You do know better," I reminded him. "You are not superstitious. You are *civilized*."

"Come on, Katrina!" He started towards me; I took another step back. "Hey, what's wrong? We're living in crazy times. New things are appearing all over the place. Others are being taken away. There's nothing we can do about it. If we don't have a little belief at times like these, what do we have?"

"Common sense," I said. "*Sanity*."

He stopped. He could see that I was unnerved now, I could tell. His facial muscles relaxed, and slowly he became calmer, his body language more welcoming. "I... I'm sorry if I frightened you."

I let him come over to me, and forced myself not to scratch his face when he kissed me on the cheek.

"I'm so sorry, Katrina. I just got carried away. So much shit has happened lately, it's like... like I've been cursed. My work, then my wife, my little girl; my reasons to exist – all gone! Then suddenly, just when I needed something to bring me back to life again, there you were. It was like all three had come back at once." He smiled. "You know you're safe with me, don't you?"

"No."

"Well," said the Professor. "You are. I would never do anything to hurt you, Katrina. Never." He kissed my forehead. My neck.

I pushed him away. "You said you wouldn't touch me."

"I just got excited. You're exciting, Katrina!"

"I'm not trying to be. And you said you'd teach me to read the writing in those books."

The Professor groaned. His jaw tensed. "Fine. But I still want something from you. If you're getting food, shelter, and tuition from me, I want you to help me."

"How?"

"There's a lot of these old machines stored at the university. Most scientists burned their notes before the Change in the Law, a kind of protest. Help me to understand what they created, like you did with this machine, and we'll see about teaching you to read."

"Okay."

It was a kind of victory. But I sensed that if I pushed for more, the offer could be retracted. I fingered the flap of my bag: learning to read the second language, in the journal, would have to come later.

\#

Eleven years old. The undergrowth rustles harshly underfoot.

"Katrina... Katrina..."

Rawg's voice is a rasping whisper. It doesn't need to be. Everyone knows. They all know you two are connected; he will forever be cursed as your brother.

A flock of birds explodes into the sky. Yellow, orange, blue. The little deer – tiny, knee-high deer, unlike the enormous ones in the 'Our Wonderful Planet' video – dart to either side of your path. You know the animals' names, their colours. Your mind is different. Pushing branches aside – stupid, stupid bendy hands -

"Katrina..."

You step out onto the beach. The water hurries up the stones, hissing, and then retreats as you step forward. The blue of the water meets the blue of the sky. Endless. It looks like nothing's out there. You think of the remnants of the boat, the vessel Father says you arrived on, stashed in the forest nearby. Wonder what life would be like for Rawg, for Father, if it had just disintegrated in that eternal expanse of water...

In your mind, you count. One Mississippi, two Mississippi, as Lorna Lane does in 'English for Beginners'. You are counting 'seconds' which form 'minutes' which form 'hours'. For some reason these are important. All you know is the repetition calms you down.

After eighty-five Mississippi's, you hear Rawg arrive on the beach. His feet crunch over the pebbles. With a thick-furred knuckle, he softly brushes your shoulder. You move away. Keep your eyes on the water. Don't want to look at the fresh, dripping scratches on his face.

"We have time," Rawg says. "Years and years. Remember?"

You might have years and years – until you are eighteen, your people's age of maturity; Father had to bargain hard for that. But at what cost? Father is no longer Leader. Rawg, an outcast. It is his first Spring of maturity; the son of a Leader would have first pick of females, would not even have to fight for a partner. The son of a Leader would not return home with scratches on his face, no female, no respect.

You hate the water seeping from your eyes.

"Come on." You feel Rawg's fingers again on your back and then he moves past you, into the forest. Glancing behind, you see that he carries your journal under one arm.

Rawg hauls logs and pieces of boat from where you have hidden them amongst the trees, and you pluck reeds, using your dextrous hands to bind them together. Rawg lays the journal on the pebbles, open on the page showing the boat, sketched as it apparently looked before your cousins tore it apart - then moves back, watching you work, quicker with your freakish hands than he could ever be.

"You're sad for me," he says. You look back at Rawg and see the rip down one side of his face which startled you, which drove you from the Edu-Centre. It is no longer dripping. "There will be other years. Other females. Even if not, we will live."

"You might never be a father-" My breath catches.

Rawg tenses. "No. And you might never be a mother."

"I don't care about that."

"Exactly. It doesn't matter. The important thing is to send you home before you come of age."

"But you want to be a father. Don't you? Otherwise, you would obey Father and stay safe."

Rawg exhales. His stubby fingers trace the wood before him. His deep black eyes gaze over the ocean.

"Come with me," you say. Your eyes are watering again, your voice wavering. You struggle through it. "When I go, come with me. We'll find you a woman like Lorna Lane."

Rawg scratches a piece of bark with a claw. "Okay," he says. Quiet, but clear.

For the first time since the morning Father returned to the Edu-Centre tired and angry and no longer Leader, you feel yourself relax. Perhaps everything will be alright.

CHAPTER SEVEN

It was long past midnight. All the semi-interesting television programs had ended hours ago, and the void was now filled with commercials. Most of them were campaign advertisements by Ferdinand Mann and other near-identical men in suits. These had become so frequent now, I would often catch myself reciting the words from memory: a parrot repeating sentences it doesn't understand to keep itself amused.

"During these last few months of the campaign, I urge you, valued American voter, to ask yourself: what *has* my opponent done for the people of this country? True, the Change in the Law came about during his time in office - but only after months of protests by the American people." Thanks to the Professor's tutoring over the last several months, I could comprehend the text running across the bottom of the screen. It was the same as the words coming out of the bald, bearded man on the television: "With our EcoTech sponsors behind us, we promise to end the unemployment crisis and lead this country into a new age of prosperity, leaving behind the mistakes of our past. Vote for a brighter future. Vote for Ferdinand Mann."

Glad as I was for my ability to read 'English', it bothered me that my journal had yet to be translated. In the meantime, I had hidden it. There was a cabinet in the bathroom which the Professor never looked into - a fact I had deduced from a simple experiment. One evening, on my second week in the apartment, I had pulled a loose thread from my pointless skinny top and stuck it across the cabinet door with two small Band-Aids. Every time I returned, I found the thread unbroken. By the end of the week, I had determined that this was a safe storage space. I didn't like the look the Professor gave my bag when I brought it to breakfast every morning: the way his nose wrinkled, and his brows drew close.

Still, I kept reminding myself: this man was my protector. Provider of food, shelter, education, and television. He hadn't touched me since the day of my first lecture. I could trust him not to harm me or my possessions.

The familiar three-person image flashed on the screen; the French voice croaked through it. *"I am sorry. Science is sorry. We wanted a better world, but no utopia is worth the destruction of animal life, nor of its people..."*

Outside the apartment, footsteps started to creep up the staircase. Before long I could hear keys stabbing the lock repeatedly, followed by the inevitable growls and curse-words.

"I have seen so much. I have seen men and women strapped to tables in institutions, screaming, as laser beams pierced their brains. I have seen impossible creatures being formed in test tubes, and rare animals being used as receptacles to grow them. Now, we have devised a means of blending animal with man..."

Finally, the Professor succeeded in unlocking the door and stumbled into the apartment, a shopping bag in each hand. Sticky red stained his lips. He turned in the vague direction of the television set where he assumed (correctly) I would be, and grinned an intoxicated grin. "Hey there, my girl!"

On the television behind me, Tati prattled on, *"We wanted to replace God, but how can we know what is best for mankind when we are no more than men ourselves?"*

The Professor kicked the door shut behind him, held up his bags, and smiled in triumph at the ceiling. He closed his eyes, as if basking in some supernatural glow visible only to him. Then he dropped his arms and let the bags fall clumsily to the floor: he had lost a lot of weight recently due to his preoccupation with his work, so he couldn't keep his arms up for long. Suddenly he started shouting, "Wait – wait, wait!"

I don't know why he told me to 'wait'. Not only had I been living with him for the past five months; I had been shut inside his apartment since the previous Monday, remaining where I was even when he forgot to lock me in, to help him with his 'History of Science' work. It was now Friday – no, Saturday; it had passed midnight. Anyway, I clearly wasn't going anywhere.

"Wait!" the Professor said again. He started rummaging through the bags. "I have a present for you... somewhere. Ah!" He removed something from the smaller of the shopping bags and brought it over to the sofa, where I was still trying to watch the television. I had grown quite attached to the television over the last few weeks. It was good company.

"Well?" The Professor flapped whatever he was carrying at me and stamped his foot. "Look at it!"

I did. First with curiosity. Then with horror. What he was holding up for my approval was a pair of pink, shiny shorts with a row of leopard-print, heart-shaped patches stitched across the backside. I looked from them to him in dismay. "I hope you made a mistake."

He looked at the shorts, and then at me. Then, with a moan, he threw them to the floor. "You never wear the clothes I give you!"

"Wrong!" I splayed my arms wide, displaying the evidence. "I'm wearing your t-shirt, aren't I?"

Strangely enough, this seemed only to inflame his temper. He groaned, gritted his teeth, and diverted his attention to the television. "What the hell is this trash you're watching?" He squinted at the screen.

"A campaign advertisement. I'm waiting for 'America's Greatest Freak Shows' to start," I explained. "It's a good show."

The Professor groaned again and retired to the kitchen, shaking his head. "You'll rot your brain, Katrina." I heard him delve into his second shopping bag; glanced over to see him bring out a bottle of the familiar red liquid: wine. "The Head of the History of Science Department bought this for me. For getting my arctic… *article* published," he said. "Then he took me out, and… bought me a little more." He uncorked the bottle, spilt some on the carpet, slopped some more into one of the mugs on the draining board - a novelty mug, in the shape a man's head with a bald patch on top and large tufts of white hair growing out of the sides - and drank deeply from it. "Would you like some, Katrina? No? Good."

"How ironic," I murmured, "that you should be celebrating the completion of an intellectual achievement by destroying your brain cells."

Words had become a great source of fascination for me. I liked learning new ones – phonetically, if not for meaning – and slotting them into sentences that I thought needed improving. I had recently learnt the meaning of the word 'ironic': a wonderful new addition to my mental dictionary.

The Professor put his cup on the counter and pointed an unsteady finger in my general direction. "Don't be so smart." He staggered from the kitchen to the dining table where his laptop computer was docked, and somehow managed to navigate his behind into a seat and switch the device on. It made its little musical noise. I turned up the television, not to cover the noise so much as to signify my distaste for it.

The Professor didn't notice. "Right," he said. "Work for tomorrow, work for tomorrow. Concentrate, Michael!" He slapped himself in the face with both hands. Then, "Katrina!" he called. "Could you pretty-please come over here and explain that... that *thing*... you explained to me last night? Please? My brain seems to be having trouble retrieving information."

Parasite, I thought.

"Oh," I said. "By 'thing', do you mean the part of Monroe's Machine where..."

"No, no, no. None of the *article* work," the Professor said, adding emphasis to the penultimate word as if I was an idiot. "The *thing*. You explained it to me last night?"

I got up from the sofa and went to him, as slowly and begrudgingly as possible.

"You could be a little more grateful, you know," the Professor said as I approached. "I give you food, shelter, clothes..." I was behind him now, looking over the top of his head at the laptop screen, and yet he continued to address the sofa. "What do you give me? Hmm?"

"Oh." I saw the image he had pasted onto his screen. "You mean the structure of Parker's Machine."

"Yes, yes; *Parker's* Machine." He nodded furiously. "Could you draw me another diagram, please? One that's simpler than this?" He gestured to the screen. "I have to explain it to *fifty* students tomorrow. Did I tell you they've increased my class size?"

I took a pen and a clean napkin off the countertop behind me and started to sketch.

The Professor groped blindly in front of him for his mug of wine which wasn't there. He looked around, located it on the kitchen counter, and made to rise from his seat - then seemed to decide that the energy expenditure wasn't worth it, sighed, and sank back down. "They seem to be paying more attention to me lately," he continued. "The students. And the bosses. It must be the article - they're realising there's life in this brain yet!"

The television cut to a new commercial. Somebody with an orgasmic voice was trying to convince America to buy a new brand of sugary cereal bar.

I sketched faster, hoping to be able to catch the last few commercials before 'America's Greatest Freak Shows' started. I enjoyed commercials. I liked the way they provided you with tasty little snippets of information to memorise, like how fifty-five per cent of Americans need more iron in their diets, and how the new EcoToaster Max toasts bread thirty times faster than the previous model. Even if most of it was not entirely true, it was at least entertaining.

The Professor glowered at the television over the rim of his reading glasses. "Commercials," he snarled. "How exploitative can you get?"

That was when the phone in the kitchen rang.

The Professor looked at me. When I didn't move, he groaned and went to answer it, leaving me to finish the diagram.

I left my half-finished first diagram soaking up wine on the kitchen countertop and moved my work station from the dining table to the sofa facing the television. There I sat, leaning on an old (and therefore expendable) copy of 'On the Origin of the Species by Means of Natural Selection' to finish my second, simpler version of the diagram, only half noticing when my pen strayed onto the cover of the book because my eyes were locked on the screen.

The Professor finished his phone call.

After a minute I looked up, curious about why he was being so quiet. I saw him standing by the dining table, looking at me in a strange sort of empty silence. What was that peculiar expression on his face?

I asked, "Are you sad?"

He smiled. A small smile. "Oh, no," he said. "That was… my wife on the phone. She wanted to know why I've stopped calling her all the time. I told her I was busy with work. Well, that was only a half-lie."

He smiled again then came over to sit beside me on the sofa. I shuffled up to give him more space. He took the remote control from me gently, and muted the television. "She read my article. Said it was very impressive. The interview in the Times, too: remember when those journalists came to talk to me last month?"

"I had to stay in the bathroom," I remembered. A flash from the television drew my attention. On the screen, bright words exploded in front of a happy family 'barbeque' scene: 'Bigger', 'Better', 'Buy it Now'.

The Professor ignored me. "She... *apologised*." He laughed. "You can't imagine how strange that was – I mean, coming from her!" He seemed pleased. "Then she said... She's bought me a ticket, you see, to fly to Hawaii. So I can spend some time with her. With Aleshia, I mean. It's a first-class ticket - she always did have too much money, that woman. She works in advertising for EcoTech Food, you know?"

I wasn't sure whether I should stop the diagram and pay attention to him or not. I decided to continue. "No. I didn't know that."

"The thing is... it's an open-ended ticket," the Professor went on. "I don't know how long I'd be out there for. Perhaps... anyway, it doesn't matter. I can't leave you." He looked at me even more intensely this time. His glasses were falling down his nose; I could see his big, glistening, performer's eyes unobstructed. "Can I?"

A direct question. I stopped drawing and looked at him. "Of course you can leave me," I said.

"Really?" The Professor beamed. "Are you *sure*, Katrina?"

"Of course I am. You can leave any time you want." Of course he could. He had the goddamn key. Cold crept up my skin: while I told myself that he was a good man, that he would make the correct choice, it was as if I could sense what was about to come.

The Professor was shaking his head now, muttering to himself. "No. It would be selfish. I couldn't do that to you. You couldn't survive on your own." With a huff, he got up and walked towards the kitchen - then paused. Turned around. "But if I made... alternative arrangements for you." Behind his tearing eyes and beneath its red-wine shroud, his mind was fumbling with an idea. "So you could have somewhere to live, at least – that would be *almost* alright. Wouldn't it?"

I shrugged my shoulders in a way I had seen people do on the television before, to signify nonchalance. "Several factors would need to be taken into account. It all depends on what sorts of arrangements you would be making for me. It also, of course, depends on your definition of 'alright'."

The Professor opened the fridge door, selected two cans of soda, and brought them over, pressing one into my hand as he sat down. "What would your definition of 'alright' be, in the context of 'alternative arrangements', Katrina?"

Television. Water. Food. Shelter. In priority order, these were what I felt constituted 'alright' alternative arrangements.

The Professor promised that he could arrange all these things for me. In exchange, all he wanted was my confirmation that what he had already decided to do - to leave me with strangers while he escaped to be with the woman who had abandoned him - really was 'alright'.

But as hard as he stared at me, I refused to say a word.

#

The arrangements were made. I was to live with two students, one of whom was connected to the Professor by some tenuous link, who shared an off-campus apartment in which a small third bedroom had recently become vacant. It was a 'good-sized' apartment in a fashionable part of town, with plenty of bars, (pointless) clothes shops, and a movie theatre within walking distance. My needs would be catered for: inside the apartment was a wide-screen television, and I would be provided with an adequate sum of money each month (or rather, my new housemates would be) to pay for food and my share of the rent.

When he got around to revealing all this to me, the Professor took obvious pleasure in listing these points; most of which meant little to me. But his explanation wouldn't come until the day before I was to be moved: driven from the one place I had come to see as home, by the only person who (despite his shortcomings) I had forged a connection with. This wasn't how things were supposed to go.

He was supposed to be my protector.

The weeks passed slowly, coldly. We didn't speak of the Professor's wife or the moving-out during that time, but there was a tension in the air. Sometimes the Professor seemed to have regressed: he would attempt to put an arm around me, stroke my hair, or grip my shoulder. I would glare, and he would go.

One morning, I awoke on the sofa to find that the Professor was busy in the kitchen, putting the finishing touches to a disconcertingly *different*-looking breakfast. As I wandered over to the dining table, I saw that it consisted of an assortment of cold meats, dry breads, and various bruised fruits: some cut in half, some piled up in bowls and disguised with sugar. There was also a red flower on my plate, which I did not attempt to eat because of the thorns.

"We need to eat everything in the fridge this weekend," the Professor told me from the kitchen, pouring the last of the orange juice from various half-empty cartons into a jug. "Celia's booked the flight for Monday. Which works well, actually, because I called a friend earlier who's looking for an apartment – her husband's just left her, poor thing – and she says she wants to move in here as soon as possible. So we only have today and tomorrow to pack up our stuff and do a deep-clean."

He came over to the dining table where I was now sitting, and put the jug down. Before he went to his own seat, he helped himself to a couple of strips of meat from a plate in front of me. I wrapped a protective arm around the rest of it, and gave him a defensive glare. He laughed. "It's not all for you, you know."

I did not remove my arm, nor did I stop staring. I was going to relocate. I needed supplies. My eyes flitted back and forth, searching for other items to protect.

The Professor shrugged. He pulled the jug away from me before I could grab it, and poured himself a glass of juice. "When she rang about the ticket, Celia said she was concerned because I haven't been calling her so often," he said. "She says I've been different lately. More aloof, more reserved – as if distracted by something. I think we both know who that 'something' was, right, Katrina?" Grinning, he hovered over my glass with the jug. I pushed it away. He raised an eyebrow. "Of course," he continued, putting the jug down, "I didn't tell her about you. That would've really set things back, if she knew I'd been living with a girl the same age as our daughter. So… I'm sure you can appreciate why we need to keep our little arrangement to ourselves, hmm? Oh, and by the way." He gestured towards me with his fork. "I'm going to need Aleshia's clothes back. Celia said she's been asking for them."

He leaned back in his chair, gazed at the ceiling, and sighed. Meanwhile, I seized the moment to remove an orange from the table, and hide it beneath the folds of my outsized 'I-Heart-California' t-shirt.

"My God," he murmured. "After all this empty time, I'm going to get to see my daughter! Celia, too." He looked at me. "She mentioned on the phone, she and her new boyfriend have been having 'disagreements' lately. Do you think that means anything?"

"Yes," I said impatiently. "It means that she and her new boyfriend have been having disagreements lately." Silently, I urged him to look at the ceiling again. I couldn't rescue any of the rest of the food while he was staring at me like that.

The Professor smiled vacantly. "Well, maybe that's all it is," he said. "Still, if they have another disagreement, and this time I'm there …"

In that irritating manner I have observed in many people, the Professor left his sentence unfinished. It hung awkwardly between us as he continued his breakfast, tipping the contents of two small bowls of fruit onto his plate simultaneously, and then reaching for a piece of bread as he forked them into his mouth.

I watched him in silence, thinking. I removed another two oranges from the table and concealed them under my t-shirt.

The Professor scraped the last few scraps on his plate together, and devoured them. Then he looked across at me. "Have you finished that?" I gave no reply, so he took our plates away to the kitchen, gave them a half-hearted spray from the faucet. "I'll clean these later. Packing is the priority for today."

I continued to watch him, still thinking.

Now the Professor noticed me staring. His brow furrowed but his smile remained. "Is something wrong, Katrina?"

I had never seen him do this before, this simultaneous smile-and-frown. It made it more difficult to decipher his emotions.

"I want to ask you something," I broached cautiously. "A favour."

"Alright." The Professor rested his elbows on the countertop. "As long as it won't take too long."

"It won't," I guessed. Bunching my t-shirt around my oranges, I left the table and hurried to the bathroom.

I opened the cabinet and removed my bag. I also rescued a small bar of soap and a pair of shiny nail clippers, which I wrapped in a towel with the oranges and stowed in the cupboard under the sink before leaving the bathroom.

The Professor was sitting at the table, tapping the wood with his fingers. He glanced up when I approached.

"Here," I said. I opened my bag, and removed the journal. The leather cover still retained some of its original earthy smell, but this was barely noticeable now, replaced by the scents of old hair-care products and twenty-four-hour deodorant. I pushed it across the table to the Professor, and sat down. "Are you able to read this?"

The Professor looked at me, frowning again, as he took the journal. He examined its cover. "Let's see."

I leaned forward in my chair, watching intently as he scanned the pages. He turned to the first page; his frown deepened. This confused me because there was nothing on that page; then I remembered that yes, there was – this was where I had copied down what the Professor had drawn on the board during my very first lecture. (For all subsequent lectures, I had asked to be provided with paper.) I reached across and the Professor moved his hand a little so I could turn to the correct page: past the sketches of the boat, five pages in from the cover. I waited as he read.

The frown did not leave the Professor's face. He scanned the page; flipped through the next few pages. Then he looked up at me. I leaned in expectantly. "Katrina," he said. "This is written in English."

"No it's not." His lie disappointed me. I had learnt English. This wasn't the same as the print in the Professor's books, or those in the Edu-Centre.

"Yes it is." The Professor jabbed a finger at something on the page. "What does this look like?"

I squinted at the strange, squiggly thing fading on the paper. It almost looked similar to – "Is it an 'A'?"

"Exactly."

I clapped my hand to my forehead, emulating the gesture for despair at the failings of one's own brain which I had seen him do countless times. "Of course! I should have seen it! They are quite similar. But *this* writing," I added, looking at him seriously, "is peculiar. Why aren't all the symbols in normal English joined up, like how they're done in the journal?"

"Because nobody joins their handwriting anymore!" said the Professor. "Cursive handwriting is archaic. I've seen one or two eccentrics do it, and a few preachers – but they're a weird, old-fashioned bunch anyway. It's *this* handwriting that's strange, not mine!"

"But can you read it?" I pressed.

"Of course I can!" The Professor turned to the fifth page from the cover again. "Do you want me to read it now?"

"Yes. No – wait!" I grabbed his shoulder. "Take it over to the sofa; that way we can sit next to each other. I want to look at it while you read."

A momentous event was fast approaching. That journal had been part of my life for so long. I wanted to be sitting comfortably as its secrets were unlocked.

#

Thirteen years old. Discomfort in your abdomen. You clutch your journal to it and hunch over. Imagine the words of your people, those of the Civilised World, seeping through its pages and into your body. The pain dulls slightly. Perhaps because of the words. Perhaps because the book is heavy, providing a comforting pressure.

On the television before you, Lorna Lane says, "As a messenger of God, it is now your duty to spread truth and love to all your fellow men."

You don't know what she means. You don't care.

Spring sunshine filters through the crack in the Edu-Centre door. Father is out, scavenging deer: the half-eaten kills of the forest-dogs. Rawg has again been drawn, by the scent of females, to wait on the outskirts of your cousins' territory, sizing up his rivals. There is room on the raft for two, he has accepted the offer to join you, and still he persists. Almost as if he doesn't trust you. He will return before Father does, bloody, rejected. Until then it is just you and Lorna Lane, females together.

"March on into your new life, Christian soldier! With God on your side, you cannot fail!"

The agony seizes your stomach again. Normal, Father told you before he left. And Rawg expanded: the older females, and the ones rejected like Rawg, will be experiencing the same when Spring is over. But how can something normal hurt so much?

"For God is love. Jesus is love!"

You wonder, will you feel pain in the Civilised World? Surely God didn't mean for you to feel this way.

Why does it feel like something terrible is about to happen?

CHAPTER EIGHT

When we were side-by-side on the sofa, the Professor opened the journal again. He took a breath and began. "Day One."

"Day One of what?" I asked.

The Professor shook his head. "It doesn't say," he said. "It just says 'Day One'.

"Day One. Finally, we are leaving California – that devil-ridden pit of social unrest – for greener pastures. The sea, so far, has been calm. I have not yet been seasick: meditation and prayer not only keep my mind focused and clear, but also seem to have a positive effect on my physical health. It excites me to know that soon, I will be spreading this positivity to others. I no longer feel like I am drowning in the swamp of faithlessness and sin that has consumed America.

"Peter is at the helm. He says he cannot see any islands yet, but he knows God is guiding him. Soon, he says, our destination will be revealed to us.

"Sometimes I cannot believe how much I love Peter. Every time I see him, I am reminded of how wonderful life can be, even when all physical possessions are lost. Is it sinful of me to consider a mortal man 'perfect'? I can't think so. My love for Peter is an all-encompassing, giddy, beautiful thing; how could any evil come of it? Katrina is asleep..."

The Professor looked at me and gave a strange little smile, a wink. I made no indication that the mention of my name was important. Inside, however, the tempo of my heart said otherwise.

He resumed. "She is an eerily quiet baby. Sometimes I worry that there is something wrong with her. Sometimes, I feel that maybe I should have reported my pregnancy to the doctors and had the scans, taken the Monroe Pill" – again the Professor glanced at me, this time unsmiling – "but I am always quick to scold myself for these thoughts. As Peter says, at the end of the day, God has blessed us with a beautiful child. And if we continue to be faithful, God will ensure that she is healthy and normal.

"I am nervous that we are drifting towards a place where no civilised man has been before. But more so, I am glad. Since what qualifies as 'civilised man' back home contradicts anything I would deem 'civilised', the prospect of moulding a new community, leading them towards the light of true civilisation, fills me with such excitement, such joy. And not only will we be helping poor, isolated tribespeople connect to God - we will be creating a wonderful, sin-free haven for Katrina to grow up in. Somewhere so much safer than Utah has become."

"Where the disillusioned Christians and Mormons came from," I recalled.

"Yes. Well remembered." The Professor turned several pages – "These are pretty drawings, Katrina" - and read on. "Day Twenty-Two. This morning, we found our island. I checked – it isn't on any of the maps.

"As we drew near, I was touched by its unspoiled natural beauty. It is a small, mountainous island, with a forest which spreads across the lowlands."

"Our Island," I whispered.

The Professor ignored me. "A shroud of mist surrounds it, curtaining it from the rest of the world. It is quite eerie, this mist. I do not know the explanation for it, but I do know that it means we will be safe here. I suspect that this mist is the reason why no 'civilised' man has ever seen this island before – they have been put off by the prospect of hidden rocks. Such traps, however, are hazards only for people whose intentions are not holy. As Peter reminds me, we have God on our side.

"Peter is building two shelters. One for us, and one to function as an educational centre. When it is finished, I will help him to unload the food and the educational equipment. For now, these will stay on the boat.

"No sign of the tribespeople yet. I hope we will meet them soon."

I shuffled eagerly in my seat.

"Day Thirty-Seven. We finished setting up the edu. centre today. I appreciate all the advice the other missionaries gave us at the hostel in San Diego, about where to acquire the right DVDs, video tapes and cassettes – we have built up quite a library of teaching materials. Soon the tribespeople will reveal themselves, and will be led from the darkness of ignorance into the light. The cassettes and videos will help them to understand English, etiquette, the outside world and, of course, the Bible."

"Not all the videos," I murmured. "My cousins destroyed some of them."

The Professor seemed not to have heard me. "Reverend Barker told me years ago that 'savage' tribespeople, although I personally dislike his term, respond better to electronic teaching aids than they do to people. The fact that such devices are like nothing these people have ever seen before gives them a power which, to a certain type of mind, seems divine. I still battle my hatred of the sick heathen who murdered the poor Reverend. Whatever the police say, I know in my heart that it was no accident. It sickens me how American law has turned against Christianity. It is terrible how so many of us have been driven from our homeland, which was once 'one nation under God', to teach the Gospel elsewhere."

"Christian soldiers," I murmured.

"Are you going to let me read this?" the Professor said. He returned to the journal. "Katrina is growing fast. Every day she becomes stronger, a little more responsive. I know that this island will be a wonderful home for her.

"Day Forty. All tired after last night's storm. The roof of our hut started to leak, so we spent the night huddled together under a blanket in the edu. centre, watching videos until morning. The videos were for Katrina's benefit of course, but ironically, she was the only one who slept through the night. This morning, Peter took the television battery out to the beach to recharge in the sun. I pray that we will find some tribespeople soon, and that our Holy Mission can begin. But I have to be patient.

"Day Forty-four. We've got one! At around six o' clock this morning, Peter shook me awake and told me to look out the window. 'Anna' had entered our camp.

"She was standing just feet away from the edu. centre door, apparently fearless. Peter came out of our hut quietly. I was terrified that he might scare her off, but Peter, as always, was gentle and guided her into the centre without having to be too physical. When she was in, Peter called for me to bring Katrina and join him.

"Anna started to show resistance when she saw that she was outnumbered, so we gave her a mild sedative. Then we sat her down on the floor, wrapped her naked body in a towel, and played her the first video: 'God Welcomes You'.

"I named her 'Anna' after a girl I used to mentor in the Drugs Rehabilitation Programme back in Salt Lake City. Like her namesake, Anna is strong, wilful, and striking to look at. She has long dark hair, a large narrow nose, thick body hair, and an elongated face. I am eager to see whether these traits are common amongst her people. Her eyes are like nothing I have ever seen before. I can only describe them as being like the eyes of a wolf at night – but that does not reflect the depth and the intelligence I see in them.

"Peter says now that we have Anna, the other tribespeople will start to reveal themselves. Then we can save an entire community. It is all thrilling!

"If I have any concern, it is for Katrina's safety. But Peter reminds me that these are people, not animals, and that we must have faith in their humanity and the grace of God. I know he is right.

"And there are some pages here that are a bit blurry. I can't read them," the Professor said, flicking forwards. "Was that intentional, to make it look authentic?"

I didn't understand. "Keep reading," I pressed.

"Okay. Day Fifty-eight. Peter's body is so handsome and strong-looking. I still cannot quite believe he is dead.

"Katrina has not cried in days. She stays silent when she sees her father. I do not know how much she understands, but I do what I can to comfort her. I cuddle her and whisper hymns to her and I pray. In spite of this I feel as if my sanity is failing me. I tried to leave the edu. centre again this morning and couldn't. My chest became tight and I could feel my heart start to hammer. After barely a minute it became unbearable and I had to go back inside. I have to sort this out soon. If I don't, what will happen when the food runs out?

"I cannot let myself fall into depression. I have to be strong. When the tribespeople come out of hiding, it will be my duty alone to lead them to Salvation. God will give me the strength to do this when the time comes. Peter's death was all part of His plan, I know. Still - I will admit, it has become agony to endure now that my 'rock' has gone. But I have to be brave. I have to keep praying.

"I have an admission to make. I know that the poisonous spider which killed my Peter was nothing to do with Anna, yet I find myself feeling hostile towards her when I should be finding comfort in her company. The way she sits and stares at Peter's body with no apparent feeling whatsoever – it seems inhuman to me. But her detachment is an effect of the sedatives. Probably. She must feel something for Peter.

"I give her regular doses of the sedative, and I keep Katrina close. I am scared to go to sleep, but I know that I must. Otherwise I might completely lose my mind.

"Day Fifty-nine. I have killed Anna.

"I woke up in the middle of the night from a fitful sleep. As always, my first concern was for Katrina, so I turned to where she was sleeping and I swear I saw a rabid wild dog leering over the basket of clothes where I put her down for the night. I didn't think. I acted on instinct. I took Peter's gun from under the pillow and shot the disgusting beast dead.

"Now, though, it is Anna's body I see lying lifeless on the floor with a bullet in its brain. I have checked Katrina over and over again - she doesn't have a scratch on her.

"Of course, the dog I saw must have been part of a dream. Or a hallucination. I know that. Yet when I look at Anna's lifeless body, I fail to feel any remorse at all. Not a touch of sympathy. It is as if my subconscious mind is still convinced I have killed a vicious dog. It is not just my sanity that I am scared of losing now - I am scared I am losing my humanity.

"Day Sixty. The tribespeople have been outside the edu. centre for hours now. I can hear them rustling in the foliage, can see their shadows on the walls. They don't speak. I am desperate to hear them speak. Even in a primitive tongue, it would reassure me that they are human, at least.

"I am scared to fall asleep but I know it is inevitable that I will. Katrina is in her basket behind me. I intend to sleep in front of her, in the hope that my body will protect her somehow should the worst happen. Maybe when they see her, they will have some mercy on her. She is a helpless little baby girl, after all. Surely, in her blissfully ignorant state, she cannot be so different from their own young?

"God help me - I saw a face looking in through the window! A male face. It was gone in seconds, but I know it saw Anna's body. They know she is dead. They will be coming for me soon. Dear Lord, that face – I swear to this – was more animal than man! I do not mean that it was a frightening face, or an uncivilised face - although both are true. I mean that, at first, I almost mistook it for the face of a wolf.

"In a way, I hope they won't take pity on Katrina. I know it's a terrible thing to hope. But if we die, I want us to die together – a Christian death.

"Dear God, dear Peter, I know I must not be afraid. Katrina and I will be joining you soon.

"And that is where it ends. Wow." The Professor closed the book, and tried to pass it back to me. I wouldn't take it, so he put it down on the floor. "You had me fooled for a second there! I like what you've done with the pages. Water damage? Makes it look old. Isn't this the notebook you used for lectures?"

I didn't answer.

After a while, the Professor patted me on the knee and got up. "I'm going to go take a shower," he said. Before he left, he switched the television on for me. The picture came up on the screen - a children's show. Grotesque puppets teaching counting in patronising voices to a small, captive group of smiling children.

When the Professor had disappeared into the bathroom, I switched it off again. I sat in silence.

#

The Professor approached me about the journal again over our evening meal: a greasy Chinese take-out, garnished with the remaining droopy salad from the refrigerator.

"Where's your book?" he asked.

I shook my head. Took another sip from the glass of red he had poured for me. "I don't know."

The journal was gone, long gone. I had seen to that, with the aid of water from the faucet and a pair of scissors I had found in one of the kitchen drawers.

"I'm intrigued: why did you have your father die of a spider bite in your book, when you told me he was murdered? And your mother – I'm sure there's something Freudian about that, having her murder someone and then be torn apart by monsters-"

"Where is Utah?" I interrupted.

"Utah? It's in the west. It was predominantly Mormon, originally. But when Christianity went into decline, back when science was still thriving and Homo-SuperiUS was all over the media, it became a sort of haven for all faiths for a while. It was really the only state where they could practice their beliefs without ridicule."

"I used to think you were all Christians," I murmured.

"Hmm?" The Professor wound a cluster of noodles around his chopsticks, slowly, looking at me all the while. "Why did you think we were all Christians, Katrina?"

I hesitated. For a moment, the image of the dead girl on the Edu-Centre floor was in my mind - and a woman in a long white dress with a crucifix brooch kneeling beside her, imploring the gods to let her own baby die rather than risk it being raised by something different. Everything was uncertain, now.

"Were your parents Christians, perhaps? There was certainly something of the superstitious about your upbringing. I could tell that as soon as I met you."

I stabbed a dumpling with my fork. "I thought the Christians believed in love and respect for all people," I said. "Even people that are different. They copied a man called Jesus who lived in a desert and had met the one true God… unlike the pagans, who believed in fake gods." For a second I was back in the Edu-Centre, staring at the television and dreaming of a superstition-free Utopia, trying to ignore the growls and hollers of my cousins outside as they fought my father for access to me. "I thought you all believed in the real God."

"Real God?"

"The one Jesus met. The one who loves everyone equally because he knows we're all perfect and can get into Heaven. He doesn't mind that we're different, only that we try to be good, and he hates killing…"

The Professor gave a strange little smile. "God is dead, Katrina."

"It must have been explained on one of the video tapes my cousins destroyed." I was staring down at my own plate now, addressing the dumpling. "Or one of the shiny discs. We never could get the shiny discs to work."

The Professor snorted. "You're rambling, Katrina. Enough is enough. You can't do that when you're living away from me – other people might not be so tolerant."

I glanced up. Stopped myself from saying the words I was already forming; replaced them with, "Are there still Christians in Utah?"

The Professor shook his head and swallowed his mouthful. "Not really. After the Change in the Law, a lot of the Christians left Utah hoping they could side with the anti-science hippies and convert a few 'lost souls' back to the flock. But of course, the hippies weren't interested in Christianity. By the time most of the Christians had accepted they'd lost the fight and returned to Utah, the hippies had taken advantage of the state's dwindling population and, well... moved in. Poor fools found themselves shut out in the rain by thousands of 'heathen' squatters. It's mainly a tourist destination now, Utah."

"So what happened to the Christians?"

"Well..." The Professor considered. "The general consensus is that most of them became homeless, or chose to be voluntary hermits. That would explain the number of preachers you see on the streets. But a lot of them just seemed to... leave."

"Leave for where?"

The Professor shrugged. "Nobody really knows. Africa, maybe, or the Far East, looking for missionary work. There's no official record of their leaving. With the state of turmoil the government was in at the time, nobody kept track. But over a period of about five years, the number of Christians living in America plummeted. Thousands of people just... disappeared."

"Maybe they went to islands?" I suggested.

"Islands? Oh... yes, maybe!" The Professor smirked. "Like your Island of Doctor Moreau?"

"My what?"

The Professor took a long, sophisticated sip of wine. "Oh, sorry," he said. "H.G. Wells. 'The Island of Doctor Moreau'. The island where the people are more animal than man."

Now, this sparked my curiosity. "Where is that island?" I pressed.

To my surprise, the Professor sniggered. "Oh – no, Katrina!" He stifled a laugh. "Poor girl. It's not real; it's fictional. Just a story. Like that book of yours. Which I thought," he added, "was very well-written, by the way. Almost publisher-worthy." He winked at me.

I took another long sip from my glass of acrid wine. Said nothing.

#

The Professor fished his copy of 'The Island of Doctor Moreau' out of his suitcase later that evening, and told me I could keep it. I got through the book in a day; it was only short. It took my mind off the thoughts stabbing and swirling; the sound of the Professor's vacuum cleaner as he eradicated all trace of me from the apartment.

I must admit, I was a little disappointed by 'The Island of Doctor Moreau'. It lacked scientific detail. How *had* Doctor Moreau achieved what he managed to achieve? How *had* he constructed a race of humanity out of the tampered-with bodies of animals? I had to keep reminding myself what the Professor had said: that it was a 'fiction', untrue. A lie, like the claims made by some of the commercials.

I wondered, as I grimaced through the descriptions of Moreau's mangled test subjects, what else was untrue. Perhaps the journal itself… but no, too much of it made sense. Too much.

Reading the book took me through Sunday. On Monday morning, the Professor called to me. "Katrina, come on! I'll walk you to your lecture. One of your new housemates will collect you afterwards."

When I didn't materialize, he came into the bathroom to collect me. He found me sitting on the floor, trying to force everything I could gather into the small satchel of Aleshia's that he had let me keep. The towel. The shampoo bottles. The Professor reached down, picked the squashed oranges out of my pile, and put them in the trash. I threw him a hateful glance.

"What?" He grinned. "They'll have oranges at your new home, I'm sure."

"How can you be sure?" I continued to glare. The Professor sighed; shook his head. He picked up my bag and left the room. I followed him out. "You *always* take what you can salvage when you are forced to relocate," I muttered at his back. "Always." Father had told me that. My brother had made me repeat it. They knew they couldn't keep our cousins at bay forever.

The Professor's classes had been taken over, he explained as I followed him down the apartment staircase, by a 'very nice lady'. She would give me tutoring after class if I needed to catch up, he was sure: the Professor had made certain that she understood my situation completely.

Of course, she couldn't possibly understand 'my situation'. Nor could the Professor; nor could anybody. But he would be gone forever soon, so I thanked him all the same.

We walked across campus together in silence. When we reached the doors to the lecture building, the Professor told me to wait. He presented me with one of his bags – it had the logo of a local grocery store on the side. "Some clothes," he said. "And the 'Island of Doctor Moreau' book I gave you. You left it on my bed."

I took the bag. "Thank you," I said.

Silence.

"Did I tell you about your new roommates?" The Professor rearranged his remaining bags to give himself a better grip. "Chemise and Courtney. Chemise will come and collect you after your lecture. She knows what you look like. Don't worry - they'll look after you."

"Alright," I said.

Suddenly, he leaned forward, brushed his lip against my cheek. I leapt back and hissed.

The Professor pulled back with a frown. "Okay, okay. Goodbye, Katrina."

And then he turned and left, down the campus path, without a backward glance.

#

Sixteen years old, and you know you don't have much time. Just over a year, since your birth date according to Father falls in a few days. But the raft is ready, and Rawg checks it daily. You are building up a stash of rations, nuts and seeds and other long-lasting foods. You have a plan.

You brush your shoulder lightly against Rawg's as you walk side by side up through the forest from the beach; a rare gesture which you hope conveys your gratitude. He nudges back.

The forest is safer at this time of year. Females settle down to bear young conceived in the Spring. Males stand guard outside nests, leaving only briefly to kill lethargic, underfed deer on the cusp of hibernation. Cool winter leaves crunch underfoot. A soft wind threads through the canopy.

Suddenly, Rawg stops.

"What's wrong?"

He waves a hand at you and turns, crashes through branches and dead leaves, following a pathway that only he can trace. You hurry behind, holding your skirt over the undergrowth. Ahead is a clearing: moonlit, turquoise grass. This is the graveyard. You can feel the subtle change underfoot when you step over someone's resting place: buried outside the graveyard, the young and the disgraced. The former Under-Leader, Rool; he will be somewhere here, in the burial plot of the unworthy. And one day…

Father!

There he is – Father. Kneeling in the clearing, his back to you. Rawg stops at the edge, just behind the trees, and you step up beside him, peer over his shoulder.

Another, younger figure kneels in the clearing, facing Father. Female. She has long, sleek, dark hair, and her chest is strangely swollen. Her arms cradle protectively around – something, hidden. You shift to get a better look; a twig snaps underfoot.

The female flinches, faces the trees. Wide, wide eyes piercing yours. Father turns. Fixes Rawg with his eyes. Silently communicating.

Then Rawg pats your back, and together you walk into the clearing.

"Her partner is missing," Rawg whispers to you. "Maybe dead, Father says. Nobody has food to spare. She doesn't know where to go."

The female's eyes never leave yours. She shuffles back a little as you near, and her arms close around whatever she is holding to her chest, embracing it closer to the swellings. Her top lip lifts, exposing sharp teeth.

"Father says she needs to come with us," Rawg says. At the sound of his voice speaking civilised words, the female's death-stare fixes on him.

Inside her cradled arms are three bundles of soft, blue-grey fur. Rising, falling, rising softly with miniature breaths. This fur will drop in the spring: you know, because Rawg explains this every year. You've imagined, but haven't seen this before...

The babies shift in their mother's arms. Three pairs of black-black eyes blink up at you from tiny faces, and for once you don't see hatred or devil-fear. Just innocent acceptance. The moonlight glints off their soft, soft hair. You feel a strange longing you haven't experienced before. Different from the desperation to go back to the Civilised World, this feels real, a part of your body. Like something ignored, forced down; now rising up, taking over.

Your fingers twitch. Wanting to touch.

Father reaches out, puts a hand on the female's arm. Whatever he communicates to her, it gets her attention. She rises with him, and keeping one arm around her young to block your view, follows him back into the forest towards the Edu-Centre.

You imagine Father speaking inside her mind, reassuring her with the same words and tone he uses with you. "Bad now. Better soon. Have to keep going."

You follow with Rawg, a few steps behind. In amongst the trees, eyes follow you. Black-black. Full of hate. Rawg steps to block you from your cousins' gaze.

CHAPTER NINE

My first lecture without the Professor was over in the usual fifty minutes. I emerged onto the campus grounds; for once, the first of my fifty-five classmates to leave. There I loitered, lost, in the spot where the Professor had been but now was not. I didn't know where to go.

The pack of students leaving the same lecture soon came out in a swarm behind me. They attempted to walk through me, met with resistance, and forced me aside, eager to get to wherever they were going. Within minutes, they had disappeared to their respective dormitories and apartments.

There, in the emptiness they left behind, I saw a girl. She looked different from the identical blond creatures I had become accustomed to seeing around campus. She had paler skin, freckles. Her lip had a silver blob on a spike speared through it. Her hair was short and red - naturally red, like mine. She was leaning against one of the aesthetically-positioned campus trees, and when she saw me looking lost outside the lecture theatre, she beamed at me. I believed that smile to be genuine, if a little too enthusiastic.

"Heya!" she said. She pushed off from her tree and stepped forward to meet me. "You're Katrina, right? I'm Chemise. It's real good to meetcha. I'm gonna show you your new home now, 'kay? Come on!"

We walked briskly side-by-side, off campus, and into town. After a five-minute stretch, the star-shaped dollar signs in shop windows were replaced by wrinkle-free suits, scarves and jackets, and gold foil-wrapped balls, possibly edible, piled high in pyramid formations. A strong smell of mingled perfumes became apparent in the air.

Chemise said, "It's total crap we have to walk so far to get to campus, I know - but you get used to it. Just need to learn to get up earlier. You take the bus ten minutes out of town, there's this store where you can buy this super-strong brand of coffee – that'll get you up. It ain't organic, but it's affordable. I mean, Courtney has a car, but she doesn't give rides. Not to me, anyway." She looked at me then.

Studied my blank face. "I guess I should tell you now," she said. "Before someone else does. I'm not one of the usual crowd here. I'm here on a *scholarship*."

She took a moment to study my face again, but of course, my expression did not change. Seeing this, she smiled. "Yeah, a scholarship! Wanna hear how I got it? You know that celebrity magazine, 'Aspire'? They run a competition each year: 'sum up in ten sentences why you want to study in LA'. I can't remember what I put, but it must have been good because it landed me here - with two thirds of my fees paid for the first year! How about that, hey? Dad's working overtime to pay for next year. I don't know how we're gonna afford it, but he says we'll find a way. Plus I'm gonna get a job over the summer, and Mom's already taken a second job – she's a telemarketer for EcoTech, the pay's good. So, fingers crossed we'll be fine!"

I nodded. I understood some of what she was saying.

"My dad's an accountant for a few of the professors," Chemise continued. "And one of them knows Michael Salvador. That's how he heard we had a room free. He's nice, ain't he, Professor Salvador? Real down-to-Earth. Always smiling, even after his wife ditched him. Everyone here knows he took it pretty badly. I mean, there *was* that fling he had with the girl he was tutoring last year – I bet people have been giving you no end of crap about that, you being so close to him and all. But he was in a bad way then, and that's old news now. It's great that he's getting back with his wife again, ain't it? I really hope it works out for them. Dad says he's one of the nicest, most genuine guys he's met here."

I said nothing.

Eager to keep the 'conversation' fresh, Chemise moved quickly on to a different subject. "I'm majoring in homeopathic medicine," she said. "That's best for a career. Well, other than regular medicine. I was thinking of taking regular medicine, but I just couldn't bring myself to. Not when all those animals had to suffer to invent the surgeries and make the drugs - it's all so cruel, you know? I'm glad they don't do it anymore. I mean, now that they've invented everything they need to keep us fit and healthy." She paused for breath. "So, Katrina, what are you studying?"

"I'm not," I said. "I sit at the back of the class and make notes. I don't study any of them."

Chemise gave a sudden barking laugh. "Yeah, you and me both, sister! You and me both. Hey, it's real great you have a sense of humour! Especially after what happened to your dad…"

She clapped both hands to her mouth. "Jesus, shut up, Chemise!" She gave me a look, eyes wide. "Professor Salvador told me not to let you know he'd said anything. It just slipped out. I'm so sorry!"

I cocked my head to one side. "Do I have a sense of humour?" I asked. I was always interested to learn something new about myself.

Courtney was silent for a moment. "Professor Salvador said you were like an Autistic-Savant," she said. "You know what that is, right?"

"No," I said. "What is it?"

"It's like…" Chemise thought for a moment. "They've got this type of mind, it's… sort of *different* from normal minds." She started making shapes with her hands, as if trying to mould an explanation in the air. "But… no," she finally said. "He's crazy. You're too young; your mom would've been given the Monroe Pill at her first antenatal appointment. Salvador likes to pretend he's found something exotic, is all." She gave me no more than that.

We rounded a corner, started down an alley which ran between two shops: 'Darcy's', which I took to be a shoe shop, and something which looked like a food store, except it was smaller than the ones in the commercials and had a window display devoted solely to olives and cheeses. My nostrils twitched at the new smells.

Chemise rummaged in her pocket, brought out a set of keys with something pink and fluffy dangling from them on a chain. "Courtney's out shopping," she said. "But I'll go ahead and show you your room. It's totally cute. You're gonna love it."

We emerged from the alley onto a small, square lawn of neatly-trimmed grass. In the centre of this was a tall, brick building; not unlike the Professor's apartment building, except smaller, and somehow smarter-looking.

"Come on!" Courtney pulled my arm, gesturing forwards. I pulled away sharply, then followed her.

Around the back of the apartment building, I could see a section of garage. As we approached the front door to the apartments, three shiny cars became visible.

"Nice, ain't they?" Chemise commented when she saw me looking. "Don't touch them, whatever you do. They got cameras in there. You go in, even if it's just for a look, and they can tell it's you. They'll find out which apartment you live in and come round. Trust me, I know. Lucky I had Courtney to bail me out that time."

Chemise skipped up the steps and through the front door. I followed behind.

"Listen, I should warn you," Chemise said as she led me up a staircase. "Courtney's great, really, but – she's got a bit of a short temper. It's not her fault. It's just... she works real hard on her studies, you know? So she gets kinda stressed." We halted before a door, but before unlocking it, Chemise paused. The pink fluffy thing swung mid-air from her frozen key. "Probably best you stay out of her way."

Chemise stood aside, holding the door for me as I entered the apartment. The front room consisted of a little kitchen (a 'kitchenette', Chemise said to call it), a table with two chairs (a third had not been brought out), two slippery black sofas, and the television set I had been promised.

Instantly, I became magnetised to the television. I dropped to my knees before the wide, black screen, and revelled in anticipation of the many hours of mindless entertainment it would deliver.

Chemise, who had wandered into the spare bedroom, apparently assuming I would follow, wandered out again to see what I was doing. From my position on the floor, I sensed her scrutinising me. But I didn't move.

"Okay. Whatever," Chemise finally said. "I'm just gonna assume you're on drugs or something. It'll make this easier to explain."

I turned and looked at her now. "What are drugs?" I asked. This word had not yet been explained to me.

Silence.

"Maybe I was wrong," said Chemise. "Maybe you *should* be on some sort of drug. Anyway!" She beckoned enthusiastically. "Wanna come see your bedroom?"

At seven-thirty that evening, Courtney came home.

She had a big black shopping bag in one hand labelled 'Project X', a bigger white one in the other labelled 'Prada', and darkly tanned legs which seemed to stretch up further than most legs did (the illusion probably being due to a combination of platform sandals, and an exceptionally short skirt). She wore a tight, white blouse, and had short blonde hair and large, round, insectile sunglasses. These she did not remove, even in the house. She looked like a praying mantis.

Courtney did not enter the apartment immediately, which I thought was strange. Instead she lingered in the doorway for a while, one hand (holding the 'Project X' bag) against the doorframe to her left, the other hand (holding the 'Prada' bag) against the doorframe to her right. One foot pointed forward; the other toe-tapped behind. Her small, glossy lips parted in a strange white smile. "Chemise," she said. "I'm *ba-ack!*"

I was sitting on one of the sofas, watching 'America's Dumbest Accidents Captured on Camera', with probably more scrutiny than it otherwise deserved. One look at Courtney had been enough for me. But on hearing Chemise's name mentioned, I turned around to see her reaction to this intrusion.

Chemise was standing in the kitchenette, where she had been engrossed in cooking for the last half-hour. Now she was staring with that same captivation at Courtney. She beamed. "Hi, honey!" she said. "How was shopping? Good?"

For some reason, this question was left unanswered.

Courtney stepped into the room and spontaneously became animated, discarding her bags by the door. "Is supper ready, sweetie?" she asked. I could only assume she was talking to Chemise; with those dark glasses, it was difficult to tell whom she was addressing.

"In a minute!" Chemise sang. "I'm about to plate up."

Courtney turned to me. She lowered her sunglasses and peered over the top of them. Her eyes were a cool, poster-paint blue. "This is Katrina?" she said.

It was Chemise who answered. "Yep, that's Katrina."

I remained silent. Held the cool blue stare.

Courtney took a good, long look at me. "Uh-huh," she said eventually.

Then she took her bags and disappeared into one of the bedrooms.

'Supper' that night was pasta with a sauce, made up of a complication of herbs and spices and tomatoes which tasted too rich to be real. Also a small bowl of olives which sat on the dining table, which nobody seemed to touch. My new roommates drank from small glasses of something clear as water, but which smelt poisonous. I was not offered this drink. Instead, I was given a far more appealing glass of orange juice.

Courtney and Chemise sat at the table to eat. With only the two chairs at the table, I sat on the sofa. This was fine by me. I was even allowed to have the television on, so long as the volume was turned down to a barely-audible level. This was a novelty for me: having the television on during meals was something the Professor abhorred.

While the television chatted to me, the girls talked to each other. After a twenty-minute discussion laden with inappropriate adjectives about what Courtney had purchased that day ("fabulous" shoes and an "adorable" handbag), their conversation turned to me. "So," I heard Courtney say, after a pause. "This is Katrina."

Chemise nodded and swallowed her mouthful. "Yeah. Professor Salvador's helping us out with the rent in exchange for, you know, taking her in. I mean, if that's still okay with you?"

In my peripheral vision, I could see Courtney's head turn. She eyed me silently: I could feel those blue-paint irises crawling over the back of my head, and my gut impulse was to get up and move out of her observational field. But I stayed with my eyes glued to the television.

"Of course that's okay, Chem, sweetie. Why wouldn't it be?" Courtney continued to stare at me, over the top of those insect-eye sunglasses which she still had not removed, even though it was now past eight in the evening.

I felt I should say something. I gave her a fleeting glance. "Hello." Quickly turned back to the television. On 'America's Greatest Freak Shows', the presenter was talking about how a man with a tail who everyone thought was an imbecile had killed his captors, run away to Russia, and become a Professor of Natural Sciences, before he was caught and executed. This all happened hundreds of years ago, the presenter said: thank goodness things have improved since then.

My attention drifted from the show. I could still see Courtney out of the corner of my eye. She flashed that strange white smile again - only this time, it was directed at me, not at Chemise. "Isn't she sweet?" she said.

Chemise glanced from Courtney to me, and back again. Said nothing.

After supper, Courtney instructed me on what my duties as newest member of the household would be. I couldn't cook, she (correctly) assumed; therefore, it would be my job to clean.

"What should I clean, and how often should I clean it?" I asked Courtney.

"How should I know?" The plates had been cleared away and Courtney was now lounging on the sofa, watching 'America's Greatest Freak Shows' with me - but scrolling through the programme listings all the time with the remote control, on the hunt for something better. "I don't do those things. Ask Chemise."

Chemise was cleaning plates behind us in the kitchenette. I looked at her for instructions but, for some reason, when she saw me looking, she looked away. "There's polish and wipes in the cupboard under the sink," she murmured at the plates. "Just follow the instructions on the bottle. Clean whatever you think needs cleaning. Okay?"

"My room needs cleaning once a week, Katrina," Courtney interjected. "And I like the bed made but other than that don't touch any of my stuff. I can tell when something's been moved." With the click of a button, 'America's Greatest Freak Shows' suddenly became 'Totally Bitchin' House Parties Exposed'. I glared at Courtney. She flashed me that smile again. "Aren't you going to give her any more instruction than that, honey?" she called back to Chemise. "Don't you want your room cleaned?"

Chemise didn't, and I received no more instructions. Cleaning was not something I was familiar with, but I made a private vow to do my best. I didn't want to lose another family.

#

For six weeks following the Professor's departure I stayed on at the university, going to the tedious lectures of his successor. This was a sturdy, middle-aged woman whose name I have forgotten, or might never have bothered to learn in the first place. She delivered facts to the masses as if she was commanding an army, and took great pleasure in frightening my peers with the phrase, 'this will be on your final exam'. Not knowing what the 'final exam' was, I assumed the threats did not apply to me and ignored them.

The only interesting thing she showed us was the entire clip of Doctor Tati's confession. She sat at her desk, pushed a button, flipped open her magazine - and behind her the film of a man, tall and scrawny, eyes wide and hands clasped, was projected onto the board:

"I am sorry. Science is sorry. We wanted a better world, but no utopia is worth the destruction of animal life, nor of its people. I have seen so much. I have seen men and women strapped to tables in institutions, screaming, as laser beams pierced their brains. I have seen impossible creatures being formed in test tubes, and rare animals being used as receptacles to grow them. Now, we have devised a means of blending animal with man. We wanted to replace God, but how can we know what is best for mankind when we are no more than men ourselves? On behalf of my colleagues Doctor Bai and Doctor Monroe, and of Homo-SuperiUS as a whole, I am sorry."

After these lectures, there were no question and answer sessions.

As the lectures were boring and repetitive, I soon stopped attending, the better to focus on my role in my new family. The fact that I was to have the job of 'cleaner', I accepted as only fair. Chemise had her job: she was in charge of the meal preparations; Courtney, the hunter-gatherer, went out each day to shop. Granted, the haul she came back with consisted mainly of handbags, clothes, shoes, make-up – but occasionally there would be food, usually cheeses and olives, which Chemise would supplement later with carbohydrates, meats and vegetables to prevent us from succumbing to malnutrition. Thus, domestic harmony was established.

But the cleaning duties were promptly thrust back in Chemise's direction when Courtney discovered another, more valuable skill of mine.

"Think of it, honey!" she said to Chemise one day, a month into my stay. I was busy in the kitchenette, scrubbing. They were in Chemise's bedroom, where they apparently assumed I couldn't hear them. "You've seen her grades! We just need to give her our notes and she can type them all up into paragraphs for us. It would basically be us doing the work. But if she happens to have a natural gift – which she must do, judging by all the 'A's she's gotten– well, why not encourage her to use that ability to help others?"

"I don't know…" Chemise said.

But I took on the duty. Once Courtney had explained it to me, it seemed logical and perfectly fair. I was new in the apartment, after all. Here, Courtney was the equivalent of Leader; Chemise was her Under-

Leader. It stood to reason that I, as the newcomer, should be given heavier duties than them. Also, it gave me something new to write - a fresh way to perfect my craft. I was lent a laptop computer by Chemise and chose the sofa facing the television as my workstation.

As I started that first assignment, I could hear Courtney and Chemise whispering indistinctly to one another in the kitchenette. The whispers became harsh and rasping; the words were still unclear but they had taken on a tone that was almost hostile. Courtney broke off when Chemise's whispers began to border on discernible – "seriously, leave her the fuck alone" - and came over to where I was working. I could sense her looking at the laptop screen over my shoulder. Then she reached out and stroked my hair. I cringed.

"Good work, Katrina," Courtney said. "See? It's only fair." She turned to Chemise.

I could sense Chemise behind us, watching from the kitchenette in silence.

#

It became clear to me that Chemise was Courtney's partner; although they did not express their love physically outside of their bedrooms. Another surprise, since 'Marriage, Sex and Sin' had implied that such partnerships only occurred between men and women, and that the 'love-making' upon which the video never elaborated only occurred after the marriage ceremony. However, I had by now adjusted to the fact that the Edu-Centre videos, like the commercials and fictions, sometimes lied.

And yet, after barely a month of my staying with them, they started to fight like enemies. Over the subsequent weeks these fights ended less with the two of them making mad, passionate, noisy love in Chemise's bedroom (where they persisted in their self-delusion that I couldn't hear them); more with Courtney storming from the apartment and slamming the door, leaving Chemise to collapse, weeping, on the living room floor. When her tears began to dry, Chemise would often look up at me. I would look down from the screen of the television or the laptop (where I would no doubt be finishing Courtney's latest essay), and wonder whether or not I should attempt to say something to her.

At these moments, there was always a sinister feeling scrabbling in the back of my brain that I should be saying something. But I did not know what that 'something' should be. Besides, with the two of them being in a position of power over me - I was living on their territory, after all - it seemed too dangerous and foolhardy to experiment with new social skills now.

\#

It was Friday night, and I was watching television when the familiar angry vibrations began.

I reached for the remote and attempted to turn up the television to block out the inevitable noise. But something stopped me. Chemise's cries were terrible to listen to, painful even - and yet something inside my brain told me that it was out of the question to cover them up. So I put down the remote. I was forced to listen.

In amongst the growls and snarls and the words 'bitch' and 'asshole', I thought I heard my name mentioned.

A minute passed. Then Courtney emerged. She gave me a look as she passed by. I think she expected me to turn away - but I didn't. I stared right back at her, and kept staring until Courtney left the apartment, slamming the door.

Seconds later, Chemise came running out from her bedroom. "You *bitch*!" she screamed at the front door. "You goddamn fucking *bitch*!" And she sank to the floor again, sobbing. I watched her.

After a minute, the sobs died away and Chemise looked up at me, her pale face streaked with tears. "Why do you always *stare*?" she cried. "Why do you always fucking *stare*? Why do you never try to *help* me, you goddamn moron?"

"Because I don't understand what's happening," I replied.

"Really?" Chemise hissed. She wiped a sleeve across her face, staining it with tears and make-up. "It's not obvious to you?" She wiped her eyes again and seemed to calm down. "No. I guess it wouldn't be," she said. "You wouldn't understand. You don't have feelings like these." She sniffed. Then the emotion welled up inside her again, and she began to wail in a disconcertingly detached, ghoulish tone. "God. God, I *hate* her!" she said. "I *hate* her, I *hate* her, I *hate* her!"

"Why do you stay with her, then?" I asked. I was genuinely confused. Chemise was at least fourteen pounds heavier than Courtney, and more intelligent. Had I been in her situation, I would have pinned Courtney to the ground and torn her to pieces with my teeth, or else used my superior intellect to torture her mind to insanity.

Chemise shook her head. "Because I love her." She gave a mad little giggle; clapped her hands to her face, and broke into a fresh peel of sobs.

'Love' is what Lorna Lane feels for Larry Larson and God. What I feel for my father and brother. Love is the foundation of a happy marriage, as explained in 'Marriage, Sex and Sin' and 'Love for the Young Christian'. It is the feeling that makes any good parent want, above all things, to protect the life of their child. It is an overwhelmingly positive emotion.

Chemise wasn't making sense.

I turned back to the television and tried to keep my eyes on the screen, but the noise of Chemise's insane cries continued to penetrate my skull. Even covering my ears didn't help. I reached for the remote – but no. As much as I wanted to, I still could not bring myself to block Chemise out. Reluctantly, I let my hands fall to my sides.

To my relief, after a few minutes, the cries abated.

Chemise got up. She walked over to me and sat down – not on the sofa next to me, but on the coffee table in front of the sofa, so she was facing me and blocking the screen. The television cast a yellowish glow behind Chemise's head. I tried to carry on watching but Chemise's head kept getting in the way. "Why won't you *look* at me?" she wailed. "*Look at me!*"

I forced myself to look her in the face.

When she saw that I had responded to her, a small smile came to Chemise's lips again. She stopped crying. "We're in the same boat," she said. "Don't you see? Neither of us belongs here. That bitch is using us. It's worse for you - God, you should hear some of the fucked-up things she says about you!" She wiped her eyes. "You barely even register as *human* to her. Do you know that?"

I shook my head.

Chemise choked up a fresh sob. "Poor, stupid Katrina," she said. "Life just happens to you, doesn't it? Emotions ricochet off you. People do things, cold and logical, without any malicious intent or cruelty. You don't get how *sadistic* people are."

I stared at her in silence. She had told me not to do this but I couldn't help it. I was aware that my face had started to shake uncontrollably. Perhaps my entire body but it was my face I noticed, because Chemise wouldn't stay still in my line of sight.

Suddenly, Chemise reached out and seized my face in her hands. Her fingers were ice-cold. I flinched. She held tight.

"God," she said. "I wish I was you!"

She kissed me.

My kiss with Chemise was warm and wet and more frightening than my kiss with the Professor, because it involved a lot of prolonged contact that I couldn't wriggle out of. No matter how hard I tried to break free, Chemise wouldn't let go. She clung to me as if I possessed some medicine which could remedy all the problems in her life, which could be sucked directly out of my jerking body.

Then Courtney came back.

There was a deadly pause. Chemise hadn't noticed Courtney's presence yet, and I didn't tell her. I saw no reason why she should become even more unhappy sooner than was absolutely necessary. I stared at Courtney over Chemise's head. Courtney stood in the doorway, stiff as a plastic mannequin, and stared back. Or so I assumed. She had her ridiculous praying mantis sunglasses on again, so I couldn't see her eyes.

Then her terrible voice erupted from her spindly, insect-like body and filled the apartment. "Traitor!"

She tore Chemise from me; let her drop limply to the floor, and manhandled me to the door. "It's sick!" she shouted over her shoulder at Chemise. "It's sick, Chemise! It's literally, like, *bestiality*! Human-on-subhuman! It's like a fucking *Doctor Tati experiment*!"

I was forced through the door; dragged down the stairs. Chemise hurried behind. "Courtney, baby," she was saying. "Listen to me…"

"Silk is so *out*," jabbered Courtney. "So you know what I've been buying today, *baby*? A whole new wardrobe. Just in linen. And I also got some Botox. Because wrinkles start early if you don't get Botox. And *then* I went to the hair salon. And I stared at pictures of ugly wannabes in a cheap magazine while some miserable Hispanic bitch spent an hour telling me how her daughter is going to be a superstar!"

"What? What are you talking about, Courtney?"

"What am I talking about? I have to do that every week. *Every goddamn week, Chemise!*" Her sunglasses slipped; she quickly jerked them into place, before Chemise could see the tears in her eyes. "That's not enough for you? You have it easy, Chemise! Nobody expects *you* to spend thousands of dollars to look like a passable human being! But I do, and I keep it up - and you still think this *thing* is better than me?"

"No! I really don't, I promise, Courtney…"

We had reached the ground floor. Courtney opened the front door. Outside, the night was eerily still. Also cold. Courtney paused, one hand clutching the neck of the oversized 'I-heart-California' t-shirt the Professor had let me keep, one hand under my armpit. She turned to Chemise. "I thought you were on my side, Chemise!" Courtney said. "I thought you and I decided that she needed to be taught her *place*?"

"We did," said Chemise.

"I was kind." Courtney sniffed. Her fingers dug into my flesh. "You said it yourself - she's messed up. She shouldn't be here. The Monroe Pills should have killed her; she's a *living miscarriage*! There's something wrong with her brain, Chemise. If she can't be useful, then there's no place for her here."

"I know…"

I craned my neck to look at Chemise. She turned away, started sobbing again.

"You find something like *this* appealing, Chemise?" Courtney said. She lifted me up by the neck of my t-shirt. "I spend a fortune making myself what everyone wants me to be and you decide that you'd rather have a *freak*. That's what hurts!"

I was thrown – literally - through the door. It slammed shut. Courtney's key turned in the lock behind me and I could hear the little metal bars sliding into place.

Inside, Chemise continued to cry. "I'm sorry, Courtney. I'm so sorry!"

I still couldn't leave Chemise while she was crying. I waited on the steps, knees grazed and bleeding, until the two of them had gone upstairs and the cries had died away.

When I could hear her no longer, I turned and I walked. I walked down the dark side-street, out through the gap between 'Darcy's' and the shop which specialised in cheeses. Back towards the highway.

#

Seventeen years old, just gone.

You know you've done nothing wrong. You know. But still your heart is pounding. Your skin is sweating, yet cold as a corpse.

Beneath you, on the piece of white fabric where their mother reluctantly laid them hours earlier, are the three babies. Soft, blue-grey hair covering their naked bodies. Eyes shut, limbs askew.

Their chests no longer rise and fall.

"I didn't..."

The female stares at you from the other side of the fabric. Her shoulders are hunched. The bulges on her chest heave with her breath.

"They were already..."

"Step back, Katrina." *Rawg stands against the far wall of the Edu-Centre, Father beside him. He looks very old next to Rawg: his hair silver, eyes dull, shoulders sagging. Rawg is posed to fight, or run. There is something about Father that reminds you of sadness.*

"But... I didn't..."

Fierce movement, and you turn to see the female bundle the three bodies into her arms and run for the door. In the doorway she halts, and looks over your shoulder at Father and Rawg. Eyes hollow. Then she disappears into the night, the cries and howls and shrieks. Might be forest-dogs. Might be your cousins. You don't know anymore; it all sounds like danger.

You turn back to Father and Rawg. "I just wanted to look at them." *Water in your eyes.* "I didn't... I didn't..."

Outside, another cry joins the chorus. A female, shrill and frantic.

Father stares at you. Then he rises. He steps towards you, eyes glazed, lips curling up to show his flintlike teeth, and for a moment it looks like – like he's going to –

But he passes.

You start to scramble to your feet; Rawg pulls you down and drags you back, his fingers agony in your skin. He ignores your struggles. You force your body still – he releases you. "Tomorrow morning, we need to go," *says Rawg.* "Father will tell us if they come before dawn."

"But..."

At the door, Father turns. His eyes are fixed over your head; behind you, Rawg translates. "If we go now, they will find us in the forest. So we will stay here. When they come, they will come together. Father will fight as many as possible while we run to the beach."

"No! Father..."

Father doesn't look back at you. This cannot be happening. You had a year. A plan. And now...

Father's retreating back. Warm and solid. You want to run to him.

"I'll come with you," Rawg rasps in your ear. "I will, like I promised. Just be quiet now."

You watch Father leave the Edu-Centre for the final time. The door closes. You hear the crunch of leaves as he settles his body before the door to wait.

CHAPTER TEN

I turned right at Darcy's and the cheese shop instead of the familiar left towards the university and didn't stop walking. I was in the grip of a strange, cold, headachy feeling, and beyond this could feel nothing else. My brain seemed to have whirred to a stop but my heart was beating fast.

The sky reddened; darkened. The clouds dispersed. Little by little, the stars revealed themselves. A crescent moon came out, glowing, against a steadily blackening backdrop, upon the Los Angeles jungle.

After a mile, the shops stopped looking familiar. The spattering of conversations I was accustomed to hearing from the cafes and apartments died to graveyard silence, broken by the occasional passing car. The roads narrowed into streets, which sprouted side-streets, interconnected in a maze along which no vehicle could travel.

I selected a street at random and followed it. It ran between rows of small, dilapidated houses, most of which were in darkness. The occasional one or two had dim lights on in the windows. These houses exuded uncomfortable noises: a man singing off-key in an unstable voice; a baby, crying. A couple arguing.

I kept to one side, in the dark behind the street lamps, and skulked on unseen.

After about three miles, the leather sandals I had salvaged from Courtney and Chemise's trash began to rub my ankles. I removed them, placed them at the side of the street, and continued to walk, barefoot.

Four miles.

The street widened into a road again. I saw a few cars parked up along the sidewalk, most with dark, scuffed paintwork. One had a smashed windscreen. The sky was now black.

I started to see people again. The night brought out a fresh new wave of humankind, the likes of which I had never seen before. Some sat in the doorways of dead buildings, drinking bottles of undesirable substances, belching, their heads swaying and their eyes rolling, swimming in the fog inside their minds. Girls in bright tops and short skirts teetered on freakishly high heels, making noises like cats to call to one another. This place smelt stiflingly of herbal smoke, spices and chemicals, barely masking that underlying damp, sickly, unmistakable stench of rot. The stench of the Civilised World.

Across the road, to my left, was a row of buildings with yellow lights glaring from all the windows. Sounds drifted from these windows: the clink of glasses, the hubbub of conversations breaking into unrestrained hollers and raucous laughter, with blatant disregard for any of the social propriety people are supposed to follow.

Sitting in the shadows of one of these buildings was a man. He had facial hair and bags under his eyes. As I passed, I heard him call out: "I get fifty dollars a week off the State, and I can't think of nothing I'd rather spend it on than you, pretty girl! How about it?"

I didn't wait to check if he was talking to me. I kept in the shadows. Kept my head down. At the first opportunity, I ducked into a side road and headed down it at a brisk, defensive pace.

Shortly, I emerged onto a street lined on both sides with the backs of buildings, mostly windowless, with barren back-yards barricaded with rotting wooden fences. It looked as if the buildings had turned away in disgust - understandably. This street was a dumping-ground for trash.

The flavour-scent of sharp citrus and sugar called my attention to a dumpster behind what could have been a Chinese restaurant. Perhaps Thai. It didn't matter, as long as the contents of that dumpster were edible. Suddenly I was ravenous.

I ran forward and lifted the lid, salivating like an animal.

"Don't bother, my dear!" A voice spoke behind me.

I glanced in its direction. An indistinct female figure was drifting down the shadowy street, towards me. Once I had registered that she carried no visible weapon, I paid her no more attention. I turned again to the dumpster and began to rummage through its contents.

"Trust me, child!" the female voice continued. "There's nothing in that dumpster except empty cans and kitchen towels. I've checked."

Something about her voice, the sweet, soft, unthreatening hopelessness of it, convinced me that she wasn't lying. Another quick rummage confirmed this. The 'dumpster' was a recycling bin; the scent coming from the building behind it. Slowly, I let go. The lid, emblazoned with the green-and-white logo of EcoTech, came down with a violent metallic clang. I slipped back down to my feet and started along the street again, in the opposite direction to the female figure. She clearly had her end of the street covered; it would be illogical to search it again.

"Wait!" The woman was calling to me again. "Wait, my child! I was given some bread by a kind man at the supermarket. I've removed the stale slices. There's enough left for two."

I turned. In the darkness, I could see little more than the woman's milky eyes and the whiteness of her teeth as she smiled at me. The vague, dark, shadowy shape of her arms stretched out towards me. A blue plastic wrapper glinted from her hands in the moonlight. I looked at the wrapper; back at her. Slowly, I approached.

The woman unwrapped the bread as I drew nearer and, when I was close enough, she pressed several slices into my hand. "Are you one of us, child?" she asked softly as I took the bread. "Or… could you be a scientist?"

I balled the first slice into my mouth, chewed a couple of times, and swallowed. "Neither," I said. Then reconsidered. "That depends on what you are."

"Oh, you know who we are. Everyone knows who we are," the woman murmured. "The few friends Jesus has left to defend him. The reminders of the old morality mankind is trying to shake off, as they pursue whatever Utopia they see glittering on the horizon… poor fools. More?" She was referring to the bread.

I shook my head. My mouth was full of the second piece.

"See, in that way we're not so different from the scientists," she went on. Perhaps she was oblivious to the fact that I wasn't really interested, or perhaps she simply didn't care. "Just another tribe of modern man's rejects. Most of those science-types refuse to see it, though." She sighed. "Such a pity, isn't it? People divide themselves up into ineffective groups in times of hardship… when really, we should all be linking hands and standing together."

Her words washed over me like supermarket music as I finished my final slice of the bread and turned to move on.

"Wait!" the woman said again.

I looked up, confused.

"Your hair… Those emerald eyes…" The woman beckoned urgently. "Come over to that streetlamp."

Seeing no good reason to resist, I did as I was told. I sidestepped into the yellow light of the nearby streetlamp and in it saw the woman staring back at me. Dark-skinned, with hair brushed back into a black headscarf and a gold talisman around her neck.

I think we recognised each other at the same instant. I froze. My heart began to beat double-time: Petunia, the preacher.

"My child!" she gasped. She exhaled, and smiled. Even if that smile was more natural than the fixed grin she had given me on our first meeting, the solid yellow-whiteness of it still gave me chills. "Oh, there's something I've wanted to say to you for so long! And now... God has brought you back to me so I can say it." Her voice trembled on the final words.

"What have you wanted to say?" I prepared to run.

"That I'm sorry." Petunia smiled again but this time her eyes sparkled with tears. "You're not a devil's child. Not really... not really."

"I might be." I locked eyes with her, feeling nothing anymore – no fear, no curiosity, no awe. Just a numb chill, and a dull, pounding headache which blocked out all thought. "I don't know what I am anymore."

The woman shook her head furiously. "No. No, you're not!" she said. "You're *God's* child. We're all *God's* children."

"Then why did you say I was a devil's child?"

"You have to understand!" the woman blurted. "We have lost everything. In these last few decades we've lost our homes, our families... The pagans are in charge again; the non-believers have power. The police who used to protect us now beat us down. Christianity is dying - and I'm *scared*! So if I see someone wearing an antichrist cross, of course I'm going to fight back. I'd be denying my faith if I didn't. And with so much against us now... first science trying to take our beliefs away, then this heathen new morality taking America like a horrible disease... I'm scared I'm going to lose it!"

"Then lose it." I glared into her sheep-like eyes. "Run from it. Save yourself."

"No. You don't understand... you couldn't."

In the pause that followed, I whispered, "Why don't you think I understand? I'm one of you, a civilised..." I trailed off, unable to finish.

The woman sniffed. "I feel like I'm nursing an old father on his deathbed," she said, quieter now. "All the prodigal children have cast him aside. But we will stay by him until his final breath. Even if it means dying of the disease ourselves – we will stand by him!" She started to cry.

Those cries caught at something in my mind. I began to feel a connection to this woman. The preacher bared her teeth against the tears but they continued to roll, faster and heavier, down her cheeks. She was clinging to a father who was already dead and gone and in the past. Instead of moving on, she was willing to die with him.

There was something *diseased* about her.

In the back of my head, a sound like forest-dogs baying. Pounding footsteps were drawing nearer. Araga-Mawg's wood-crafted talismans beating against bare chests. And there was my brother's voice: *Run, girl, before they get you too…*

When I spoke, my voice croaked. I swallowed to moisten my vocal chords; tried again. "I don't think I want to be your God's child," I said. "I don't think I want… *anything*… to do with this."

I pulled away from her and ran down the street, not looking back.

I found somewhere safe to lie – behind another dumpster, in the dark – and bedded down for the night.

I had been lying there for just a few moments when a pair of dishevelled-looking stray dogs approached me, sniffing inquisitively. Tired, I rose up onto my elbows. The smaller of the dogs lay down, and crawled on its stomach until it was partway beneath the dumpster. Its dark eyes glistened; its tongue lolled from its half-open mouth. It wagged its tail at me.

I snarled.

That sent them both running, tails between legs. I was not prepared to return to their sorry ranks just yet.

As I lay down again, my lips twisted into something which might have been the primitive beginnings of a smile. Or perhaps I was just baring my teeth.

#

Seventeen years old. Alone at sea.
It wasn't your fault.
It wasn't.
You reach back into the past, trying to remember. The way they felt under your palm: so soft, so new and innocent. The warmth of

three helpless lives under your curious hands. The way your stomach lifted, and love and excitement rose in an unstoppable wave-

You play it over in your mind like a video tape. Over and over; until the scene jumps and flickers black-blue-white, and you can't tell what's happening anymore.

All that remains is the rush of the sea, and Rawg's voice: "Run, before they get you too..."

Father's voice: "Have to keep going, girl. Have to keep going..."

CHAPTER ELEVEN

I awoke at dawn the next morning from a light, dreamless sleep.

I didn't really know where I was, let alone what lay in wait for me there. I tried to force myself to stay still, to remain in relative safety behind the dumpster until I came up with a rational plan.

But there was a restless energy inside me. It began as a fluttering in my stomach and a cold throbbing in my head, then it seeped into my limbs. I crawled out from behind the dumpster, scrambled to my feet and, before long, was being carried with speed by my disobedient legs along the empty street. I had no idea what I was hurrying towards - or from. My legs, however, were determined to move, and I had neither reason nor will to disobey.

The softness of dawn gradually abated as I walked, the pale light supplicating to the harsh, rising sun. The light grew steadily brighter and the air became warm. My head was free of thought. In this state, although still restless, I found myself experiencing some mindless, superficial enjoyment of the morning.

After half an hour of walking I turned a corner and found myself standing on the outskirts of an urban labyrinth: a tangle of pedestrianised walkways, winding through clusters of semi-dilapidated houses and shops.

Here, I became aware of a sound. A fast, rhythmic, heartbeat sound. It was pulsing from somewhere in amongst the labyrinth, and it stopped me.

Music.

Of course, I had heard music before in California. It was impossible not to. Even the children playing in the streets brought their music-players along for company - turning the dials to top volume, apparently determined to share their noisy new discovery with the entire street. I never understood this music. To me it was a sometimes mildly interesting, often merely irritating, undercurrent to the far more captivating aspects of civilised existence: literature, education, dialect, television. It made me shut the windows of Courtney and Chemise's flat on hot days so I could concentrate on my essay-writing.

But *this* music spoke to me. It was alive in a way nothing else seemed to be at this time. It had a heartbeat, a soul, and on top of this... *real* emotion. Anger and lust and restlessness and joy. Primal feelings, which seemed to be buried so deep beneath the pretension and the confusion and the gloss of every aspect of civilised life I had experienced so far, that I had started to doubt their existence here. This music was carnal, tribal... familiar. Comforting, like a womb.

I wanted it.

I dived into the labyrinth, pursuing the heartbeat rhythm through a network of streets and side-alleys, ducking under clotheslines hung with colourful fabrics, running past cafés and houses, from which the smells of caffeine, herbs, and cooked breakfasts were starting to seep.

Finally, I tracked it to a little shop opposite a boarded-up 'Youth Hostel' and something called a 'Freegan Café'. It had a big, black symbol – a musical note, I think – painted on its window. The lettering above the door proclaimed that this building was called 'The Groovy Kroovy Music Store'.

A bell rang behind me as I opened the door but I paid it no heed, stopping inside the doorway. Before me, a dozen rails of CD cases radiated from a long, horizontal black desk at the back of the shop. Behind the desk stood two men, staring curiously back at me. One was tall and pale with bouffant black hair, clad in a long, dark coat ridiculously at odds with the climate. The other had tanned skin and long blond hair, torn khaki pants: he would have been camouflaged against the wood on the back wall if not for his black t-shirt.

As the song ended and the music started to die away into silence, I asked them, "What is that beautiful song?"

There was a click as the music player was switched off. The man who had done this – the man in black – turned and arched his eyebrows at me. He said nothing.

"That would be 'Countdown to Extinction'. From the Megadeth album, 'Countdown to Extinction'... obviously!" said the long-haired man.

While the man-in-black looked on scornfully, the long-haired man leapt over the top of the desk and came towards me, beaming. "The best song Megadeth ever recorded," he continued, stopping before me. "I mean, listen to that bass..."

"What is Megadeth?" I asked.

There was a groan from behind the counter. I flinched, then peered over the long-haired man's shoulder at the man-in-black. He was holding his hand to his forehead, eyes shut, as if battling a particularly nasty headache. "Snake," he said. "Please throw the philistine out of here, before I do something to it which will seriously damage the resale value of this blasted shop."

My long-haired ally's expression did not change at this. "Ignore him," he murmured. "To him, not knowing who Megadeth are is like not knowing who the Beatles or the Stones are."

I restrained myself from asking.

"Megadeth was one of the first thrash metal bands, back in the twentieth century," the long-haired man continued. "They were pioneers of heavy metal music. In fact – hang on a second." He turned his back to me, and flicked through the rack of CDs behind him with astounding dexterity. He picked one out with barely a glance at the title and presented it to me. "This is the album you heard," he said. "It's only fifteen dollars. I swear you won't find a better price in any other store."

"Practically charity," snarled the man-in-black behind the counter. "No wonder we're going broke."

I took the CD case and examined it. The creatures on the cover photograph were so fantastically dishevelled, so hunched and grim-looking, that there was almost something... *savage* about them. That savagery was dangerously appealing.

These rugged, wild, beautiful people...

"I don't have any money." I looked up into the long-haired man's eyes. "Chemise and Courtney always handled the money." I recalled Chemise taking me to stores, showing me the bills and coins, explaining their meaning. Never allowing me to hold them.

"And are Chemise and Courtney here?" The man-in-black scanned the shop, his hand to his brow. "No? Go away, then. Come on, Snake!" He slapped the counter commandingly. "We have this infernal delivery to sort."

My ally smiled softly at me. Then he started to turn away.

I panicked.

"Wait!" I shouted. "You can have full use of my body as payment. Would that be okay?"

My ally whipped around and stared at me. "Huh?"

"It's valuable," I insisted. "There's a lot it can do... cleaning, writing. I've used it in exchange for a place to sleep before. That CD can't be worth more than a place to sleep, can it?"

"Not a bad offer."

My ally and I turned towards the counter. The man-in-black was watching us, his hand stroking his chin. Then he leaned over the counter, staring past my ally, directly at me. He looked me up and down. He seemed to like what he saw, because he smiled. "Do you really want that CD so much, my dear girl?" he asked.

I nodded furiously. "I need it."

"Dougie – no." My ally looked at me again. Frowned. "What are you doing, Dougie?"

Dougie ignored him. "Come over here, my dear," he crooned at me. "I'll show you what I want you to do." His voice was soft and musical.

I hurried to the counter. Snake stood back to let me pass. He followed me with his eyes, brow furrowed, but said nothing more.

I jumped over the counter sideways as Snake had demonstrated. Now I was standing next to the man-in-black: Dougie. At over six foot, the man towered above me, the padded shoulder of his coat coming to at least a half-foot above my head. I peered up at him expectantly, awaiting instruction.

"Now then," Dougie said. "Come over here." He guided me into place, in front of the little machine which the money went into and came out of. I had seen these in shops before, on my occasional grocery-shopping expeditions with Chemise - but never from this side of the counter.

"Right!" Dougie snapped his fingers at me. I stopped wondering at the money-machine and turned to attention. "Watch closely. In the unlikely event that somebody wants to make a purchase today, you will press *these* buttons to key in the price you see on the red sticker. That's the *red* sticker, understand? If they notice the original price underneath, and try to get some of their money back… come and get me."

Button, red sticker, key in the price… I had to remember, I knew, but my mind was caught up in the rhythm of the song I had heard. My eyes wandered to the CD case in my hand. "Okay."

"Good. Then it's *this* button to subtotal. You key in the amount of money they've given you, and then you press 'cash'. We don't take cards here. Give them the amount of money it tells you to on the screen - no more. If you need to open the drawer again because you've forgotten to give them change... well, don't. Just smile, and eventually they'll go away. Trust me, we need all the money we can scrounge."

"Alright." I tore my gaze from the CD case, and gave Dougie a smile and a nod to fool him that I had given him my full attention.

Dougie nodded bleakly. "If you need us, we'll be in the back room with the delivery." He gestured to a door behind him, which was open on a long, grey room full of cardboard boxes. "That gormless idiot over there," he said, nodding towards my ally, "insists on being called Snake."

Snake stuck out his tongue: it had been slit strangely at the tip, and had silver jewellery stuck through it.

"He will be responsible for any queries you might have. My name is Douglas Harrison, but you can call me 'boss' for today. Come, Snake!" He struck the counter again then disappeared into the back room.

Snake came forward slowly. Before he passed me, he lingered, and asked if there was anything else I wanted to know before he went to assist Dougie.

"Yes," I said. "Can I please listen to the Megadeth song again?"

"Well, yeah," he said. "You can listen to whatever you like."

We crouched behind the counter together; he showed me where the broken-down CD player was and how to work it. "It's one of the players for the old CDs," he explained. "It works fine on the type-two CDs as well, but nobody's supposed to know that. You put your disc in here, and..."

"Okay, okay, I've got it." I waved him away and, with eager fingers, started to extract my new CD from its box.

"Well done." Snake watched as I coaxed the sluggish drawer open with frantic fingers and fed the CD into the machine. "It's a tricky thing to work. I'm impressed."

"Don't get too used to it," Dougie called to us from the back room. "I predict that in a week, all technology in this shop will be utterly obsolete and we'll be back to record players again."

I shut his voice out as the music started to play - a song even more exhilarating than the first. The singer snarled and screamed with unrestrained ferocity, like a wild dog backed into a corner. The instruments screeched up a whirlwind behind him.

Snake said some more words before he left the room, but I couldn't understand them. Nor did I wish to.

I had found Heaven.

#

Come eight o' clock that evening, I was still in the shop. I had nowhere else to go, after all.

I had handled five out of the six total transactions we had processed that day; now that the shop was closed I was helping Snake get things ready for the next day. We were working our way up and down the aisles together, putting all the CDs that the 'good-for-nothing browsers' had messed with back into alphabetical order.

"What did I tell you? Obsolete! It's already started – again!" Dougie announced this, loudly and theatrically, from behind the counter as he wrote up the day's takings.

Neither of us responded. Dougie looked up from his ledger. I caught his frown out of the corner of my eye. "I don't see why you two are bothering to sort those blasted things," he scorned. "It's like sorting shillings, or euros. Pointless!"

"Oh, shut up!" Snake called from our end of the shop. "Don't be so dramatic!"

Dougie ignored him. "Can you guess what was in that delivery, my dear girl?" he asked. "Some nice new music by a freshly-signed band, maybe? Well, no. Actually, it was sixty-one boxes of new Polymer Mini-Records. Sixty-one boxes! What is a Polymer Mini-Record, I hear you ask?"

"I never asked," I said. Snake sniggered at this.

"What is a Polymer Mini-Record?" Dougie repeated, louder. "Well, Snake and I know all there is to know about them – don't we, Snake? The delivery came with a pamphlet. They're the 'next big thing' in music, apparently, and we must tell all the customers to scrap their horrible old CD-Type-Two players and – how did they put it, Snake?"

Sighing, Snake slipped 'Jon Bon Jovi's Greatest Hits' into its rightful place alongside 'Jackson Five' and 'John, Elton'. "Run, and…"

"Ah, that's right. 'Run, and get yourself a Polymer Player before you find yourself stranded in the dark ages'. Yes."

"Polymer Mini-Records *are* supposed to be completely scratch-resistant," said Snake. "That's kind of a plus, right?"

Dougie snorted. "Scratch-resistant? That's what they said about the Type-Two CDs. And the Sound Sticks. And the New Vinyl Records. And the old CDs. Your naivety really is astounding, Snake. Have I taught you nothing?"

Snake turned to me. "Are you on the Judas Priest section yet?" he asked. "Some maniac has mixed them in with Joy Division. Just a heads-up."

I had discovered an oddity - a Black Sabbath CD in a Judas Priest box - so I did not answer him. Besides, I assumed he was just trying to find an excuse not to listen to Dougie.

"It's always the same," Dougie continued with a groan. "Every two months – some new format, ever-so-slightly better than the last. And we're forced to buy into it! An entire shop's-worth of stock becomes valueless, and we have to dispose of the lot."

"*You* don't!" said Snake. "You keep it all in your apartment, you hoarder! You should see it," he whispered to me. "He lives in the room upstairs and it's full of CDs, records, cassette tapes – it's like a museum."

"Nothing sentimental about it. Saves money on garbage disposal, doesn't it? Have to put the old stuff somewhere... even if it is from the 'dark ages'." Dougie smirked. But his eyes glistened as if he was going to cry.

Snake leaned in to me. "He keeps every bit of stock we don't sell, even stuff from before I started here, in alphabetical order in boxes and on shelves. Every little bit of useless trash from the past. He throws nothing out."

"Why not?" I whispered back.

"Are you quite *done*?" Snake and I whirled around. Dougie shook his head; his eyes were clear again. He glared at us venomously. "It's not even for the money," he continued.

"What isn't?" Snake sighed as he was dragged back into the conversation.

"What isn't? Honestly, Snake, pay attention. These new CDs."

"Polymer Mini-Records," I corrected him.

"Whatever. The point is, if they were doing it for the money – granted, I still wouldn't like it, but I could accept it as a businessman. Developers bring out new products all the time. That's not the reason they're ruining us, though - it's *boredom*."

"Oh, God. This again." Snake rolled his eyes and grinned at me.

"Yes, this again," said Dougie. "Because this illustrates my point perfectly. You see, this is what happens when you take away millions of people's reason to live. We're stuck with thousands of out-of-work scientists, desperately trying to squeeze a bit of meaning out of their lives, through the only outlet that still exists for the scientific mind: product design." He abandoned his ledger, ducked down behind the counter, and returned holding a crushed cardboard box. He tapped the logo on its side: a triangle within a circle, white on green, with big bold text underneath.

"EcoTech Music," I read.

Dougie nodded. "They should be shut down," he said.

"Yeah, well," said Snake. "That's the way the world's turned out. Nothing we can do about it - right, kid?"

"It's tragic," Dougie cut in before I could answer. "What the scientists have become. If the poor bastards were animals, there'd be a cull. Then maybe the turnover in technology would slow down. Then maybe I could shift some stock and get some *sleep*!" He winced.

It was then that I noticed the heavy, dark bags under Dougie's eyes.

When Dougie had gone into the back room to set the burglar alarm, I asked Snake about these eye-bags, and the other unusual aspects of Dougie's appearance and personality. He was thin. His stubble was uneven, like that of a homeless person, and his hair, though bouffant, was thinning. His emotions fluctuated wildly. "Is he sick?" I wondered.

Snake smiled. "Sick? No, don't worry. He's not sick." He threw a quick glance over his shoulder at the back room, then whispered, "He – *overindulges* a bit, that's all."

"What do you mean, 'overindulges'?"

"Well, you know. He messes with some pretty strong stuff." I looked blankly at him. "You know. *Drugs*," said Snake. "Those chemicals mess with your mind after a while. Change how you see reality."

A memory surfaced. Crouched behind foliage with my brother, watching the Dead-Talkers kneel on the beach as Araga-Mawg paced the line, taking something from a large, dried leaf on their reed-matted belt and placing it between the lips of each one. *Chemicals*. Minutes later, the Dead-Talkers would rise on shaking legs, mumbling and howling at something invisible on the horizon. "You mustn't take them too much."

"Right. That's why I never take anything much stronger than weed. I mean, except at the weekend and at concerts. The strong stuff screws you up. Could you pass me that CD?"

Reluctantly, I relinquished hold of the Judas Priest/Black Sabbath CD case, and watched as Snake, oblivious to its contents, put it on the 'J' shelf. "We'll tidy more tomorrow," he said. "No-one ever comes in before midday, anyway."

Once we had finished tidying for the night, the three of us sat on the floor between the 'glam rock' and 'thrash metal' aisles. Dougie brought in a bottle of something translucent and sharp-smelling from the back, and distributed it evenly among three mugs, one for each of us. We started talking. At some point in the conversation, Snake realised that he hadn't asked my name yet, so I told him.

"So, Katrina," Snake said. "Where are you from?"

I took a sip from my mug; instantly wished I hadn't. "The university," I said, wincing at the taste. "But I left."

Dougie snorted. "Damn the university." He had poured himself a full mug of the liquid, but like me, seemed reluctant to drink. "Damn the *snobs* at the university, in particular. Little Gucci-wearing cockroaches should be wiped out."

Snake smiled down at his drink. "Yeah, I know. They hop on the hippy bandwagon but only because it's trendy. They'll vote Ferdinand Mann because he's always on TV. All their tie-dye comes straight from a designer store. Right?"

"When they hold protests – it's meaningless. Science is dead. The idiots have what they want. Silly kids are just copying what they've seen on television."

Snake took a swig from his mug and smiled. The drink seemed to make him more agreeable. "Yeah, tell me about it. 'Vote Ferdinand Mann'? The guy's a bureaucrat! 'Say No to Science'? I mean, thirty years ago, those same kids would have been protesting for 'Supreme Rights for Science', and volunteering in those places that bred rats for research…"

"Don't pretend to reminisce," snapped Dougie. "I'm the old man here."

"What? Oh, shut up." Snake giggled. "You're twenty-five." He finished off the contents of his mug, and leaned in towards me. "Dougie had just broken up with a college girl when I first started here," he said in a loud, smelly whisper. "Elizabeth. She was studying – what was it, film?"

"Reality television studies," said Dougie. He made a growling noise. "Cruel, vacuous woman. A user. Like all the plastic, soulless succubae that call themselves students." Now he took a small sip from his mug; wrinkled up his nose as if he was forcing down acid. "Still, she was attractive," he said. "And at the end of the day, if you're only with a woman to screw her, what does personality matter? You can fulfil the need for companionship with less attractive beings." He gestured to Snake.

"Here, here!" said Snake. He raised his empty glass to Dougie, then tried to drink from it. Seeing him struggle, Dougie slid his own mug across to Snake. Snake took it eagerly, without seeming to notice where it came from. "To beautiful, plastic, soulless women!" He drank successfully this time.

"Here, here!" I groped for my own mug and copied him, pretended to drink. "To beautiful, plastic, soulless women!"

The reaction I got for copying Snake confused me at first. Dougie snorted and looked at Snake. Snake looked down at the floor, away from me. I would have guessed his mood to be 'sad', or even 'disappointed', although I didn't know why he would be.

"Are you from a commune?" Snake asked me. "You act as though you are."

I took a chance. "I am," I said.

Snake grinned. "That's awesome!"

Relieved, I sat back. The risk had paid off. And it meant that, for the first time since my arrival in California, I had a background. No longer would I have to avoid questions which might otherwise have led me to reveal too much. "Do you like communes?" I asked. I took another sip from my mug, accidentally; but a third of the contents gone, it had stopped tasting quite so bad.

"Like them? Hell, I wish I'd been raised in one!" Snake proclaimed.

"Yes," said Dougie. "Having met your father, I can see why you would."

"'Do this, do that. Cover up that tattoo. Go back to college'." Snake said. He shook his head, grinning fiercely. "Bourgeois bastard!"

I was about to request clarification when Dougie murmured, "Yes... I suppose I should count my blessings that I never knew mine." He turned away and examined the back of his hand.

Snake nodded several times with enthusiasm, and refuelled with another gulp of the clear liquid. "Right. You know what my dad said to me last time he called? He said, 'You are a self-indulgent, drug-addled fiend, and if you don't clean up your act I'll never speak to you again'." For this, he affected a deep voice and a peculiar accent. "I mean, seriously? *Drug-addled fiend*."

"What does that mean?" I asked.

"I'm surprised anyone knows what that means. I hope you told him to get back in his time machine and return to an age when they still used words like that," murmured Dougie.

"Better. He's got a new car - I told him I hoped the damn thing would explode with him in it!" He laughed - a hysterical, intoxicated laugh. "Wipe out two environment... environ*mentally* poisonous, mindless machines at once. God, try saying that with a slur!" He laughed again.

"You want your father... dead?" My chest tightened.

For the first time that evening, Dougie fully acknowledged me. He nodded towards Snake, and arched an eyebrow in my direction. When I didn't react, he shook his head and ignored me again.

"I bet your dad's cool, though?" Snake turned to me. "Raising you in a commune. That's, like... awesome. Real awesome. Or was it one of those feminist communes? Were you raised by your mom?"

"I don't have a mother," I said. "My father is dead."

Silence.

I tried to take another sip from my mug, but I felt too sick. So I looked away. I tried to read what it said on the 'health and safety' poster at the far end of the shop.

Finally, in a calmer tone, Dougie broke the silence. "Why don't you go and put some music on, Katrina?" he said. "See if *you* can figure out how that new Polymer Player works. It's in the back."

As I passed him on my way to the back-room, Snake opened his mouth. But then Dougie scowled at him, and he closed it again.

In the back room, I located the Polymer Player: a three-foot black metal box with its name etched in silver above a line of slots and dials. I knelt down before the machine. Closed my eyes. Clicked my tongue.

#

They never said I could sleep in the shop. But they didn't try to remove me, either, so there I stayed.

I spent the first night lying on the floor beneath the cash register. (This was before I discovered that the counter was a much more comfortable place to lie.) I woke up only once that night; sweaty, and a little sick. I reached out to the CD-Type-Two player, slipped my new CD inside, and turned up the volume to the point where I couldn't hear myself think any more.

I went back to sleep easily after that.

CHAPTER TWELVE

Time passed. Since my continuous presence in the Groovy Kroovy Music Store went uncommented on, I accepted that I was not going to be removed any time soon, and started to relax. Snake and Dougie weren't quite like brothers; but they offered me food, water, shelter, and a constant stream of mind-numbing music. Snake educated me on matters he found important – instruments, band names – and Dougie remained present, if not an active character in my life for the most part. It was enough.

Something I believed to be enjoyment began to seep into my life.

After two weeks of my being there, Snake entered the shop at the agonising hour of half past six in the morning on Dougie's day off. He shook me awake with the news that Dougie had bought us tickets to see a band play live that evening. As the newest member of the Music Store, it stood to reason that I should be given a relevant education.

"No need to pay him back. He charged it to his mom's credit card." Snake gave me a wink.

As usual, the day passed with maybe six or seven customers making purchases, and a few more 'filthy time-wasters' browsing. When twilight fell, Dougie materialized outside the door, tapping his foot.

Snake sat on the counter, swung his legs lazily, and watched Dougie for a good long while before letting him in. "You look nice," he said with a smirk, acknowledging Dougie's familiar trench-coat and aged black boots made by a Doctor Somebody. "Good to see you made an effort, man."

We ran to catch the electric EcoShuttle at the end of the street. It carried us west of the Music Store, past dilapidated houses with flowers in their window-boxes and colourful clothes hanging limply on their washing-lines.

After half an hour, the shuttle pulled into a vast parking lot, solely occupied by minivans and banged-up old cars. By now it was dusk. Most of the EcoShuttle passengers had disembarked at previous stops. The one remaining passenger hurried past us as Snake escorted me off the bus. Dougie squinted at the man's watch, and ushered us forward at a similar speed.

A dark, hulking building loomed out of the dusk. Dougie propelled me towards its door. As I passed, I noticed a Polymer Mini-Record poster pasted to its peeling wall. 'Run, and get yourself a Polymer Player before you find yourself stranded in the dark ages.' Around the poster, angry words and curious symbols had been painted in white. They looked like the illustrations the Island's young ones used to draw on rocks, I thought, and the sickly-sweet sense of home blew past me on the breeze.

Inside, the building was a lot like the Professor's auditorium in layout, with rows upon rows of seats curved in a semi-circle around a main platform. But this was public entertainment on a far larger scale. The cavernous room swarmed with hundreds of people all of whom, unlike the Professor's audience, actually seemed enthusiastic about the performance they had come to see. Their chatter bordered on deafening.

This auditorium was a lot darker than the Professor's. I had to let Snake and Dougie guide me to our seats. When I realised where we would be sitting - exposed and vulnerable in the front row - I stiffened.

Snake and Dougie, however, exuded confidence in this situation. Their outfits, I noticed as I looked about me, were similar to the outfits worn by the other spectators. Half were dressed like Paradise birds in attention-grabbing finery; others were clothed darkly, in plastic and leather, looking like predators in the undergrowth: wanting to observe without being seen. I couldn't tell what Dougie wore under his trench coat, and he seemed disinclined to share it, but Snake had opted for the brighter look and had even painted his face. This was clearly their territory.

And also my territory, for all anybody in the audience knew. I was dressed comfortably for once, in baggy shorts and an oversized t-shirt, which I had been allowed to pick out myself from the Music Store's unsalable stock. The t-shirt had an upside-down silver crucifix on the front.

"Why didn't you get standing tickets?" Snake asked, as we edged along the row behind our seats. "Arena gigs are way too impersonal as it is."

"Because I like to sit," said Dougie. "If you want to jump the barrier and dance the night away with the groundlings, go ahead. I'm an old man. I need to sit."

"Oh, shut up." Snake sniggered. "You're five years older than me, if that." We stopped abruptly, having reached our seats. Snake helped me scramble over the tops of chairs to get to mine.

"Be that as it may..." Dougie began. Then he broke off to speak to somebody in one of our seats. "I think you'll find that you are *trespassing*," he said. "Unless you wish for me to do something very surprising with the penknife I have concealed in my pocket, please leave as soon as possible and go and join the other groundlings in the pit.

"*Be that as it may*," he resumed, as the 'groundling' slid away into the darkness before the stage, "I paid for these tickets." He took them from his inner coat pocket and reached across me to wave them in Snake's face. "Therefore, *I* get to select where we sit."

"Paid for them with mommy's money." Snake winked at me.

Dougie withdrew his hand. "It's a loan," he said. "I intend to pay it back, with interest, when the shop starts making money."

"When pigs fly, you mean," said Snake. Dougie smiled.

I was about to question what kind of pig was capable of flight – it sounded like a lie or a fiction to me – when the lights switched off.

Around me, the hundreds of spectators sat down as one. Snake hissed at me to do the same. The vibrations of several hundred pairs of feet tapping expectantly on the floor, like heavy rain, rippled through my seat. An excited chatter started briefly then vanished into silence.

"Are we going to see Megadeth?" I asked Snake in a whisper.

In the darkness next to me, I heard Dougie groan.

Snake laughed. "No, of course not," he said. "This is a band called 'Broken Record'. You'll like them. They started off doing covers of twentieth century hits, punk and stuff. But now they're pretty popular in their own right."

"As you can see," said Dougie, "from the number of faux-hippies and skinny-jeans-wearing freaks they've managed to attract here - like flies to a *turd*!" He raised his voice at this last bit. "To think, five years ago they were playing their first concert in the back room of some no-name dive bar for an audience of thirty. You could reach out and touch them if you wanted. No chance of that now - those thugs guarding the cowards would break your neck like a chicken." He pointed. I could just about make out the three muscle-bound men in the darkness before the stage, with the word 'security' on their t-shirts.

"Any other circumstance, I'd say 'a chicken couldn't break your neck'," said Snake. "But as it's your scrawny neck, I won't." He snickered, then whispered to me, "Don't listen to Dougie. He's bitter because his gods have gone mainstream. Trust me: they're still brilliant. There's no better way of initiating a newbie like you into the music world."

The stage exploded into sound and light.

The vibrations from the explosion ripped through the audience; through my body; right through to the follicles of my hair.

For a second I was completely, blissfully deaf. My lips contorted into what could have been a grimace of pain, maybe a smile, maybe both.

When my hearing came back, I could hear voices, cheers, *howls* from the groundlings in the pit. And behind me – more cheers, yells, screams. To my left and right: Snake blew a double-whistle on his fingers, shouted something I couldn't make out; Dougie, like many others in the audience, leapt to his feet. Under the veil of darkness, he was applauding wildly. There was another noise, too: as if from somebody in distress on a distant horizon - the ghost of a scream. A girl's scream. Detachedly, I realised that it was coming from my lips.

Then the music started to play. *Thud... thud... thud.* A dull, heavy heartbeat. Slow. Now faster, faster, faster – until it beat in time with mine.

"Oh, God," I heard Dougie say loudly, before I lost contact with him and floated away. "It's one of their new songs."

He started to clap – discretely - in time with the heartbeat.

"Come on." Snake nudged me to my feet.

The light from the explosion died down. In the remaining glow, four hulking figures stood, poised, ready. From left to right:

Figure One: Hair down to his hips. Muscular. Tall. A hunter.

Figure Two: Shaggy hair, shoulder-length. Crouched with predatorial eagerness behind a black-and-silver drum kit.

Figure Three: Hair cropped short on the right side; flopping over to the left as thick, bestial locks. Wielding a guitar.

Figure Four: Also holding a guitar. Hair curly, matted... in a way which suggested such freedom, such carelessness, such wildness...

The drummer struck his kit. At this, all four members of the band looked towards the stage lights. In the glow, I could see that each was wearing make-up, black and white and red, in intricate patterns around their eyes and lips and over their cheeks and foreheads. Their naked torsos were covered in tattoos.

My breath caught in my throat.

Then the guitars were released. They sounded like forest-dog cries. I had heard guitar music before, of course. On television. CDs. Polymer Mini-Records. But nothing compared to this. Here they were *live*, and unobstructed by TV screens. Wild creatures, loose in their natural habitat. At this moment, I realised something; something which, since my time with the Professor, I had doubted.

I realised that God was alive.

It filled this auditorium. Filled the people in the auditorium, as if we were starving, empty bodies; like It was the only thing alive. We were all connected in our love, our worship. Simultaneously, we all supplicated; we allowed It to enter us. Even Dougie was now swaying silently, his eyes glazed and fixed on the stage. When I gave in to the music, it felt as if two hands had reached inside my body and raked all thought and negativity to the side, leaving a glowing core of mindless enjoyment. I felt exposed, vulnerable – but willingly, *blissfully* so.

The music could do what It wanted with me now. I was ready.

The man with hair down to his hips stepped forward. I became one with the legions of screaming girls, hearts leaping together as we bore witness to the physical embodiment of the music: the Messiah.

The Messiah put his lips to the microphone. The guitars died down. I leaned forward, ready and eager to receive his message.

A pause.

Then the Messiah spoke. "This song," he said, "is called '*Brother*'."

The auditorium screamed.

My heart stopped. The front-man spoke in words, instead of in grunts and growls. This was wrong: I wasn't supposed to hear what he was actually *saying*. It was the sound, the energy, the mindless passion that I wanted. Words evoked new feelings, *complicated* feelings. And worse: memories.

He sang.

"Brother, Brother, where are you? I need you by my side. I cannot understand this place. I need you as my guide. Brother, when we were children, you taught me how to fight. But now she's gone and broke my heart. And I'm confused – I don't know what to do. Brother..."

#

My brother. Rawg.

He was at least four years older than me. Since his mother died, he had stayed close to his strong, protective father. Who later became our father.

Any other child would have used this forced sharing of a parent to fuel resentment for the little impostor. But not Rawg. I suppose he took after Father in many ways. Physically, he had the same brown-flecked thick hair, the same bottomless dark eyes, the same thin black lips - which never parted in a snarl, unless it was in my defence. But more importantly, like Father, he had intelligence.

Without Rawg, the raft would never have been built in time. His thick, hairy fingers were clumsier than mine but he was always keen to have an input in the design of the vessel, and took it upon himself to go off into the woods and find fresh supplies whenever they were needed.

Looking back on it now, I don't think he ever planned to make it across with me. He lied to spare my feelings. Perhaps he thought I'd be too scared to go alone, if he didn't leave it until the last minute to tell me, when it was a case of 'go now or die'...

Evening. Father was dead.

I had reached the raft, was standing next to it on the beach, getting my breath back, waiting for Rawg to arrive. He had poor muscle definition, which made running difficult. I, ironically, was the brawny one of the family.

Finally, I saw him cresting the hill. I got on the raft, ready and waiting. Then he stopped.

The shadows of our cousins started to collect behind him.

He continued to stand, staring at me. I continued to wait. I knew perfectly well what was going to happen. I just didn't want to admit it to myself.

Suddenly, I heard him shout: "Run, girl, before they get you too!"

He knew that, if I had waited for him, they would have caught up with me.

I was lucky. All I understood of the noise they made on approach was a mindless, bestial baying; Rawg would have been able to hear more. Every curse, every bad word, every threat to kill his little sister - he would have understood.

I cursed myself continuously on that journey for only being able to understand English. If Rawg had not had to holler at me, if my stupid brain had been receptive to their *subtle little ways of communicating silently* – well, perhaps then he could have told me to go, without them realising that he was helping me. Perhaps then he could have gone on living in relative peace on the Island.

I told myself I was being pessimistic. Maybe they hadn't turned on him as they had turned on Father. There was always a chance...

Of course, I know this was self-deception. Rawg was – is – undoubtedly dead. But I told myself that anyway. It kept me from self-destruction during those crucial first few days.

#

Back in the auditorium, I was glad of the darkness. Were it not for the darkness, Snake and Dougie would have seen me crouched on the floor with my elbows to my ears, silently sobbing. I was in agony. God had waited until my defences were down - then shot an arrow through my soul.

"Brother."

The word resonated on the Messiah's accusing lips as the drumbeat died away and the guitars hummed into silence.

The arena exploded into applause.

"Bravo," I heard Dougie murmur from somewhere above me. Then, "Now play your old stuff, you goddamn pop-music sell-outs."

A hand gripped my shoulder. I flinched. "Are you alright?" Snake's voice. "Katrina? What are you doing down there?"

I fumbled for an excuse. "I fell over," I said. "I'm not injured. Don't worry." Hastily, I scrambled to my feet.

"Okay." Snake sounded as if he was going to follow with a question but he was cut short. On stage, the Messiah began to speak.

"Did everyone enjoy that? Yeah?"

The answer to this came in the form of a scream from the entire arena of devoted disciples.

"No," Dougie said.

"Yeah," I sniffed. I wanted to go. Not just from the arena. I wanted to go, to disappear, from existence. When my barricades were down, life was simply too painful.

"Alright!" The Messiah flicked his hair. He had been standing at the end of the stage with his microphone in hand, but now he stepped jovially back and replaced the microphone in its stand. "Here's a bit of Black Sabbath for you guys!" The arena burst into a fresh new wave of applause.

"Good enough," Dougie said.

An angry beat started up. As soon as the guitars began to screech and squeal, I forgot what I had been thinking about, gratefully welcoming the sounds into my head. Around me, people were stamping their feet, clapping their hands: a ritual which everyone instinctively became a part of, including me. Once again, I was mindless: one with the mass.

God had struck me down. Perhaps this was divine punishment for my desertion; perhaps just Its sadistic pleasure. But now It had redeemed Itself, and I welcomed It back inside me. If there remained a slight feeling that something unresolved should have been making me sad, I drowned it out with stomps and claps until I barely noticed it was there. I was free again. The Messiah was beautiful again.

And that was how it remained until the end of the concert.

Finally, the last word from the Messiah's lips died away. A thousand lights flashed wildly from the stage. More lights shot over my head; impossible, neon rainbows.

My mind was exhausted. My pulse was racing. I felt exceptional…

Then the world went black.

#

I awoke on a hard bed in a strange room. This would have terrified me if I had not seen Snake sitting by my bedside. He smiled. "Katrina – you're awake!"

"Am I?" I looked at the ceiling, then at the walls. Everything was peculiarly bright-white. "I thought maybe I was dreaming. Where am I?"

"In hospital. Katrina, you had a seizure!" Snake leaned in closer; clasped my hands in his. I pulled mine away – but gently, politely, so as not to offend him. He seemed to understand, and sat back in his bedside chair. "Have you had seizures before?"

I shook my head. This made me dizzy. I lay back in bed and let the room spin. "Why do I feel strange?" I heard Snake attempt to construct an explanation, fail, try again. I groaned. "Where's Dougie?"

"Dougie's in the corridor, talking to the doctor," said Snake. "He's going to be back soon."

"How long am I going to be here for?"

"Not long," said Snake. "We hope, anyway."

"Good."

Inside my head, I could still hear the beat of Black Sabbath. I nodded my head in time. "But this beat won't last forever," I murmured to myself. "I have to get out. I have to get to *real* music soon. Or else I will die."

I could see, from the corner of my eye, Snake's smile become a frown. Then suddenly he looked to the door. "Aha!" he said, too cheerily. "I think I can hear Dougie coming back with the doctor."

I listened. Over the wonderful beat of Black Sabbath in my mind, I could hear footsteps. They came to a halt outside the door.

"Your friend has had a *fit*," I heard a man say. "Understand? She's lucky not to have sustained any serious brain-damage. That bleed was serious. Whatever you do: *you must not take her to any more concerts.*"

CHAPTER THIRTEEN

At my second concert, I didn't get a seizure.

I writhed and swayed with the other 'groundlings' on the arena floor, eyes closed, arms waving in the air. From their front-row seats, Snake and Dougie looked on: Snake I think with a kind of pride, Dougie with detachment.

I let the music take my body over and over again. Revelled in the vibrations it sent rushing through my nerves. I let it explore every nook and cranny of my pointless, fleshy corpse. My mind was up in Heaven; my soul was with God. I was safe.

These songs - or what I could understand of them through the growls and the shrieks and the groans - were not about brothers, or fathers. In fact, I never heard another metal song which so much as touched upon these themes. These songs addressed the body, not the mind; they spoke of sex, warfare, physical things. My mind was unneeded when this music was animating my body - it could go, disappear, and take its pain with it.

When the electric EcoShuttle stopped at the end of our street that night, I snatched the shop keys from Snake and ran the rest of the way to the Music Store. I reached the door a half-minute before Snake and Dougie, and fumbled frantically to unlock it; finally broke through. The bell chimed once, then twice, three times as Snake and Dougie came in behind me.

I dropped to my knees before a delivery box which had been abandoned in one of the aisles, and leafed through the Polymer Mini-Record sleeves within until I came upon the darkest, most savage-sounding title I could find. 'Anger', by something called the 'High-on-Acid Hippy Slaughter Band' (or 'H-O-A-H-S-B' for short).

"Katrina!" I could hear Snake somewhere in the background, coming nearer. "You can't open that - that's merchandise!"

"Oh, leave her," said Dougie. "We won't sell half of that. By the end of the week, they'll have perfected the cassette tape and we'll be selling those again. Mark my words." He sighed. "Anyway, I'm going home now - make sure she locks up." The bell chimed again as Dougie left the shop.

I scissored through the biodegradable plastic wrapper with my finger and removed the record from its sleeve.

I ran behind the counter, jammed the record onto the Polymer Player, and forced down the needle. Waited. Nothing. I removed the record, wiped it frantically with the sleeve of my denim jacket, and tried again. Still nothing.

Only now did I become fully aware of Snake's presence behind me. "You can't work it, can you?" I turned, and he came forward. He reached out a hand towards me. "Give it here."

I thrust the record in his direction.

"I'm surprised you've forgotten how to work this thing," Snake said, taking the record from me. "Seriously, I thought you were going to be our in-house technical whizz-kid…"

"Put it on!"

Snake sighed. He fiddled with the player. Within seconds, music was playing.

It filled the shop: furious electric guitars, pulsing drums, screaming vocals. Then it became quieter as Snake dimmed the volume.

"What are you doing?" I demanded.

Snake turned to me and frowned. "You know we can't have it too loud. It'll disturb the neighbours. It'll disturb *Dougie*."

"Turn it up!" I said. "Turn it up, turn it up!"

A pause. Then the music became louder by half a degree. With a sigh, Snake drew back from the record player. He turned to me again. There was something sad about his expression as he regarded me. I couldn't tell why, but there was. And it annoyed me. "Why are you staring at me like that?"

"Katrina." Snake spoke softly. "Are you… *sure* you're alright?"

"Yes!" I said, louder than I intended.

The way Snake had spoken – so low, so soft – was somehow extremely irritating. My head was still buzzing with music, aflame with energy. It was as if Snake wanted to quench this. To calm me down, to make me unhappy.

But one look at Snake's face dispelled these suspicions. He seemed so innocent and confused, so non-threatening.

"I'm fine," I said. "Now the music is on, I'm fine. Really."

Snake continued to stare at me for a while. Then he nodded. "Fine." He started towards the door. "Just remember to lock up before you – no, actually…" He came back, and took the keys gently from my hand.

I let them go without resistance. My mind was with the music.

"I'll lock up. You make sure you get some sleep." Before he left, he cast a brow-furrowed look back in my direction. I quickly dismissed it.

I was somewhere else.

The bell over the door sounded as he left. When he was gone, I jumped up onto the counter and lay down. Pressing my face against the countertop so I could feel the player's vibrations through the wood, I let the 'High-on-Acid Hippy Slaughter Band' lull me into a pleasantly empty, mindless sleep.

#

Saturday night. I must have been working at the music store for almost two months.

I was sitting on the floor in the back-room with Snake, playing 'chess'. A new set had been sent with the latest delivery by mistake. Snake had plans to see a band later that night and, up until recently, so had I. But Dougie the Druggie had confiscated my ticket, and forbidden Snake from taking me to any more gigs for a month. He had said it was messing with my head, that my mind was no longer on the job.

"Don't worry – I'll sneak you out next week," Snake consoled me from across the chessboard. I shrugged, and toyed with one of the pieces silently. When Snake was gone, I told myself, I would put some angry music on and turn up the Polymer Player to full volume. Dougie had lost all right to be offended by my music.

Snake's rucksack was by the door, packed up and ready to go but he had opted to stay behind for a while to teach me how to play, so I would have something (besides music) to keep my mind occupied after-hours.

"Now, that's a bishop. And that's a knight. A knight can jump, but a bishop can't."

"Why not?"

"Because… you know, I've never really thought about it."

"Pointless rules." I knocked a bishop over viciously with my finger.

Snake stood the piece up again. "You're pissed at Dougie. I know." He hesitated. "Yeah, he's overreacting, as he always does. Always doom and gloom. But... he has a point. I mean – you need something more in your life than music, you know?"

"Like what?"

"Like... I don't know." Snake ran a finger over the white, polished heads of his pieces. "But like Dougie says - you can't just sit in a happy bubble all your life. You've got to face reality." He slid a pawn forward. "Anyway, your move."

Later, as Snake finished explaining why the move I had made with my pawn was 'illegal', Dougie stepped forward. I wondered if Dougie had been standing there, watching us in silence, for a while. He seemed to like watching people have fun.

The sound of Dougie's heavy boots hitting the floor startled Snake. He flinched. Something cylindrical and white fell from his pocket, rolled across the floor, and stopped at Dougie's feet.

Dougie stooped to pick it up. He examined its label. His face morphed into a peculiar expression which I didn't recognise. He looked at Snake.

Snake was frozen. Wide-eyed, he stared at Dougie. Slowly, Dougie approached.

For a moment I thought Dougie intended to kill Snake. Discretely, I took the longest, sharpest-looking piece from the chess board, concealed it under my t-shirt, and waited.

But all Dougie did when he reached us was pass the cylinder back to Snake. "Are you aware how many deaths are caused by these things, Snake?" His spoke in a slow, grave monotone.

Snake took the container uncertainly. "But, I mean... everyone takes them, right?"

"Do they?" Dougie's lip lifted in a humourless smile, showing sharp, white, perfectly straight teeth. "Well, it wouldn't surprise me. The world has gone to shit. Stands to reason you would want to hide from reality. I hope you all have fun on your *Soma-holidays*." Then, in response to Snake's blank stare, Dougie said, "A chemically-induced escape from reality. 'Brave New World' reference. No?"

Snake shook his head.

"Philistine," said Dougie. And Snake started to unscrew the lid, fingers trembling. "Pathetic."

Snake tipped what looked like tiny white breath-mints into the palm of his hand. Dougie swallowed harshly. "I hope you understand what a complete and total hypocrite this makes you, my friend. Contrary to popular belief, I don't take substances to change the way I see the world."

"Maybe you should," said Snake

Dougie's glare would have killed a lesser creature. Snake dropped the bottle on the floor, and hurriedly swallowed the pills. I leaned over to read the label – 'Antidepressant'. The word sparked a memory, somewhere in the recesses of my mind, and another name – Doctor Helen Monroe – swam to the forefront. For a second I was in the Professor's auditorium, and he was pointing at a big machine and saying... *something*...

But these thoughts were quickly drowned out by the ever-present bass riff in my head.

"Just make sure you don't take too many," Dougie warned in a disconcertingly musical voice. "I can't have my only semi-sane employee dying on me." He looked at each of us. "If anybody needs me, I will be rearranging my music collection to make room for the Polymer Mini-Records. They should be out of date soon." He left without another word.

Snake and I stared after him.

#

Tuesday night. Month uncertain.

Snake, Dougie and I sat in Dougie's apartment, crouched on cardboard boxes in amongst the debris and dusty CD stacks. The lights were off, the curtains closed, the only light coming from the dull glow of Dougie's tiny, muted television. On the screen, footage ran of green-clad people cheering and crying; a map of America slowly turning green.

Dougie had banned me from music for the entire day. My mind was aching, my defences down. Dougie was cruel. I licked salty sweat from my fingers, remnants of the poorly-cooked pizza Dougie had presented us with hours ago, and tried to focus. But Dougie and Snake's chatter had turned philosophical as the night drew on, and their voices grated on my brain.

"The Monroe Pill - that's what started all this!" Snake said suddenly, as if in revelation.

I flinched. "Don't do that!"

Dougie looked at him wearily. "What are you talking about? The Monroe Pill was one of the reasons people loved science; not a reason for its demise." He nodded at the screen. "Ferdinand Mann's wife had a Monroe Pill termination, don't you remember? The whole country was celebrating her honesty."

"Yeah, but hear me out. It depends on what version of the Pill you're talking about, doesn't it? I mean, sure - people accepted the Pill when it was only killing off the really messed-up babies..."

"Killing babies?" As much as I tried to concentrate on the screen – another state, a big one, flipping to green – their words seeped into my brain. "Why were they killing babies?"

"Foetuses. Not babies," Dougie corrected. "But go on."

"Well, people got uncomfortable when it started wiping out other brain conditions. Like... I don't know. Autism? Because that wasn't really an illness, was it? More like an eccentricity. And Beethoven was autistic... or bipolar... or something. I read that in one of your books." He grinned, apparently proud.

The new words drifted around in my brain, trying to imbed. "Autistic-savant," I murmured the word, half-remembered from somewhere.

"Irrelevant!" said Dougie. "Illness or not, people love wiping out the little differences that blight their populations. They're obsessed with normality. Otherwise they wouldn't still be using the Pill today, would they?"

On the television, people in green shirts bared their shiny white teeth, leering at me through the screen.

"True..." Snake said.

"Anyway," continued Dougie. "The real reason the Monroe Pill was invented in the first place was because most scientists were neurodivergents anyway. They knew those conditions were beneficial. Most of history's great scientific advances were made by such beautiful minds."

"Okay, but... wouldn't that make them want to *ban* the Monroe Pill? To stop those conditions being wiped out?"

"No! Honestly, Snake, do you really think Homo-SuperiUS was a philanthropic organization?" Dougie gave a sinister little chuckle. "They wanted to create an elite overclass, reserving those coveted traits for their own kind.

"They were bad people," I recalled. A cluster of people in blue t-shirts stared sadly through the screen.

"If they were bad, then so is everyone. Even the Ferdinand Mann supporters are complicit. You don't see them rejecting the Monroe Pill, and with the Pill killing off any riff-raff with unusual neurological patterns before they left the womb..."

"Killing?" A memory-flash: Courtney spitting at me, venom in her eyes. *Living miscarriage.* I moved closer to the screen. The people were gone, the map was back. Greener.

"Yeah, yeah," said Snake. "I went to school; I get where you're going with this. Eugenics, right? Dougie the Druggie's paranoia strikes again!"

Dougie shook his head. "I tell you, it's true. The scientists claimed all the best psychological abnormalities for themselves. Meanwhile, what's left for the artists? Run-of-the-mill depression - and even that, they can kill with a little white tablet. No wonder the music scene is stagnating. Oh, surprise-surprise – Washington's green." He nodded at the television as more of the map changed colour. "Think about it, though. They kept Tati. He would have been a prime candidate for a Monroe Pill termination if he'd been conceived in our generation."

"You think Tati was... what, schizo?"

"What's schizo?" I asked.

"Schizophrenic," said Dougie. "And of course he was! That was why Bai and Monroe made him give the public apology. When that journalist discovered the chimpanzee they'd mangled and demanded an explanation. The other two said to themselves, 'We've got a chimp bleeding out on a table with bits of other animals' brains stuck to it –"

Too much. I shrunk in on myself and hissed.

"Bits of a cat's brain," said Snake. "I took history of science in high school. They'd blended the chimpanzee's brain with bits of a cat's brain..."

"Stop it," I muttered. Explanations from the Professor's lectures. Photos projected on the wall, which I overlooked, dismissed as lies. People didn't enact cruelty. But now...

"Again, irrelevant! Bai and Monroe said, 'Whatever explanation Tati gives for that, it's going to look nuts'."

"Right. So all the stuff he was saying about - animals and people being blended together, and laser beams through brains-"

I cringed.

"-you reckon that's all crap?"

"No, Snake, it's all *true*. But the world was meant to think it was 'crap'. We were meant to think, 'the man's clearly insane, it can't be as bad as all that'. Monroe and Bai would have thrown him in an institution, and everyone in Homo-SuperiUS could have gone about their lives. But the populace believed him, and it all came crashing down."

"So you reckon it's all true? Laser beams through brains?"

"Correct. The old hospitals were overflowing with candidates for that sort of experimentation."

"And blending animal with man? What were they doing with that?"

"...I don't know, Snake. But I'd bet anything that chimpanzee experiment was some sort of trial run."

"So you would blame him, for everyone turning against science?" said Snake, returning to the original topic of conversation. "You would blame Doctor Tati."

"Doctor Tati." Dougie nodded. "The Doctor Moreau of Bordeaux, didn't the papers call him?"

"You wouldn't blame… the albino one, what's-his-name…"

"Bai," said Dougie.

"Bai, or Monroe? I mean even if Tati did spill, they were all involved, weren't they? In the monkey… no, the *chimp*-brain experiment."

"Honestly, Snake," said Dougie. "I blame them all." He smiled a wicked smile. "Ah. Behold our new Commander in Chief."

On the screen, a somehow familiar bald man with a beard stepped onto a stage. He waved grandly, and moved towards the microphone.

"Alright," Dougie switched the television off. "That's it. EcoTech's in charge. Might as well shut up shop."

"He'll be like this for a while," Snake murmured to me. "Why don't you go back down to the shop, get some sleep?"

Relieved, I ran downstairs to the Polymer Player. Dougie had made me abstain from music for the entire day. As I listened to the music, I thought about what Snake and Dougie had said. Monroe, Bai and Tati, the picture on the papers, on the television screens, the names in the Professor's lectures – a destructive force, intent on wiping out difference. Ferdinand Mann and all those American people, continuing their legacy.

Run, girl...

But I was safe here. I turned up the music. Blocked the bad thoughts out.

CHAPTER FOURTEEN

It was my first outdoor rock festival. The sun was blisteringly hot. Waves of young people in green T-shirts, rolled up to reveal glistening midriffs, ebbed and flowed around me. A screen on stage displayed the image of a bald man with hair on his chin, smiling, eyes bright over round glasses. "As your president-elect, it gives me great pleasure to open this music festival. We won, California! Together we will drag this great country from its dark past into a new era of glory!"

The image faded to show another: Bai, Tati and Monroe pinning their monkey – no, *chimpanzee* - down on the table. Wanting to get into its brain, Dougie said.

No. No.

All around me, the young people started baying. Jostling, hungry dogs.

They'll all take that Pill.

"Start the music!" I screamed. A hand slapped the back of my head. I whirled to see a spike-haired young woman squaring her shoulders at me. A predator preparing to pounce. "Shut up," she said. I lunged for her, but then a hand was on my wrist, dragging me into the crowd. I screamed again and yanked it free.

"Hey," said Snake. "Sorry. Seemed like something bad was gonna go down there." He grinned and held up a white plastic bottle. "Dougie said you needed sunblock. Here, let me…" He squeezed some nasty white paste onto his palm. Extended his hand towards me.

"Get away!" I wriggled past him into the throng. Seeing Dougie approach me from the left, I moved faster into the jungle.

The music had started. A strong, heavy beat growing faster, faster. The bodies around me, tall as trees, blocked my view of the stage. I stopped moving, closed my eyes. The heat from the sun, from the throngs, scorched my arms and legs and face, seeped through my long black shirt and denim shorts, burning them to my body. The pain felt like a release. Somewhere, a rough male voice roared. A pack of wild metal instruments howled.

Father. Rawg.

I could see their faces, familiar, loving, alive. Watching me, waiting for me in the trees.

"Katrina!"

And I was falling, falling, the world swimming to complete darkness.

#

Now lying on the floor of the cave belonging to Araga-Mawg. The Healer.

Standing at my feet: Father, aged by the worry creasing his face. Beside him stands Araga-Mawg, naked except for the dog-skin which conceals their ambiguous genitalia.

The cave is dark, wet; yet the ornaments of deer bone, forest-dog teeth, deer skulls and stones which line the edges of the cave give it an aura of authority and sophistication. I can hear noises from the beach nearby: whoops and howls and hollers. I am impatient to return to the safety of the Edu-Centre. But of course I can't, not just yet - because my head is gushing blood, and I cannot stand.

Of course, at age fifteen, I believe I am immortal. But it is clear from the tremoring of Father's shoulders that he is not so sure. "It's alright," I try to tell Father. "I only hit my head on a rock."

Which is true. I only omitted the fact that said rock had been launched at me by one of Rawg's peers, when he saw me peering through the leaves to watch Rawg's endless fight for females on the beach. Knowing Rawg is outside the Edu-Centre and putting himself in danger would only worry Father more.

Father and Araga-Mawg stare at each other, exchanging silent messages that I cannot pick up on. My father lifts his eyebrows at Araga. Araga remains still. Father looks deep into Araga's eyes. Silence.

"Can I have something for the pain?" I venture. Ordinarily I would just have gestured silently towards the leaves and fruit-skins of concoctions strung across Araga's reed-matted belt, to avoid the ugly temper my alien language skills provoke in anyone other than Father and Rawg. But my headache is spreading through my body, and it hurts too much to move.

Araga glares at me. Then they turn back to Father.

I look from one to the other, trying to guess at what they might be telling each other. Father's jowls are quivering ferociously. Araga remains still but tense.

Suddenly, Father says in civilised words: "Fix my daughter!"

Araga-Mawg slaps him hard across the face as if he is an insolent child.

Even I recoil. This has never happened before. What is going on?

But it seems to work out for the best. Seeing Father's furious expression, Araga-Mawg backs down, and gets to work on me with handmade bandages and ointments. But even under Father's supervision, Araga's manner is cold. I feel like a raft being repaired and sealed by a craftsman, for a client the craftsman would rather see drowned...

#

I awoke in another clean, white hospital bed. I felt like I was floating, then sinking, then floating again, in thick molasses.

Once again, Snake was seated by my side. He seemed genuinely happy when I regained consciousness, and said some words that I couldn't quite make out due to the ringing in my ears. I gave him an affectionate smile and a nod.

A few minutes later, an elderly doctor came into the room, herded from behind by Dougie, who was carrying some vending machine snacks. Dougie nodded at me then threw a bag of mini cheese crackers at Snake before taking a seat in the other visitor's chair, to my right. He leaned back in his seat with blatant indifference to the company and opened up a packet of cookies. He shook it temptingly in my direction, but when I failed to rise from my sickbed, he sighed, and tucked the packet into his inner coat pocket.

The doctor cleared his throat. The three of us looked at him in anticipation. Snake seemed concerned. Dougie was glowering at the doctor as if he was a parking attendant or a tax inspector.

"Well," the doctor said to me in a sickly-sweet voice. "You certainly are lucky your big brother found you when he did."

A gesture from Snake when the doctor wasn't looking indicated that he was the 'big brother'.

"You've sustained some pretty severe head injuries, young lady," the doctor said. "Those Doctor-Martin's-Boot prints will be on your forehead for a while, I dare say... Uh... well now, we've done some tests, and I am sorry to say you appear to have a *little* damage to the brain. Nothing too severe. Certainly nothing to worry about for the moment. But we would like to keep you in for another week, to be sure. And we'd also like to run some more tests. Okay?"

At this, Dougie's eyes doubled in size.

Later, when the doctor had left the room and I had drifted into a doze, I heard Snake and Dougie talking across the bed. Their words woke me, but I continued to pretend to sleep to hear what they were talking about.

"But we've got to pay," Snake hissed.

"I never suggested she attend this concert. Why should I pay for its consequences?" Dougie.

"Because it's the right thing to do! It's not like we pay her anything to work in the shop."

"Don't pay her anything? Honestly, Snake! She gets free food, pays no rent... God help me, thanks to your insistence, I even paid for her ticket to that concert, too!"

"But..."

"Listen." Dougie paused. "I'm not heartless. I have some affection for that poor girl. But we're broke. If I had the money, I would pay for her to have every test, surgery, whatever she needs to repair the damage. But I don't, so I can't."

"But your mother..."

"Talked to her financial adviser about the shop's real prospects. I've been cut off. Understand? We'll have to do a 'dine-and-dash', or whatever the medical equivalent is."

"Let's just wait for him to come back," said Snake. "See how much it is. Who knows? He might let us off lightly if he knows the situation."

"Oh, for the love of God, would you listen to yourself! It's those little white pills talking, Snake; not you. Time to face reality."

I would have offered the use of my body as payment again, rather than listen to them argue. Time spent in a hospital bed couldn't have been that much more expensive than a room to sleep in. Certainly not as expensive as a CD. But at that point the concussion returned like a grasping hand, and pulled me under again.

CHAPTER FIFTEEN

The night I came back from the hospital, Snake made a bed for me on the shop floor. He laid me down then checked his watch. Suddenly, he was babbling apologies because he had a dinner-meeting with his father, saying he would cancel it – but Dougie gripped his shoulder, looked him in the eye, and promised that he would watch me through the night.

Dougie brought in a folding chair from the back room and set it up by my mattress. He spoke little as he watched me, responding to my moans with gentle 'go to sleep's. But his expression did seem to be one of genuine pity.

When I awoke in the middle of the night, I had a painful throb in the back of my head. Through the darkness I saw Dougie's shadowy figure reclining in the chair. I reached out to his foot and pulled on it weakly. He stirred. "What's wrong? What do you need?"

I tried to speak, but my voice came out as a dry, guttural croak.

Dougie started to rise from his seat. "I'll bring you a glass of water."

"No!" I grabbed Dougie's foot, and with great effort I asked him to put my new Polymer MiniRecord on.

But he refused. "You must rest, Katrina."

I didn't see why he was being so cruel. I asked him again, several times, then begged. Still, he shook his head. "You've had enough."

He knelt by my mattress and touched a finger, lightly, to the bandage around my forehead. "Does it still hurt?"

I shook my head for 'no', and the room started spinning.

Dougie's voice developed an echo and became eerily soft, strangely soothing. He said, "What are you running from, Katrina?"

I couldn't feel my lips move. "I'm not running."

"You are running *metaphorically*. Don't play dumb." Then I felt his hands in my hair. The ringing in my ears became the sound of a gentle breeze, and I was floating like a leaf in the wind just above the forest floor, watching the sunlight through the canopy above me and letting Rawg's bristly fingers stroke the fringe back from my strange, soft, human face. "If you tell me why you're running," said Dougie. "I'll tell you why I am. Do we have a deal?"

I smiled. The sun broke through the canopy and fell, warm and splendid, on my face. "Why are you running?"

A pause. Dougie's hand stiffened, and lifted from my head slightly; continued to stroke my hair. "Snake believes I'm twenty-five, or younger. That's a lie. I'm thirty-two."

"That's no reason to run," I whispered.

"Not in itself, but listen. When I was twelve, they changed the law. I was old enough to know what was going on, and I was old enough to realize how it was destroying my family... It's important you understand that, or nothing else I say will make sense." He paused. "How old were you when your father died, Katrina?"

Another hand, thick-furred and warm, brushed my cheek. The question meant nothing to me. "I don't know."

"Were you close to him?"

I smiled. "I think so." In the distance, the sounds of the forest-dogs playing, calling and howling; the rustle of the leaves above me.

"I never knew my father. My mother was rarely in the picture, either. The family fortune set her up for life: with no motivation to work, she spent her time pursuing mindless ecstasy in the arms of horrible men. I suppose I should feel sorry for her. I was close to my grandmother, though." Dougie sighed. "My grandmother wasn't like other people. She was quick, intelligent. She knew things nobody else should know, and she kept secrets. I stayed with her every summer in Santa Monica, by the beach. It seemed there was a different journalist in her kitchen every morning when I came down for breakfast... I even had my picture taken with her for that old magazine, Scientific American. Are you listening?"

I tried to nod. A breeze curled gently through my hair.

"Anyway, I watched as those journalists turned from loving her, to hating her, to wanting her dead. She started taking those horrible little white pills. I was with her when she..."

He paused. I could feel his eyes outside my fantasy, scanning my face, searching for recognition. I lay still, played dead. Strained to hear the forest-dogs calling; strained to feel the breeze, the hand against my aching skin.

Dougie exhaled. "You can't ignore what's happening around you." He took his hand from my hair. "Reality will catch up with you sooner or later. The longer you block it out, the harder it will be to accept."

I tried to smile again, to reassure him that nothing really mattered. But my muscles were starting to cramp and, above me, the leaves were looking more like the stains and patterns on the Music Store ceiling, the breeze sounding more like the perpetual ringing in my ears. "Snake does it."

"Yes. And I love Snake, I really do, but his way of dealing with reality, by shutting it out with those pills… it isn't healthy. You can become addicted to those things. People have overdosed." Dougie hesitated. "Do you know that's how Doctor Helen Monroe died?"

"Helen Monroe?" I blinked away the remnants of the fantasy, and now back in the Music Store, I was struck by the sadness, perhaps disappointment, I recognised in Dougie's pale face.

"It doesn't matter."

When Dougie went to get me some water, I crawled out of my makeshift bed. Holding a hand to the side of my head to keep the bandage in place, I managed to reach the Polymer Player and switch the music on myself. I didn't recognise the song, but it was mindless and heavy.

When Dougie returned to find me sprawled on my mattress in the grip of euphoria, all he did was shake his head and sigh. He went to the player and turned the music down a few notches.

"The day you and Snake decide you want to see the real world, I'll be there to guide you through," I heard him murmur distantly. "But I am not prepared to help someone who refuses to help themselves."

The words were lost on me. Lulled by the music, I managed to sleep through the rest of the night. When I awoke, late the next morning, I felt pleasantly numbed.

PART TWO: ALEXANDER BAI

Hunched over pieces of dismantled freezer on the floor of my cabin in the desert, I start to realize that the sunlight is burning my naked skin again.

I shake free of my memory-trance and look quickly around the room, reacquainting myself with my surroundings. The kitchenette behind me, now a mess of cups and spilled coffee granules; the door, with its chain safely across; the desk, twenty-six test tubes still unoccupied in a line across it, and the window behind. Somewhere to my left, the CryoBag. A whine, urgent now, emits from the synthetic cube. The power draining.

The walls seem to be lit with a much fiercer, brighter light than when I started work this morning. I take a final look at the network of wires covering the side-panel I am currently holding. Then I hurl it to the floor among the other fragments and go to the window.

Of course, I stop before the thinning floral fabric which serves as a curtain. I am not going to open it. I'm not an idiot. I can't remember if it was me who drew the curtain in the first place or if it was already drawn. Whoever drew the curtain, it was a good idea.

The desert sun is high in the sky now. It must be midday. Over the last three days I have learnt to dread this time, when the sun becomes bright enough to penetrate the fabric and light the entire cabin. I imagine people, hiding where I cannot see them, staring through the curtain at me. Nobody must know what I am doing. Night-time is my preferred time to work. My eyes seem to have grown accustomed to operating in the dark.

I stand looking through the thin fabric. I can see the vague shape of the building opposite. It is staring directly at me. A cabin larger than mine, the only other building for miles. So far I have seen no one emerge from it, no vehicles draw up to or drive away from it. If they did, would I leave? Short answer: no. Even if this area had been inhabited, I would still be living here. I had no option but to choose this location.

Perhaps an ordinary person might call it 'fate' that such a perfect, isolated building landed in my path when I so desperately needed a base. But this, of course, is drivel. The gloopy by-product of weaker minds. It was chance – that is all.

Besides, it isn't *perfect. The goddamn solar-powered Eco-Freezer resists my attempts at repairing it.*

Time is short.

I take a quick look at the portable CryoBag, which now lives under the desk in the shade. Two more days of power within that synthetic cube, maximum. I have to keep working. I cannot let all this be for nothing.

I can't let Alexander Bai win.

I stop by the kitchenette before I return to work, boil a little more water, and heap three tablespoons of instant coffee into a stained cup. Do I like coffee now? Maybe my taste buds have changed, along with everything else. My tongue – I stretch it out, tap it against my weird front teeth – feels different, thick, alien, like something stitched badly inside my otherwise human mouth.

Or maybe I just don't care about the taste anymore. It tastes like nothing. Flavourless medicine.

I hate that I still need sleep. Already my mind is drifting away from its purpose. Cup in hand, I sit back down on the floor and try to seize control, but my consciousness slips through my jittering fingers and carries me back to the past.

CHAPTER SIXTEEN
ONE YEAR BEFORE

A dream, or perhaps a memory.
The Edu-Centre, warm and familiar.
Two hands, reaching out in front of me.
Soft, warm, breathing. I want to hold them to me. I want to feel their plush fur beneath my hands, their breath against my chest.
The hands close over the sleeping pile. A burst of warmth and soft flesh makes my heart leap – and then those hands are pressing down, bones cracking, blood seeping between my fingers.
"Katrina..."
Rawg and Father stand together by the Edu-Centre wall. Their eyes are large. I can read their minds now; I can feel seventeen years of care and love and sacrifice crumbling.
"Run, girl. Before they get you too..."
Make it worth it.
"Have to keep going..."
Prove yourself.
I woke, my head pulsing.

I cannot remember what day it was. But I can remember waking early that morning when the winter sunshine streamed in through a gap between the shop-window blinds. It fell upon the green-and-white EcoTech poster, stuck lop-sided above the Polymer MiniRecord discount bin. The poster read: 'MusiChips - the little piece of the future you can hold in your hand'. Below the heading, a Snake-lookalike held up one of the little silver sticks, beaming in religious ecstasy at his purchase. Along the bottom, the text was black and bold: 'EcoTech Loves Music.'

"Yes," I whispered. "Loves it enough to drain it of its genius then dispose of its empty corpse." I wasn't sure what this meant, but Dougie had said it a few days ago, and it had a memorable ring to it.

I squinted at the clock on the wall; saw the little hand pointing at the 'seven' and the big hand at the 'twelve'. The second-hand clicked loudly as it travelled around the face.

I looked up at the ceiling again and tried to make sense of where I was. My ears were buzzing. My eyes were blurry. My head was pulsating with the steady rhythm of whatever wonderful band-in-a-basement Snake had scrounged tickets for us to see the previous night. Beyond this, I could think of nothing.

And yet, somehow, I knew I had been dreaming.

It was one of those dreams that are like syrup: which refuse to completely let go of your brain for minutes, even hours, after your eyes have opened. A surreal dream. I had been having them more and more with every wild night out, every fabulous gig, every song listened to for that exquisite first time through state-of-the-art, enormous headphones with the sound turned up to 'max'... Only rarely worrying that, one of these days, I would reach a stage where the syrup wouldn't come off, and I would be doomed to spend the rest of my life wandering the streets as a brain-damaged 'junkie', stuck forever between realities. I lived for the moment. And Snake and Dougie would protect me if anything went wrong. Probably.

Besides, I didn't really feel that mine was a brain worth saving.

With dawning consciousness came the inevitable cravings. Sluggishly, my fingers crept behind the counter to the new player, felt for the MusiChip, and pushed it back into its slot. The music was unleashed with a growl: some angry song about how beauty is a facade thinly veiling the true evils of human nature.

For a moment, the image of a blonde girl in insectile sunglasses was conjured inside my head. It started spinning demonically. So I turned the music up until I could hear only the steady heartbeat throb of the bass. Into the ether she vanished.

As the song drifted to a close, I became aware of another noise. A sort of tap-tap-tapping on the doorframe outside.

At first, I thought it was my imagination. So I turned over on the counter, groaning, forearms to my ears, and tried to get back to sleep again. My cheek touched one of the pieces of paper on the counter. I peered at it, trying to focus. I could tell it was from Dougie, not Snake, because some of the words had been underlined multiple times. 'KATRINA: DOOR MUST BE LOCKED AT NIGHT. EMPLOYEES MUST BE FULLY CLOTHED AT ALL TIMES. PLEASE REMEMBER!' It was a new one.

The noise persisted. After a few more rounds of tapping, a voice started to call: "Hello? Excuse me? Excuse me? Hello?" The door shook. The speaker was trying to get in.

This was not normal.

The fact that this was not normal penetrated what was left of my grog and administered a shot of adrenaline straight to my brain. I rolled off the counter, landing almost-on-my-feet like a cat on marijuana, and dragged my body to the door.

I was barefoot; on my left ankle, the silver-spiked leather cuff which Snake and I had won from Dougie in an intoxicated game of 'no-rules chess', and which Snake had let me keep. Wearing loose denim shorts, bleached almost white by the sun, unbuttoned for maximum comfort. On top, my upside-down crucifix t-shirt, five sizes too big for me and made to fit a man. That shirt was so long that, if I stood a certain way, it gave the illusion that I was wearing nothing on the bottom. My long, unwashed, wiry hair scratched my skin through the thin material.

The door teetered and rocked as I drew closer. My brain was now able to pick out a male shape behind the glass, dark against the sunshine. He was bent at the waist, peering in at me.

Whoever this person was, he was clearly not one of our regular crowd. His figure was neither obese nor skeletal, but on the skinny side of healthy. He appeared to be wearing a suspicious amount of clothing; his entire body, from collar to wrists to ankles, was covered with fabric. And that insistent voice – "Hello? Can you answer the *door*, please?" – was soft, even slightly feminine. It reminded me of somebody I had almost forgotten: a well-spoken academic, who had foolishly believed my brain was something special. And yet this voice trembled a little, as if unsure of itself. Like the voice of a child. It was not an unpleasant voice to listen to, especially with my ears being in such a tender state.

I reached the door and opened it out of habit. Then I went over to the window to roll up the blinds and flip the 'closed' sign to 'open'.

"Right. Finally! Thank you. Hello."

"Hello." Beyond that one pleasantry, I was far too preoccupied with the sign to pay the man any heed. It is amazing how similar 'open' and 'closed' can look when your brain feels like it has lost a fight.

"I'm looking for someone," the man said. "You might be able to help."

I picked a side, turned the sign. Then I retreated to behind the counter and waited in silence. A few moments passed before the man realised that I wasn't going to respond to his statement.

"Listen, you obviously can't hear me! Can you turn the music off, please?"

He sounded serious. I turned the player off.

"I said," he pressed, "that I am *looking for somebody*."

"Stevie Nicks?" I asked.

"Excuse me?"

"We've had a big delivery of Stevie Nicks. Five whole boxes. It was a mistake, but the MusiChip people won't take them back." We had also been sent a surplus of 'Best of the Buzzcocks', but I kept quiet about that in the hopes of maybe being able to keep them.

"What are you talking about?" the man said.

I decided to make an effort. I came out from behind the counter and pointed the man in the direction of the correct aisle. Then I went back to the counter and leaned over the front of it to change the till roll. I was too drained to walk around to the other side.

"No," the man said. "I am not looking for Stevie Nicks. I can't think why anybody in their right mind would assume that I am looking for Stevie Nicks. No, I'm looking for a *person*."

"Stevie Nicks is a person," I corrected him, still bent over the counter. Where was that goddamn till roll? "Well, *was* a person. Dead now, unfortunately, like so many great artists. But her music lives on. Brilliant music! I could play you some?" I knew all the spiel by now; could turn any thread of a conversation into a sales pitch, no matter how tenuous the link. Snake and Dougie had programmed my broken brain well. "Or we've got Black Sabbath, Judas Priest, Led Zeppelin, the Rolling Stones. All *gods* of the music world – and all at low prices! You won't find the same music for less in any other local store. Snake checked himself, just last week."

"No! What are you talking about? I am not here to buy music. My name is Alexander… no, that's not important. I'm looking for a person. A *living* person. A scientist."

"There aren't any scientists anymore," I said.

"Alright. A science *student*, then. 'History of Science'. She was majoring in the History of Biochemistry and Genetics at UCLA, but she dropped out. One of her roommates said she'd passed by this store last month, and thought she saw her working here."

Groggy I might have been, but I still had enough of a brain to realise who this man was talking about. I grinned. "Oh, really?"

"Apparently, yes."

I had found the till roll by now – the little bastard was hiding behind the pencil holder - but I chose to remain bent over the counter nonchalantly, fiddling with drawers, pretending to search. This angered the man.

"Will you please, *please* turn around and talk to me?" he snapped. "I cannot have a conversation with your behind."

"The other customers don't mind," I said. "The *paying* customers. In fact, it usually improves sales."

"Yes, I would imagine it does..."

Silence. I had embarrassed him, perhaps. I grinned wider. "So," I said. "If this person is a student scientist, or *was*, then what would she be doing in a place like this? It isn't an 'intellectually stimulating' environment."

"Well, sometimes people don't think they're good enough," the man said. "They quit early to avoid failure in the future, and do something beneath their abilities. It's only natural. But hopefully she'll see sense after I've spoken to her."

"You seem to think you have this all figured out," I said. "Maybe she just realised that a life of pleasure is more rewarding than a life of learning facts. Facts which will continue to be true whether they're understood or not."

"Maybe that's how it is for people like you," said the man. "But for a genius…"

"Oh? Is she a genius?" My smile returned. "What's her name?"

"Her name is Katrina, but she might be using a false name if she doesn't want to be found. And yes; according to the university's records, she has a high IQ. It's important that I find her – I have this photo, here. So if you could look at it, tell me whether or not…" He stopped. The game was up. I had turned to face him.

Only now that I looked at him properly did I realise there was something strange about this man. He looked like a man from China or Japan, but for some reason he was colourless. No, not 'colourless'; that sounds too negative. How should I describe his colour?

White. Not Caucasian-white; white like marble. No – *whiter*. A tone that I didn't believe existed on the spectrum of human skin tone. It was not just his skin; his hair was white silk, shoulder-length, springing from a parting along the centre of his skull and waterfalling down the sides of his head in two perfect, symmetrical waves. The only non-white parts of this man were his pale blue eyes, and the pale blue shirt he wore with his white suit. A suit! On a man not much older than myself. This man was clearly not accustomed to being in this part of California. There was a strange little lump the size of a cherry stone under the skin of his left temple.

If I was surprised by the appearance of this man – 'Alexander', he had called himself - I managed to cover it almost immediately. He, however, had more trouble.

"My God," breathed Alexander. He took me in with one slow, sweeping look from my feet to my head. When he met my eyes, he glowered. "What have you done to yourself?"

The implications of this sentence were paradoxical. He was clearly angry at me (fair enough) but for abusing something he apparently saw as valuable – i.e. also me. Even with my year of experience with civilised humanity, I couldn't quite comprehend this. It made the situation more than a straightforward confrontation. I was confused now. The strange man was in control.

With effort, I willed my smile to remain. "I'm afraid I don't understand you. What have I done to myself?"

Alexander stared at me with an expression like a virus-ridden computer trying to solve a complicated mathematical problem. "You are happy to remain here and let your brain rot… in pursuit of a mindless existence that any halfwit could achieve… when, from what I've heard, you have one of the most incredible brains to study science since Homo-SuperiUS disbanded?"

"Yes," I said.

"Yes? You think it's alright to do that? Life gets difficult and you take that as your cue to push the self-destruct button? *Really?*"

It was peculiar how personally he seemed to be taking this. He started to pace up and down in front of the counter like a tiger in distress, raking his long white fingers through his long white hair, and muttering fragments of neurotic speech to himself.

I stood and watched, transfixed. This was like theatre.

"I was told…" Alexander started to emerge from his crisis state with real words – but then he trailed off.

I ventured a step closer. "What were you told?"

Alexander came to a standstill in the middle of the shop, and turned to me. His face was blank; his pale eyes wide and glazed.

"You're upset about something, aren't you?" I prompted.

"Of course I'm upset!" Alexander's voice simultaneously roared and trembled. "I was under the impression that I was going to meet a great scientist, someone who could understand how any device worked just by *looking* at it… and I turn up after days upon days of searching and hoping… to find this beautiful brain is locked away beyond my reach inside the head of a woman who doesn't even seem to care if she *rots it to death*!" He smacked his fist against his thigh. "If your brain was an animal, I would report you to the authorities and have it taken away from you!" Tears were forming in the corners of his eyes. He sniffed and turned towards the window.

I was surprised at this outburst. Not least because I had never been referred to as a 'woman' before.

"The world has become a sea, stagnant with human scum," Alexander murmured to the window. "Everywhere I go, I get the same peace and love and marijuana crap. I can't get a decent answer out of any of them. I was sure, *so* sure that you were going to be different, someone I could finally understand. So I looked for you. And now I've found you. And you're the same as the idiots I had to wade through to find you!"

He was breathing heavily. I stood and watched, waiting, whilst he grappled with whatever was going on inside his mind. "Okay," he told himself. "Calm down. Don't be an idiot, don't be an idiot." Finally, he became calm. He turned to me again. "Are you intelligent, like they said you are?"

I pondered this. "I've had no reason to doubt it."

"Okay," he said. "Let's do a test, then, shall we? We'll start easy: what is Pythagoras' Theorem?"

"I don't know."

He gave a bitter little laugh, and continued. "How does somatic cell nuclear transfer work, in the context of reproductive cloning?"

"I don't know."

"And what is Pi to fifteen places?"

"One fifteenth," I responded instantly.

Alexander frowned. "Excuse me?"

"One fifteenth of the pie per place. Unless the pie wasn't complete before it was divided up between the places. But you made no mention of that. And not all fifteen people might like the pie – or some of the places might be vacant. In which case, some of the pie would remain."

Alexander looked at me for maybe five full seconds without saying anything. This wasn't normal behaviour.

"Would you like some pie?" I offered. We didn't have any, but it broke the silence for a moment.

Wide-eyed, Alexander continued to stare. "No, I don't want any pie, thank you. In fact, I think I'd better leave." He turned to go.

"Wait."

That little taste of puzzling through the pie-problem, regardless of how wrong my answer had been, had left me hungry for another chance to exercise the underused organ between my ears. Or maybe… maybe I just didn't want the unusual stranger who had called me a 'genius' to leave thinking I was a fool.

The little lump of skin above Alexander's left temple had interested me since I noticed it, partway through our first conversation. Beautiful and blue though they were, the extreme paleness and milky quality of Alexander's eyes suggested blindness. Yet, he could see. A theory came to me. A few clicks of my tongue in quick succession, and my sleepy brain was able to squeeze out enough information to confirm my suspicions. I could see what lay beneath that lump.

"That's a clever little device," I said.

Alexander turned. "What device?"

I waited a few seconds. I chose not to give him any eye contact, much as I wanted to; nor did I smile, in case my conceit drove him away. "That device above your eye," I said. "I haven't seen anyone with one of those before, and it's well hidden - but I guess that, without it, you would be almost completely blind."

Alexander's eyes widened. With paper-white fingers, he lifted up a lock of that floppy white hair of his and touched the little lump – a lump which could easily have been overlooked by a normal person as a simple human defect on his otherwise inhumanly perfect body.

"Why didn't you just have surgery?" I asked. "Snake's sister lost her sight when she was five, and they took her to the hospital. He told me a surgeon cured her for next to nothing."

"How did you…?"

Proud as I was, I didn't want to upset him again. I downplayed my self-satisfied smile, and kept my eyes locked on the floor.

When I looked up, he had left the shop.

I hurried out of the store, black dots swirling in my vision as the sun hit me. I saw Alexander across the road outside the Freegan cafe. It was always open early for take-out drinks, sometimes little cakes and cookies made from the richer supermarkets' expiring ingredients. The glass window slid open and a woman with thick, curled, dyed-green hair appeared. Her eyes fixed on me, and Alexander looked over his shoulder to see me approaching. He rolled his eyes. "A green tea, please."

"This guy with you, Katrina?" the woman asked me.

I arrived beside Alexander at the window. "Yes. We're together." Alexander gave me a nasty little look, but I stood my ground. The man had no right to spark my interest and then leave.

The woman looked between us and grinned. "Well, about time you met someone! I'll get you your usual, okay?" She disappeared into the kitchen behind the window.

"You know her?" Alexander asked me.

"I must do," I said. With the constant stream of browsers in and out of the music store it was difficult to remember faces. She could have been one of Snake's girlfriends.

Alexander's mouth formed a thin line. "She thinks we're courting."

Beyond the counter, mounted on a wall in the kitchen, was a little television. A somewhat familiar bald man in a suit was speaking, muted; but there was text at the bottom of the screen to convey his words. It had been a while since I read anything. I leaned over the counter.

"No, I wouldn't make that comparison. Homo-SuperiUS worked in its own interests only. EcoTech will work with the government for the good of the planet and the American public. Besides, I would hope that the people of this great country would have learnt from past error and moved beyond-"

"What do you think of the President?"

Alexander's voice startled me. "I don't think anything of the President," I said. In the kitchen, the green-haired woman grimaced over the coffee machine. Automatically, I amended, "And what is your opinion on the subject?"

"He's riding a wave of public hysteria," said Alexander. His voice was a low growl. "But he didn't cause it. He's no coward, but with any luck he'll be out of office before his term is over."

The green-haired woman arrived with two paper cups. "Oh, no charge," she said. I glanced in the direction she was looking to see Alexander putting his wallet away. "You guys enjoy your date. Oh, and tell Snake to call me, yeah?"

We sat in the dirt outside the cafe - Alexander following my lead hesitantly - and I sipped gently at my hot milk whilst Alexander held his tea in cupped hands, as if warming them. His eyes were fixed ahead.

"What do you need my help with?" I asked.

Two people emerged onto the empty street. Alexander watched them: a young couple, unwashed locks and naked torsos, the boy pierced, staggering down the street with arms wrapped around each other. His brow furrowed. "Do you like it here?"

He hadn't answered my question. I decided to play along. "I like the music," I said.

"Is that all?"

I took another sip of milk, tried to think. "I like... I like the people I live with." Even as I said it, I wondered whether this was true. As time had gone on, Snake and Dougie had faded more into the background: a means to food and shelter, their attempted conversations an inconvenience.

"But they clearly don't care about you. You're underweight, unwashed - you look ill."

"That's an inappropriate observation to make, Alexander." Even I knew that.

"It's true, though." Alexander sighed. "What about intellectual stimulation? Achievement? Your life could be worth something, you know. Isn't there somebody out there you want to make proud?"

Have to keep going...

Last night's dream stirred in my mind. I gripped my cup. Milk rushed over my hand, sticky and hot.

"It's not yours, your life," Alexander continued. His voice sounded detached, distant: like Snake's voice when he'd been smoking too long. "Somebody cared about you enough to raise you, educate you. Your life belongs to them. Is this how you want to repay them?"

The shop. I had to go back to the shop.

Before I could formulate an excuse, Alexander said, "Look. Would you mind going away for a moment? I need some time to think."

I was on my feet and hurrying, milk sloshing to the ground, spray touching my legs and bare feet.

#

About half an hour later I was sitting on the stool behind the counter, distracting myself by making a tower out of the Stevie Nicks MusiChip boxes, when a white hand appeared suddenly before me and struck the counter. The tower fell. I looked up.

"Right," said Alexander. His hair was all displaced, and his shirt had darkened around his neck and navel with sweat. His eyes had gone pink and moist at the edges. "I have made a decision. You're coming with me."

"Am I?" I said.

"Yes. Unless you're happy to stay here and let your brain rot."

I fumbled for a clever response to this, a reason why I should stay. Nothing came. What did appear in my mind, overshadowing the wavering faces of Snake and Dougie, was my father. As vivid as he had been in my dream, he curled his top lip and gave me a look which sent me vaulting over the counter and hurrying after Alexander to where his car was parked – down a nearby side-street, out of sight of the Music Store.

Well, I say 'car'.

Alexander's 'car' was a formidable behemoth of a thing, with wheels up to my midriff and a step to help you up to the door. It had been spray-painted the same gentle baby-blue as Alexander's eyes: such a strange colour for an aggressive-looking vehicle.

Leaning against the Behemoth, Alexander's eyes went to my feet. He frowned. "You'll need shoes, of course."

"Will I?"

"Yes. Go and get them."

Sighing, I went back to the store. In my haste to leave I hadn't even locked the door. That was worrying. I pulled on a pair of big black boots – Doctor Martins, an old pair Dougie had bought second-hand for me – and scanned the store for other supplies. Food, or maybe clothes. From the radiating rails, hundreds of MusiChips stared back at me, soon to be dead and replaced. It took a moment to hit me: I had accumulated nothing from this life that it would be useful to take.

Father would not have been proud of me.

Soberer now, I closed the shop door and locked it. Then a thought struck me. "Hey," I said. "Shouldn't I wait to tell Snake we're going? He'll be in at nine."

Alexander paused at the driver's door, but didn't turn around. "I don't know who 'Snake' is," he said. "But if you're nearly half as intelligent as I was told you are, then you are certainly too good to associate with people with names like that."

I accepted this without comment.

I hid the key under the doormat, as I had been told to do if I ever had to leave the store unattended. Then, without looking back, I ran to the Behemoth, whose passenger door had been left open for me. I scrambled up into the seat next to Alexander, who was already waiting behind the wheel. It had been a long time, but I could still remember the safety procedure - shut the door, seatbelt on. Alexander watched me do all this, then started the engine.

We drove down the colourful bohemian street, and out onto the highway.

To my delight, Alexander turned the Behemoth towards the mountains: the wild backdrop to civilised California which I had yet to explore. He increased his speed.

I had not realised just how tired I was. After no more than five minutes in the Behemoth, the engine began to lull me into a doze. Another ten, and I had passed into a light, achy, dreamless sleep.

#

Sleep. That would be nice right now. But these days it is a luxury I cannot often afford.

There is a mattress in this cabin in the desert. It is almost comfortable... Yes, I think I can afford to sleep tonight. Today has been a productive day.

It has taken me almost a full five days to get the goddamn solar-powered Eco-Freezer working, but this evening, finally, I heard the healthy 'whirr' of life emit from within the casing.

The moon and stars are out now. The steady beating of living machinery within the freezer has been going on for so long that, while my heart is still wild with exhilaration and relief, it is starting to lull me to sleep.

What would have happened, had the freezer not done what I needed it to do?

That thought shudders me awake.

I am proud of the result. Resurrecting the freezer so it would do its original task would have been difficult enough, but it put up a tremendous fight when I tried to connect parts of the CryoBag. The poor thing coughed and spluttered so many times, I almost gave up out of pity. But now, thankfully, it has accepted its new parts.

Three or four years ago, this wouldn't have been nearly so hard. It seems the more modern the technology, the more difficult it is to work with. I wonder if that is something Ferdinand Mann instructs his EcoTech minions to bear in mind when they are making a new product? To stop people like me from tapping into the machinery and working out how to fix the older models. EcoTech doesn't understand that I cannot buy the latest model. It doesn't realize that without a working freezer, all of this - everything I have been working towards, body and soul, for the (admittedly short) entirety of my life so far - would be for nothing.

But if it did know what I was doing, EcoTech would probably alert the government. And they'd have the military take me away. So really it is just as well that things have worked out like this.

The ceiling above my mattress is riddled with cracks and mildew stains. One looks like an amoeba; another almost like a crucifix.

Will I ever be able to lay outside and do some real stargazing? Given all that has happened, it seems highly unlikely that I'll ever be safe outside again. Alexander Bai will be looking for me. And, more importantly, he'll be looking for the specimens.

I glance over at the freezer. The EcoTech symbol on its door seems to be the only unspoiled part of it, but within the damaged shell there is a living core of technology.

"You're worth it," I whisper to the specimens inside. "You're worth all this madness."

A desert wind interrupts the night-time stillness. I can feel its vibrations through the floorboards beneath my mattress. I can hear it churning up dust outside. As the wind gasps, the starlight seems to *grow fleetingly brighter, lighting up another stain on the ceiling... a stain which looks like a familiar face.*

My naked flesh rubs fiercely against the floorboards as I scoot off the mattress and closer to the freezer, but I barely feel the pain. I place a hand on the freezer. Beneath my palm – coolness, humming: the stirrings of potential new life.

Tomorrow my real work begins. I will do everything in my power to make that potential a reality.

"I'm here," I whisper. "I'll never, ever let him hurt you."

CHAPTER SEVENTEEN

When I awoke we were pulling into a gas station. As the Behemoth slowed, I glanced around, taking note of the little things which entered my visual range. A man, dressed for the cold, walking down the sloping sidewalk to my right. A white cloud of bird droppings obscuring a top corner of the windscreen. The dull greyness of the sky.

Then Alexander stopped the vehicle. I hit my head against the back of my seat and was fully awake. The sound of the driver's door opening made me turn.

Alexander slipped down from his seat and shut the door without looking at me. He disappeared around the back of the Behemoth.

I twisted in my seat to peer out the back window. I could see houses many miles in the distance downhill, clustered together as one big settlement, rather than as the individual neighbourhoods they had been before. I tried to estimate how far we had come but my brain was doped and foggy and refused to do as instructed. I needed music. Fast.

There was a tap-tapping on the driver's window. I turned, saw Alexander looking in at me. He started making 'come here' signals with his hands and mouthing things I couldn't make out. I undid my seatbelt, crawled across to the driver's door, and opened it. He stepped back as I stuck my head out. "Do you want something?"

Alexander ignored my question. "This is going to take a while," he said. Then, "I don't suppose you know how to put gasoline in a car?"

I shook my head. I probably could have figured it out, but my head felt too heavy, thoughts coming slow.

"No? I didn't think so." He fumbled in his inner pocket and brought out a thick roll of banknotes bound with a rubber band. "Then go and pay, please, while I figure this out. There's a hundred dollars in there. I think it should be enough for a full tank of gas. We're at pump two."

I took the money, slid out through the driver's door, and headed for the shop which Alexander indicated with a vague wave of his hand. Alexander watched, presumably to make sure I was headed in the right direction; then he returned to the rear end of the vehicle, and puzzled over it some more, hand on hip, chewing his bottom lip in frustration.

"Should I get somebody to help?" I called back to him.

"What? No!" Alexander shouted at me. "I can figure this out myself. I'm not an idiot. Go!"

Fifteen minutes later, I came back to the car with a plastic bag and the remaining banknotes. Alexander was back in the driver's seat, hands poised on the steering wheel. "Did you manage to put the gasoline in?" I enquired as I got in beside him.

"Of course I did," said Alexander. "It was simple. I'd just overlooked the obvious, that's all." He glanced at me and noticed the plastic bag. He frowned. "What's this? I didn't tell you to get anything."

"No, you didn't," I agreed. "This is a plastic bag with a Rolling Stone magazine and a bottle of Cherryade inside. The man in the shop was helpful when I described what I wanted."

While I was putting my seatbelt on, Alexander stole the Cherryade out of the plastic bag and studied the label. When I became aware of the robbery, I tried to snatch the bottle back. "Did you buy this with your own money?" Alexander asked. "No? Then this is technically mine, and I'll read the ingredients if I want to." He held it out of my reach but didn't take his eyes off the label. After a moment, his eyebrows rose sharply, and his lips thinned. "Have you seen what they put in this drink?"

"Aqua, sugar…" I recited from memory. Snake often bought the same brand, and I'd read that label many times before.

Alexander held the bottle out so I could see the label and pointed to one of the ingredients – several letters and a number. "Do you know what this is?"

"An ingredient."

"That additive has been banned in most of Europe. It will rot your brain." Alexander pulled the bottle away from me and launched it through his half-open window; then he rolled the window up and started the engine. We pulled out onto the main road. I turned in my seat to watch the bottle disappear from view through the back window.

"But I need energy," I pleaded. There was still time to go back and reclaim the Cherryade.

"Then go back to sleep," said Alexander. "Get some energy the natural way. And stop behaving like an addict – it's too pathetic for words."

"I'm not pathetic!" I turned to him, teeth bared. "If I was pathetic, you wouldn't have come all that way to find me."

"Do you want me to take you back?"

I didn't. I wasn't sure why I didn't: my head felt like it had been stuffed with something thick and muffling. "I've got a headache," I mumbled.

"I repeat," said Alexander. "Go back to sleep."

I gave him a hateful look. But Alexander had returned his focus to the road. So I dozed, and the scenery around me blurred, but I could not get back to sleep. My brain ached for instant gratification. Inside my head, a heavy-metal baseline was playing on a loop, irritatingly quiet, crying out to be subsidised by a MiniRecord or a MusiChip. With nothing to animate me, I was a floating, empty carcass. Looking around drearily for something to soothe the ache, I noticed the shape of a musical note on the dashboard. Mindlessly, I leant forward and pressed it.

The painful sound of static filled the car - but this quickly subsided, leaving behind a golden beach of music. Tinny and electronic, but music nonetheless. As I listened to the beat, my headache started to fade.

I was allowed a split-second of peace before Alexander's bony white finger came down and turned the music off. I glared up at him, furious, desperate.

"No music," he said. "I need to concentrate." He never took his eyes off the road.

It was not just the incessant music in my head, or the headache, or the desperation for instant bottled energy that made me uncomfortable. As we climbed to higher altitudes, the temperature dropped considerably. I did not realise I was cold until after another half-hour of travelling. My brain was certainly not functioning at full capacity.

Alexander glanced across and saw me writhing. It took a moment for him to understand. His lined suit and sensible shoes, although unsuited to LA weather, were clearly keeping him at a nice, steady temperature in these conditions. But eventually he grasped what was wrong. "Oh, you're still dressed for Los Angeles. Hold on – I know how to do this, I've done it before." He pushed a button. The dashboard breathed hot air into the car. He glanced at my bare legs, then back at the road. Seemed to consider for a moment. Then he gestured to the back seat. "There's a warm blanket somewhere back there," he said. "Wrap that around you. And some socks; put those on."

As much as I hated the man for taking away my music and making me suffer, I appreciated his directness. I rummaged in the back as instructed, and returned with a long, thick blanket, and a pair of woollen socks. All white.

After I had slipped the socks on and arranged the blanket around me, I began to feel more comfortable. Something human returned to my brain. I even felt well enough to attempt a question. "So," I looked at Alexander, "Why did you choose me?"

Alexander kept his eyes on the road. "It's a long story. I went to the university in San Diego first. I asked if they had any professors or students with few friends or family ties, willing to assist me with a technology project which would require them to be away for a long time. They said no. So, I found the number for UCLA." He said the name with scorn. "I was invited to come in and talk to the head of some pathetic pseudo-science department. He looked through the student records. One of the first students he came up with was you. No last name, no parents named, no address; just a glowing reference from your former professor, describing some incredible achievements and a high IQ score."

"A high IQ score."

"Yes. Not the most reliable measure of intelligence, true, but your professor apparently slipped you several tests and you never scored lower than one-hundred-forty. The head of the department found an address for you, but when I showed up there, all I got from your roommate was a photo and a description of a shop where you might have been working. But I persisted. Your lack of an identity made you too good an opportunity to miss."

"Oh," I said. "How flattering." I rarely indulged in sarcasm, but I thought I had pulled this off rather well. The sting it seemed to give the pale stranger gave me a sense of cruel satisfaction.

"Don't think I chose you lightly," he snapped. "Had it not been for that reference, I would not even have considered going to the lengths I did to track you down. In fact, had it not been for that reference, I would have left you where I found you the moment you opened your mouth."

I chose to ignore this. "Which roommate did you ask about me?" I pressed.

The Behemoth bounced over a bump in the road. Alexander's hands gripped the steering wheel tight, and he checked anxiously in all his mirrors. "There were two roommates," he said. "A white girl and a Japanese girl. I think they were lovers."

"Was the white girl tall with short blonde hair?" I asked.

Alexander frowned. "Not very tall, no. Medium height. Red hair. And I seem to remember she'd had her nose pierced." He squinted over the top of the steering wheel. "Actually, come to think of it, I don't think the Japanese girl had been a roommate of yours. She didn't seem to know you. I don't think she was a student, either. She mentioned something about modelling... Now, will you please be quiet and let me drive?"

I settled back in my seat. Good for Chemise.

I still had my copy of Rolling Stone in my bag. I took it out, let it fall open on a random page: a feature about a new rock band from San Diego, all shaggy hair and beards and ripped clothes and dark, tribal make-up, staring with bestial ferocity through the page. Strangely enough, for a moment, I could have sworn that I was looking at a picture of four of my cousins, staring at me vengefully. My separation from music was causing some strange psychological effects.

I bent the page in half to cover the picture up. I tried to read the article instead, but the words merged and blurred, so I gave up. I dropped the magazine and turned towards the window, waiting to fall asleep again.

While I waited, I watched the scenery. The elevation of the road grew steeper. The sky darkened. The pine trees along the roadside grew denser; became thick forest.

I passed from consciousness into semi-consciousness, and from semi-consciousness into a black, dreamless void of sleep.

#

I woke again the next time the car stopped but this time it took longer for me to stir. By the time I was fully conscious, Alexander had already left the car.

I leaned across to look out of the driver's window and saw him talking to a man in a chequered shirt outside a small house. Alexander was wrapped up in a thick white coat, and, shockingly, was up to his calves in *snow*.

I knew what snow was. Different types of weather had been explained to me by the Edu-Centre video, 'Our Wonderful Planet'. However, seeing it for real was an entirely new experience for me.

I looked around, but could see no other houses, cars, people; not even a suggestion of road beyond the Behemoth's own winding tyre-tracks. The snow dominated the landscape.

A map was open on Alexander's seat. Attached to it was a sticky-note, with a message scrawled across it in black ink: 'If you get lost, PLEASE check into a motel and start out again in the morning. DO NOT drive in a temper. Good luck.' I leaned across to Alexander's side and rolled down the window.

"I don't see why you won't help me!" Alexander was shouting at the man in the chequered shirt. "I'm local! I have *family* up there!"

The man was shaking his head. "I know that town. Never met anyone up there looking like you. I'm sorry, but you're going to have to turn around and go back to where you came from. I'm not going to be responsible for letting some tourist kid get lost."

"Kid?" Alexander bunched his fists. "Listen, *sir*, I'm going up there whether you help me or not. But if you would just give me some directions, it would make the process a lot safer."

"Hey!" I called from the car. Alexander and the man turned. "It's alright," I said. "That's my boyfriend. He's a mountaineering expert. I asked him to take me up the mountain, and he doesn't like to disappoint me. He's a 'hopeless romantic'." I tried to smile winningly, and to make my eyelashes flutter as I remembered Chemise doing when she haggled for cheaper groceries.

The man looked from me back to Alexander. Alexander met his eyes but didn't say anything. "Stupid kids," the man muttered. "Alright!"

He gave Alexander some directions which meant nothing to me. I rolled the window up again and settled back in my seat to watch the snowflakes. A fresh flurry had started to trickle from the heavy, grey sky.

A minute later, I heard footsteps. I glanced over to see Alexander approaching the car. Behind him, the man was gesturing to me. I guessed what he wanted and rolled the window down again.

"Now," the man called to me over the wind. "I'm going to tell you what I told your boyfriend. Be safe, and make sure you stop the minute you get to this guesthouse he's taking you to. If that thing you're driving shows any signs of struggling, stop at the nearest house. Tell them Joshua sent you. There's only one town up there with a guesthouse, although they're damn stupid to accept folk this season."

"Don't worry," I assured the man. "I'll take care of him."

Alexander gave me a hostile look.

"Yeah, well - take care of yourself, too!" called the man. "These mountains may look beautiful, but they are dangerous. Be warned."

"Alright."

The man did not look reassured.

I rolled the window back up, and moved aside to let Alexander get in. I gave him a wide grin.

"Why did you tell him we're a couple?"

"You needed him to grant you a favour, so I helped. It worked in the café: we both got free drinks."

"I suppose." Alexander didn't seem to like that I was correct: he spoke through tight, tense lips.

"People like assisting romantic pairs," I explained.

"I know. It's basic biological instinct," said Alexander. "Protect the young heterosexual couples, and you're protecting the next generation of humanity."

"Exactly." He was right. But people aren't supposed to talk like that.

"Put your seatbelt on," Alexander muttered.

We crawled on for another ten or fifteen minutes. I looked at Alexander. He had his eyes on the road.

I leant forward, slowly. Looked up - Alexander was still focussed on the road.

Quickly, I pushed the music button then leant back again in my seat. But this time, only static came out. I frowned, confused. I tried fiddling with the buttons but to no avail.

Now Alexander looked at me. He opened a compartment concealed in the dashboard and removed something from it that I hadn't seen in months. A CD. "Move, please." He brushed my hands away and posted the silver disk into the slot above the music button.

He glanced at me again. I met his eyes. "Only *quietly*," he emphasised. I nodded.

The music which came out of that machine – *Alexander's music* – was twinkling and wordless. Full of different sounds and instruments, yet somehow dull, meaningless.

Nevertheless, it was music. I took this as a minor victory and fell asleep again.

#

When I next awoke, I found that the Behemoth had stopped. Dead.

Ahead of us, filling the windscreen and beyond, was a fence. It was made of wire but was far too tall to climb. I could have stacked six replicas of myself on my shoulders, and still we would not have been able to reach over. Just in case anyone did manage to climb it, little wire rings of spikes had been coiled along the top like man-made poison ivy.

There was a large gateway in the fence in front of us. It was locked.

Beyond the fence, a short drive away, was a large building covered in snow.

I looked across at Alexander. He was sitting in silence, arms folded, staring at the gate. Groggily, I undid my seatbelt and opened the door to leave. Alexander's hand gripped my shoulder and pulled me back. "Where are you going?" he demanded.

"Out," I said. "We've stopped."

"Out? In this snow, in those shorts? You'll freeze to death! I haven't brought you this far for you to die on me now. Close that door." I did, and he pressed a button on his side: the door clicked. "You have to stay in the car until we get there."

"Get where?" I tried my door. It was locked - but there was always the window.

"A scientist should ask questions, but for the moment, just observe," said Alexander. "Or I'll get a headache. I haven't slept properly in days." He continued to stare ahead.

Thirty seconds passed. The silence was unnatural, disconcerting. I made to turn the music on. Alexander made no move to stop me. Soon, Alexander's soft, ethereal, hypnotically dull music filled the car, barely loud enough to cover the whistle of the wind outside. I wasn't sure whether this made the situation better or worse, but I left it on.

After a minute or two, I was startled by a metallic whine from outside the car.

Alexander shrugged his shoulders, stretched out his hands, his fingers, and gripped the steering wheel again. He smiled.

Slowly, mechanically, the gates swung open.

Alexander moved the Behemoth slowly through the gates. When we had cleared them, they wailed shut behind us, coming together with a 'clank'. It sounded final.

Alexander glanced over at me. "Are you cold?" he asked.

"Yes."

"I'll have a warm bath run for you when we get inside," he said. "I'm not sure what we're going to do about clothes for you yet. We really should have bought some in Los Angeles."

"You should have." Alexander gave me a look. "I didn't know it was going to be cold," I said.

"Well-"

"Plus, if I'm going to be working for you, then you should provide all the necessary equipment – including appropriate clothing. That is how jobs usually work."

Alexander's lips narrowed. "Sorry," he said: it sounded like a struggle. "I'll think of something."

We continued towards the building. On our way, we passed a weathered wooden sign sticking out of the snow. I read it aloud to myself. "Sierra Nevada End-of-the-Road Lodge. Welcome to Civilisation in the Wilderness. Open May to October. Closed in Winter...

"It's closed," I told Alexander.

"I know," said Alexander. "It's been closed for forty years."

But it wasn't closed. There were lights on in some of the windows and, as we drew nearer, a small group of people came out through the front door. They were all men, and all wearing white.

The men assembled on the porch and stared, squinting, as if trying to penetrate the steamed-up windows of the Behemoth, as Alexander drove us closer.

Cold and hunger were forgotten as a wave of adrenaline coursed through me. I glimpsed beyond the doorway: a vast hallway, leading to a wide staircase. The men – six on each side of the door –

moved as one, hurrying down the porch steps like two streams of a waterfall, towards us. Their toothy smiles gleamed bright in the twilight.

#

I blink.

I'm awake.

I'm back in the cabin, and the sun is dipping below the desert horizon, the mildewed walls growing silvery in the moonlight. I try to grip my scalpel, but my hands – goddamnit! *– my hands have grown restless and clumsy and useless.*

Caffeine is the obvious cure.

But, when I go to the tiny kitchen to pour myself a tepid cup of instant coffee, a strange familiarity creeps over me; a peculiar deja-vu. This sensation remains even after I return to my desk. It is as if something should follow my visiting the kitchen – as if there is something missing from this cabin, missing from my life. My attention shifts from the delicate procedure I am performing and, scalpel poised in mid-air, I let my eyes wander to the empty corner of the cabin... where a single electrical socket lives, empty and sad.

I am looking for the television.

Unfortunately, there is no television in my little cabin in the desert. There is a radio though, and for that I am grateful – even if the radio seems to be perpetually tuned to an inane soap opera featuring a man named Juan and a woman named Frieda. They met in a hospital when Juan was a nurse and Frieda a patient, as far as I can gather. They eloped. Their mindless, mundane conversations about Juan losing his job or Frieda's sordid past or whether or not to start a family are somehow comforting to me as I dance on the edge of sanity, teetering precariously over the void.

It is close to midnight now. The desert is cold. The solar-powered heater I have fixed up would be enough to keep me warm but it must stay at a distance while I work. The specimens I have lined up in jars along the desk - dead and floating though they may be - could be destroyed completely by the heat before they can be made useful. And, of course, these specimens must come first, my own welfare second.

I will put them back in the freezer soon. They shouldn't all be out now. I just like to look at them sometimes, to remind myself of why I'm doing this.

Juan and Frieda prattle on, stilted 'stay with me's and 'I love you's seeping out of the radio into my mind. It's not enough. My brain aches for comfort.

CHAPTER EIGHTEEN

"Dinner will be served at eight, Katrina," a soft, male voice said. "Is that alright with you?"

The voice clearly expected a response, meaning I must have looked more awake than I felt. Reluctantly, I swam upwards into a state of passable semi-consciousness.

As my senses refocussed, I found that I was lying on something soft, staring up at a spotless, white ceiling. I struggled up into the closest I could comfortably get to a sitting position and looked around. I was on a white double-bed, in a room with white walls, a white rug on the floor, and no windows or pictures. To my left, I could see a door: closed, also white. The bed had four tall posts, and from each one hung a piece of thin, white curtain.

Standing at the foot of the bed was the man who had spoken. He was dressed in a long, white coat, white trousers, white shirt. All spotlessly clean. I would have found him sinister. But then he smiled at me - a warm, welcoming smile, spreading beneath his red moustache - and his eyes became human. "You certainly are looking a lot healthier after your bath, you poor creature," he crooned. He came around to my side of the bed and handed me a glass of water. I grabbed it and downed it in one go.

"You were so pale when you arrived. We thought you might have been ill. But we have a good doctor here, and he said you were just overly-cold and a little travel-sick." He held out a red pill. "This should help your headache."

I had finished my water, so I swallowed it dry.

The man then took something out of his inner coat-pocket: a rolled-up magazine. He unfurled it and held it up for me to see. "Mr. Bai – *Alexander* - thought you might like to read this."

The magazine, which looked to be in a state of near-decay, was called 'Scientific American'. It must have been a couple of decades old, at least. On its cover was a faded picture of an elephant; beneath this, the words 'final issue', printed in bright red; and in italics, 'What will the Change in the Law mean for our endangered species? Doctor

Lau at the San Diego Frozen Zoo makes predictions for the future of conservation'.

"I would not like to read that," I decided.

The man smiled. "As you wish." He obviously didn't believe me, because he put the magazine on the bed, by my hand. "Is there anything you'd prefer to read? We have quite a library of novels between us, and plenty of other magazines... although most are a little out-of-date."

"Yes," I said. "I'd like to read my Rolling Stone magazine."

I didn't want to read my Rolling Stone magazine. The thought of coming across that picture of the rockers who, in the absence of music's influence, had reminded me so much of my murderous cousins, made me feel ill. But I was interested to see what this man, so eager to please, would do when asked to deliver something I could only assume had been thrown away.

"Of course," said the man. "It's right there." He nodded to my right. There it was, on the bedside table: my Rolling Stone magazine, laid out neatly beside a small, white music player, and a stack of CDs. "When Mr. Bai remembered the magazine, he went straight back to the car to get it for you. He also suggested the CD player. Although," the man added, looking again at Rolling Stone and then back at me, "I can't think Mr. Bai's classical albums are really to your taste." He picked a CD from the pile and looked sadly at its cover.

In his silence, I could faintly detect the rhythmless whine of a flute drifting from the music player. *Alexander's music.*

"No," I agreed. "This is terrible."

"To be honest, I don't think they're to Mr. Bai's taste, either," the man said softly. "This isn't the sort of music he listens to when he thinks he's alone. I suspect he only keeps these silly CDs because he thinks it makes him an 'intellectual'." He chuckled to himself and tossed the case back onto the pile. "Perhaps you should ask Mr. Bai to let you listen to his *other* music collection sometime? The secret one he actually likes." He patted my shoulder gently and got up to leave. "I'll bring your meal in here, if that's okay with you? I'm sure Mr. Bai will show you the dining room tomorrow, but right now he's otherwise occupied. Do you have any special dietary requirements?"

"No. Yes!" I said, deciding to test him. "Nothing white."

The man smiled again and left.

I waited, interested to see what he would come up with.

I attempted to follow the faint, heavy-metal beat that was still playing in my head, trying to work out what the song was. But Alexander's intrusive music made it impossible to decipher. With a groan, I crawled across the bed and gave the little white music player a smack - but nothing changed. I ran my hand down the side of the machine and tried pushing buttons and turning dials. This only made the problem worse: the volume increased.

I sighed. I lay down on the bed with my head raised slightly off the pillow, turned to face the box - and clicked my tongue. I closed my eyes.

It took longer than it should have taken me to conjure the machine's insides onto the black shroud behind my eyes; however, after a few minutes it became apparent that it was built to respond to sound. All I had to do was clap, and the music stopped. I smiled, satisfied, and lay back down on the bed.

I cannot remember what the song in my head turned out to be. But I enjoyed listening to it, and humming along, as I flicked through 'Scientific American' magazine's final issue.

#

At first, I thought the man who brought my meal was the same man who had given me the magazine. They were identically dressed in white coats, white shirts, white pants. But then I noticed that this man didn't have a moustache. He also didn't speak.

He waited by the door until I acknowledged him, then came forward with the tray of food. He waited silently at the foot of the bed whilst I ate, watching me.

I ate ravenously. Greenish vegetable soup; a slice of brown bread, honey, no butter (butter is white); a sliver of cold apple pie; an apple – dry. The innards of the apple were almost white, but I let this go: at least the moustached man had tried. These people seemed willing to listen to me. As soon as I had finished, the man came forward, took the tray, and disappeared through the door, shutting it behind him.

I nestled back into the bed and re-read the article in 'Scientific American' which had been marked with an in-turned corner. It was the title article, 'Controversy over Frozen Zoo Closure in San Diego'.

"The Frozen Zoo's purpose is to cryogenically preserve the genetic material of endangered species," read a quote in bold. "Cloning is only used if absolutely necessary. Any claims that we are cloning long-extinct species for mere curiosity are unfounded."

Another section had been underlined in red by somebody who had read the article before me. "No scientist other than Doctor Lau could be found for comment. However, a recently-hired laboratory assistant, who did not give his name, told our reporter: "[the proposed Change in the Law] is a testament to mankind's stupidity. They say our research is immoral, but look at what we have achieved - cures for polio, cancer, dementia. The only reason people have turned against science now, is that they believe they have taken all they will ever want from it. But one day, with or without the ban, science will come back, and with it will come some new and amazing discovery which will lift humanity to new heights. No-one will be complaining then.""

I was totally engrossed in 'Scientific American', and it was only when I finally put the magazine down, an hour or so later, that I realized somebody had been in my room. My door had been left ajar and two books had been laid at the foot of my bed. Hungry for something new to exercise my recovering brain, I pounced on them.

'How to Clone a Mammoth' was a fifty-page paperback for idiots. I devoured that one instantly. 'Humanity and Parahumanity', by Doctor Jean-Luc Tati and Doctor James Bai – Bai, like *Mister* Bai, the moustached man's name for Alexander - was a longer and far more detailed book. It took me an hour or two to process.

When I had finished reading for the night, just as I started to drift to sleep, I heard the door to my bedroom open softly. I looked up from my pillow.

Alexander was standing in the doorway, staring at me. In the electric glow of the lights from beyond my room, I could see that he was wearing a white shirt and pants, and a white coat. But Alexander's coat was longer than the other men's coats, and he had paired it with thick, white rubber gloves.

"I came to tell you... goodnight," he mumbled. "And that breakfast will be served at seven. Tomorrow. In the dining room. I'll come and get you."

I stared at him blankly.

Alexander lingered. It seemed he was waiting for a response, but I couldn't imagine what he wanted me to say. Then, hesitantly, he came into the room.

I felt my back tense and my shoulders rise defensively as Alexander approached. A familiar, unwelcome animal response. I grappled my instincts into submission and made a point of giving him direct eye-contact to show that I wasn't afraid.

Alexander came to the side of the bed, and paused there, looking down at me. His pale, ice-blue eyes gleamed in the dark. I held his stare. Still he didn't speak.

His eyes dropped to one of the books on the bed, 'Humanity and Parahumanity'. He picked it up, began to leaf through it. "How long before you finish reading this?" he murmured.

"I've finished it," I said.

He looked at me; frowned. "And what did you think of it? Be specific."

I considered. "It was obvious... *eventually*," I admitted. "It took me a while to work out what 'natural telepathy' meant, but after that it was simple. It just seemed to... over-complicate the obvious."

It was difficult to read Alexander's expression. He continued to stare at me. "And do you believe in it?"

"Believe in what?"

"That certain species can communicate telepathically?"

"Well, of course they can!" I snorted. "Belief has nothing to do with it." It was difficult to process the extent of Alexander's ignorance. "How else could a pack of dogs sense a herd of deer from miles away? How else could they tell other members of the pack what they know? How else could they execute a perfect killing if they couldn't tell each other what to do?"

How else did *all* my cousins find me after Father's death, when only one thought to track Rawg to the beach?

"My thoughts exactly." Alexander smiled. There was something soft about his eyes now, something wondering and childlike. I felt the tension leave my body. Poor boy. From what I had seen of his struggles on our journey into the mountains, his unusually slow social knowledge, I deduced that he had an infant's understanding of life outside this sterile, white enclosure. But he apparently wanted to learn.

"I'm glad you do believe. Otherwise there would be little point in any of this." He dropped the book back on the bed, and pointed to the other one, the book on mammoth-cloning for idiots. "And this one? Did you understand this?"

"Of course I did," I said.

"Good ... that's good."

Alexander lingered a little longer. Then, "Breakfast is at seven," he said again. And he left, quickly.

#

Alexander Bai's eyes. So seemingly trustworthy.

They are full of deception. All of them, waiting to catch me unawares.

I am sitting under the window where the cabin opposite cannot stare at me, trying not to let the feel of the dusty floorboards against my backside distract me as I clear my mind.

The specimen I was working on last night is still sitting in its test tube on the desk. It is waiting for me to add another chemical to its preserving fluid but right now I cannot remember what that chemical is. My scientific knowledge has been crowded out of my head by these unwelcome memories.

I could kill for some music. Some Black Sabbath. Some Judas Priest. Ideally, some Megadeth. Loud, mindless music by harmless old musicians. I can remember what their songs sounded like now, and I want them back - to block out the bad thoughts so I can concentrate *for a bit.*

Why was I senseless enough to have only stolen Alexander's ancient 'Best of the Eighties' cassette? Such a gross error of music selection is excusable only by insanity. I should have reclaimed my stack of MusiChips and Polymer MiniRecords from Alexander; I could have stashed them with the stolen specimens inside the CryoBag before I escaped. But I had to move fast. I don't want to think about what would have happened if Alexander's men had caught me...

Ah! The radio has clicked back on. Thank goodness for that.

I have not yet learnt how to work the radio. It seems to switch itself on and off on a whim. I force my mind to focus on it, wander to my seat and sit down. It is Frieda and Juan again, as usual, in their inane soap opera. I recognise their voices instantly.

I have been getting into this little show. The soap opera mundanity is mindlessly soothing, in a way similar to that of Black Sabbath and Judas Priest, although not nearly as exhilarating. Anyway, I am glad that I am enjoying this show, because I have no desire to expend any of my precious energy working out how to change the channels. I am stuck with Juan and Frieda and have spent a lot of time with them over the last week. They have no desire to trick and abuse me. We are almost friends.

A couple of days ago, Frieda found out that she is going to have a baby. She keeps referring to it as 'she', which is strange, because I know it's a boy. Idiot writers.

Here is a sample:

Juan: Food is running low, Frieda. I'll have to drive into town and get us some supplies. No - don't look at me like that, Frieda. I don't like to leave you in your condition but your nutrition is even more important now. I promise I won't go anywhere I'll be recognised.
Frieda: It's not that. I'm not concerned for my own safety anymore. I... I could feel her inside me again today, Juan. This morning, while you were fixing the roof.
Juan: That's good, isn't it? You said yourself - it lets you know she's alive and strong.
Frieda: These last few days... she hasn't felt nearly as strong as she did at the beginning.
Juan: You worry too much, Frieda. Come over here to me, darling. I'll take your mind off it...
Frieda: Oh, Juan – why do you speak so condescendingly? You never used to speak to me like this, even at the hospital. Nurses are supposed to condescend to their patients, not husbands to their wives, not nowadays! Maybe you don't understand these things because you're not a father yet. You won't be until the baby's born. But I am already a mother, Juan; I know how important she is and I want what's best for my child!
Juan: What's best for our child is a mother who doesn't worry about nothing all the time!
Frieda: Nothing? Juan, if she... if she *goes*, Juan, that will be the end of it! I couldn't go on living, knowing I'd denied my child a future.
Juan: Well, it's not as if we can call for a doctor, is it? There isn't one for miles. Besides, even if they don't recognise you, they will recognise me. They'll have my face on file with all the other minions who worked at that despicable hospital, and if they see me... that really **will** be the end! If I could intervene medically myself, I would, but...
Frieda: No. No you wouldn't, Juan. Because you don't care like I do. You haven't seen her yet. You can't feel her. To you she's an alien presence in the dark, something separate from yourself... but I can **feel** her, Juan! She's **inside** me!

Juan: Frieda, please don't get like this again...
Frieda: You think she's strong, Juan, but she isn't. She's unstable. Oh, so unstable and vulnerable!
Juan: Frieda - for the love of god, don't wail like that!
Frieda: I'm scared... I'm scared we're going to lose her to the darkness!

CHAPTER NINETEEN

When I awoke the next morning, I made it my mission to dissect the music player on the bedside table, and to reconstruct it in such a way as to make it play Black Sabbath. Only partway through the process did I realise that my mission was not only impossible, but utterly insane.

My mind was returning. Slowly.

When Alexander came to my room, he found me sitting cross-legged on the bed, re-reading Tati and Bai's book. He ignored the white panels and pieces of machinery scattered around me. "Which chapter are you on?" he enquired.

"Five," I said, still reading. "'Coming to Terms with the Limits of Human Intelligence'."

Alexander nodded. "There's some breakfast downstairs, if you want to follow me?"

He was being uncharacteristically indirect. Perhaps he thought imitating normal speech patterns would give me a sense of comfort, but it didn't. It annoyed me.

"If I don't want to follow you, will there cease to be breakfast downstairs?" I asked.

"Oh, there will still be breakfast," said Alexander. "You just won't get any. Come on."

Satisfied, I slipped off the bed.

"Wait." Alexander stopped suddenly and snapped his fingers. "I forgot to say – there are some clean clothes for you, in there." He gestured to the closet by the door. "If you would like to dress first?"

"I am dressed."

"I meant, if you would like to put on *day*-clothes rather than *night*-clothes."

The knowledge had been in the back of my mind since I awoke the previous day. But everything had been so distracting, and with my mind not what it once was, I had ignored the change. Only now did I fully register that I was no longer wearing my denim shorts and t-shirt. I examined a sleeve of my new satin pyjamas.

"Your old clothes are being washed. You can have them back soon," Alexander said. "In the meantime, wear what we've provided. One of my men had a pregnant sister staying here, a long time ago - it turns out she left some of her maternity clothes behind. They're all in the closet. I've also included one of my belts, to make them fit you."

I continued to examine my strange new pyjamas.

"If you have any questions," said Alexander, "you can ask them over breakfast. Come on, now."

"In a minute." I opened the closet doors and examined the contents. Lots of big, thick jackets, puffy trousers. The air inside the building was warm, so I selected a loose shirt, jeans, and a leather belt snaked around a wire hanger. I made Alexander stand outside while I put them on.

"There are slippers – there." Alexander pointed out a pair of white, fluffy hotel-slippers by the foot of the bed.

"Yes," I acknowledged. "There are."

Leaving the slippers where they were, I followed Alexander out onto a vast, horseshoe-shaped, white-carpeted landing. Along the surrounding walls, many doors (all closed) were positioned at regular intervals. As I walked, I counted the doors, estimated the spaces between them; recalled the structure of the building from outside. My brain constructed an image of twenty-five identical rooms, all similar in size to mine. I smiled. My brain was alive.

"Are you coming, Katrina?"

Ahead of me, Alexander was standing at the top of a wide, curving staircase. He beckoned for me to follow him down.

On the ground floor, we crossed the hallway to the dining room. It was long, spacious, empty. Two folding-chairs faced each other across one lonely table in the centre, above which hung a grand electric light with multiple golden tentacles: freshly-polished but broken. Wires sprouted from the cable connecting it to the ceiling. The floor-to-ceiling windows lining the back wall let in pre-dawn light, and displayed scenes of thick, endless snow and grey sky. It made the room feel like a cave.

On the table was a jug of pink liquid and a box of golden cereal. No milk. Usually cereal is served with milk. Also glasses, cutlery, and bowls for two.

Alexander sat in the chair facing the window. He gestured to me; I sat opposite him. "Have something to eat," he said.

I took a couple of fistfuls of cereal for myself, then pushed the rest back generously across the table to Alexander. I poured the pink liquid into my glass, smelled it, tasted it, confirmed that it was good – it tasted like strawberries - and poured liberal amounts over my cereal.

All the while, Alexander watched me in silence. I looked up, caught his eye. He looked quickly back down at his cereal, as if frightened to meet my stare.

"Who put these pyjamas on me?"

Alexander looked up again: now we were having a conversation, perhaps it seemed more natural for him to meet my eye. "Two of my men. I asked them to. Don't worry, nothing inappropriate went on - they're medical men, professionals. Both gay, anyway."

"Oh." 'Gay' means same-sex mating, like Chemise and Courtney. I didn't care about this irrelevant information: I was just glad to have the mystery of who dressed me solved. I waited a while before trying another question. "Are you called James Bai?"

"No. I'm Alexander. I told you."

"But the man called you Mister Bai, and the book..."

At this point, the red-moustached man I had met the previous day came into the dining room with a watering can. Alexander had his back to him and didn't turn around; not even when the man spoke.

"Good morning," said the man. He padded over to one of the dead, potted ferns which cowered by the windows. Slowly, looking at us all the while, he started to water it. "Is the breakfast alright, Mr. Bai?"

"It's fine.... well, no." Alexander turned to face him. "Actually, Harley, I was meaning to ask - what possessed you to put strawberry milkshake powder in the milk this morning?"

"That was for our guest." For some reason, the moustached man winked at me. "I thought it would be nice to add a little colour to things for once. Besides, there was a time when you would *only* drink milk if it was bright pink, Mr. Bai..."

"Yes, alright," snapped Alexander. "Thank you, Harley."

"Of course!" I said.

Alexander jumped, and whipped back round to face me. "Yes? What is it?"

I beamed. Connections were forming. My brain was functioning. "I've just realised, you can't be James Bai... because he was a doctor. And that man said you're just a 'mister'."

Alexander struck the table with his palms. Behind him, I could see the moustached man looking at us uneasily.

"*Mister*." I wasn't exactly sure which word had provoked the reaction, but I assumed it was the latter. I looked from Alexander to the moustached man and back to Alexander again. But the repetition of the word provoked no further reaction, so I resumed my breakfast.

A minute passed. The moustached man lingered: a tense, silent presence in the background.

Finally, Alexander said, "My full name is Alexander Bai. And you're right: it is 'mister', not 'doctor'. You don't get many chances to study for a PhD all the way up here, in a disused hotel, built by a madman who couldn't understand that it's impossible to get enough tourist income when you have to close down for six months of the year... but the solitude works fine for us!"

"It would be difficult to get to the university from here," I agreed.

"And qualifications aren't everything. I'm educated. I'm intelligent. I make up for my lack of qualifications in work. I am *devoted* to my work. As any scientist should be."

"You can't be a scientist," I said. "There are no scientists anymore."

Alexander didn't respond. He drained his glass, pushed his bowl away, and stood up. "Right, I've finished. Have you? Good."

I hadn't.

"There should be some new books in your room soon," Alexander said. "I picked a selection out last night. Harley, could you get one of the men to bring the books up to Katrina's room?"

Harley nodded and left the room, casting a final, brow-furrowed glance over his shoulder at us as he went.

"You can spend the next three hours reading. Then I'll show you what I've brought you here to do," Alexander continued. "No – *don't* pour yourself another glass of milk. You've already cost me enough in food and gasoline. If you want this hospitality to continue, you are going to have to prove your worth."

I shot him what I hoped was a suitably defiant look. Then I retreated to my room with my half-full glass.

#

When I returned to my room and saw what had been left for me there, I was astounded.

Two towers of books flanked my bed, with at least twenty thick volumes in each. Three hours to read forty books. Alexander's expectations of me clearly went beyond mere optimism - this was nothing short of insanity. But if this is what I had to do to 'prove my worth', I would conquer it.

I took the first three books off one of the piles, sat on the bed, and started to read. The first book was on genetics and cloning. The second (reviewed as 'highly perceptive' by Doctor James Bai, according to its cover) outlined a theory that dolphins had an organ in their brains to enable intra-species communication. The final one I flicked through was about the practice of artificially inseminating tigresses at San Diego Zoo.

'By freezing the gametes of captive specimens and using them to inseminate later generations, we might be able to repopulate this species without resorting to the now-illegal practice of cloning,' one chapter began.

After skimming these three at speed, I went back to the piles, crouched down, and scanned the spines of the other books. Judging by the titles, they all fell under the general umbrella of 'biology'. Other than that, they seemed to have been selected at random. I tried to think of something which might connect them but couldn't. I picked another book, took it back to the bed. As I read, the mystery continued to play on my mind.

It was more than three hours before Alexander Bai returned.

Again, he materialised silently in the doorway. Again, I did not realise he was there until I happened to glance in that direction. Again, he was watching me intently.

There was something different about his countenance now. Somehow, he seemed less confident than he had at breakfast.

"I haven't finished yet," I explained when I saw him. "I'm only on stage three of 'Stages of Feline Foetal Development'. I'll be finished with this one soon; then you can show me what you want me to do."

"I'm sorry."

I assumed Alexander hadn't heard me properly. "I said..."

"No, I'm sorry I was so short with you before." He ventured a few steps into the room, slowly, uncertainly. "It was my problem. My insecurity. You didn't mean anything by what you said - I know that now. I was rude."

"Were you?" I asked, distracted: 'Feline Foetal Development' was full of fascinating diagrams.

"Oh." Alexander noticed a book on the floor which had slipped off my bed. He picked it up, examined its cover. "Thomas and Harley used to read this to me when I was... oh, seven? I saw it in the library last night. I don't know why I put it in the pile." His eyes flicked to me, then back to the book. "You might not know their names yet, but you've met them. Harley was present at breakfast this morning. He's sort of the... 'general domestic', when he isn't assisting me with my research. Thomas is the medic. He's one of the men who dressed you and helped you in the bath last night."

"I had a bath last night?"

Alexander looked at me. "He said you were a little dopey; I didn't realise you'd actually passed out!"

The thought of hands on my sleeping body prodded a memory, a monkey forced down on a table... But to Alexander, this seemed to be extremely funny. He smiled, showing two rows of perfectly white teeth. A flash of charisma flickered in his pale eyes. A lock of white hair became displaced.

Then, like a performer, he quickly regained composure. He gazed at the book, studying the text and the creases on the cover as if it were a profoundly fascinating, valuable relic he had unearthed.

"The Time Machine," he murmured. "What a classic." He paused; stroked its cover. "If I could travel in time... I would go back to when I was a boy. Not to change anything. Just to watch that idiot playing mindlessly, no sense of responsibility, or maturity, or duty... No, I wouldn't change a thing." He looked up at me. "Read the others later," he said. "I want to show you the laboratory before night."

#

The only way to reach the laboratory was to take an elevator. Alexander ushered me to the ground floor again and showed me where it was concealed: behind the wide, curved staircase which led up to the first floor.

I should have been frightened of the elevator. I had seen elevators before, in some of the larger university buildings. Horrible, claustrophobic electronic boxes which could so easily go wrong. But Alexander was there behind me, and his ease must have been contagious.

Alexander's fingers scurried over a pad of silver keys on the elevator wall, pressing numbers. 2-0-5-2. He hit the button labelled 'Basement' and the metal doors clanged shut.

It took a long time for the elevator to reach the basement. After fifteen seconds of standing in the dim light, the calming effect of Alexander's presence started to slip. I shifted nervously. Alexander turned to look at me; whether it was with disgust or concern, I couldn't tell. He said nothing.

Finally, the doors squealed open onto a dark, empty corridor. Gratefully, I stepped out.

Two electric light-panels in the ceiling came to life as I passed beneath them. By their harsh glare, I could see two doors leading from the corridor: a wooden one, marked 'Changing Rooms', at the far end and, to our right, a pair of glass sliding-doors, slightly ajar, labelled 'Hot Tub'. A metal panel behind these doors blocked access to the 'Hot Tub' room.

"Go on," Alexander whispered behind me.

I let him usher me forward. Our footsteps made echoes on the floor-tiles.

The sound of a machine whirring grew louder as we approached the 'Hot Tub' door, then softened to a muffled hum once we had passed it.

"We'll visit that room later," said Alexander, as he encouraged me through the 'Changing Rooms' door. "I want you to see my work room first." He pulled on a string light-pull. A naked bulb, hanging from a wire overhead, flickered into semi-life. In its dim light, I could see a dark wooden table, a few feet out from the wall at the far end of the room. It was strewn with paperwork. Beside it, a rug with a swirly pattern covered a small section of the black-tiled floor.

At our end of the room was a cage. Empty. Its bars reached from floor to ceiling. It was big enough to contain one of the humming machines you sometimes see in similar cages, with signs next to them reading 'Danger of Death'; or perhaps a small lion, if it was persuaded not to move. At this end of the room, the light was weakest.

Alexander saw me squinting at the cage. "Hold on."

He went to the table, picked up a torch, flicked it on, and shone it around the room. I followed its beam as it touched various objects: the hanging bulb, the light pull, the cage (the light glinted off its silver bars), and finally Alexander's desk, where he was standing, watching me.

Then Alexander turned, and the torch-beam settled on a scroll of paper mounted on the wall behind him. "Come here," Alexander said, and he moved behind the desk. "I want to show you this."

As I came up behind him, Alexander unrolled the paper. He held it at the bottom, unfurled, for me to see. "Can you tell what this is, Katrina?"

I nodded. "A tiger."

The sketches were in pencil, annotated with tiny, scrawled handwriting which I couldn't read, no matter how close I got to the paper. The image in the centre showed the whole animal. Surrounding this were several smaller sketches, showing parts of the tiger in close-up: mostly cross-sections of the brain and the skull. I paid these satellites little attention, though. They did not interest me nearly as much as the whole of this stylised beast, which had dagger-like teeth protruding over its thick black lips, and powerful shoulders hunched over the top of its streamlined head. Its primal posture and small, intense eyes were familiar. But there was something else about it; the extra muscle, those massive paws in relation to its body, which gave the tiger a strength the likes of which I had never seen in nature.

This was a creature that walked alone.

I stretched out a skinny arm, my own muscles having dissolved to nothing during my time in California, to touch it.

"No." Alexander spoke softly from somewhere behind me. "Not a tiger. Smilodon Fatalis; a kind of sabre-toothed cat. They died out long before tigers evolved."

I glanced at him. He was looking at the picture, not at me. There was a strange smile on his thin lips. "Isn't it beautiful? My father drew the sketch - *Doctor Bai*, that is."

Alexander was correct. It was beautiful.

A creature that had ruled the world of the past. Not with brainpower or trickery or tools, nor with religion and superstition, but through sheer *strength*, pure *power*, and the natural determination to survive. Something from a simpler, faraway time, brought to life in pencil. My heart pounded like a hammer, as it had when I first laid eyes on those gorgeous savages at my first live rock concert. Only this time, my head was clear.

My fingers made contact with the paper. Alexander's hand touched the back of mine, and gently brushed it away. "No touching. Please."

Alexander allowed me a couple more seconds with the sketch, then tugged at my sleeve and led me away.

There was a pair of doors down the wall from the 'Changing Rooms' door, made of thick, lightly-tarnished metal. Alexander prized the metal doors apart with his fingers. "No need for extra security down here," he said. "No undesirables would ever find this place, let alone think to come down to the basement. When he first took over the building, my father insisted on reinforced security panels for the doors, and locks, keys, code pads – you must have seen the one in the elevator – and, of course, the men obliged. But we disabled most of them years ago. It makes it easier for me to get down here, day or night. Whenever I get a flash of inspiration."

He pulled the doors wide.

It was only half the size of the dining room upstairs. But after the confines of Alexander's 'work room', it seemed positively immense. This room was painted the same matte white as the rest of the basement, but it was a cleaner white. The entire room stank of sterilisation.

In the centre of the floor was a deep pit, about twice my height in diameter. It was filled with something ice-cold, and poisonous, judging by the aroma of mixed chemicals. I stopped inside the metal doors and stood, staring at this crater, not sure what to make of it.

"Go on," I heard Alexander whisper behind me. His hands touched my shoulders, gently pressing me forward. I shrugged him off, then proceeded with caution.

"Don't touch," he warned. He took a few steps with me then hung back, letting me go on ahead. "Just look."

I crouched at the edge of the pit and looked down. My mouth went dry. Something white, hairless, ghostly, but *organic*, was drifting in translucent goo.

"My father... *Doctor Bai*, of course... had the sides of the hot tub removed, and altered the pit for it. See, you can access it without having to take it out of preservation. You notice the membrane – the film, I mean - over the top of the pit? It can be penetrated by certain tools, but it reseals immediately afterwards to prevent contamination. Ingenious, don't you think? Of course, we keep any risk of contamination to a minimum here anyway. That's why we didn't wait to give you a bath your first night here. We wanted to remove the city toxins from your skin... and warm you up after the trip, of course."

"What is it?" I glanced back at Alexander and saw that this question had provoked a smirk.

"Oh? Don't you know? Can't you guess?" Alexander came over to the pit now and knelt beside me. "Can't you tell, just by *looking* at it? I was told that, for you, one look is all it takes."

Curled loosely as if cradled by invisible arms. An enlarged head, closed eyes, and four tiny paws. It didn't look dead. It didn't look like anything from the Civilised World. A spirit of a baby, trapped on its way to the afterlife.

"Tell me."

With a sigh, Alexander relented. "About eighty years ago," he said, "in the La Brea tar pits, a body was found: a female Smilodon. People have been finding them there since the first big excavations in the twentieth century, half-preserved in the tar. But this one was special. They had her transported to the San Diego Frozen Zoo - that's where they used to preserve and study the remains of endangered and extinct species..."

"Before it closed down after the Change in the Law," I murmured.

Alexander nodded. "She was dissected. And by some miracle, underneath the damaged flesh and meat of the female carcass, the scientists found her uterus perfectly preserved. And... *in use.*"

"What do you mean?"

Alexander smiled. "Somehow, even in death, she had managed to protect her offspring. A female cub, almost ready to be born. So perfectly preserved, you would hardly know it was dead."

My eyes travelled again to the little body. Beneath the membrane, tiny, colourless paws moved gently in the translucent goo. And that face - closed eyes, miniature ears, soft-looking jowls were all intact, as if the baby animal was merely asleep and waiting for a mother's touch to wake it up.

"The zoo still had the pickled foetus on display decades later, when my father took a job at there as a lab assistant. The job was beneath him, of course, but he wanted to gain some insight into the techniques they were using to preserve ancient DNA. They put him to work in the room where they were keeping the foetus. As stupid as it sounds, when he saw this creature… he fell in love. For the first and only time, so he said."

"That doesn't sound stupid," I murmured.

"Anyway, when they closed the Zoo down, my father 'rescued' the foetus and brought it up here. He hired various assistants – my father was a wealthy man, he could feed and clothe an army. He never left this place. Over the years, some men died. Some went out for fresh supplies and refused to come back. But the loyal ones, the ones who knew my father would succeed no matter what… they remained with him for decades."

"Why did your father stay here?" I asked.

Alexander smiled. His eyes moistened at the corners. "His work. It meant everything to him. Once he had the resources and the men to keep him alive, he was able to commit himself totally to his work. Nothing else in life mattered."

"What was his work?"

Wiping his eyes on his sleeve, Alexander turned to me. "Have you been listening to anything I've said?"

"Yes. Doctor Bai brought a Smilodon up to the mountains to protect it. Then he died." I battled the frustration. "You didn't say anything about 'work' until now."

"You don't think he acquired the Smilodon to admire its beauty, do you?" Alexander snorted. "That's an *artist's* way of thinking! Lazy, idiotic! My father was never content to be a passive observer. He wanted to use his *whole* brain. He wanted to *do* things!"

Alexander's reaction frightened me. I was trapped in an underground room with the man, after all, and was too afraid to operate the elevator by myself. I paused, rigid, waiting.

After a moment, Alexander seemed to calm. His breathing slowed.

"What did he want to do?" I ventured.

"Well," Alexander gave me a nasty-looking grin. "You've read his books. He was a cloning man, a scientist. Can't you put two and two together?"

"I'm not stupid," I snapped. "It's four."

Alexander bared his teeth at me. "He wanted to resurrect the creature, of course!"

Alexander said this with such conviction, as if it was obvious. For a moment I questioned my intelligence: had I really allowed my brain to rot?

But then the implications of Alexander's words got through to me - and the question of my intelligence ceased to be important. The Dead-Talkers would never discuss their craft with a defective little reject: I was always pushed aside. But I saw the reactions on the faces of the onlookers. I knew it to be true: *the dead could be brought, temporarily, back to life.* They could be spoken to. 'Telepathy' - that was the human word for it.

But before Alexander had said this, I had never considered it possible for someone of my own kind to witness the living dead - not only that, but to take on the role of Dead-Talker themselves.

"Is that possible?" I asked. "Can you really make a dead creature come alive?"

Alexander's smile stretched. I could see his white teeth again, bared in defiance of the impossible. A lock of pale hair fell out of place against his moist brow. "If you're asking whether we could resurrect this exact specimen – no, that would be impossible. But clone it? Yes, I should think so." He paused. "I'm sorry. It's just… this has been such a big part of my life for so long. I forget sometimes… people probably don't think about such things anymore. I don't… really know how other people think."

"Neither do I."

But Alexander wasn't listening to me. "You see what I'm trying to tell you, don't you?" he said. "Now I am in charge, it falls to *me* to find a way of accomplishing my father's dream. That is my purpose in life. And… it can be yours, too, if you want it to be… Katrina?"

Something was unfurling inside me. Perhaps the same adolescent desire that lured Rawg out from the safety of the Edu-Centre every Spring, in search of a mother for his young. The feeling Father might have experienced when he held the tiny pale human infant that was me for the first time. The feeling that drew my hand towards three tiny, soft-furred creatures curled on the Edu-Centre floor. A forceful, primal sense of purpose.

I found myself saying, "Yes."

#

It was an agreement which, for better or worse, would lead me here.

It's late. Probably past midnight. The cabin is eerily moonlit again.

Two hours ago the radio cut out, leaving me with nothing but the whistle of the desert breeze and the creak of the wooden walls to accompany my work. A macabre soundtrack to an increasingly uncomfortable procedure.

The specimen before me on the table is something long-extinct. A once proud creature, reduced to shrivelled tissue in a jar of gloop. It still has a foot, and a bit of skin. It used to be called an 'African lion'.

I try to hum something comforting but I can't remember any tunes. I pause. My scalpel hovers over the jar, glinting ominously above the creature like a dagger in a dark street, whilst I think. Why can't I remember? Is my mind too damaged to recall my favourite songs? Maybe there's nothing to remember. Alexander always said my music was tuneless, after all.

But Alexander Bai was wrong about a lot of things.

My palm strikes the table harder than expected. The lion-piece starts to float slowly, hypnotically, around its jar. I watch it.

Poor, noble beast. Reduced to nothing. Your home destroyed, your skins sold, your captive descendants cloned and drugged and put on display then sold off, one by one, as the people demanded more flesh and funding for research. The Change in the Law came too late for you.

Yes, so many people were wrong about so many things. How lucky it is that I am now aware of the injustice. How lucky that I agreed to Alexander's proposal.

How lucky that I am intellectually equipped to set things right.

CHAPTER TWENTY

Lunchtime. I sat across from Alexander at the dining table, contemplating his proposition as I drank green soup from a chipped bowl.

Alexander watched me in silence. His soup remained untouched.

"So." I put my soup down.

"Yes?" Alexander leaned in.

"How does this plan to clone a Smilodon back to life link with what your books call 'animal telepathy'?"

"Tenuously."

"I see." I made a mental note to look this word up in a dictionary later, if I could get my hands on one.

"It's a matter of scientific voyeurism, really," said Alexander. "It's just... such a beautiful creature. My father wanted to see one in the flesh. And so do I."

This wasn't the full answer, I could tell. Celebration of beauty was the priority of artists, for whom Alexander had already shared his contempt. He was keeping something from me.

Alexander must have noticed my doubt, because he went on, "Well, alright. It's not pure voyeurism. There is a connection."

"What's the connection?"

Alexander fell silent again before he responded. "You see, my father did a lot of work with domestic animals. Cats and dogs. That was how he made his money: at one time it was fashionable for people to have their favourite pets cloned. He knew his subjects inside and out, from the anatomical specifications for each dog breed to the structure of a healthy animal's brain. An obsessive, I suppose some people would have called him. But his interest in animal telepathy took over and he became involved with Homo-SuperiUS, started looking at the brains of wild animals - and noticed a difference."

"What difference?"

"The part of the brain my father believed to be responsible for animal telepathy... it seems to be smaller in more recently evolved species. And it's particularly small in the brains of domestic animals, like the dogs and cats my father was cloning. Human breeding intervention seems to stunt telepathic development. This makes research difficult, of course, because even the wildcats and the apes the scientists had access to were bred by humans.

"We want to find the living brain of an early animal, a purely wild animal. A brain containing the telepathic organ from which that of a thousand later species originated. Theoretically, the telepathic organ of such an animal should be larger, stronger, easier to study. If we could observe telepathy in an early mammal... perhaps that could bring us closer to understanding why human beings lost this ability."

I recalled sitting on the floor of the Edu-Centre, watching Rawg and Father communicate overhead, eyes locked, minds closed to me. Rawg, helpless, screaming to me across the beach... I would be lying if I said such an investigation sparked no interest in me. Primarily, though, I just wanted to see the baby Smilodon alive.

"It's a pity, I suppose, that we were unable to acquire an even earlier mammal." Alexander sighed. "Perhaps a primate, even..."

"No!"

This threat was enough to project me from my seat. Now I was standing over the table, leaning towards Alexander, bristling. A man in white who, throughout our conversation, had been discretely watering the same plant that had been watered this morning, slipped out into the hall.

Alexander's eyes widened. He leaned back in his seat. There was confusion in those eyes; perhaps even fear. "What... do you mean, '*no*'?"

"That animal is perfection," I said. "You know it is. If you pick a more manlike species, I shall refuse to cooperate with your exercise in voyeurism, Alexander Bai."

Alexander exhaled. "So, does this mean you're on board?"

"By 'on board', I assume you are asking if I will cooperate." I shrugged with exaggerated nonchalance, excitement bubbling beneath the surface. "I suppose I will."

Alexander nodded, and his shoulders relaxed. "Good," he said. "That means I won't have to go to the trouble of kicking you out into the snow and letting you freeze to death." He laughed softly and smiled.

I smiled back.

We had reached an understanding.

At this point, the moustached man from earlier came into the dining room, as if Alexander's words had conjured him, and asked if we would like anything to drink. "To celebrate Katrina joining the family," he added, looking from me to Alexander and back again. His smile suggested he was aware of something that I was not.

Alexander glanced away, clearly embarrassed, and waved him off. "Nothing for me, Harley – go away."

"Wait!" I said, catching Harley before he left the room. "Pink milk."

Alexander opened his mouth but Harley nodded and left before he had a chance to speak.

"That man doesn't have any offspring," I acknowledged when Harley was out of earshot.

Alexander frowned. "How can you tell?"

"By the way he behaves towards you. You are his substitute child."

"You think so?" Alexander seemed to consider for a moment. Then, "No, it's sycophancy, plain and simple. But you're right; he doesn't have children. He's gay."

"Oh," I said. "You said the man who helped me in the bath on the first night was gay as well. Was it the same one?"

"Yes, it was Harley who gave you the bath," said Alexander. "But all the men here are homosexual. Wonderful workers, too. They were picked from laboratories and pro-science rallies by my father."

I tried to work out why the men's sexual preferences would have made them more appealing workers to the now-deceased Doctor Bai. Back on the Island, the adolescents who paired off with members of their own sex showed as little interest in productivity as any of the young opposite-sex couples, and the videos in the Edu-Centre never touched on the subject. "Was he gay?" I asked.

"Who, my father? No," said Alexander. "Sexual feelings were beneath him. He was completely asexual – didn't like women or men."

"But he reproduced," I said. "If he didn't like women, how could he have had you?"

At that moment, Harley returned with a large jug of pink milk and two glasses. His presence brought our strange, fractured conversation to an end. Harley put the jug down on the table and moved to place one of the glasses before Alexander.

Alexander waved it away. "No, no. None for me. In fact, none for her, either," he said, nodding in my direction. "We have a brainstorming session to begin. Put that in the refrigerator, please. If you need us this afternoon, we will be in the laboratory."

"'Us'. 'We'." Harley smiled. "It's so refreshing to hear you speaking in plural, Mr. Bai! Even if you are only referring to a friend. It's a start."

"What on Earth are you talking about, Harley?" Alexander said. "Yes, I am speaking in plural. About me and my lab partner. Now go away."

Harley made to take my glass away, but I held it back and stared challengingly across the table at Alexander. "Why can't I take it with me?"

"Contamination," said Alexander. "You should know that."

"Does your rule apply to the whole house?" I asked.

Harley put both glasses back down on the table and left the room quietly.

"The whole house?" Alexander said. "No, of course not."

"Oh, good." I glanced over my shoulder at the staircase. "We'll brainstorm in my bedroom. All the books are up there anyway, so it makes sense."

"Sorry?" Alexander didn't seem to understand what was going on.

"What do you want to carry?" I asked him. "The glasses, or the jug?"

"We always – *I* always brainstorm in the laboratory," Alexander said.

"Yes, and you've barely progressed on your own so far."

Alexander's features contorted into an expression of utter misery. Not wishing to upset him further, I grabbed the glasses and ran upstairs to wait.

#

I lay on my bed, staring up at the white ceiling. Whilst I scanned it for inspiration, I chewed on the tip of a plastic straw which one of the men had interrupted us half an hour ago to give me. I hadn't requested one, but I appreciated the gesture.

My pink-milk glass sat half-empty on the bedside table; the end of the straw wasn't touching it. I no longer wanted to drink or eat anything. I was thinking.

At the foot of the bed, Alexander sat in silence. He bounced slowly up and down, making the bed move. His bony hands cupped his glass; his fingertips tapped rhythmlessly on the rim. Now he took a sip.

"Any ideas?"

Alexander shook his head.

The 'brainstorming' session – brainstorming was an overly complicated word for 'generating ideas', it turned out - had begun almost an hour ago. At first, I had been ready to delve head-first into what the books called 'reconstructing the genome': repairing the age-damaged Smilodon DNA with genes from living organisms. In my mind, I had listed all the species I had come across in the Professor's books that resembled the Smilodon; tigers, lions, leopards, jaguars; cheetahs, to some extent. Many were extinct, I knew: lost when science turned its back on conservation to focus on human advancement, in the days of Homo-SuperiUS. But some still existed in private collections and wildlife parks; even, perhaps, in the wild, where some specimens might never even have seen a human being before. Bengal, where the tigers came from – that was where I wanted to begin my search for a suitable donor, whose fur and blood could be used to rebuild the baby Smilodon's damaged cells...

But Alexander had cut me off mid-flow and explained that such a journey would be pointless. Doctor Bai had already made several cloned embryos of the Smilodon foetus, all of which were in storage. It was a finite supply, so mistakes had to be kept to a minimum, but it was enough to mean that embryo supply was not our current concern.

"But you've already done the hard part," I had moaned; and Alexander had countered, "No. That was the time-consuming part - not the hard part."

The 'hard part', Alexander had explained, was making the embryo grow. Electricity could spark the cells into life but, without a living host, the embryo would surely die. This was the impossible barrier Alexander had been hurling himself against since the death of his father. The barrier he wanted me to overcome.

James Bai had created a potential life. It was up to me to find a way of bringing it into this world.

I removed the straw from my mouth. "Surrogate mothers?" I suggested. 'How to Clone a Mammoth' had mentioned using elephants to bear the babies. I got up on my elbows to see Alexander's response.

Alexander shook his head solemnly. "We tried it," he said to the wall. "We failed."

"What went wrong?"

Alexander sighed. I felt the bed rise beneath me as he stood up. He walked over to the wall, turned, and leaned back against it, gazing up at the ceiling. "She was a Siberian tigress," he said. "The biggest living cat. The only animal that could possibly carry a Smilodon. My father was lucky enough to acquire her as a cub from San Diego, before he left the Frozen Zoo. Unfortunately, there were deformities in the embryo – both mother and offspring died a few weeks after implantation."

"But implantation was successful?" I considered. "And there's no other cat with a womb that could hold a Smilodon?"

"Have you been to a zoo, Katrina? How many big cats have you seen alive lately?"

I had never been to a zoo. But I got Alexander's meaning.

"And even if I could source one, how would I explain what we wanted it for? I would be locked up." Alexander bared his teeth at the ceiling. "You know the Law."

"Does it have to be a cat?" I asked.

"Short answer: yes," Alexander said. "Not for similarities in body structure, but for diet - it has to be carnivorous. All the largest land mammals are herbivores; the foetus wouldn't get the nutrients it needs from an herbivorous surrogate. We could, hypothetically, use a dog... but I doubt there are any dog breeds large enough to carry a Smilodon foetus to term..."

"That's right," I murmured. "No dog could be strong enough to carry such a magnificent creature."

"It would have to be at least as big as a tiger." Alexander nodded. "Anyway, I've been over all this with Harley before."

"Where did you put the tigress's body after she died?" I asked.

Alexander frowned. He paused while he thought about this. "I wasn't alive back then," he said. "The situation with the tigress happened before I was born. I think the men said they buried her around the back of the building; I don't know precisely where. We still have some tissue samples from her, though - they're in the storage room, with the samples my father collected from San Diego. Why?"

"We could clone another one?" I suggested.

Alexander snorted. "Another tiger? And whose uterus would that grow in?"

It had been a random idea which had somehow slipped through the filter of rationality and come out of my mouth. 'Clone another one', indeed! But I wanted to spite Alexander. I didn't like his tone.

Whose uterus would that grow in?

I searched my brain for a clever comeback, but all I could think to say in response to Alexander's perfectly reasonable question was: '*mine*'.

I didn't say it. Because this got me thinking all over again.

A uterus, according to Alexander's book 'Reproduction in Mammals', is made up of a lining of cells called the 'endothelial cells', in which the embryo implants. These cells form a sack, and the inside of the sack is filled with a fluid called the 'amniotic fluid'. An organ called the 'placenta' takes blood and nutrients from the mother and pumps them into the foetus; it also removes waste, taking it out of the body via the mother. A clever design of Mother Nature's - and luckily, without a patent.

"We would need a huge container,' I mused.

Alexander did not respond. While I had been inside my head, he had been talking to somebody at the bedroom door. I resurfaced to hear the end of their conversation.

"Listen, Harley," Alexander was saying. "We *haven't* finished with the drinks. We *don't* want any food. Go away!"

"I might just come in to change the bed linen, then. And the towels. You don't want to leave filthy towels for your guest..."

"Do it *later*, Harley." Alexander shut the door firmly and marched over to the far wall. He stared at it, arms folded. It was difficult to read his expression - whether he was angry, or merely upset was unclear.

"I would have liked some food," I said.

Alexander didn't look at me. He kept his eyes on the wall. "It's always the same," he said. "It's always the *same*, goddammit!" He beat the wall with both fists.

"They always offer you food at inappropriate times?" I asked.

"Food. Drink. Stationery. Or they want to clean the room, or water the plants. But that's not what they really want. No. They're checking up on me. It's been the same ever since my father *di*..." A whine seeped from the depths of Alexander's throat in place of that word.

Unable to see Alexander's face, I studied his posture: the quiver of his shoulders, the stiffness of his spine. "Stopping in the middle of a word is worse than stopping in the middle of a sentence, Alexander Bai," I told him, kindly but firmly. "Say what you were going to say."

Alexander turned from the wall. Like a wild animal, he crept over to me cautiously, and perched on the bed next to me. "They loved my father," he said. "They were in love with his charisma; they worshipped his brain! That's what they were selected for: not intelligence or ability, but how completely they fell for him. He cultivated that love until they would have done anything for him. Until he became a god to them. But now he's gone… Two years, gone… and *I'm* what they've got left. So they hang around me like religious drones without a messiah, waiting for me to give a command or perform some miracle. And I *should*, I *should* be able to complete this damned experiment for them… but I can't! I'm not… can *never be* my father! He's *dead*!"

That final word had a profound effect on Alexander. As soon as he had said it his eyes grew wide, and his lips began to quiver. He looked at me, a scared, lonely, fatherless child, and the tears started coming; welling in his pale blue eyes, spilling down his perfect white skin.

I couldn't stop myself. Some force beyond my control made me leap at him with, "It *hurts*, doesn't it? It's like… there's a hole inside you. You try to cover it up but the hole's always there, and everything you try to layer on top of it eventually starts to crumble… and nobody ever talks about it, so you pretend it never happened… but sometimes you're alone, or you wake up in the middle of the night, or somebody says something that reminds you, and *you see him*! You remember his scent, and the way his hands felt, and his voice. The things you did together – sitting on the beach at night, watching the stars; walking home through the trees. Sleeping in front of the television with his arms around you. There's no pain like it, is there?"

Alexander's eyes stopped watering. He stared at me for a few seconds longer. Dry-eyed, expressionless. He opened his quivering mouth to speak.

"I can't do this." He hurried from the room: a strangely skittish, adolescent action.

Without a thought, I leapt off the bed and pursued him; across the landing, down the curved staircase.

By the time I had reached the foot of the stairs, Alexander was at the end of the hall with the front door open. He was wearing his white fur-lined coat and pulling on his boots. He looked up, saw me. Hurriedly, he left the building with one boot half-off, slamming the door again.

I don't know what compelled me to keep chasing him. Perhaps it was merely a hunter/prey reflex. But something inside me needed to catch up with Alexander, the same way something inside me needed to be with Chemise when she was crying over Courtney. I knew I was faster than Alexander, and so I continued to run, eyes locked on the door.

However, as I passed the dining room, I was halted by one of the men. It was the same one who had spoken to Alexander earlier: Harley, with the moustache. He reached out, gripped my shoulder tightly. "What happened?" he said. "Hey!"

I tried to wriggle free but he put a hand on my other shoulder and pulled me into the dining room. Gently but firmly, he turned me around to face him. "What happened?"

I hesitated. But his eagerness to find out what was wrong with Alexander seemed to suggest fatherly concern, so I relented. "We were talking about his father," I said. "Then his eyes started watering and he ran off."

Harley sighed. His moustache twitched a little as his lips moved. "Please don't talk about Mr. Bai's father. It gets him so upset."

"But..." I wanted to say so many things in response to this. If Harley thought himself a better authority than me on the feelings of a young person robbed of their father, the man was an utter fool.

"Uh-uh," Harley interrupted. "Best not to mention it."

I stood my ground and glared at him. I wanted to make it clear that I would not be taking orders from him, from *anyone*, anymore.

Eventually, Harley sighed. "Oh, go on, then." He gave a smile but his eyes appeared sad. "Go to him. You know what? I think a female influence might be just what Mr. Bai needs right now."

I slipped into somebody's fur-lined boots, grabbed a winter coat, and ran out into the snow.

After a few minutes' search, I spotted him, standing before the fence. The pure whiteness of his body showed up starkly against the tarnished wire. If he'd been anywhere else, I doubt I would have spotted him. Everything but his eyes matched the snow. Perhaps he wanted to be found.

I went to him. Stood beside him.

For a long time we stood, staring through the wire. The sun emerged briefly from between the clouds. It glinted sharply off the snow beyond the enclosure, throwing harsh light back into our eyes. For a moment, the sky above us was clear. And everywhere about us was whiter than starlight. It should have been beautiful, really - but what I remember more than anything else about that moment was how high that goddamn fence was.

After a minute, I asked Alexander, "Why are they keeping us fenced in?"

"They're not," murmured Alexander. "This is to keep the rest of the world out."

He looped his fingers through the wire and shook the fence to show its sturdiness. Something about the way he did this made him seem like a caged animal.

"Oh." I didn't understand but I nodded, humouring him.

The endless snow stretched before us, unchanging. I looked across at Alexander. His face was blank.

Then he started to speak in monotone.

"When I went down to Los Angeles to find you... that was the first time I'd ever left the compound. I mean, I'd seen LA on television before, but I'd never actually been there myself. The men were so flustered when I told them I needed to go. I guess they thought I'd either fall in love with the outside world and stay there, or be killed by it. But I insisted. Finally, they let me have the keys to the car."

I nodded. "My father wouldn't have wanted me to go alone either. He expected my brother to accompany me."

"They... didn't mention a father or a brother at the university."

"Both dead." I shivered.

"Sorry."

"You didn't do anything."

"I didn't ask about your family. I was too absorbed by my own problems. I'm like that sometimes... too often."

"It's okay." It was. He understood: words, or their lack, didn't change that. "What did you think of Los Angeles?"

"Noisy," said Alexander. "Overcrowded. Beautiful in its own way, I suppose... but vicious."

"Confusing," I added.

"I was trying to put gas in the car one night, and this woman came up to me. She looked young from a distance... but then she came closer, and I saw that she must have been in her sixties at least. She touched my shoulder. And then... she started running her hand down my back, really slowly. Almost in a motherly way, as if she loved me. Until she reached the top of my thigh – then she stopped. She kept her hand where it was, and with her other hand, she brushed the hair away from my ear. And she whispered in my ear... she whispered, 'Give me ten bucks, and I'll...'"

Alexander broke off and shut his eyes tightly. A single droplet formed in the corner of one eye, and dropped down his cheek, leaving a glistening streak. He seemed suddenly aware of it and brushed it away, baring his teeth. "I hung up the gas pump and got out of there as fast as I could." Alexander opened his eyes. "But I threw ten dollars at her first. She could have been a scientist. My father said that's what some scientists ended up resorting to - especially if they had children to feed."

I nodded slowly. I turned away from him; looked into the whiteness. "What happened to your mother?" I asked.

I could sense him turn to me, but I didn't look back. I kept my eyes on the world outside the fence. "What happened to your mother?" I repeated.

Again, Alexander was quiet for a moment. Then, "I never had a mother," he whispered.

"Of course you did," I said. "Everybody has a mother." I assumed his comment was another offhand remark; an illogical cliché. I told myself I had no time for them - even though, looking back, I now remember that I once used the same cliché to refer to my own situation.

"Well, what do you want me to say?" Alexander's voice hardened. "Whenever I asked my father, that was always his response. *You never had a mother, Alexander. Only me.*"

"He was lying," I said. "You must know he was. Everyone has a mother."

Alexander shook his head. "I think I told you... before my father came here, he was a famous scientist in the field of cloning? People wanted clones of their dying pets. My father pandered to their requests. But he took it one step further - instead of creating an identical copy, he would change the animal slightly. Remove a faulty gene, give it a faster metabolism, a nicer temperament – anything the owner requested, and sometimes things they didn't. The new animal was always stronger, better than the original."

"Amazing." Although the thought of tampering with the body and brain of an animal sent something of a shiver down my spine, this was, admittedly, incredible. By now, I had a good understanding of cloning from Alexander's books: 'The process by which a genetically identical copy of a single specimen is made. In animals, this is usually achieved by transferring chromosomes from a living organism into an empty egg cell, and allowing this to develop into a foetus which is genetically identical to the original specimen'. But to manipulate the offspring; to mould them to your vision of perfection? That was simultaneously repulsive and wonderful.

"Child's play." Alexander bared his teeth. "All the time he was doing that, he was preparing to transfer the same techniques to a different animal; to attempt something which had always been illegal, even when science itself was legal. I take it you know what I am talking about?"

I lied that I did; I didn't want to interrupt his flow.

"I have my father's eyes, his hair," said Alexander. "The same short stature. Maybe a faster metabolism: he was rather overweight. I had the same visual problems he had, before he corrected mine with the implant. I have the same nose, same lips, same cheekbones. The same double-jointed middle finger." He flexed the freakish digit to demonstrate. "And the same temper. According to Harley. So, can you see why... I don't think I have a mother?"

I did now.

"But I get so confused!" Alexander rested his forehead on the fence, letting the wire bear his entire weight, as if his body had decided to give up. "By my age, my father was already starting his doctorate and had several books published. He was becoming a distinguished scientist. Whereas I... well." He turned his face, against the fence, towards me; looked at me with large, moist, child-eyes.

Irritated as I was that he had not finished his sentence, I didn't give him any prompting. I forced myself to wait patiently until he was ready to speak.

Finally, Alexander said, "Twenty-plus years of intensive training - since I was practically a *toddler*, for God's sakes - and I still cannot get my brain around how this blasted experiment is going to work!"

I thought about this. "Maybe intelligence doesn't work like that," I ventured. "Maybe your intelligence lies dormant - until something sparks it into life."

"What sort of something?"

"Well." I thought. "You've been locked in here for however many years you've been alive. Coming to LA and finding me was a good start." I threaded my fingers through the fence and peered out through the cross-hatching, at what must have been Alexander's whole world for the last 'twenty-plus' years.

After what seemed like a long time, I felt Alexander put his hand on my shoulder. The inevitable goosepimples started to prickle along my back at the unexpected contact. But I did not remove the hand.

I let Alexander turn me away from the fence. Together, we walked back up to the Lodge.

#

Goosepimples start up my back again.

I shiver them away. Have to focus.

After five specimens, the procedure is becoming simple. I use my scalpel to break down the organic material from the freezer, add this to one of the test tubes then introduce the chemicals.

I wonder if Doctor Tati ever reached this point, when he could do this sort of thing without thinking...

I put down my scalpel and look at the ceiling.

Doctor Tati. Probably the most hated man in the history of science. So hated that the involvement of his peers, Doctor Monroe and Doctor Bai, in the experiments he confessed to is often overshadowed. And now – here I am, more or less replicating his experiments.

What does that make me?

I remember something a lonely truck driver told me, years ago. About how people had no right to condemn Doctor Tati's experiment, because they never understood its purpose. Well, when I discovered the true purpose of Tati's experiment, I was more horrified by the motive than I had been by the procedure. The motive behind Tati's experiment is what made it evil.

My motive is different. This time, no innocents will suffer for humanity's whim.

As I turn back to test tube number six, I cannot help but wonder... what would Alexander's reaction be, if he were to discover what his former pet genius is about to do to the world?

CHAPTER TWENTY-ONE

Harley was standing on the porch, rubbing his hands together, breathing silver plumes into the icy air. He waved at us as we arrived and beamed broadly. I was able to confidently label him as 'Harley' now: that bristly, red moustache, and his frequent presence in Alexander's life, made him stand out from the other near-identical men-in-white drifting about the building.

"Hello, you two!" he called. "What have you been doing, hmm?"

Alexander turned away from Harley's stare, so I took it upon myself to respond. "Brainstorming," I lied.

"Oh, good!" Harley smiled. "Any new ideas?"

"Yes," I said.

Alexander looked at me.

"Oh," said Harley. "How exciting!"

"You have an idea?" Alexander mouthed to me.

Subtly, I nodded.

Harley came down the steps to meet us. "I'll get you each a hot chocolate," he decided. "Would you like that?"

"Yes," I said, answering for the both of us. Alexander looked as if he would benefit from a hot chocolate. "But first, I am going to ask you a favour."

"Of course," said Harley. "What is it?"

"I want to see where the tigress from Doctor Bai's experiment was buried," I said. "Will you show me?"

Harley fell silent for a moment. Then he laughed. It was not a normal laugh. "Why?" He grinned – too wide. "You're not planning on doing any grave-robbing, are you? There are plenty of tissue samples from her in storage."

"No graves will be robbed. I just want to see."

"Yes." Alexander spoke up. "So would I." He took a step closer to Harley. Harley took a step back. "You told me when I was a child that she was buried somewhere in the compound - but you would never show me where. I want to see now. If only to put the past to rest before we start afresh."

Harley laughed again. "As you wish. Come with me."

I tried to keep in line with Alexander and Harley, but they were slow, and I found myself overtaking. I looked back at Harley. "Go ahead," he said. He smiled and made a little waving motion with his hands. "I'll tell you when we get there." As I moved on, I heard his voice trail away, "So, you two seem to be getting along…"

With Alexander and Harley trudging behind me, I marched steadily on through the snow, glancing back every so often for a nod from Harley to confirm that I was going in the right direction.

Once we had passed the Lodge, it was not that far to the fence at the back of the compound. I stepped carefully over the Behemoth's icy tracks. These formed a wide curve which ran from the front gates, around the side of the building, and ended at the door to a long garage which protruded from the Lodge's back wall.

Beyond these tracks, the snow was untouched and thick, and the uphill incline made the going slightly harder. Barely twenty feet from the back fence, Harley called, "You can stop now. The grave is right in front of you."

Alexander stopped beside Harley. No footsteps now. Softly, the wind hummed and whistled. The sun kept trying to penetrate the snow-clouds. Leering through the mist, the wire fence glinted intermittently as the light touched it.

"Thank you, Harley," Alexander said. "It's good to know." I heard him start to turn away.

I crept forward. Treading lightly over the snow, I detected an area of ground beneath which a hollow had been forged. The area where a body is buried always feels slightly different from regular ground; I had learnt, through childhood walks in the graveyard with Father, how to recognise the subtle differences in the soil.

I dropped to my knees. Lay down. Rested my cheek against the snow.

"Katrina?" I could hear Alexander say, somewhere behind me. "What are you doing?"

She was down there. The brave creature that had suffered in vain to bring a new, stronger life into the world.

"Paying my respects," I called back.

I lifted my cheek. With my finger, I drew a little spiral pattern in the snow: my cousins' symbol for 'maternity'.

"That's nice, Katrina," Harley said, as I got to my feet and turned towards him. "But I think we should go inside now. Please? I'm cold." He shuffled from foot to foot, demonstrating.

Alexander said nothing. However, it was clear from his expression that he was thinking. He seemed concerned.

I cast another glance back at the tigress's final resting place. Then I followed Harley and Alexander.

As I stepped over the snow, I strayed slightly from the path I had made to the tigress's grave. I noticed a difference in the ground beneath my feet again. I stopped.

It was Alexander who first realised that I was no longer following. He motioned for Harley to stop. "What's wrong?" he called.

I stepped twice on the spot, to make sure that my feet hadn't been deceiving me. There could be no doubt about it.

"There's another body here!" I shouted.

Alexander stared at me. Then he looked at Harley. Harley shook his head. "No," Harley said, loud enough for me to hear. "There was only the one tigress. Come on, both of you!"

Alexander looked back at me. "What makes you think there's another body?"

It would have been pointless to try to explain, intelligent as they both were. Even I was unsure how I could detect this second grave. "Trust me."

Harley had already started back, hugging his coat around him and rubbing his shoulders to highlight his distaste for the cold. Alexander lingered a moment longer, looking at me. Then he turned and went with Harley. Realising that they would not be coming back for me, I followed at a sprint.

As I neared them, I overheard Alexander saying to Harley, "...it's not unusual for a genius to be a bit... I mean, look at Doctor Tati...", to which Harley replied, "Yes, look how he ended up." As I approached, Harley turned and saw me. He gave me a strained smile. "Oh good," he said loudly. "Katrina's caught up."

He started talking to Alexander again, loud enough that I could hear. Only this time, he talked about pointless things like how regrettable it was that they had been able to secure only one tigress, and how that had only come about due to James Bai's disregard for the law.

"Of course, I understand why they have these restrictions on giving away animals," Harley said as we passed the garage. "Endangered or not, it isn't fair to use any live animal in non-medical research. It's simply unethical. Especially when you consider that the experiment might all come to nothing..."

"Stop it," Alexander said. For the first time on the walk, he looked straight at Harley. "Let's not get into this again."

I frowned, confused.

We stepped over the Behemoth's tyre tracks and made our way around the side of the Lodge. Partway down the wall, a door opened, and one of Alexander's men-in-white stepped out. The man held a cigarette between his fingers; smoke lifted into the air as he brought the little white stick to his lips. Then he turned, saw us.

I tried to give him a smile.

But the man's eyes had settled on Alexander. Quickly, he threw the cigarette to the snow and stamped it out with his boot, cast a smile hastily in Harley's direction then disappeared back into the Lodge.

"Why didn't we go in through that other door?" I asked Alexander. We were at the front of the Lodge now, about to ascend the porch steps.

Alexander's foot paused on the first step. He turned to me, but it was Harley who answered. "Because that's the kitchen," he said.

This response seemed to satisfy Alexander, who nodded and went up the steps. Assuming I had missed something obvious, I nodded too, and followed him. Harley brought up the rear.

At the door, Harley stepped aside to let Alexander and me enter. I let Alexander in ahead of me and hung back. I looked hard at Harley. "There were two bodies," I insisted.

Harley shook his head and held my stare. "So you keep saying. I don't see how you think you can tell, but you're wrong. Go inside, now. We can't have you freezing to death on us!"

#

That evening Alexander and I went down to the laboratory. Alexander brought his office chair through from his work room, and I crouched at the edge of the pit. Together, we sat and watched the Smilodon foetus as it floated, ghostlike: an Earth-bound spirit, waiting to be reborn. While we watched, I told Alexander my idea.

"It's simple," I said. "We'll drain this pit. Create a lining for the base made of 'endothelial cells', like the book said. There must be a chemical or something that can encourage cells to grow. We'll have a layer of them, covering the inside." With my hand, I indicated the concave shape of the pit; more to help myself visualise the plan than to explain to Alexander what I meant. "The Smilodon won't know it's growing in a 'hot-tub' instead of a womb. Not as long as it's covered with womb-cells."

"I'm with you so far," Alexander said, nodding. "Although I can already see one flaw."

I ignored him. "We'll plant one of the embryos in the lining. Once the placenta grows, we can create a sort of stream under the lining. We'll link it up to two tanks." Again I gestured: two large cylinders, side by side, at the edge of the pit. "One can be for the removal of waste; one of us will have to empty that every so often - we can work on a rota. But that doesn't matter now. The other tank, we can fill with some sort of solution, like... blood."

"Blood?" Alexander scoffed. "And where are we going to get that much blood?"

"We can synthesise it."

"Oh, can we now?"

"Give me the tools - *I'll* synthesise it," I said.

"No, you can't. You're an undergraduate with no lab training."

"I have more college training than you." As Alexander choked, I thought back to the books he had given me. "It's just a matter of taking little samples of blood and making all the components multiply, isn't it? We've both got plenty of blood."

"That's a bit of an oversimplification," said Alexander. "It would require some of the molecules to be synthesized from scratch, and the technology that would enable us to do that isn't supposed to exist, but... alright. Let's say it's possible. What about the endothelial cell lining? Where do we get those cells?"

"From a womb, of course," I said impatiently. "We have one here. And then we encourage those cells to multiply - with a chemical, like I said."

"Alright." Alexander stood up. "Alright, I'll go take a look. But I'm not making any promises. I don't see how it could work." He disappeared into his work room.

I had no idea what he had gone to do, and I wanted to find out, but the surreal scene before me held me hypnotised. I decided to wait five minutes. I counted the seconds under my breath, following the subtle movements of the floating foetus with unblinking eyes.

When three hundred Mississippi-seconds had elapsed and Alexander had still not returned, I sighed. With a final fond look at the foetus, I tore myself away from the pit and went into the work room.

As I approached the double-doors, I became conscious of the ever-present sound of whirring machinery in the laboratory. Usually, in the work room, this sound was barely noticeable. It was present in the 'Hot Tub' room, but only as a muffled hum from behind the back wall. I stopped; listened. The volume of the noise had risen considerably. It sounded like the breath of an aged creature, labouring to stay alive.

I forced my way through the metal doors.

In the work room, Alexander was closing a door in the wall behind his desk. I hadn't noticed this door before: its label, 'Staff Only', was just visible in faded, grey paint. When Alexander closed the door, the whirring sound became muffled again.

Alexander locked the door. Slipping the key into his pocket, he turned and saw me. "Ah – there you are." He was carrying something - a glass jar of thick, translucent liquid. He held it out to me as he approached and pushed it into my hands. "This is the only uterine tissue that we have in storage," he explained. "It's from the tigress. But I'm afraid there's only a slim chance that we can salvage any cells; my father hasn't taken much care in preserving it."

I held the jar up to my face. Inside, something small and sad floated, with all the life and vitality of a dried banana skin. With a frown of disgust, I handed it back to Alexander. "It's completely dead," I said.

Alexander looked back hopelessly at the 'Staff Only' door. "Well, I'm afraid that's the only suitable tissue we have in storage."

Now I realised what Alexander - with that classic human tendency to overlook the obvious - had failed to understand. "No! I didn't mean that we use cells from the *tiger's* womb; I meant *mine*."

Alexander turned back to me. "Yours?" He sucked on his lower lip. Blinked once, twice, as if to clear his vision. "Your uterus?"

"It's alive. Mammalian. Unused. It's sure to be full of cells: I'm at the most fertile point in my reproductive cycle."

Alexander stared at me for a long time. "Yes," he said eventually. "That could work."

"You'll have to cut me open," I said. "Please numb me first."

We went back to the Hot Tub room. I crouched down by the pit and Alexander came to crouch beside me. Together, we watched the foetus float: alien and ghostly, enchanting.

"Amniotic fluid," I murmured. "We'll need amniotic fluid."

"I can make that."

"Are you sure?"

"Of course I'm sure!" Alexander snapped. "It's basic biochemistry. I'm not completely useless." He paused. "Sorry… Katrina, are you sure you want to do this?"

"Obviously," I said. "Don't you?"

"It's my father's dream. Of course I do." Alexander continued to stare, hypnotised, into the pit. "Yes… I want, more than anything, to grow an artificial womb from the cells of a human female, to resurrect an extinct animal to satisfy my dead father… God, I'm screwed up!" He gave a shrill little laugh. "Maybe it comes with not having a mother."

"I never had a mother, either," I admitted. "And yet, we both turned out perfectly normal."

Alexander looked at me. "You think so?"

"No," I said, surprised. "I was trying to make a joke."

"Oh." Alexander chewed his lip. "Well, it's not like I can criticise. I don't have much of a sense of humour either." He turned back to the pit. "You know, in some… well, in *many* ways, Katrina… you are uncannily like me."

#

The morning after I told him my idea, Alexander took me back into his work room and together we drew up plans: who would do what, when we would do it, and how. Alexander was keen to have as big a role as possible in the practical side of things, perhaps to compensate for not having come up with the method. I was happy to oblige.

The next day, Alexander and I, clad in long rubber gloves and sterile white coats, lifted the delicate little body from the pit and transferred it to a large pickling-jar of translucent fluid.

"To keep it preserved," Alexander explained. "Don't look so worried, Katrina! All the other tissue samples have been through the same process."

Once Alexander had sealed the jar, he took it through the double-doors to the work room. I followed; watched curiously from behind as Alexander unlocked the 'Staff Only' door and pulled it open.

The door turned out to be a gateway to the most peculiar storage room I had ever seen. A long, pristine-white pantry, smelling faintly of alcohol, and lined with rows upon rows of wooden shelves. On these shelves lived all the other tissue samples in Alexander's possession, floating in their jars in the dark. Perhaps hoping for resurrection themselves.

I watched Alexander move jars of lion and tiger fragments aside to make room for our foetus. "I should have done this a long time ago," he said. "It's not like we need her out of storage; not since my father created the embryos. We shouldn't be needing any more DNA from her. I guess I only keep her in the pit for inspiration."

"How many embryos did your father make?" I asked, not caring, but needing the distraction. Anything to take my mind off the scene before me. Those rows of sad, pickled bodies...

"A dozen," he said. "Hold on; I'll show you." He lifted something out from beneath a lower shelf: a blue box, about the size of a small refrigerator – and, judging by Alexander's groans, just as heavy. It was emitting a loud, steady whirr. The box had padded straps attached to the back, so that it could be transported by hand or over the shoulder if necessary.

Alexander lowered the box carefully to the floor. "It's called a CryoBag. A portable cryogenic freezer. Practically impossible to lift, granted; but necessary, in case of emergency evacuation. My father designed it." He lifted the lid and beckoned me over.

I went to him. Peered inside.

"There was a space of about twenty years between the tigress dying and my father's own passing," said Alexander. "He had given up on seeing the experiment through to completion himself. This is what he spent those years creating, down here in the lab, while I grew up. I was given strict instructions never to disturb him while he was down here. I only disobeyed these orders once, and... well." He smiled and touched the side of his jaw; here I saw something, almost invisible against the white of his skin, which could have been a scar. "Never again. If Harley hadn't intervened, I doubt I would have gotten off so lightly." He closed the CryoBag. "We only have these twelve. We must make every one count."

"I intend to make every one count," I said, highly offended that Alexander felt he needed to emphasise this to me. It was as if he didn't believe that I was as passionate as he was about our Smilodon. "In fact," I boasted, "I will only need to use *one*."

But I couldn't get the thought out of my head. As Alexander sat me down on the office chair and helped me to peel the sticky rubber gloves from my hands, I could picture them: twelve young Smilodon cubs, running and gambolling through the work room. Rolling on the ground, play-fighting, as the Island's youngsters did every year after winter's end, when their mothers brought them out, hairless and mobile, from their dens and into the sunshine. Alexander and I would start with one, but I wouldn't let it be an only child. Not when it was the only one of its kind, being raised by parents of a different species...

I looked up at Alexander. He was gazing absently at my fingers, lost in his own thoughts.

#

What a pity.

What a pity it is that humanity is so quick to place a mould over whatever they see or hear. A mould based on whatever moralistic or pseudo-scientific dogma they were fed as children. So quick to disregard anything that does not fit this mould.

I was never like that. No. I never succumbed to the desire to form a mould of my own... no matter how comforting that promised to be. I wanted to keep an open mind, to know the truth - about civilisation, about the world, about humanity. And now I do.

And it has been beneficial. Because now I know what repairs have to be made.

I finished working on specimen twenty-two this morning. The scalpel is in the kitchen sink, and test tube twenty-two is now in the freezer, where the liquid inside will congeal around its organic contents, cushioning them until I am ready for them. Then they can fulfil their purpose.

There are four more empty test tubes lined up along the desk in my shack in the middle of nowhere. The twenty-six test tubes I managed to steal from Alexander before I heard his footsteps behind me, turned to give him that final farewell glance, and ran for the hills. Twenty-six test tubes... and twenty-eight tissue samples. Needing new homes. Or else they go to waste.

Twenty-six test tubes.

Twenty-six test tubes is not enough.
Damn Alexander!
Damn me…

CHAPTER TWENTY-TWO

When evening fell and Harley came down to the laboratory, looking inquisitive but keeping his questions to himself, to tell us that dinner was ready, Alexander announced that he was going to stay late that night. He said that I should go and eat, however; then get some rest to be ready for tomorrow.

"Why, what happens tomorrow?" I was standing in the corridor, halfway between Harley, who was holding the elevator door for me, and Alexander, who was at the work room door, rolling a fresh pair of rubber gloves over his hands. Above me, the light-panels in the ceiling flickered nauseatingly. Somebody would have to fix those before the Smilodon was born: I couldn't have it developing epilepsy.

"Well." Alexander wrangled a glove over his bony wrist, not looking at me. "I spoke to Harley about your idea to harvest the endothelial cells from your own uterus. He said we could perform the procedure tomorrow morning."

"No time like the present." Harley's jowls lifted and, beneath his moustache, his teeth became exposed: large and dangerous.

"I'm ashamed to say, I don't know much about... these sorts of things." I heard Alexander shuffle back a few paces into the work room. He was clearly eager to get started on whatever he intended to do tonight. "But Harley said that if we don't do the procedure within the next few days, we'll have to wait a full month for another healthy sample. Something about your... 'cycle'. That is still okay, isn't it, Katrina?"

Harley's bottomless brown eyes bored into my face. I tore away to face Alexander; saw that his eyes were on me too now, glinting through the half-dark of the corridor like the eyes of a prey-bird on a mouse. My leg muscles tensed, ready to run.

"Of course it's okay," I said – perhaps too loudly.

I hurried down the corridor, pushed Harley aside, and dived into the elevator where I stood, stiff and silent, my eyes closed against the thick blackness, willing my heart to stop racing.

Against the black shroud behind my eyes, I could picture Father, his face the night he told me he had renounced leadership so that I could live. And Rawg, forever childless: dragging himself back to the Edu-Centre alone, night after night, that final Spring.

Intruding on this, the memory of three little balls of soft fur beneath my hand.

I didn't touch them. I didn't...

"Have to keep going," I murmured to myself. "Have to keep going."

Nobody woke me the next morning, but somebody – probably Harley – had left an apple and a glass of pink milk by my bed. There was also a note, asking me to put on comfortable clothes and come down to the laboratory when I felt ready.

I selected a pair of maternity pants from the wardrobe and fastened them around my waist with Alexander's belt. Then I rummaged beneath my bed for the pink sweater I had been wearing for the last three days.

Retrieving it, inside-out, I noticed the hand-written label stitched to the inside collar: 'Property of Sonja'. As if the owner, presumably the sole pregnant female in the building at the time, had felt the need to take precautions against her sweater being accidentally given to one of the men. What a strange woman.

I pulled it on.

I picked up the apple. And now the sickness stirred. I could picture them: Harley and Alexander, waiting for me downstairs. Waiting with scalpels. Waiting to cut me open.

I steeled myself. Then I consumed the apple, core and all, the sourness searing my throat, my stomach churning. I noticed the mirror on the wardrobe door and glared at the scrawny girl I saw staring pleadingly out at me, swamped in maternity clothes, apple juice dribbling from her lips.

"This is going to happen, whether you like it or not."

I swigged down the pink milk and left the room.

When I returned to the Hot Tub room, I found most of the floor space taken up by large, plastic bottles. Each was labelled with a peeling 'Bleach-Based Pool Cleaner' sticker. But of course, there couldn't have been bleach in them, because bleach damaged the environment and wasn't sold any longer. EcoTech's *SynthetiBleach* was the best thing on the market now, according to the commercials: almost as effective as regular bleach, and well worth the fifty-dollar-per-gallon price tag. Nevertheless, there was liquid in these bottles. A mysterious, gloopy, translucent liquid.

I spotted Alexander sitting against the far wall, cross-legged, screwing the lid tightly onto a final bottle. He looked up at me and smiled. There were heavy bags under his eyes. "Surprise! What did I tell you?"

I tried to pick up one of the bottles to examine it but could barely lift its weight. "What's in these?"

"Fluid," said Alexander, proudly. "More than enough to fill the pit, I should think."

My eyes widened. "You're filling it with bleach?"

Alexander laughed. "These were empty containers Harley found in the garage. They've been sterilised. It's amniotic fluid inside them – or a close enough substitute, anyway. And now… I am afraid we need the lining."

I nodded. I was prepared for this.

Alexander rose stiffly. He smiled at me again. This time, I got the impression that he was trying to appear reassuring. "I had the men erect another table in my work room," he said. "Please, come on through."

I followed him through. There was, indeed, a table in the room which hadn't been there before. A white folding table, standing between the cage and Alexander's desk, directly beneath the naked, hanging bulb.

At one end of the table stood Harley, wearing rubber gloves and an apron. He grinned at me. "Hello, Katrina."

"Harley is going to perform the procedure," Alexander explained. "He's worked in surgical theatres before." He put his hands on my shoulders, and for once, I did not recoil, my body too stiff to resist the touch. I let him guide me forward.

"I was a surgical nurse, briefly. Between my lab assistant career and working for Doctor Bai," said Harley. "I've assisted with quite a few caesareans in my time."

"Don't worry. I'll be here to observe," Alexander said. And he removed his hands from my shoulders.

I felt a chill.

The light from the bulb glinted fiercely off the table now; off the shining, sterilized floor; off Harley's white laboratory coat – right into my eyes. I was seeing swirls, black dots. I had to look away.

"You're not having second thoughts, are you, Katrina?"

I made myself glance up. Alexander was now standing beside Harley. Both men were smiling at me - identical smiles, full of glistening, sharp, white teeth.

Alexander patted the table.

"Hop up," smiled Harley.

Harley numbed me effectively for the procedure. But barely an hour after he had announced our success, the numbing-agent started to wear off. A throb, growing stronger, angrier, began to consume my lower body.

Alexander was back in the Hot Tub room, unreachable. In a weak whisper, I managed to communicate my discomfort to Harley, who was cleaning his hideous sharp instruments by my makeshift bedside. He said the pain was normal.

When the agony became too great and I started to writhe, he held me down on the table by placing a hand on my chest. He injected something into my forearm and carried my now-limp body to the elevator as the world around me turned black.

#

After a week or so of my being confined to bed, Harley told Alexander, who was watching over me from my door, that I had sufficiently recovered from the procedure. The pain was unlikely to come back and if it did, I was strong enough to handle it. I was, in his words, a "tough little thing".

Once Harley had gone downstairs, Alexander asked gently if I would help him bring two empty oil canisters down to the laboratory. Grateful to be allowed back on my feet again, I stumbled to the bathroom to dress.

After checking that I was tightly swaddled in the mysterious 'Sonja's' maternity clothes, Alexander led me downstairs, and out to the garage. This was where Alexander's Behemoth and two small, low-crouching vehicles – 'snowmobiles' - were housed. It also stored gasoline, oil, cleaning products, and food: masses of it - dried grains, piled high in sacks; towers of canned pulses, vegetables, protein supplements. Everything to keep man and vehicle fuelled for an entire winter.

Experimentally, I wormed my finger into a plastic rice sack, and dabbed a few grains on my tongue. I wrinkled my nose at the taste.

"Katrina!" Alexander called. "Don't get distracted. We've work to do."

He beckoned me over to a mountain of empty containers, piled high at the furthest, darkest end of the garage. I approached, stepping carefully over boxes and bottles which must have fallen from the main bulk in previous landslides.

"Sorry. I know this must seem incredibly disorganised. But it's not as if we can drive these things to a recycling centre," Alexander muttered. "Anyway, this space was built for a hundred cars: there's plenty of room here to store everything. For now, at least."

I picked up a bottle from the floor and tried to read the age-worn label. A sour, repulsive smell lingered on its gunk-encrusted lid.

We eased two empty canisters from the pile and dragged them through the snow, into the Lodge, down to the basement. These were to be the bodies for our nutritional and waste disposal apparatuses.

"Won't be long now, Katrina – won't be long now!"

Alexander brought a roll of netting through from the storage room. We stretched it over the pit, a few inches from the base.

"Your cells are developing quickly," Alexander told me, as he secured the net along the edge of the pit. "I'll have them transferred to this scaffold soon; before long, we'll have our lining."

Synthesising the blood took Alexander another month. He retreated to his work room to do this. Meanwhile, I sat at the edge of the pit, watching proudly as my cells grew over the scaffold. Whatever magical chemical Alexander had used, it gave my cells superhuman abilities: they spread across the pit like a conquering army. I had never felt so powerful.

Alexander's blood molecules, however, multiplied with pitiful, anaemic slowness. This led me to win a bet, and a hypothetical five dollars, and Alexander to spend days lamenting his own physical, as well as intellectual, shortcomings, as he waited for the last of the blood to develop.

Poor Alexander.

But he shook off his self-pity when I lied that the pains in my abdomen had returned, and asked him to take over the next stage of the project.

The alterations to the canisters were completed. Alexander hauled them through from his work room, and pushed them into position by the pit. He tucked the tubes – segments of hosepipe, which now led from the adapted cylinders - under the lining and, carefully, he poured in the blood-solution.

Then we filled the pit with the amniotic fluid. Bottle by bottle, throwing each fading bleach container out into the corridor as we emptied it, our excitement bubbling over into a fever, until the room was empty and it was just us standing there again, at the edge of the pit, gazing down into the liquid.

The womb was complete. Now all we had to do was implant the embryo.

#

That night, we slept on the floor of the Hot Tub room - dubbed by myself the 'Womb Room'. Slept late into the afternoon.

The next day, Alexander shook me awake and summoned me to his work room. Doctor Bai's 'portable' CryoBag lay open on his desk, which was buckling under its weight. Alexander told me to close my eyes. He whispered to me, "The choice is yours. Point into the bag, Katrina - no peeking."

When I had done this, he ushered me back through to the Womb Room to wait until he had harvested the embryo that I had chosen. He kept the double-doors open, so I could see what he was doing.

According to Doctor Bai's book on cloning domestic species, the fertilized ovum of a cat will begin to divide naturally after two to three days. After this, the cells will continue to divide every ten to fourteen hours, creating a small cluster. Doctor Bai's Smilodon clusters were four to five days old before they were frozen, Alexander told me – tiny; invisible to the naked eye.

But *there*. Definitely *there*.

That was apparent in the paternal care Alexander demonstrated as he lifted my selected test tube from the vat of cold, vaporous liquid within the bag, and carried it through to the womb room in his white-gloved hands. As he lay on his stomach by the pit and stretched out his skeletal arms as far as they would go, the beads of sweat standing on his painfully-furrowed brow reminded me…

…*this is* Alexander's *baby, as much as it is mine.*

The long, silver poking device shook between Alexander's rubber-coated fingers as he speared the needle through the pit's membrane cover, and drove it closer, closer to my cells. He paused.

Then he pressed the plunger at the end of the device. A slight movement stirred the liquid around the needle's tip.

"Done," he said. I could sense the relief emanating from Alexander.

He lay on his stomach for several more seconds, eyes wide. Finally, he got up.

I went to him.

We stood together by the edge of the pit. Alexander's hand crept into mine; I accepted it, hating the clamminess of his skin, but knowing he needed the reassurance. We said our silent prayers to the gods we weren't sure we believed in, and we waited.

We must have watched that pit for hours. Finally, there came a point when both of us were struggling to stay awake. The next time Harley came down to check up on us, Alexander reluctantly appointed him night sentry, and the two of us went up in the elevator to bed.

"God... I hope this works," whispered Alexander. At the foot of the staircase, he froze. It was as if the thought of failure had just struck him.

I was almost at the top of the staircase now. I turned to him. His white face had become dull over the preceding weeks; drained. His skin had tightened and the bags under his eyes had darkened and become heavier, so that his eyes now appeared too big for his face.

I forced myself to smile for him. "It will be alright, Alexander. Go and get some sleep."

I continued up the staircase, went to my room, and closed the door. I lay down on the bed, staring up at the ceiling, listening.

Finally, from across the landing, I heard Alexander's bedroom door click shut. Satisfied, I let myself sleep.

#

The next morning, I was roused by Alexander hollering my name through the building. "Katrina! Katrina, get down here now!"

I slid out of bed. Pulling on my bathrobe, heart beating double-speed, I ran barefoot out onto the landing and followed the sound of Alexander's voice to the staircase.

Alexander was standing on the bottom stair, looking up at me. He was wearing his white laboratory coat over his pyjamas. His face had contorted into an expression I couldn't recognise as 'good' or 'bad'. What was clear, however, was that *something* had happened.

"Alexander? What's happening?"

He did not answer. Instead, he beckoned to me urgently then gestured towards the elevator. "C-Come to the *laboratory*, Kat!" he finally spat. "Now!"

The force of that final word sent me hurrying down the stairs without a second question.

In the elevator, Alexander said nothing. He restrained his mania to an awkward shuffling from foot to foot. This did nothing to quell my apprehension - not to mention my elevator-related paranoia. I hissed at him, "Stop it," but he continued.

As soon as the doors opened onto the basement floor, Alexander exploded out of the elevator and sprinted down the corridor. The light-panels overhead were still on: he must have been down here recently. I ran behind, following him through the right-hand door into the Womb Room.

Alexander came to an abrupt halt at edge of the pit. I hung back by the doorway.

Noticing that I was missing, Alexander looked around, frowning. "What are you doing?"

"I'm barefoot," I said. "I don't want to contaminate anything."

Alexander looked down at my naked feet, my gnarled toenails, poking out from under the too-long legs of my pyjama bottoms. He smiled, and said, "It's alright, Kat. Just this once." And he beckoned again.

I ran to him. Stood beside him.

Together, we looked over the edge of the pit, into the amniotic fluid. It had the same colour and consistency as before. I glanced at the nutritional and waste-disposal tanks: they were still making their faint 'whooshing' sounds as fluid passed in and out, refreshing the stream of faux blood which ran beneath the endothelial layer.

"What am I supposed to be looking at?" I asked Alexander. "I don't see anything unusual."

Alexander pointed to the space between the two tanks. Here he had positioned a white, plastic tube. A foot-long section of the tube was poking out from the surface of the pit; the longer section stretched beneath the surface, into the fluid. The membrane had puckered around it.

"You have stuck a foreign object through the membrane," I observed, trying to conceal my panic.

Alexander ignored me. "Cover one eye, and look down there," he urged.

I gave him a suspicious look as I crouched down between the two tanks, covered one of my eyes with my palm, and rested my other eye against the glass top of the long tube. I looked down into the pit. As I looked, the tanks heaved and lowed on either side of me, rhythmically, healthily.

I could hear Alexander's voice behind me – soft, almost a whisper. "Amazing, isn't it? It's dividing so quickly! I mean, I've seen it happen before. My father used to show me bacterial samples multiplying, when this was his lab - and there were the photographs, diagrams in books, the video tapes… I've even been unfortunate enough to witness one of my own failed experiments divide once, then die. But nothing compares to this. To think, one of those cells could become part of a new arm, a heart, a brain. It's alive, Katrina! We've done it. We've created a healthy life!"

I took my eye away from the microscope. Shakily, I got to my feet. My heart was beating to an unfamiliar rhythm. My eyelids seemed to have lost the ability to close.

I turned to Alexander. He was standing behind me, leaning against the wall, watching from a distance. That expression on his face: the widest, whitest smile I had ever seen this side of a television screen. "So? What do you think, Kat?"

None of the words in my vocabulary could express how I felt at this moment. And so I threw myself at Alexander Bai.

I pinned him against the wall, my left hand over his left shoulder, my right clamping his right shoulder, and forced my lips against his.

Alexander tasted of sterilisation. Unsavoury creams and ointments. Mint toothpaste. Mouthwash. His lips were inorganically soft; his body warm.

"We've done it." I pulled back to whisper in his ear, "We've done it. A child. We have a child!"

"Katrina?"

I blinked.

Alexander was standing, as he had been before, a few feet away and facing me. He arched a brow. "You're staring. Why?"

"Because…" The taste on my lips: no longer real, a spirit, fading. My heartbeat slowed.

Alexander twisted his lips. He brushed a loose strand of silky hair behind one ear; his double-jointed middle finger flexed.

I tried and failed to arrange the thoughts in my head. Then, "Music!" I said decisively.

Alexander told me to wait and left the room. I heard the elevator ascend. While he was gone, I squatted again in the space between the two canisters and looked through the lens of the microscope.

I swear, in the short space of time that my attention had been diverted, our creature had grown to several times its original size. And with every passing second, it was growing bigger; stronger. The ancient cat was drawing on its primordial strength to claw its way gloriously into the present.

I withdrew, backed out from between the canisters. I shuffled to the edge of the pit, and looked down into the area where, although I could not see it yet without Alexander's technology, I knew our little force of nature was developing.

I could feel in my arms: a soft, compact weight, the head nestled against my chest, four little paws batting gently at the air. Feather-soft hair beneath my fingers, warm with life. Its tiny chest rising and falling, rising and falling...

I heard the elevator returning to the basement; footsteps approaching. I turned as the door opened. Alexander came into the room, his arms full of CD cases and tiny boxes. He cast a quick glance in my direction as he made his way to the double-doors. "Just give me a second." He disappeared into his work room.

Moments passed silently. Then I heard a drumbeat. It increased in volume.

A pack of guitars, violins, vocalists burst into the room, filling with a wonderful blast of music which sent all the hairs down my back standing to attention.

Hastily, the volume decreased. Alexander emerged from the work room. "How's that?"

"I liked it louder," I said. "Turn it up!"

Alexander stood beside me. "This is loud enough," he said. "The vibrations could upset the embryo's growth if they're too intense."

Of course, I knew this. I just wanted Alexander to be the one to say it: that way, I still had the freedom to protest on behalf of the music.

"What music is this?" I asked. "This isn't what we listened to before."

It wasn't what I would have selected for myself, either. It was slow and maudlin, rather than wild and libidinous; its lyrics were deep and contemplative, rather than forceful and outspoken; it was delicate, emotional, vulnerable. And yet, it did share some similarities with my kind of music. Both had a strong beat. Both had passion.

"It's by a band called the Smiths," said Alexander. "It's from my 'Best of the Eighties' cassette." He squeezed past me, murmuring an apology as he ushered me back, and took my place before the microscope. He squinted down the lens and adjusted the knobs. "Do you like it?" he asked. "The music, I mean?"

"I thought you only played that horrible twinkly music?" I said. I had ignored his question primarily out of politeness – I did not want to offend him by criticising his tastes – but also out of confusion over what my answer should be. The fact was, a small part of me thought it might quite *like* Alexander's music.

"This is from my other music collection," said Alexander.

"Oh yes," I recalled. "The secret one Harley told me about. The one you actually like."

"Well… Yes." Alexander said no more.

We remained like this, taking turns with the microscope, one of us crouched and one of us standing, while we listened to the melancholic tones of Alexander's music until one of the men came downstairs and interrupted us by clearing his throat. He told us that Harley had sent him to take over watch of the embryo for us, while we went upstairs to eat.

Hungry as I was, I found it near-impossible to tear myself away. It felt unnatural to leave the embryo under the watch of somebody other than Alexander or myself. If it hadn't been for Alexander's gentle reassurance that this man would be able to handle any possible problem that might occur in the half-hour we would be away, I doubt I would even have made it as far as the door. It seemed so wrong to leave that vulnerable creature, growing like a miracle in my womb, with a stranger.

I explained this to Alexander in the elevator. He laughed, but then frowned and tilted his head, which made me think that what I'd said had perhaps disturbed him.

#

If only I had understood then, what I understand now.

The human race is cruel.

That is an understatement.

But they are my people... were *my people; I forgive them, of course. Cruelty is in their nature.*

Nature fucked up.

'Fucked up.' Did my mind always use curse words? I can't remember – No, I don't think so. It's changed.

Like everything about me: changed.

What I am working on now is a solution: a chemical 'solution'... to be a 'solution' to Nature's mistake. Wordplay... that's also new.

A similar solution, in the scientific sense of the word – a mixture of molecules; a chemical substance - was invented by that infamous 'sick bastard' of a scientist, Doctor Jean-Luc Tati. The man whose chimp-brain experiment and subsequent confession gave the American government the ammunition they needed to destroy Homo-SuperiUS, take down the scientific establishment, and regain power.

But my solution isn't the same as Tati's.

Tati's solution, if applied to the organ of one animal, could make that organ accept tissue from the same organ removed from another animal. A little piece of heart stolen from a cat, melded with the heart of a chimp, for example. Or brain with brain.

The result would be the transference of some of the properties of the donating animal into the receiving animal: a different heartbeat; a shorter sleep-wake cycle; a more intellectually capable brain.

The donating animal: sacrificed.

My solution is better because it can fuse anything *to* anything *else. Biochemical superglue. Imagine: the entire brain of a chimp merged with the entire brain of a cat. Nothing carved up or stuck on. The best parts of both brains alive inside the same skull, neither animal having to die.*

Imagine!

When my solution is ready, I will combine it with my dear little specimens in their test tubes. They will dissolve, and will wait until... until...

I'm not sure yet.

I don't know where I'm going to find the new specimens with which to merge my test tube-dwellers. They will have to be living specimens.

Tricky...

I will deal with that when I come to it.

I failed to find all the test tubes I needed to house each specimen, so yesterday I was forced to discard two of them. Doing so was easy enough.

However, after they had been buried in the gap between the kitchen floorboards and were beyond all hope of resurrection, I felt a sickness start to rise in me. It welled up gradually, filling my body until I could bear it no longer and was reduced to crouching on the floorboards on hands and knees, painfully dry-retching – not vomiting, because I haven't eaten anything in so, so long. The sickness consumed my mind. I felt sick at myself, and guilty, so painfully guilty – for denying these two innocents life, for using them and discarding them as if I was a god.

As if I was Alexander Bai.

When I had finished retching, I felt I should cry. So I got up on my knees, closed my eyes and braced myself. But I didn't cry. I think that, after all the changes I have been through, I might have lost the ability to cry.

Now, though, I am fine. They were two samples of Bengal tiger tissue – perfectly replaceable, as I have many, many duplicates of that species. And they were discarded for a greater cause, after all.

I am sitting at my desk now, progressing further with my solution, a coffee by my left hand (which I now sip – ah, revitalising, beautiful liquid! How could I ever have hated you?). I listen to Frieda and Juan on the radio. That wonderful, inane soap opera...

Frieda (to herself): Oh! I can't remember when I last felt so helpless. No – wait, I can! It was in that terrible hospital. The people there – oh, such sick and twisted monsters! Rabbiting away, going through the motions of nursing, keeping us drugged and bound and stupid like logs in a warehouse!

Frieda often embarks on wild, nonsensical tangents like this. It's becoming more and more common as the series goes on. I am starting to suspect that the writers are under the influence of alcohol, or something stronger.

Frieda (continued): Those monsters! They knew, once we were gone, that there would be none of our kind left... all the wild, beautiful minds extinct... because of that terrible pill they force down expectant mothers' throats! When the last of us died, that would be it. We would be forgotten and they could get on with their lives... forever pure, forever normal, forever boring and stupid and hypocritical... Oh my God, they were waiting for us to die! It's them - they should be the ones to die!

This is doing nothing for my fragile state of mind. I am seriously considering switching the radio off – but no, it seems Frieda is calming down now, thank goodness. Whatever those idiot writers were taking, it must have worn off.

Frieda (continued): Okay, calm down. Don't remind yourself, Frieda. You got out: Juan rescued you. He didn't have to, but he rescued you because he wanted to. And he'll protect you. I have to keep her alive. That is my destiny. The reason why I was saved and nobody else was. Nature made Juan fall in love with me, and now I owe Nature a service. I can't sit around here and let her wither away!
(Juan enters.)
Juan: Frieda? What is it? Are you still worried about...?
Frieda: She is not getting the right nutrients, Juan. She is going to die.
Juan: Frieda...
Frieda: No, Juan; listen. I've made a decision. I'm going to go outside. I'll walk to the outbuilding – not far. I won't even go in. I'll just go up to it and back again.
Juan: No! You remember what happened last time, Frieda. You don't want to give yourself another panic attack. Especially not in your condition.
Frieda: If I can't fight this now, what sort of mother am I going to make? I can't rely on you to be the only one to go out hunting, getting water, shopping, feeding the chickens, keeping us warm and clothed...

Juan: Why not? I'm not going anywhere!
Frieda: Yes, Juan. I know. You have been my saviour and I love you for it. But this is something I have to do myself. For our son.
Juan: It... it's a boy? Really?
Frieda: Uh-huh. We need to keep her alive, Juan. We need to keep her working. We discussed this. If she doesn't succeed – what kind of a world will our child be born into? I couldn't bear for him – for **anyone** *– to go through what they made me go through. Because not everyone will have somebody like you to save them!*
Juan: I'm nothing special...
Frieda: Yes, you are! Now, you were planning to go buy food tonight, yes? So go. Just please, buy a little more this time-

I take another sip of coffee, and let the voices wash over my head. I ceased days ago to understand what is going on in Frieda and Juan's lives.

CHAPTER TWENTY-THREE

Those first few weeks of the embryo's growth were as tense as they were magical.

We only had the one microscope between us; Alexander set his stop-watch so we could take equal turns with it. When not using the microscope, I was allowed to distract myself with whatever I wanted to listen to on the CD player. Alexander had Bauhaus, the Cure, Depeche Mode – bands made up of miserable Twentieth-century boys singing maudlin songs, aged before their time. They had their appeal. Still, I found I was only truly relaxed when it was my turn with the microscope; when I could watch the embryo for myself and be certain everything was okay.

During his turns, Alexander would often notice me fidgeting and beckon me over to the microscope. Sometimes he would put his hands on my shoulders – the touch felt good, comforting, as it had from Father. I would look down into the fluid while he explained what was happening in hushed tones; perhaps out of respect for the embryo, or perhaps so we could still listen to Bauhaus while he spoke.

The placenta grew, like the books said it would: a round, flat, pinkish-grey organ. A primitive circulatory system was now developing inside the embryo, Alexander explained; it was starting to produce its own blood cells. Already it was a life, separate from Alexander and myself but dependent on us.

Its face started to form next: large, dark circles for eyes; a gelatinous mouth, jaw and throat. Ears bloomed at the sides of the head as tiny folds of skin. Then came the limbs: little buds at first, becoming more recognizably mammalian every day.

My fear that the embryo could die faded. Replacing it was a sense of awe, of sublime peace.

And also, something else.

Something had been nagging at the back of my mind since the day Alexander and I had visited the tigress's grave. As soon as I felt our creation was old enough to do without me for a short time, I decided to pursue it. My faith in Alexander was so strong that, one morning, I found myself able to leave him alone with the four-week-old foetus and go outside.

When Harley found me, I was lying in the snow at the back of the compound. My ear was against the ground, my eyes tightly shut. I heard the snow crunch as he approached.

"What are you doing, Katrina?"

I opened my eyes. With my head so low to the ground, the fence around the compound seemed impossibly tall. It reminded me of something from television. A prison-camp fence.

Harley's footsteps stopped just behind me. He cleared his throat.

I stood, brushing the snow from my coat, and faced him. He was scowling at me.

I met his scowl with an unblinking stare. "I was right," I said.

"Oh? What were you right about?"

"There *are* two bodies buried here," I asserted. "One over there, by the fence." I gestured to where the tigress was buried, a short distance away from where I was standing. "And one down here. Beneath me."

Harley stared at me for a long time. I held his gaze. "There are two bodies," I repeated. "Did you know?"

"I honestly have no idea what you're talking about. There was only one tigress."

"I know."

Harley shifted from one foot to the other. His eyes darted away. "Look - come inside, why don't you? Get yourself warm." He started back towards the Lodge.

I followed, dragging my feet deliberately. "Alexander seems oblivious to these things," I called to Harley. "A lot of people seem to be. Sometimes I forget how ignorant you all are; I was taught from an early age how to recognise if I was treading on a grave."

"It isn't a grave," said Harley. "Come on."

"I can also tell what is in that grave." I stopped. "And it seems to me that you know, too. Otherwise you wouldn't be denying it so hard."

We were almost at the Lodge's back door, the one which led to the kitchen. Harley had his foot on the first step. He paused, not looking back. Then, "Come on," he grunted. "I'll let you in through here, shall I?" He started up the steps, put a hand on the doorknob.

"Tell me what you know," I said. "Or I'll have to ask Alex why he has a dead human buried in the grounds of his house." It was an educated guess. With animals such a rarity, that second body could be nothing else.

Harley turned to me. His eyes were wide, his lips small and pursed under his moustache. His left hand tapped restlessly against his thigh. "And you would," he murmured. "Wouldn't you? You two have become close now." He threw a quick glance over his shoulder at the window in the kitchen door, as if checking to make sure it was deserted inside. "Alright. Alright, you are part of the family now – I suppose you should know everything. But you have to promise me that you won't tell Mr. Bai. Okay?"

There was something strange and eager in Harley's tone. His hand continued to tap his thigh, faster, harder, and his eyes kept flitting to the kitchen door. It was as if he wanted to do this, tell me his secret - and as soon as possible. Perhaps that was why he believed me so readily when I lied to him - "I promise."

Harley nodded stiffly. "Would you like a hot drink?"

Minutes later I was sitting at the kitchen table, a mug of herbal tea warming my blue hands. Distracted, I had forgotten to put on Alexander's gloves before I went outside.

I had never been in the kitchen before. It was larger than I had expected, from other kitchens I'd seen; yet it was still smaller than the vast, empty dining room, and much more comforting for it - although the walls were painted the same predictable white, and the floor was made of cold, white tile.

Forming an 'L' shape along two of the walls were several fridges and freezers, two large, black ovens, at least three microwaves, various kettles, and a generous stretch of empty counter space. A kitchen typical of a hotel, I assumed. I figured the extra meat and milk required to sustain Alexander and the men between shopping trips warranted the extra storage space.

The kitchen's sole domestic statement was the table. It sat in the middle of the room, large and circular, spread with an off-theme chequered cloth. This must have been where the men ate their meals together, after serving Alexander, alone, in the dining room.

Harley came towards me, stirring his own drink. He sighed as he took the seat across from me, gazing into the depths of his cup.

I leant forward. "Well?"

Harley took a long, slow sip from his mug. Then he put it on the table again. He wouldn't look at me. "Her name was Sonja," he said. Even this seemed to be too much for him; he picked the mug up again desperately, as if it contained vital medicine, and took another long sip.

Sonja. The pink sweatpants and baggy fleece beneath my coat had her name stitched into their linings. My hands wrestled impatiently on my knees. "Well?" I said again.

A pause. Then Harley gave a defeated moan, and relinquished hold of his mug. "She was living on the streets, a – a *schizophrenic*," he said. "At least, I think that's what she was. They say they've eradicated schizophrenia with the Monroe Pill, along with the rest of the psychiatric divergences. But there are still some out there. It won't be eradicated until those born before the pill was created... well, until they *die out*, poor things. And, once in a while, an abnormal birth slips through the net - the Pill isn't as perfect as they claim. And one or two mothers refuse to take it..."

"Is any of this important?"

"I suppose not." Harley swallowed. "Bottom line, she was... unstable. But she came here of her own free will, I assure you of that - there was no struggle. We simply asked her, did she want to help an aging but brilliant man with an important task, and she said 'yes'..."

"Was she your sister?"

Harley frowned for a second. Then he smiled: "Ah, that was what we told Mr. Bai, wasn't it? To explain where those clothes came from. The poor boy's too trusting. No, we picked her up off the streets of San Diego. This was, let's see... twenty-three years ago. In the spring."

The smile disappeared. Harley's eyes grew vacant. He was somewhere else now, seeing things I couldn't see: a Dead-Talker taken over by a spirit. "Doctor Bai's tiger had died the previous winter. The poor thing's womb had been destroyed beyond repair by that first attempted Smilodon. There was no hope of the experiment being repeated, not with that tiger, and really no chance that such a creature would fall into our hands again. Not in Doctor Bai's lifetime, anyway - he was an old man, even when I met him. He'd taken that tigress as a cub from the San Diego Zoo - he knew a keeper, used to be a genetic engineer, who was happy to look the other way. Thomas and I raised that little cub ourselves, while Doctor Bai worked down in the basement on God-knows-what."

His eyes flitted to the wall behind my head. He traced a restless finger around the rim of his cup. "When the time came... we held her steady, calmed her down, while Doctor Bai slit her throat. Sounds ghastly, I know. But it's the kindest way, really. It's quick. And after what we'd put her through, the poor creature was in such pain. We put what we could salvage from her body into storage and then buried her in the grounds." He cast a glance behind him at the back door; his eyes returned to his mug. His finger continued its endless journey around the rim.

I brought my own mug to my face and inhaled the fragrance – ginger, lemon – but couldn't bring myself to drink. With a gulp to suppress the nausea which had spiked at Harley's words, I urged him, "Go on". There was anger in my voice, but I doubted Harley noticed.

The life had left his eyes. When he spoke, he addressed the table. "Well... it took us a long time to convince him, but Doctor Bai finally came around to the fact that his plans wouldn't come to fruition in his own lifetime. Which meant there was only one option available to him: he had to have a child. A group of us were dispatched to find a mo... a *'vessel'*, is how he put it, a 'vessel', for his son to grow inside.

"She – Sonja, the homeless girl – she met Doctor Bai only twice. Once at the beginning, and once at the... *end*. The first time, something sort of 'clicked' inside her head. I'm not sure what it was about him: maybe his charisma, his presence, or just his appearance - that full white beard, those piercing ice-blue eyes. The same as Alexander's eyes... anyway, when Sonja saw Doctor Bai, she decided that she was in the presence of God himself. Yes, she was religious too, poor thing. A double catastrophe.

"And when we'd done the operation, and Alexander started growing inside her – well, what else? She was the Virgin Mother, carrying the Messiah. The poor girl spent the next eight months wandering around in a state of mindless elation. It was all we could do to get her to eat and drink - she told us she didn't need to anymore, not with *God Himself* inside her."

"Why didn't Doctor Bai explain that he wasn't a god?" I asked.

"Because I think, in a way, he believed it was true," said Harley. "That, and he didn't care much for Sonja. Doctor Bai's only interest was in the baby - that was why we were told to take care of the girl. To make sure the 'vessel' didn't break. But, after getting to know her, she stopped being a vessel to us; I mean, we *genuinely cared about her...*" Harley paused.

Dozens of questions presented themselves to me at once. I made myself select the next one chronologically. "How did she die?"

Harley sighed again. That sigh became a moan. He ran his hands down his face; looked at me over his fingertips. "Are you sure you want to hear this?" He obviously didn't want to tell it.

I would be lying to say that my interest in the matter wasn't partly rooted in voyeuristic curiosity. But it was a voyeuristic curiosity about a person I had developed genuine feelings for. What these feelings were exactly, I wasn't sure. But I felt them. "Yes," I said. "I do. Go on."

Harley removed his hands from his face and squirmed into a different cross-legged contortion in his seat. "Alright - but I want you to know, I feel uncomfortable telling you this, okay? Especially when Mr. Bai doesn't know."

"I understand." I nodded. "Go on."

Harley's eyes flitted to the dining-room door; to the mug in his hands. Then they settled on me again. "Mr. Bai was born early. Not too early, but without any neonatal care equipment to hand we were scared we were going to lose him. Sonja was screaming the place down. We had her lying on the sofa in the lounge to begin with, but it became apparent she would need a Caesarean... which meant we had no option but to take her to the basement. Which meant disturbing Doctor Bai. He had taken to locking himself in his work room, creating embryos for his son to use - so Alexander wouldn't have to waste any time. Anyway, two of us – myself and Matthew, he's no longer with us - we went ahead to explain the situation to Doctor Bai, and to coax him out of his room. Strangely enough, he didn't fuss. He just grunted, picked up his work, and went into that room you two call the 'Womb Room'. He left us with the work room table and some of his equipment to perform the operation.

"Sonja calmed down after some pain relief. Matthew and Thomas held her steady, and I was able to remove Alexander with minimal trouble. It was miraculous, really. For all the poor girl had put him through - forgetting to eat, refusing sleep and vitamins; not to mention the premature birth - he was a healthy baby, if small.

"Matthew went through to the other room to give Doctor Bai the good news. He was with us in seconds. He looked Alexander over, decided he was adequate... everything seemed fine. I mean, it's not as if any of us could have foreseen what was going to happen."

I didn't want to ask. But I had to know. For Alexander's sake. "What did happen?"

Harley lifted his cup to his lips, closed his eyes, and took a long sip. Then he put it on the table again, clasped his hands around it, and turned his face to the ceiling, as if praying. "Doctor Bai told me and Thomas to take Sonja off the table and hold her upright. We were confused, but we did as told. Doctor Bai came up to her... She was completely doped on painkillers by this point, even more out of her mind than usual. But when she saw Doctor Bai, she recognised him instantly from that first encounter eight months before. Her face broke into this... *incredible* smile. 'I did it for you!' she kept saying. 'I did it for you. I did it for you.'

"Doctor Bai ignored her. He told us to hold her steady. We did: I mean, we had no idea what the man had in mind. He asked for the scalpel. Matthew passed it to him - he tried to clean it with an antiseptic wipe first, I remember, but Doctor Bai said 'no'.

"Then Doctor Bai rolled Sonja's head back. She was in ecstasy – that smile never left her face. Not until the scalpel touched her neck, and then she..."

He broke off. "It was only for a moment. The pain, I mean. Very quick. The kindest way, really."

Silence. Harley's hands had become like spiders, moving restlessly over the table. He cast his gaze downwards, watched them squirm. He still wouldn't look at me.

"I don't think Doctor Bai liked women much," he muttered. "He saw them as weak, useless. The incident with the tigress, the fact that she was unable to contain his work - that couldn't have helped. I suppose that was why he surrounded himself with male company. And I suppose, to him, he was simply getting rid of an empty vessel once the product had been delivered. The man was single-minded. He focussed on *results*.

"We cleaned up the mess, buried Sonja behind the building, next to the tigress. Doctor Bai was never aware of the graves. He would have disapproved. And, of course, we never told Alexander... *Mr. Bai*, I mean."

Harley's spider-hands died on the table. He looked dully down at them.

"Why did you let him do that?" I asked. The whimper in my voice was difficult to control. "I thought you liked her?"

"We did! Of course we liked her!" Harley's hands were alive again, moving rapidly around each other, as if moulding a ball. Only now that I examined him closely did I notice the dullness of his eyes, his prematurely wrinkled skin. His shoulders were hunched defensively; his head hung low. His breath whistled shallowly between sentence-fragments. "Of course we liked her... poor thing... she was the mother of Doctor Bai's child... I mean... without her... we wouldn't have him... our Alexander! We picked her out. We brought her up here. Spent every evening for eight months in her company. Chatted to her, ate our meals with her, monitored her health. She always beat me at Scrabble in the lounge – we played every Friday. Oh, God. Delusional, maybe... but she was a *sweetheart*. She didn't deserve to die!"

"Then... why?" Slowly. Carefully. Trying hard to understand. I said, "Were you scared of Doctor Bai?" I didn't see how they could have been. I wasn't sure how many men had been working for Doctor Bai twenty-three years ago, but Harley had mentioned three including himself. If they had joined forces, they could easily have overpowered one man.

With a sniff, Harley collected himself. "I suppose it was partly fear, yes. We were all scared of him – terrified, at times." He stretched his shirt sleeve over his fist, and mopped a few stray tears from his cheeks; wiped away a pathetic stream of mucus from beneath his nose. "But it was more than fear. That man was something special. There was something... *omnipotent*, about his presence. The man was a demon, yes, but he was the sort of demon you would willingly go to Hell for. That voice, that smile... he had to be obeyed. Plus, we didn't know what he was going to do until he was actually doing it and then..."

"Did you like him more than Alex's mother?" I asked.

"Oh, good lord, no!" Harley exclaimed. "I hated the man! I hated him ever since I saw what he did to that beautiful tiger. How he treated the poor, broken body afterwards – it was deplorable! When he was gone, we didn't bury him – as soon as Mr. Bai gave permission we took him out to the grounds and we burned his body. Burned his clothes." He looked at the top I was wearing: Sonja's. "But I also loved him. We all did. That was what we were chosen for, at the beginning. Our skills were one thing, but there are millions of unemployed lab assistants out there - and thousands of medics, too, since the younger scientists started retraining as doctors. Doctor Bai chose us because we fell for him. Love makes more of a slave out of you than fear ever could."

"How could you feel any affection for somebody like that?" It seemed illogical to me.

Harley shook his head. "Oh, my dear, you already know! You see it every day. The way his hair sometimes flops out of place; the wonderful authority in his voice. His *eyes*! His devotion to his work. And underpinning it all - that touch of vulnerability, reminding you that he is a human being after all. It makes you want to look after him, even though reason tells you he's perfectly capable of looking after himself – that, in fact, he could easily snap your neck or drive you crazy if he felt like it. It's the same with Alexander as it was with his father."

"You're wrong," I said, perhaps too loud.

But Harley wasn't listening now. He was watching me intently. "You must understand," he said. "Mr. Bai adored his father. Doctor Bai always kept a distance between himself and Alexander when the boy was growing up. It was left to us to raise and educate him. Mr. Bai never saw anything but his father's good side: always the illusive genius working tirelessly in his lab, always the tortured soul creating improvements for a failing human race. Never the monster. Mr. Bai grew up with a skewed impression of his father, you see; he *worshipped* the man.

"Which is why you cannot tell him anything about this, Katrina. Animals are one thing, but if Mr. Bai knew what his father was willing to do to a human being, to the woman who *carried him* no less... well, it would destroy him." Harley continued to stare at me, unblinking. There was something close to fear in his eyes. Fear of *me*.

"Sometimes animals have to die in research," he said. "No deaths - no advancement. It's the ones that are kept alive, to suffer on for years with drugs burning through their systems, or... with *extra bits* added to their bodies... *they're* the ones I feel sorry for." He gave me an awful, trembling smile. Then the smile disappeared. "But I suppose even those experiments are sometimes necessary," he said. "Terribly sad. Awful. But necessary."

Harley shut his mouth. For a moment, he seemed to be on the verge of saying something else. But then I heard footsteps beyond the kitchen doors – one of the other men, going to water another dead plant, perhaps – and Harley looked up abruptly like a startled rabbit.

I stood. "Take me to the basement," I said. Almost two hours had passed since I had left Alexander down there. I had told him I was going up for a glass of water; he would be worrying where I was.

"You're perfectly capable of using the elevator yourself," murmured Harley.

I glowered at him and he was on his feet.

I strode ahead, ignoring the plant-waterer as I passed through the dining room. Harley followed me, doglike, into the elevator. Timidly, he reached past me to push the number keys and the 'basement' button.

I felt that familiar sick panic stir in my stomach as it began to descend. As we jerked and slid down to the basement floor, Harley glanced at me. "I know it might sound manipulative," he said. "But sometimes we have to lie to protect the ones we love. If you really care about Mr. Bai as much as I think you do, you will keep what I've told you *our secret*."

I said nothing.

The elevator reached the basement floor. The doors opened. There was Alexander, standing in the corridor with folded arms.

"Why aren't you with the embryo?" I asked, concerned.

"I have been. Where were you? I thought you went to get a glass of water."

I could feel Harley hovering behind me but, as I couldn't slap him away like a mosquito, I did not acknowledge him. Harley was irrelevant.

I observed Alexander, standing alone in the corridor, hugging his lab coat around his slender frame. "The rate at which that animal's neural tube is developing – it's incredible, Katrina! Four weeks and we're already well past brain stem development. I have the microscope trained on the cranial end of the neural tube - do you want to miss the most important stage in this creature's development?"

His hair was so soft; his eyes so wide, and blue, and lost. Skin like porcelain – it could crack at any time.

"I got lost," I said. Without a backward glance, I ushered Alexander away from Harley, into the Womb Room.

#

I sat on the floor of the Womb Room with a book open on my lap. 'Your Pregnancy and You', it was called. I had found it crammed into the pocket of a fleece-lined ski jacket that the men had left out for me, since the winter weather was now at its worst.

'By the end of the first trimester,' the book said, 'the baby can now be called a *foetus*.'

Taking into account the corresponding development of our embryo – the face, the limbs, the primitive organs taking form under the delicate translucent flesh and, recently, *movement* - I calculated that we were roughly at the end of the first trimester. The book's previous owner – Alexander's mother, my spirit guide into the realm of maternity - had underlined the word 'foetus' several times in red marker and drawn a star next to it. Next to the corresponding star in the margin, Sonja had written: 'And soon-to-be NEW-BORN!'

"Foetus," I told the Smilodon, as I watched the pit. "You are a *foetus*."

Alexander was sitting between the canisters, staring down the microscope at the creature's 'neural tube' which fascinated him so much. His hair had fallen over his closed eye, but he didn't seem to care. His teeth were clenched in concentration; his white lip curled into the prettiest grimace I had ever seen.

I didn't need the microscope. I could see it now with my naked eye: a four-inch-long furless worm, with dark eyes, a mouth hanging open; a stalk of a tail curled towards its chest; head tucked towards the tail; stubby buds of limbs moving slightly in the amniotic fluid. With the exception of the tail, it looked like the images in the book.

I whispered to the embryo, which was now a foetus and soon-to-be new-born, "Don't worry. We're not going to make the same mistakes our parents made. Alexander and me – we're going to raise you *right*."

"What?" Suddenly Alexander was staring at me from across the pit.

I shook my head. "Nothing. I said nothing." I gave him a smile. "Change the music, please."

He was a father. He wouldn't understand these things until the baby was born.

#

What kind of mother would I have made?

What kind of mother would Sonja have made, if she had been allowed to live?

Perhaps there is a reason we were denied motherhood. She, a schizophrenic; me, a... what was the word Chemise used?

Savant.

My mind is clouding. The specimens need a protector, a nurturer; something I don't feel prepared to give them right now. My trembling hands. My whirlwind brain. Perhaps everyone was right...

No. That is insanity!

Right?

There is a dictionary on the shelf above the freezer. It is one of only three books in the cabin - the other two being 'One Flew Over the Cuckoo's Nest' and 'Self Sufficient Living for Dummies' - and it looks to be at least two decades old. I look up the word 'Savant' in this dictionary. Here is what it says:

"'Savant Syndrome'; noun. A condition in which an otherwise intellectually-subnormal individual exhibits some genius traits in certain disciplines, e.g. memory, logic, scientific understanding. Often associated with the now-extinct condition, 'Autism'. Rarely seen in developed countries since the implementation of the Monroe Pill."

The 'intellectually subnormal' bit makes me laugh. But it's a nervous laugh. I look behind me at the current specimen ready to be subjected to the chemical.

Some *genius traits...*

A lot has happened to my brain in the last year. A lot of weird things have been done to it. But I hope I have retained those genius traits somehow. My work depends on it. The world depends on it.

"I am not stupid," I whisper to myself.

I look up. The strange mildew stain on the ceiling, the one which looks like a painfully familiar face, is grinning at me.

"I'm not fucking stupid, Alexander!" I scream – and then I hear something.

No. There's no chance...

I run to the window. The sound of tyres on sand ebbs away into the distance, and squinting, I'm sure I can see tracks.

Maybe. Maybe not.

I return to the specimen. The final one to be altered. A female, it used to be. I look down at its single eye, the only intact part of it remaining – and scream again.

CHAPTER TWENTY-FOUR

One night, a dark-haired man-in-white appeared at the Womb Room door, and cautiously murmured that he would be happy to watch the foetus for a few hours – "If you and Mr. Bai would like to go up to the lounge and relax for a while?"

Alexander thanked him and went to the door. "Come on, Katrina."

I lingered by the edge of the pit, looking down. Alexander went to me, touched my shoulder. "You need the rest as much as I do. Come on."

Reluctantly, I let him direct me to the elevator. The man-in-white went through to Alexander's work room to turn the music off.

The 'lounge' was located on the ground floor, near the Lodge's front door. It was tiny compared to the other rooms: it had probably once been used as a staff room, Alexander explained as we walked side-by-side down the hall. Most of the furniture was what had been left behind when the Lodge was still a hotel: a rickety sofa with space to seat two or three, an armchair in one corner, a chipped wooden coffee table. There were also several shelves in the corners, which held yellowing magazines, novels and slightly-less-aged video tapes. The dining room was a far nicer room to relax in, he added, which was why he had never mentioned the lounge. It was strange that the men had suggested it tonight. Perhaps they were cleaning the dining room again. "They get bored," he said. "So when they've run out of books to read, they clean. Continuously. It drives me insane."

We entered the lounge. All the lights were off, and a curtain had been drawn across the only window. Harley, his back to us, was placing a lit candle on the coffee table, which he had positioned between a television set – like the one from the Edu-Centre, a cube with a bulging eye for a screen - and the sofa.

Alexander halted by the door. He seemed disturbed.

Harley put his candle down on the table and looked up at us, beaming. "Ah - hello, Mr. Bai; Katrina," he said. He gave me a cryptic look which I couldn't decipher.

"Hello, Harley." Alexander leaned over to me, whispered, "It doesn't usually look like this. We *do* have electricity in here." Then, to Harley, "What's wrong with the lights, Harley? They were working fine in the hall. Are the bulbs dead?"

Harley shook his head. "No, no, Mr. Bai. You can have the lights on if you want. I just thought candles might make a nice change for tonight. Oh – excuse me." He stood up, slipped past us, and left the room. I watched him over my shoulder and saw him disappear into the dining room.

When he had gone, Alexander said to me, "I don't know what the man is playing at. We can have the main lights on if you'd prefer."

"Oh – no," I said, attention fixed on the television. "You can see the screen better in the dark."

When Harley returned from the dining room, he was carrying a tray, delicious smells accompanying him. "I took the liberty of cooking for you two *without* instruction," he said. "I haven't used this recipe in a while - I hope it's alright." He excused himself as he slipped past us again.

I could see that the food he was carrying was pizza - cheese and tomato. He moved the candles to make room for the tray and set it down on the coffee table. Alexander peered at it.

"Do you know," Alexander inquired, "the saturated fat content of a pizza, Harley?"

"On average, eighty-five per cent of your recommended daily intake of saturated fat," I said. Chemise often bought pizza when she couldn't stand the thought of preparing another extravagant meal for Courtney; I used to look at the nutritional values on the backs of the boxes when I had nothing else to read. "And a whole one contains, on average, half of your recommended daily calorie intake."

"Exactly," Alexander said.

"Oh, shush," said Harley. "You always used to eat pizza. Besides, Katrina must be getting tired of your restricted diet. I made it to be accommodating to your partner. She's doing a lot for you, in case you haven't noticed." He winked at me - a gesture I knew usually signified either sexual attraction, or a shared understanding. Given what I knew about Harley's sexual preferences, I could only assume that the latter had been implied.

I sat on the sofa. Alexander continued to linger behind it. "Katrina also says she wants to watch the television," he said to

Harley. "I don't see how we are supposed to select a film with all the lights off."

"No problem at all. I have one ready. You're watching 'Gone with the Wind'. Is that acceptable?"

I turned in my seat to see what Alexander's response would be. He lingered for a moment. Seemed to consider. Then, finally, he gave a small nod of approval, and sat next to me on the sofa.

"What is 'Gone with the Wind'?" I asked him.

"You'll love it," Harley interrupted. "It's very romantic. It was Mr. Bai's favourite film when he was younger."

"Yes - thank you, Harley," Alexander said shortly. "You can take a break now. I'm sure I can manage things from here."

"Just trying to be accommodating to your new friend," Harley said. He put a little metal wheel on a stick down on the tray and straightened up. "You could make more effort yourself, you know, Mr. Bai. You don't always have to act so cold."

"Katrina doesn't want to stay away from the foetus for too long," Alexander said. Then he looked at Harley directly for the first time that evening, and said, "Thank you for the effort, Harley. It is appreciated. But we really should be starting the film now; neither of us wants to waste too much time."

Harley nodded. "That's perfectly understandable, Mr. Bai. As you wish." He left the room. Alexander moved forward to pick up the television remote, which was on the coffee table.

Reflected in the television screen, I could see Harley's face as he stood for a moment in the doorway. He caught my eye, checked quickly to make sure Alexander's attention was diverted – and then mouthed something to me. I think it might have been 'thank you'. Then he disappeared down the hall.

Alexander aimed the remote at the television and pressed a button. The screen flickered into life with a black-and-white image. Quivery string-music started to play. It reminded me of the introductory music to some of the old Edu-Centre videos; I think 'Marriage, Sex and Sin' used to start with music like that.

The film began.

Half an hour in, I looked across at Alexander. I can still remember the expression of innocence on his face as he watched this film from his childhood. All pain and anxiety pushed to the back of his mind.

I should have envied him, I suppose. He had reached a state of infantile regression which I, deprived of that veil of blissful ignorance even in childhood, could never hope to achieve. But I didn't envy him. Instead, I felt a sort of comfort in the fact that he was no longer feeling pain.

At that moment, I believed completely that *Alexander* was the one who needed protecting.

#

Later that night, I searched the kitchen for soda, hoping to give Alexander a taste, but disappointingly found nothing more exciting than seltzer water and apple juice.

That was, until I prized open a locked cupboard beneath the sink and discovered a bottle of clear liquid labelled 'Vodka'. It must have belonged to one of the men. It was tasteless, flat, and colourless, unlike soda. But when I mixed Alexander's juice with a generous helping of the vodka, the results proved to be much more fun.

After drinking the concoction, it took little encouragement for Alexander to get his keys, stumble over the snow to the garage and bring his snowmobile around to the front of the Lodge, where I stood on the porch in my fleecy winter coat, waiting.

I hurried down the steps and mounted the snowmobile at the front. Alexander got on behind me. He wrapped his arms around my waist; I batted them away.

I revved the engine as I had seen the men demonstrate. The machine vibrated into life beneath us, like a sleeping predator waking from a long slumber. I smiled. I pushed down on the accelerator.

We were off.

Leaping and bounding over the snow at God-knows-how-many-miles-per-hour, the wind raking my hair and freezing my knuckles blue. The stars shone down on us from a clear ink-black sky, lighting my path. This is how a forest-dog must feel when it hunts down its prey, I thought; finally, *finally*, I was experiencing it!

I remember taking my hands off the machine and waving them in the air. With my arms stretched towards the heavens I screamed, at the top of my voice, the words to Megadeth's 'Symphony of Destruction'. My words were lost to the wind.

Behind me, Alexander started singing, too. I think it was something by Morrissey. Entirely inappropriate, poor Alexander; he had completely missed the point of the exercise.

Of course, my control of the snowmobile wasn't perfect. So it should have come as no surprise to either of us when I crashed, going forty miles an hour, into the wire fence, completely demolishing the section to the left of the gate.

A sound broke the silence. An undulating, whooping cry.

The shock subsided, leaving little pain: I was unharmed. I dragged myself to my knees, melted snow seeping through my clothes, vision wavering, and searched for the source of the sound. In the distance the men, tiny black specks, poured from the lodge like ants evacuating a colony. Finally, my eyes landed on Alexander. Splayed on his back in the snow.

He was laughing.

When Alexander visited me in my room the next morning, limping a little but otherwise unharmed, he sat on the edge of my bed and smiled. He said that he had told his men that he would rather not have the fence repaired. He didn't like living in a cage any more; besides, no sane person would come up this high into the mountains now that the Lodge was closed. In fact, people never came this far anyway – "which was why this blasted hotel went out of business in the first place!" This provoked another bout of his weird, wavery, unpractised laughter.

Life was good, Alexander told me. He saw no point in maintaining a reminder of his dead father's paranoia.

#

I don't miss him.

I have enough to occupy my mind without Alexander Bai.

For instance, my hallucination a few nights ago. The tyre tracks...

A hallucination is what it must have been. I cannot see the tracks anymore; through the near-complete darkness of the desert night, I can barely see the house opposite...

What I do miss are Alexander's films.

I would give a lot to watch a film now. Gone with the Wind; even an Edu-Centre video. Something to take command of my flittering brain. To let me escape for a moment.

My mind is hazy. My fingers shaking. Every now and then I have to sit down on the floor so I don't fall. My experiments, waiting for me on the table.

I sit and stare at the empty socket in the wall.

I love television. Like a parent, it is the imparter of knowledge. It is also a wonderful source of comfort, like a parent. It speaks to you in a multitude of voices: male, female, genderless; young and old. Some long-dead. Resurrected, by the power of the television.

With television, you can hear the spirits speak without the need for a Dead-Talker. I found that out when watching 'Modern Pop Culture' in the Edu-Centre with Father. After a lengthy interview with a spike-haired man in face-paint, the disembodied voice narrating the video suddenly revealed that this man had died twenty years before the film was produced. Before I even had time to process this, the television showed another living-dead man. And then another – this one from way back in the early twentieth century. Television gives ordinary people the power to bring any dead temporarily back to life.

The television cannot judge you because it is blind. It cannot insult you because it can't speak. It cannot hurt you because it can't touch. Everybody bathed in the warm glow of the television is equal before the television.

And if you grow tired of it... well, you have the power to switch it off.

Sometimes I wish I could plug myself into one. Become one with the television, let my body decay and my mind disappear.

Perhaps it is already happening.

My mind constantly drifts and spins and morphs: an alien thing.

My body has become a strange, wavering entity, reworking and rewiring itself, like a trapped animal trying to squeeze out through reality's bars, desperate for somewhere more hospitable.

My tongue, outsized and rough, wrestles against my front teeth.

I look down at my hands and try to flex them, but they have grown stiff and clumsy with thick, stubby, hairy fingers. Like Rawg's hands. Like Father's hands.

CHAPTER TWENTY-FIVE

One day during the Smilodon's second month, I sat on the laboratory floor to sketch. I had taken to sketching in a notebook Alexander had lent me, whilst I guarded the foetus. It kept my mind active, and restless hands busy. Stopped me from dreaming up worst-case scenarios.

As I shaded in the shadow cast by Alexander's hair, my pencil slipped from my fingers and rolled under Alexander's empty chair. I crawled over to retrieve it and saw with a sickening, poisoned feeling, what had happened.

My eyes went to the two empty oil canisters which Alexander and I had converted into tanks to maintain the flow of glucose to, and extraction of bodily poisons from, the foetus. Connected to the stream of fluid under the endothelial lining, replicating a mothers' bloodstream. Essential to the foetus's survival. Meticulously constructed.

They had stopped working.

Somebody had walked across the pipes leading from the tanks. They had been crushed.

It took a few seconds for my mind to process this. Then I screamed. "*Alex! Alex! Alex!*"

By the time he came running in from his work room, the amniotic fluid had started to turn a sickening shade of green.

"What's wrong, Kat? What happened? Are you okay?"

"Don't you see what's happened? How could they have failed, Alexander? Tell me!"

While my body quivered with panic and fear, his remained completely, deathly still. He looked at the tanks. Then slowly he turned and peered through the darkening fluid at the foetus. He looked up at me. His voice was like that of a waking Dead-Talker. "You… were supposed to be… keeping an eye on it…"

"Don't blame this on me! You designed the goddamn things! It was the only part of the goddamn experiment you had to design - and you got it wrong!"

"You can't… fix it, Kat?"

The helplessness in his voice threw me. It forced me to admit to myself what all the screaming and cursing had been blocking out. The truth that I couldn't bear.

"No," I said. "No, I can't fix it. Not in the time we have before…"

Alexander approached me at a funereal pace. He took my shoulders firmly, stared into my eyes. I flinched, but fought the instinct to tear away from him and run. Something about his hands on my shoulders was comforting, reassuring. As I concentrated on Alexander's eyes, the pressure of his hands, I could feel my heart rate slow. The rest of the world faded into the background.

"Listen to me," Alexander said. "Stop panicking. If there's nothing you can do about this… Well, I guess I'll have to accept that. But I want you to *try*."

Alexander's face was a flawless, white mask. His pounding pulse, the occasional twitch in his left eye, were all that spoiled this illusion.

I forced myself to ignore these. I mimicked Alexander's supposed calm. And then…

An idea.

Not the best, most rational idea I've ever had; nor the safest. But when the life of her child is in danger, a good mother knows that nothing else matters.

And, good father that he was, Alexander didn't hesitate to follow my instructions.

The anaesthetic took its time to take hold. I wasn't quite numb when Alexander cut me open. The pain was like a fire down my abdomen.

Then a light, like a rip down the centre of reality, opened above the pit. In the disorienting glow I could almost see Father, a dark shadow; and Rawg, eyes staring with the same desperation as when he had watched me leave the Island, our cousins closing in on him…

"Have to keep going, girl."

The vision faded.

I dropped to my knees before the pit, looking down at that helpless scrap of naked flesh and organs. Our foetus. My sight kept clouding, black spots passing before my eyes - but the fluid seemed to be clearing.

Thank God! I thought – *we were just in time! My quick thinking and Alexander's skilled hands have saved our child.*

It wasn't Alexander's fault, I told myself. I had sent him into the work room to dig out a new CD. I could have gone myself, but no - I had stayed behind, to continue my stupid picture of Alexander Bai's stupid face. Disgustingly self-indulgent and overly-anxious mother that I was, I had immediately broken down and blamed Alexander for everything.

The sublime image of ghostly beauty before me was more than enough to numb the pain in my abdomen. I could still feel the tubes moving inside me, brushing against me; perhaps I was bleeding a little, too - but not enough to matter.

I gazed at the tiny creature and thought of it steadily gathering strength from my body, safe in the womb that Alexander and I created. I breathed in deeply, and exhaled. My pounding heart slowed.

Movement behind me. Out of the corner of my eye, I could sort-of see Alexander working. Repairing the tanks which would sustain the foetus when my body ceased to be able to. This is only a short-term solution, I reminded myself.

"I should be finished in an hour," Alexander said. "Do you think you'll be alright for that long, Kat?"

The painkillers and various other chemicals Alexander had pumped into me were making me giddy. "Of course," I swooned. "I could stay like this forever."

Alexander snorted. "You're delirious," he said.

I managed to stay kneeling for almost the entire hour *and a half* that it took for my overconfident Alexander Bai to fix those tanks. At one point, the foetus's toxins must have overcrowded my system, or else the loss of glucose and oxygen from my blood became too great; either way, I began to slip into unconsciousness…

But I was unharmed. Alexander was there.

He held my shoulders and kept me from dropping into the pit; stayed with me, until my head cleared and I was able to kneel again without assistance.

"Listen to me. You're doing well, Kat," Alexander whispered to me. "But you have to stay awake a little longer. Okay? When this is over, I'll get one of the men to look after things here for a while. We'll go upstairs, and we'll listen to that horrible CD Harley gave you. Yes, we'll have some vodka and we'll listen to the Buzzcocks again." He started to sing, coaxingly, in my ear. "Come on, Kat. You're the one who calls that trash 'music'. Sing it with me."

Bleary-eyed, I gazed down at our images, reflected faintly in the film over the pit. Alexander's soft, white, angel-hair against my tanned, earthy face. His white-gloved hands clutching my t-shirt.

#

I wish I could remember those words now...

Due to my foolishness with packing, I find myself without the aid of decent music tonight. Fuck Alexander for leaving 'Best of the Eighties' lying around. Whatever happened to my music?

No music. No television.

I can't go on much longer without something to comfort me. Such weird things have been happening lately.

Take last night, for example. At several hours' past sundown, I became aware of a meaty smell which curled under the door of my cabin and wafted over to my desk, where I was sitting and working in the near-complete darkness. Mindless, ghostlike, I drifted over to the door, and opened it.

This was the first time I had opened the door in weeks - but this thought has only just occurred to me. At the time, all I noticed was what was on the doorstep.

Two chickens, plucked. And several boxes of dried fruit.

I bundled these items into my arms and brought them inside, shutting the door behind me with my foot. Ordinarily, of course, such an out-of-the-ordinary occurrence would have at least aroused my suspicion. But I suddenly realised I was ravenous, and animal hunger overrode everything else. I stacked the fruit boxes by the sink in the kitchenette for later, and devoured the chickens raw.

The sudden revitalisation this gave me was astounding. I was able to continue working at a faster pace through the night, and well into this morning.

The test tube that is now in front of me is full of a gloopy, white liquid. My solution. It looks the same, smells the same, as the fluid I was exposed to back at Alexander's laboratory. Will it react the same when I add it to the specimens? That remains to be discovered.

I look over my shoulder. The freezer glints back at me in the moonlight. Twenty-six specimens sleep inside, waiting, satisfactorily altered, floating in their new chemical cocktails. The big test will come soon, when I add the white solution to one of them and try to merge them with a living piece of organic tissue.

"I'll pick one of you at random," I whisper to them.

And then, because it sounded insensitive when I said it aloud, I quickly add, "Don't worry. I'm not Alexander Bai. I would never do anything to hurt you."

CHAPTER TWENTY-SIX

In the days that followed the near-disaster with the tanks, I suffered from a long, brain-destroying bout of insomnia. All night I would lie awake, thinking about those tanks shutting down, the foetus failing, withering away.

A week later, I decided to take matters into my own hands.

Alexander came down in the elevator early that morning to find me staring across at him from the other side of the pit. I was grinning so widely, it felt as if my trembling, taught skin might snap.

When he saw the look on my face, Alexander paused. He started towards me again but at a slower, more careful pace. He stopped at the edge of the pit.

Here, he must have then felt the powerful heat radiating from the pit, because he jumped back suddenly. "Katrina!"

"Yes? Is there something you would like to ask me, Alex?"

He was staring at the pit now, trembling a little. Slowly, he raised his head to me. I was still grinning.

"Why is it so *hot* in here, Katrina? What have you done?"

My smile could stretch no further. It broke and I let out a short barking sound - the closest I ever came to a laugh - and ran around the edge of the pit, on tiptoe, towards Alexander. He watched with wide eyes as my feet veered close to the edge, and stepped forward as if he would have to catch me. Really, he needn't have bothered: mentally unstable I might have been, but as far as physical stability goes, my innate ability to stay on my feet remained unhindered. I stopped before Alexander, still grinning. "You'll never guess what I did last night, Alex!"

He took my elbows in his hands and looked down into my face. "Tell me," he said. "Tell me, Katrina! What the *hell* have you done?" He shook me.

This brought me back down into the gloomy depths of sanity. So, instead of being jovially cryptic, dropping clever hints to confuse poor Alexander further and withholding the revelation until the last minute, I said-

"I heated up the fluid under the cell lining."

"What? How did you do that?"

The smile crept back. "Always the scientist, Alex; always asking 'how', never 'why'. Anyway, you won't get an answer. It was all like a dream. I can barely remember."

Alexander let go of my elbows. He went to crouch down by the side of the pit. Then he recoiled with a rasping shriek. "That is more than just 'hot'." He spun round. "Alright - *why*? Why on Earth would you do such a thing, Katrina?"

"Ah!" Now was my time to show off. I searched for something with which to demonstrate and noticed a half-eaten cereal bar in Alexander's pocket - one of those cardboard-flavour ones. I snatched it from him.

"Hey! What are you doing?"

I got to my knees, dug my gloveless fingers under the endothelial lining, lifted it - and slid the bar into the blood-red fluid.

"Have you gone mad?" Alexander had to restrain himself from coming any closer to me until I had moved away from the pit, rubbing my blistered hands. From a safe distance, we watched as the cereal bar broke into segments, then crumbs, then crumbs of crumbs, until it had disappeared altogether.

"I strengthened the cell lining," I explained to Alexander. He was still staring into the pit, at the place where his cereal bar had been. "The heat won't damage it; the blood-liquid won't get through to the amniotic fluid or the foetus. But it is still semi-permeable – the lining, not the foetus. But the foetus is too. Are you with me so far?"

Alexander shook his head. "Strengthened the cell lining? How…"

"Ignore the 'how' for now, Alexander Bai. Listen to me. Anything we drop under the lining will be broken down to tiny, tiny molecules. Those molecules will be able to slip through the membrane, and be absorbed by the foetus."

"What would we want the foetus to absorb?"

"Food, of course! It doesn't just work with cereal bars. I've tried – we can throw *real* food in there, Alex! Food that can be broken down into energy molecules. And those energy molecules will travel from the blood, through the lining and be absorbed directly by the foetus's body. We won't have to rely on those faulty tanks anymore. We can relax! Today, I'll work on an alternative waste-extraction system, then we can get rid of those stupid things altogether. Our foetus will be safe!"

Apparently, Alexander did not share my enthusiasm. He stared at me. The expression on his face was impossible to read: it was as if he was wearing a mask, frozen neutral. "You do realise," he said slowly, "what will happen if the cell lining becomes damaged in any way?"

"But it won't," I said. "I made it stronger."

"How did you make it stronger?"

"With a solution. I came down here last night, and I made a solution. A solution that binds the cells together."

"Where is the rest of this solution?" It seemed as if Alexander didn't believe me.

"Nowhere. I used it all. Then I sterilized all the apparatuses - we must keep contamination to a minimum..."

"Alright, what went *into* the solution?"

I thought. "I... don't remember. It just sort of - *came* to me."

Alexander's hands. They were shaking. "Then how can you be sure that the lining won't be seared apart at any moment? Do you know what would happen if a substance *that hot* got into the amniotic fluid?" Alexander peered into my face, searching for some sign that I understood. He found none. "The foetus would not survive the heat, Katrina! It would be broken into molecules too. We would lose it forever."

This scenario had never occurred to me. With Alexander's words, my elation vanished. I fell to my knees, moaning.

Alexander let me moan for a while then took a step towards me. He nudged my body, cowering and squirming on the floor, with his toe. "Can we reverse it?"

"I don't know!" I cried. "I don't know what I did!"

"Alright. Alright." Alexander removed his foot from my body. "It's not your fault. You were tired. People do stupid things when they're tired."

"They don't destroy their own innocent creations by burning them away to nothing," I said. "No, they don't, Alexander Bai – that is unforgivable!"

Alexander crouched down, a safe distance away from the edge of the pit. He made as if to move towards it - then remembered, and stayed where he was. "Well, the lining doesn't appear to be damaged.

So you must have applied *something* to it, even if you don't remember what it was or how you did it." He was silent for a moment, thinking. "And how could you create so much *heat*? I must say, Katrina, given that you've barely slept for almost a week now, this is incredible. It's completely insane, true, but *ingenious*."

"Maybe, if I could find a way to cool it down again – quickly, after the disintegration…" I removed my hands from my face, looked up at Alexander. "All the foetus molecules could reassemble?"

Alexander shook his head. "Don't be stupid." He didn't take his eyes off the pit. "You know as well as I do, that wouldn't happen. If it did… well, you'd have to make sure there wasn't any unabsorbed food in there first. Or else they might combine, and it could end up with… a cluster of raisins for a frontal lobe, or something." He laughed, weirdly. Then he looked at me with a stiff, painful smile, which I could only assume was meant to be comforting. "Look, we'll just have to be careful. You say you reinforced the cell lining? I don't know how you could have done that, but I trust you managed it. The foetus is probably safe. We'll just have to make sure someone has their eye on it at all times."

"*Her*," I whispered.

Somewhere far away, I heard the elevator doors open. "Ah. One of the men, come to summon us to breakfast, no doubt." With another forced smile, Alexander beckoned to me. "Come on, Kat. Get some breakfast."

I refused to leave until the man-in-white had come into the room, and I had heard Alexander explain the situation to him, emphasising how vital it was that the foetus should be watched at *all times*. Only then would I allow Alexander to usher me to the elevator.

And then…

Actually, I can't remember what happened next. I'm having a blank moment.

I get them more and more now, these blank moments. After everything that happened to me in Alexander Bai's laboratory, something strange must have affected the part of my brain which stores memories. Some of my memories just… aren't there anymore.

Other memories have become distorted. Dreamlike. So I can no longer be certain of what is real, and what is not…

...Oh good God I've killed one.

Fuck.

Fuckfuckfuckfuckfuckgoddamn SHIT!

I'm back in the cabin. The clouds of memory have dispersed. I can see what I have just done.

Specimen six. Formerly a pickled fragment of muscle and flesh from a lioness. It dissolved when I added the solution. Nothing can bring it back!

Test tube six, selected at random, is empty.

I don't know what happened! Perhaps the concentration of the solution was too strong. It broke the poor thing into irreparable, tiny-tiny, molecular shards when I added it to the tube. Or else it was too weak: it couldn't pull them back together again once they came into contact with the secondary material.

The secondary material, a mouse I caught in the kitchen this morning, is scrabbling at the sides of my stained coffee cup. It is wet from the concoction I poured on it, perhaps disturbed by the burning sensation irritating its skin, but is otherwise unaltered. The lioness DNA failed to assimilate with its body. My prototype hybrid never materialized. A once proud creature has been lost forever.

I had eaten. I had slept. I don't know what could have caused me to make this mistake!

Brain damage...

No.

I try not to think about it. My brain is whole and normal.

But if I do have brain damage, I cannot help but wonder... does this mean that what I am doing now is... well, wrong?

Sometimes, I think my mind has become a dangerous creature. Something even I need to be protected from, not to mention others...

I hurl the coffee cup to the floor. The wasted contents of test tube six spread over the floorboards, and the mouse runs for safety.

Of course, I have other specimens. Plenty of others. This experiment is far from over.

Yet... specimen six was a life. A potential life, anyway. I wasted it. Destroyed it in the name of research. Just like Alexander would have done...

NO.

No, Alexander was working for – what did he call it? 'Scientific voyeurism'. I am working for a greater cause.

The mildew stain on the ceiling is looking down at me. Smirking like a condescending teacher at a problem student.

My facial muscles are stiff, my lips paralysed from underuse, but I direct my eyes upwards and think the words – "This isn't over!"

Maybe there was something wrong with the mouse? Some reason that particular individual couldn't absorb the new genetic material. Maybe it was diseased? I should have checked.

The old me WOULD have checked, or at least asked Alexander to check; he was the one who knew about these things. But I didn't think. No. I never thought. What is WRONG with this new brain of mine?

No. No, don't think like that, Katrina. Alexander created a problem. You are creating a solution. 'A solution – to be a solution'. Get it?

Incredible. Even if everything else about you has changed, your abominable sense of humour certainly has not. That's something to be grateful for, isn't it? Embrace it.

You are going to put your work to one side for the moment and listen to the radio. Yes. The radio always makes you feel better. Juan and Frieda - you haven't listened to them in a while. What gibberish are they spouting today?

Juan: She's not going to do it, Frieda! You must realise that. If she's trying to do what you think she's trying to do...
Frieda: What I know she's trying to do, Juan!
Juan: Either way, it's insane! No human being could possibly achieve that.
Frieda: But she's not human, Juan. She's better than human! What could a human being do for our cause? Don't you see? That is why we always fail - because deep down, there isn't a human being alive who wants to eliminate...
Juan: Would you listen to yourself, Frieda! 'Not human'? Do you really believe that? You're delusional. This is some weird symptom of the pregnancy – it has to be!
Frieda: Why are you so unwilling to accept this, Juan? You were a member of the Cause long before I was. If she succeeds, everything we've been fighting against will finally be a thing of the past! And the way she plans to do it, intelligent life will still have a future. Why can't you believe in her, Juan?

Juan: Because the things you say you've been hearing from her, Frieda, are the ramblings of a madwoman! You saw her when she opened that door. Those crazy eyes, that matted hair...
Frieda: Exactly. She isn't human!
Juan: No. I've seen this happen before, Frieda. Some people get so caught up in the Cause, usually because of a personal vendetta rather than any desire to save the planet, that their minds become broken. They start to develop this insane belief that their personal struggle makes them the only person who can change the world. She's not... 'Parahuman', Frieda; she's just a broken human!

I have a strange, jittery, cold feeling inside me. Come to think of it, I don't think I've felt any real emotion other than fear in a long time. Is this how it's supposed to feel?

My hands have started to shake, and I can't make them stop.

Maybe it's the coffee. Yes.

Let's see: coffee is to hangovers, as... what is to the effects of coffee?

Frieda: I believe in her, Juan! What does that make me? Crazy?

Frieda is usually such a strong character. A reclusive housewife and emotional disaster, maybe, but she always defends her corner. I don't like it when she sounds this weak and pathetic. I don't. I think they should FIRE those goddamn alcoholic writers!

Juan: Crazy? Well – sometimes I wonder.
(Pause.)
Frieda: Oh. Right. I see. So you admit it: you made a mistake. They were right all along, were they? I should be sent away, and locked up in that hellish hospital again, and violated...
Juan: Shut up!
Frieda: ...again and again by the system, because you made a mistake in believing me when I said I wasn't crazy!
Juan: Don't be stupid! I only meant... Look, maybe you should stay inside for the time being, okay? Take care of yourself and the baby, and let me worry about the Cause for a while. And try not to listen to her for a few weeks. Would that really be so bad?

Frieda: Oh – alright. Alright, Juan. You want me to stay inside? To cook your food, to sleep in your bed, to mindlessly devote myself to your *ambition of having a son while you steer us in whatever direction you see fit - is that all you want from me? Well - I won't comply! I won't comply!*

I WON'T believe in you, ALEXANDER BAI, and I WON'T comply. NOT THIS TIME.

I want to turn the radio off.

I get up from my seat and search the room; search it from corner to corner, for the radio. Where is it?

I check in all the obvious places. On the higher shelves of the dusty, empty bookcase which takes up the longest wall of the cabin. No. On top of the refrigerator - there is a chance that, caught up in my work, I always overlooked it when I went to use the fridge. But no. On the windowsill; all over the kitchenette.

Then in the less obvious places: under things, in drawers, down the sides of the grotty, discarded mattress I have been using as a bed whenever I remember to sleep. Even through my own bags because I cannot trust my own GODDAMN mind not to have FORGOTTEN that I brought the goddamn radio myself but never unpacked it... before admitting to myself something I must have known all along, but up until now, never had a reason to think about and accept.

That 'something' is that there is no radio here. There never has been.

I go back to the desk and hold my poor, diseased head in my hands.

But – let's be logical. What could it be? Schizophrenia? That can cause audio hallucinations, I know; I leafed through Alexander's copy of '1000 Medical Mysteries Solved' back at the laboratory. Bipolar disorder, maybe?

If only I had access to an MRI machine, I could see for myself what's going on up there. Alexander showed me several diagrams of the human brain during our time together. Poor little blindly-trusting me didn't even consider why an animal expert would be so interested in human brains...

But NO! Now is not the time to reminisce!

If only I had an MRI machine, then maybe I could compare an image of my brain with those pictures of normal brains on file inside my head (I hope to God I still have the key to those files), and work out what the hell has gone wrong.

But I can't. I don't have the technology - and it feels like I've lost a limb. I could make one? But, no: I wouldn't find the parts here, would I? Damn!

Even a book would suffice. 'Abnormal Neurology for Dummies', or something like that. But no. There are only three books in this cabin: a guide to self-sufficient living, an aged dictionary, and an even older copy of 'One Flew Over the Cuckoo's Nest', mocking me from the bookshelf. Other than this, the bookshelf is empty.

GODDAMN EMPTY!

FUCK!

And I am alone in the desert, hiding behind a paper-thin blind from a house with no-one in it. Living off instant coffee, raw meat, and three hours' sleep a night.

No music.

No Alexander.

FUCK ALEXANDER!

My only company: a mind that I barely recognise as my own anymore, to go with a body changed beyond all recognition. A mind that generates voices which might well be saner than I am.

AND WHAT THE HELL IS THIS EXPERIMENT I'M DOING?

It seemed sane a while ago, but now I don't know. Is it? Is it all worth it?

Alexander Bai has broken my brain.

But I will go on.

Yes. Of course I will.

I will see this experiment through to completion, even if it is all a figment of my imagination. As the street-preacher Petunia once said to me, though not in the same words: everyone needs something to believe in. Something to die for. Something to kill for. It is what keeps us going – even if that 'something to believe in' is about as real as pixie dust, or religion, or everlasting love. And so...

What do you know? It turns out I can cry. If only for an experiment doomed to failure.

And so, pushing the tears to the corners of my eyes, I march steadily forward into the abyss.

CHAPTER TWENTY-SEVEN

'During the first month of the second trimester, your baby's eyelids, eyelashes and nails will form. She will be able to yawn, stretch, suck her thumb, and make faces, as her nervous system starts to function.'

At the bottom of this page in 'Your Pregnancy and You', the book's previous owner had written a list, in blue and pink crayon, of possible names for her baby.

I read through the names in pink.

'Faith'. 'Angel'. 'Justice'. 'Sonja'.

\#

Alexander and I took turns watching the foetus constantly, day and night. I remained sleeplessly paranoid for days. But as the creature continued to develop healthily above the stream of boiling fluid, I became more trusting that it would still be alive when I awoke, and allowed myself some rest. Eventually, Alexander convinced me to delegate a few more hours of guard-duty to one of the men. To give us time to relax together without distraction.

Harley, I remember, was the top contender for this duty. Although we had barely spoken since the day he swore me to secrecy about Alexander's mother, I knew that all the years Harley had spent at Doctor Bai's side, as well as his unparalleled patience, made him ideal for the job. Plus, as a former caesarean specialist, he had experience with newborns.

Later, other men were allowed to share the duty. I became used to the identical, white-coated figures materialising in the lab and, while I never learnt their names, I did learn, to an extent, to trust them.

Although it became easier to entrust guardianship of our foetus to the men, I would always be reluctant to leave. Alexander would have to guide me out of the Womb Room, thanking whichever man-in-white had given up his time to watch our pride and joy as we passed.

"You know nothing's going to happen to it," he would whisper to me in the elevator. "And *he* knows what to do, if anything goes wrong."

"Yes. Yes - but he's no substitute for us!" I must have said this a hundred times.

"You're too devoted to this project, Kat," Alexander said once. Then he paused. "But then, who am I to criticise?"

Alexander's words always calmed me somewhat. But when we reached the ground floor, it was always the lounge I would retreat to, where I would escape from my anxiety with that fail-safe cure: *music*.

The stereo system - large and cumbersome, designed for the old CDs - was in the far corner of the lounge, tilted so as to project sound throughout the room. Alexander's twinkly, pretentious CDs were stacked in alphabetical order to one side of it. He would always keep his 'other music collection' under the bed in his room; however, pieces of it did start to trickle their way down to the lounge, forming their own pile next to the boring-music stack, as I made more requests.

From this new stack, I would select my cure. Always something with easily-ignorable vocals and a strong beat. I would load up the player, turn the volume to 'max', and become lost in the vibrations.

Not one for dancing, Alexander would sit on the sofa and watch me.

Once the music had allowed me to push my anxieties to the back of my brain, I could enjoy the thrill of the prospect of new life - new life, which *I* was going to bring into the world. No matter what I was listening to - whether the lyrics spoke of love, or lust, or of tearing down the establishment – the song always seemed to agree with, and heighten, the joy I felt. I was in raptures.

And it was not just the thought of the foetus provoking these raptures.

I found that I had only to think of a *part* of Alexander Bai – his soft blue eyes; that small, perfectly-white smile when he was caught off-guard; that rebellious lock of hair which seemed to have a mind of its own, and would flop down over his eyes if left untended for too long - and it would inspire an ecstasy in me. An ecstasy which made me want to dance and squeal and howl at the moon, a Dead-Talker seeing the Spirit World across the void; and then crash to my knees in tears, begging Rawg's forgiveness that I had obtained that illusive magical thing which summoned him to the beach every spring.

One night, Alexander called down to me from the landing. "Kat! If I hear 'The Power of Love' one more time, I swear to God I'm going to scream. Come to my room – I want to show you something."

He spoke so casually, as if my entering his room was perfectly normal, something we had done a thousand times before, when really, what lay on the other side of Alexander's perpetually closed door was a mystery to me. Curious, I switched off the player and went upstairs.

It was a featureless, white room, almost identical to mine. I had expected more furniture in Alexander's bedroom: perhaps a poster, or a framed photograph; even a few stray socks on the floor – but no. Even the bed looked unslept-in, the dressing table untouched.

I lingered in the doorway, taking in the emptiness, the unnatural cleanliness. Every night, Alexander went to sleep in this sterile cage. Every morning, his presence was wiped away with – by the smell of it – antibacterial wipes and polish. A perfect, safe environment for the Lodge's most precious captive specimen.

Standing in the centre of the room, Alexander gave me a smile. This gave me enough encouragement to enter the room; however, I couldn't help wrinkling my nose at the overwhelming stench of disinfectant.

Alexander got down on his knees by the bed, lifted a corner of the sheets, and pointed out the three shoeboxes underneath which housed his 'other music collection'. I could select CDs and cassettes for myself and take them down to the lounge, he said; or to the basement, where I could have them playing *softly* whilst we worked.

"Take as many as you like," Alexander said to the back of my head as I pawed through the box. He hesitated, then said, "You know, if you would prefer, Kat... you can sleep here tonight? I mean, only if you want to. It might help the insomnia."

I replied truthfully: I would *not* prefer to sleep in Alexander's bed. My bed was perfectly comfortable, and my room didn't smell of disinfectant. The location was not the problem.

"Oh." Alexander almost seemed disappointed. "Sorry. I'm sorry. Silly question."

Another week and, somehow, he was sleeping in mine.

We did not touch each other when we shared my bed. We simply lay there, side by side; sometimes in silence, sometimes having half-brained, pointless conversations, which for some reason neither of us felt too embarrassed to let the other share.

And somehow, Alexander was right. Sleep did come easier when I was lying beside him, warmed by his body heat, listening to his rhythmic breathing. When I closed my eyes, I was lying in a cocoon of soft fabrics beside Father and Rawg: safe and protected in the embrace of family.

#

'At this stage in your pregnancy, hair is beginning to grow on your baby's head. A soft, fine hair called 'lanugo' now covers her shoulders, back and temples. This will be shed during the first weeks of life.'

For all but the last few stages of its development, the Smilodon's fur (or 'lanugo', as 'Your Pregnancy and You' liked to call it) did not turn dark as Alexander had predicted, but stubbornly remained a ghostly, pale shade.

I remember pointing at the pit one day. "Alex," I said. "Look!"

Instantly, Alexander was at my side. "What is it, Kat? Is something wrong?"

I looked up at him and grinned. "She's got her father's white hair."

"What?" Alexander saw my grin, and snorted. "Oh, don't be ridiculous."

#

'Gender can usually be determined by the end of the fourth month of pregnancy, by means of an ultrasound scan. However, doctors often prefer not to disclose the sex of the baby until after the Monroe Pill has been administered, halfway through the fifth month.

'If yours is one of the twenty per-cent of pregnancies to be ended prematurely by the Monroe Pill, please do not be disheartened. Save this book for future pregnancies. In these cases, it is normal for mothers to experience feelings of guilt and regret. These will pass with time.

'It might be helpful to ask yourself: In a society that is constantly moving forward, what sort of future could my defective child hope to have? Would it have enjoyed its life of exploitation and bullying, without employment, friendship, or love?'

'Remember, you have made the best possible decision – not only for society, but for your unborn child.'

"It *will* be loved," I told the book. I held my invented image of Sonja in my mind, a slender angel with Alexander's silky white hair and milky blue eyes, and looking skywards promised: "It will be loved. No matter what."

#

Since his cardboard-flavour cereal bar had not harmed the foetus, Alexander relaxed his contamination rule, and said that we were allowed to bring food down to eat in the work room. He started to bring down snacks from the kitchen. I would take them back to the kitchen, and replace them with new, better foods. Things that Alexander had never tried before.

There was a list attached to one of the fridges in the kitchen, on which the men could write anything they needed. When spring approached and the roads became less treacherous, Harley would take the list down to the nearest town in Alexander's Behemoth every month and return with fresh foods.

Gradually, as I discovered times and methods by which I could enter the kitchen unseen, the items on this list became increasingly exotic.

'Fizzy fruit sweets'. 'Cola'. 'Chocolate'. 'Ice cream'. 'Sour cream potato chips'.

'That green soda in the can with the lightning bolt on it', which I remembered from my stay with the Professor, was once at the top of the list. Sadly, I never received it. Harley explained that a lot of products like this had recently been banned by the new government, on the grounds of them being a 'danger to public health'.

Other items started to disappear from the list, too. The rice cakes, for example - they went. The plain wafers, the vitamin paste, the watered-down apple juice. Alexander never commented on the absence of these pointless products. I doubt he even noticed.

New music was added to the shopping list, too, to diversify Alexander's laboratory playlist. One morning, I went up to the kitchen to get some chocolate and lemonade, leaving Alexander with the unearthly, wailing tones of Pink Floyd, and returned to find him listening to Ozzy Osbourne. He was even waving his pure-white locks slowly from side to side, in time to the heavy, wild beat.

I didn't comment.

#

Whenever we were given the opportunity to take an evening break from our guardianship, and if I was too tired to dance, Alexander and I would sit and watch the old television set in the lounge. At first, I was disappointed to find that we could not receive the typical Californian programmes this high in the mountains. However,

Alexander *did* have an impressive collection of old films, recorded onto ancient video cassettes. I suspect that Doctor Bai, for all his cruelty and misogyny, did have one redeeming feature: a passion for television.

"Why do you like fiction?" I once asked Alexander, scanning titles of romances and dramas.

"I don't see a problem with watching things that aren't true," he said. "If they make you happy and keep you going. As long as you can separate fiction from real life and return to the real world when the film ends."

Which made some sort of sense, I supposed.

Searching through these video tapes in the lounge one night, I was excited to find two entire shelves of documentaries. Most were about cloning and genetic engineering. Some were wildlife documentaries. One, I recognised. It was 'Polite Society'.

"Don't look at that," Alexander said when he saw me slip it out from amongst the others. He snatched the tape from me and put it back. "Something my father used to make me watch. To help me understand the social conventions of the outside world. It's… embarrassing."

I simply nodded. I didn't want to know whether Alexander shared Rawg's interest in Lorna Lane, with her perfect curvy body and her glossy yellow hair.

One night, Alexander and I were on the sofa in the lounge, watching 'the Cabinet of Doctor Caligari'. It was a black-and-white silent film about a doctor who hypnotises a sleepwalker into committing horrendous atrocities; the poor sleepwalker, unaware that the doctor is manipulating him, goes along with it.

Towards the end of the film, I leant across the sofa; rested my head on Alexander's leg. My motivation for doing this wasn't clear to me. Perhaps I was merely tired; too tired to understand what I was doing. The foetus's development had been progressing rapidly. I had spent the last few days staring at it with even greater intensity than usual. But I had been tired before and, even though I had slept beside Alexander, I had never before known such self-abandonment.

What surprised me more than my own actions, was Alexander's reaction. I felt his body go rigid, his legs stiffen, when he felt my weight against him. Yet he did not try to remove me. After a moment, he relaxed. He started to stroke my hair.

And it didn't feel like a violation. It felt... *nice*. Like a soft breeze blowing from across the sea: my partner's fingers in my hair, soothing my scalp, repairing my fracturing mind.

The evil doctor loomed behind his brainwashed victim on the flickering screen, and I nestled closer to Alexander Bai. If there were any thoughts in my mind at the time, they were clearly not worth remembering.

#

'Her eyelids will be developing over her eyes. Her outer ears will be forming. Her inner ears will be starting to differentiate into more complicated structures - through which your baby will very soon be able to hear your voice. You don't have long to wait now, new mother!'

#

The day the outer ears started to develop visibly was a day of great excitement. After all, it meant that soon the little Smilodon would be able to listen to my music. There was so much I had to teach her.

I scribbled a 'top ten songs' list in the back of my sketchbook, which became a top twenty then a top fifty; when I discovered that some of the songs were missing from mine and Alexander's music collection, I wrote the album names in big red letters at the top of Harley's shopping list, overlapping less important articles like 'milk', 'eggs' and 'bread'.

I danced around the lounge to the Buzzcocks later that night, getting dizzy. Perhaps it was because my blood sugar levels were low. I had been too excited to eat for days.

"You're going to hurt yourself, Kat!" Alexander warned from the sofa behind me. He had to shout to be heard over the music.

I ignored him, kept dancing, until the room began to slope and slide. My feet tripped over each other. I was on my back on the hard wooden floor, the ceiling spinning above me.

Alexander leapt from the sofa and ran to me. He leaned over, looked desperately into my face. "Are you alright, Kat? Say something!"

His concern was so ridiculously over-the-top, it was almost humorous. I gave him a taunting smile.

We remained that way for a long time: him looking down into my eyes, me looking up into his; almost perfectly white, but for that faint touch of crystal-blue if you peered closely enough.

Meanwhile, the Buzzcocks played something about falling in love; the lyrics lost to the wailing of the guitars, to my own thumping heartbeat.

#

'Your baby now has little left to do but grow. During the final trimester, a good mother-to-be should begin preparing a healthy, stable home environment for her future little one.'

#

Alexander introduced me to more of his own films. Old ones, like *Pretty Woman*. Even older ones, like *Casablanca*.

At first, he would sit motionless on the sofa and watch the screen. But, as our film nights became more common, I became aware of him looking every now and again in my direction. There was always a slightly concerned expression on his face, as if he was coming to terms with the fact that these idealised films of his might not make the same impression on another viewer. He even asked me for approval several times. "Did you like the film, Kat?"

I would respond, "Not really. But the ending was good."

Because it was not the plots of these films which interested me, as much as their endings.

In videos such as 'Love for the Young Christian', 'Marriage, Sex and Sin', and 'Polite Society', marriage was presented as a solemn exchange of vows, sealed with a kiss. Never had I seen it as something more symbolic, as a way of sealing up the past.

But that was what marriage was, according to Alexander's films. A way of putting an end to the sadness and the heartache the characters had endured and letting them start afresh with the promise of a perfect life. So perfect, that the film always ended before the audience had a chance to glimpse it.

One afternoon, when I had gone up to the kitchen to find the popcorn and orange juice I had ordered, I added something to the bottom of the shopping list.

'A ring. (Preferably diamond.)'

Then, pleased, I gathered what I wanted from the fridge, and hurried back to the elevator. And I waited, in anticipation, for shopping day.

#

I'm feeling rather good about myself now. You see, I worked something out today that I think you'll want to hear.

Are you ready?

You see, the building opposite my cabin is inhabited. By two people. A man and a woman.

Their names are Juan and Frieda.

They almost never go out. That is why I have never noticed them before. But today, Juan drove his car out of a garage hidden at the back of the building. I watched it leave, making tyre prints across the desert which are still visible through the curtain - dispelling any doubt I might have had that what I saw was real.

And I've worked out what the voices are. They are Juan and Frieda's thoughts.

Which means two things:

'A' – I can do something Alexander can't do.

And 'B' – I am not insane!

My self-confidence has returned to me. Not even my memories can hurt me now!

My research will continue.

PART THREE: THE DAY IT ALL CHANGED

CHAPTER TWENTY-EIGHT

I cannot remember quite how it happened. It all happened, to exploit an apt cliché, 'as if in a dream'.
A terrible, unending dream.
I cannot remember, for example, waking that morning and realising that Alexander - who had spent every night for the last month or more sleeping by my side - was gone. Nor can I remember the feelings which came to me upon this discovery. Was I concerned? Or was I relieved that he would not see what I was going to do?
I cannot remember getting out of bed or collecting the ring in its neat black box from wherever I had hidden it. (If I had to guess, knowing the naïve little idiot I was back then, it was probably somewhere miserably obvious - like in a bathroom cabinet, tied with a loose thread secured with Band-Aids.)
But I can remember other details very clearly.

#

I drifted down the wide, white staircase to the Lodge's ground floor in my bathrobe and slippers. I remember the sterilized air, the echoes, the emptiness. None of the men-in-white were around, which meant I must have woken especially early with the excitement. There were no creaking footsteps, no voices whispering behind closed doors, no prying eyes to follow me.

The word 'Alex' on my lips; I chanted it softly to myself.

He wasn't in the dining room. He wasn't in the lounge. I suppose I'll never know where he was: perhaps outside or in his own bedroom. At the time, the only place I could think of was the basement. And so, steeling myself, I went to the elevator.

I stepped inside, alone. The doors closed. The box went dark. My body broke into the predictable shivers. Slowly I reached out, made myself push the number keys – '2-0-5-2' – and the basement button; quickly withdrew my hand, clutched the ring box tightly to my chest. The elevator descended. I closed my eyes, and pictured Alexander's luminescent white face, his pale eyes watching me in the dark.

I stepped out of the elevator into the dark basement corridor, still clutching the ring box to my chest. The light panels on the ceiling came on one-by-one as I progressed down the corridor. Calling Alexander's name like a pathetic, mewling kitten…

\#

Oh - some days, I wish I could go back in time and shoot myself in the head for my weakness! Those that are weak of mind, weak of heart - all must die, according to Nature's Law. Funny how humanity, with all its scientific knowledge, its machines and Monroe Pills, has not yet eradicated the foolish. Rather, it has used its science through the centuries to help them to survive and breed.

Mankind is naïve, I suppose. It does not think that a bigger predator might someday come along, exploit these weaknesses, and wipe the whole species out. So, in a way, science has given me an advantage…

\#

I must have checked the Womb Room first, because I distinctly remember seeing the foetus before everything changed. Ghostlike, pale, and vulnerable; and now a four-limbed, twitching, soon-to-be *breathing* creature. White, like Alexander. Wild, like myself.

Our child.

I remember thinking, detachedly, how different the world would become once the impossible creature was born. And for the first time, I wondered how it would cope in a world where it did not fit in. Would it be received as a freak, an outcast - hunted down, or driven away?

But I don't remember worrying too much about this. I suppose I must have believed wholeheartedly and unquestioningly that, with the united forces of Alexander and myself to protect it, everything would be alright.

\#

Weak of mind. Weak of heart. Stupid, stupid Katrina…

\#

No Alexander in the Womb Room. I drifted through to the work room.

\#

A hazy moment in my memory. Images flicker and blur like those on a broken television…

\#

And now I am standing in Alexander's work room. He isn't here. I should probably go back upstairs. I think - *Maybe he has gone back to bed?*

But... no.

I glance from the empty office chair to the wall. There is that captivating sketch on the unrolled parchment. The first picture I ever saw of the Smilodon. The picture which started all of this.

I move closer to the picture, as if hypnotised. I feel wood against my legs. I glance down. Here is the desk, and on the desk is a leather-bound book.

Alexander's journal.

It looks like mine used to. Thick with pages and covered in leather. The promise of secrets and truths within.

In the absence of Alexander, I take a chance. Grab the journal, curious to see the Alexander Bai that its leather cover obscures.

On the first page, Alexander's name. Also the words: 'Journal to Chronicle my Fulfilment of Dr. James Bai's Dream'. Always a pretentious one, my Alexander.

I skip the next few pages.

On the fifth page - something strange. Five sketches of animal heads: all big cats. Part of the skull has been erased from each animal to reveal a cross-sectional diagram of its brain. For each brain, a small, dark-shaded section has been circled in pencil. Each circle is labelled: 'telepathic organ of Panthera tigris?', 'telepathic organ of Panthera leo?', 'telepathic organ of Acinonyx jubatus?', and so on; always with the question mark.

Very strange.

On the seventh page is an image I recognize. It is a sketch of the Smilodon; just the head this time, its face staring out at me. So expertly drawn, it almost seems three-dimensional. I reach out to touch it; run my fingers delicately over the page. I murmur, "Soon we'll meet each other, little one. Soon."

The Smilodon has also been drawn with a side-panel removed from its skull. However, in this case, the brain has only been drawn as a basic shape, with minimal detail. A circle has been drawn in roughly the same region as for other five brains. Next to this, another label: 'telepathic organ of Smilodon fatalis?' Again, the question mark.

Curious, I turn the page.

It takes me a few moments to work out what I am looking at. But as soon as I realize, I become nauseous.

Sometime in the distant past, the Professor, and later, Snake and Dougie, had talked about the infamous 'Chimp-Brain Experiment' performed by Doctor Tati, Doctor Monroe, and… and Doctor James Bai. *Alexander's father.* I had blocked it from my mind. Like the Island of Doctor Moreau story, it didn't seem real.

But now - here is a drawing of a cat, tiny face and big black eyes. A cat – one was used in the experiment, Snake had said: its brain operated on by the abominable Doctor Tati. Underneath this is some familiar handwriting.

'Doctor Tati's solution enabled Doctor Bai to attach the section removed from the domestic cat's brain to the brain of the chimpanzee, with no rejection of the foreign material. As a result, traits typical of the more primitive animal (the cat) – in this case, its sleep/wake cycle - were assumed by the more advanced animal (the chimpanzee). This method of transferring brain matter between brains of dissimilar species could have monumental consequences, if the same method is applied to…'

The poor cat has been sketched unconscious on a section of table. From this picture is an arrow, pointing to the next image on the page - the cat's head; the side of its skull removed, its brain exposed. A circle shows the area from which part of the brain has been cut. A picture of the grey mass of brain-matter has been drawn - floating where it should not be, outside the animal's skull.

From this sketch, another arrow, pointing to a picture of an ape - its head cut open in another cross-sectional diagram. A circle indicates where the part of the cat's brain has been implanted.

A part of my own brain remembers the Professor; thinks how annoyed he would be if he saw Alexander's bizarre, morbid sketches in a scientific journal, when a linear diagram would have been preferable. I think, *Alex draws like me.* But I quickly silence this thought. The utter disgust I feel at the comparison shocks me – I think, *I could never draw something so obscene and cruel!*

There are more notes on this page. Legions of them. I only read the one beneath the final diagram:

'Cat's brain matter implanted within corresponding region of chimpanzee's brain. Immediately after procedure, the latter acquired the former's sleep-wake patterns. These remained until the chimpanzee's death. Chimpanzee was destroyed after three days, before long-term health effects could be determined. Cat died after twenty-four hours.' And underneath this, Alexander has written: *'NOTE (to self): Remember, destruction of test subjects is a necessary sacrifice for a greater cause'.*

I'm shaken, but curiosity drives me on. With trembling fingers, I turn the page.

Page ten begins with a sketch of a Smilodon – *our* Smilodon – lying unconscious on a section of table.

Next to this: an arrow, pointing right.

Here is a cross-sectional diagram of the Smilodon's head; the side of its skull removed, its brain exposed. Here is a circle around where the supposed 'telepathic organ' should be – but the region is empty. Here is a small, grey lump of something gelatinous-looking, floating where it should not be, outside the animal's skull.

Arrow.

Here is a picture of a head. A human head. It is a head which – which I *recognise*.

Part of the human's skull has been cut away, revealing its brain. Around part of the brain is a circle – in red ink, this time. And within this circle: something gelatinous-looking and grey, and by now familiar. The telepathic organ. The text underneath reads:

'Evidence suggests that a sample of the telepathic organ from a Smilodon will be less specialized to the species than that of a more recently-evolved feline. Therefore, it will be better suited to inter-species transference. *NOTE: While evidence shows that removal of the organ will result in the death of the original animal, there is no evidence to suggest that the procedure will shorten the receiving specimen's lifespan. However, this is still a risk. It is therefore important to use a human test subject with few friends or family ties, whose loss will leave negligible impact on society and the public's perception of science.'*

That familiar face, with the grey lump of our Smilodon stuck to its brain, continues to stare at me hideously from Alexander's journal.

'That is why I must use myself as the initial test subject.'

Alexander's face.

*'RESULT: Telepathic abilities in humans? Enhanced linguistic capabilities? Safe method developed by which such abilities could be

transferred to others? With creative marketing - social re-acceptance of science?

'NOTE: Animal must be allowed to reach maturity (five years approx.) before surgery, in order for telepathic organ to fully develop.

'NOTE: Body of animal must be disposed of carefully, preserving as much tissue as possible for further analysis and possible replication of the experiment with another specimen.'

I stare at the journal. My brain is whirring. Connections are forming.

Was this the ultimate aim of Homo-SuperiUS? To wipe out abnormalities and then enhance the human brain... using pieces stolen from other species?

To do such a thing with *our* Smilodon – this was undoubtedly Alexander's plan.

#

Even now, looking back – I cannot describe the feelings which came over me.

I was now a mother who had found out that her partner intended to murder their baby. Not just murder it, but carve it up! And not because of insanity. Insanity, at least, is pitiable. Alexander's plan was built on cold, hard sanity: the assurance that he had sovereignty over the natural world, a world he could never come close to understanding. And because he could not understand it, he wanted to taunt it, to torture it, to butcher it until it would yield to him.

Because he was a scientist.

Because he was human.

#

The naked lightbulb in Alexander's work room flickers. In my mind I picture it, hanging by the torture-cage where the tigress once existed; above the table, where Harley cut me open.

And still, I cannot turn away from the journal. Alexander's face, staring out at me from the page... it looks as if it's about to say something. I focus on its pencilled lips-

Movement. Behind me.

I turn.

Chemise is leaning against the tigress's cage. She is wearing a short leather skirt, dangerously spiked wrist-cuffs, and has a righteous grin on her face. "Ooh," she croons, shaking her head. "You stupid,

stupid girl." She moves forward. Her hands reach out with childlike, grabbing possessiveness towards me.

I step back - too late. Her hands clamp my face. She yanks me forward, forces her lips against mine, and sucks.

Now I can feel those hands in my hair. They are gravitating down my body, touching tender, private parts of me that I would rather not be touched. It is her right to do these things to me, or so she feels. She is, after all, human. And I am… *what am I?*

Chemise disappears. I blink.

Now the Professor is in the work room, sitting cross-legged on Alexander's desk. He grins. "I can't stay," he says. "My little girl, and my wife - they're waiting for me." He starts to slip down from the table. His eyes are hungry. "But there's so much I still have to learn from you, Katrina. Everything about you – your brains, your beauty - there is so much of you that I still have to sample. Please, Katrina - give it to me. Give it *all* to me." His lips drip thick white saliva.

I turn; I need to run. That man could rip my brain from my skull without a second's remorse. He's human; and *what am I?*

My legs give way beneath me. Blackness swallows my vision. I feel dizzy. Have to close my eyes…

When I open them again, I am lying on the counter of the Groovy Kroovy Music Store, my near-naked body being seared to an ideal golden-brown by the Californian sun. Five bedraggled, long-haired men surround the counter. Leering at me. Their eyes feel like spiders, wandering over my body.

I try to move – but my limbs won't cooperate. I manage a twitch: now my head is swimming. "*Help*," I whisper.

Between two of the men, I see Snake schmoozing a customer, a sycophantic smile on his lips. He turns towards me. Sees me.

"Help!" I say, as loud as I can manage.

But that smile never falters. Snake's eyes are glazed. He refuses to see, through his boozy contentment, that my world is hell. He turns away, back to the customer.

"What's happening to me?" I hiss. And Snake can hear me, I can tell, because he's moving further away from me now. Snake doesn't care. Never did care. I know that now. None of them cared.

"It's called an existential crisis, girl. It's what happens when we reach a certain level of understanding. Don't try to fight it."

I don't have to turn my head to know that Dougie is behind me. I can smell his breath – strangely clean; no trace of alcohol, tobacco, or that herbal smell which I had almost forgotten; that herbal smell which was so common, particularly in that part of California, and which I had smelled on almost everyone except Dougie.

"Dougie – help," I whisper.

I can hear Dougie laugh behind me. "Help? Better ask Snake for help, dear; he's the one with the pills. All I can offer you is truth. But I think you've figured that out for yourself now, haven't you?"

Helplessly, achingly, I nod.

"Good girl." And now, for some reason, Dougie tenderly kisses my forehead. I can feel his lips, cold and wet and strangely soothing, against my burning skin. For a second, I feel relief.

Then the heat, the aching, the pain returns. I wake up.

I am in the Womb Room, standing at the edge of the pit. The heat rising from it is making my skin blister and burn. I'm turning red.

Red. Like the unexplained, horned creature which sometimes appeared on the Edu-Centre video tapes. Those horrible, *lying* video tapes.

In the pit below me, the foetus floats. She doesn't know what is happening. Poor thing. She is innocent, as I once was. An untainted new life.

Now - noise. Somewhere far behind me, the elevator is descending. Alexander is coming.

My body is burning. Fear is building.

But I dare not move. Because there, standing on the other side of the pit, is Father.

All five-foot-four of him. He towered above my cousins, above all of them: I was always so proud of that. His grey hair is thinning with age but still retains that healthy sheen. His eyes – endless sparkling black, like the night sky – have a lightning bolt of indomitable defiance in them.

"*Run, girl.*"

Father's voice is soft, measured. He always tried to speak my native language as slowly and as accurately as he could with his unsuited tongue. The tone is so sweetly familiar, I can feel the tears I restrained on my way across the ocean spring in my eyes again.

"*Run*, girl," he repeats. "*Run*, before they get you too." And with that, he vanishes.

The elevator clanks as it reaches the basement floor.

I step back from the pit. Now I realize that I am still carrying the ring box. Although my first impulse is to hurl it as far as I can, I make myself place it down, calmly, by the side of the pit. Then I stretch out my arms. Loop them behind my back. Flex. I have seen professional athletes do this on television, before they prepare to dive.

Somewhere behind me, footsteps. I can hear a voice, I think it's Harley: "Don't panic, Mr. Bai – we'll find her for you."

I look down into the pit. The blood-solution, like lava, steams and bubbles angrily beneath the reinforced cell layer. Above this, in the clear liquid, safe for now - is the Smilodon foetus, and soon-to-be newborn.

I feel the pit's heat burning my body. I know that this is the creature I love. My child. I mustn't be afraid.

I reach down. My hands are scalded as I force my fingers into the pit, seize the cell lining, and tear it asunder. The blood mingles with the amniotic fluid, the reinforced layer of my harvested cells dissolving into the mix, and the entire contents of the pit start to boil. I smile.

Then, keeping my eyes on the foetus, I dive.

I don't feel any pain. As my flesh peels from my bones, I think I can hear Alexander's voice, distorted by the fluids in my rapidly disintegrating ears, screaming words that I can't quite make out. And then I hear Harley's voice. "No, don't you *dare* go in after her, Mr. Bai! She's gone. Now get the damn foetus out of there before it dissolves, too."

CHAPTER TWENTY-NINE

So, now you know.

But if everything I've told you really happened, I hear you ask... how can I be here, telling this story to you? Surely I would be dead, deceased, gone?

Well, 'gone' I might have been. Physically, at least. My body had disintegrated into tiny, tiny little molecules. Scientifically speaking, Katrina was dead.

But only for, oh... two months?

Good old Harley must have rescued the foetus before it, too, dissolved. I imagine he had a hand in undoing the damage I had caused the pit, too: I doubt Alexander would have been in the right state of mind to repair the cell lining, resynthesize the blood, and create more faux amniotic fluid without some assistance and prodding from his substitute father.

After two months, the patched-up pit was drained, and a somewhat deformed but otherwise physically intact new creature entered the world.

To Alexander Bai, now little more than an anaemic scarecrow with a nervous tick and yellowing eyeballs, it *seemed* to be a Smilodon cub. But this was not the case.

True - it *was* more animal than man. But there was something intelligent working behind those small, intense, emerald-green eyes.

It was allowed to live for three years, and for those three years it spent its life in a tiny cage, watching in the light of a single naked bulb as its captor scribbled notes and measured growth hormones into syringes, and paced, and cursed. It developed rapidly, under the watchful and vengeful eye of Alexander Bai, who, following my self-destruction, seemed to find no pleasure greater than in seeing the creature we had created together suffer at the hands of his malevolent sycophants.

So really, three years were all that were needed for the creature to grow big enough and clever enough to make its escape.

If it had been just a Smilodon, without a human's cunning, I doubt it would even have occurred to the creature to get away. But thankfully, with my molecules making up a good portion of its brain, this was not the case. After three years' imprisonment, it broke free.

I broke free.

I remember the last time I saw Alexander Bai. I was standing in the front doorway of the Lodge, naked under my stolen lab coat, taking one last look at the long, empty hall.

Alexander hurried out of the elevator and appeared from behind the staircase. He stood, staring at me, for a long, long time.

I cast an eye over his body. Malnourished and mad he might have been, but there was still something about those pale eyes, wide and lost; the soft, white hair; those thin, trembling lips. For a moment, he was my Alexander again. My Alex.

Then Alexander looked down, and he saw the portable CryoBag I was carrying in my almost-human hands, bulging with all the tissue samples and bits of scientific paraphernalia I had managed to grab as I fought my way out of the basement.

Alexander Bai stared at the CryoBag, then he looked up at my face again, into my eyes: on-level with his for the first time in three years, now that I had struggled my way into a bipedal stance. His expression changed.

I slung the CryoBag over my shoulder and ran like an animal.

#

You see, I am damned if I'm going to be the only one of my wonderful new kind in a world full of humans. What is the point of an army of one? I have picked up a lot more than manic depression and a touch of schizophrenia from my time with Alexander Bai. I am now a fully-fledged scientist.

I am Doctor Moreau!

And I won't stop. I won't ever, ever stop. Not until I have created my new race. My animals without savagery. My people without human malevolence.

I am surrounded by countless tubes of different substances with various viscosities. One of these must be the solution... the solution to my problem. The contents of each tube has become a different colour, which is highly confusing since I have only just realised that I have become completely and utterly colour-blind! *I am having to rely on other senses to tell them apart. Smell. Taste...*

There's a piece of me inside every tube. So I suppose every taste is an act of auto-cannibalism. Charming thought.

Bothers me?

Not at all!

I have four primitive, wooden walls enclosing limited floor space. I have five shelves, a refrigerator, a kettle, and a mattress. I have... no air conditioning. This is all starting to sound like a riddle. Here are your clues – so, what am I?

I dare not open the front door anymore, because of all the sand. I must not let my specimens become contaminated.

What am I?

I have not eaten in four days. The crate of dried fruit is running out. The refrigerator is occupied by specimens in tubes. Even the supply of coffee is dwindling. I am running on adrenaline alone. My head is pulsing with it.

What am I?

My heart is throwing itself against my ribcage again and again, relentlessly, like a madman behind bars.

What am I? I am…

…Wired! Completely wired.

Good. A certain degree of insanity is required for a genius to make a breakthrough. Homo-SuperiUS knew that.

At this point, even I am not that sure what it is I am working on. But my brain seems to know what it's doing, and so I shall let it do its thing. I'll keep you informed, though. This memoir of mine is not over yet. We still need a satisfactory ending.

What am I?

Good God… I wish I knew!

I wish I knew…

#

My father thought he knew what I was. And one day, when I was a child, he started trying to show me.

He woke me early that morning. Quietly, he led me away from my cousins, shielding my eyes from the glares and the curled lips of the other early risers with his thick, bristled hands. He took me down the dirt track through the forest along which no other would dare venture, because it had been cleared by strange tools and worn down by alien feet. Feet like mine.

We came to a clearing in the forest. There, with a silent gesture, Father presented the old cabin: damp, covered with foliage but somehow still standing.

Inside we opened up the chests of picture-books, videos, and a television, which my birth parents had brought over from their native home. And, day after day, while my cousins cowered outside with hackles raised like frightened dogs, we taught ourselves the ways of the Civilized World. Learnt their words. Civilisation. Knowledge. Heaven. Damnation. California...

California. Part of that mysterious world which I was always aware of, growing up, like a distant relative – but which I never really knew, faults and all, as I do now.

When I was a child, it always seemed close and comforting; a loving grandmother, who I had never got around to visiting. It was only when I left childhood for adulthood, and actually journeyed to California, that I realised how separate it was from my little island. And I realised how removed it must have seemed to the beings I had grown up alongside, who had never even considered that there was a 'rest of the world' before my birth parents arrived.

And now, I find myself struggling to adjust to yet another new world. A world of new feelings, thoughts, and sounds. Where people can enter my head at will, and tell me their secrets.

But if I close my eyes, and keep them closed, and focus my mind on something else and keep it focussed - then I can somewhat mute the volume. It would have been unusual for the old me to think back to the past. Yet it helps.

That first memory of California as I approached on my raft, yet to feel the sand beneath my feet, or meet its people – this memory is one of my favourites. The salt smell of the sea. The motion of the waves. Even the wind, which froze my face and tugged at my hair. All of these sensations help me feel alive.

I was not thinking of anything, really, at that point. Being on the raft is the first situation I can remember being in where my mind wasn't constantly engaged by a task; the last where it wasn't burdened by a human concern. I was liberated. The inside of my head was like a deserted art gallery: vast, but mostly empty; lined with pastel landscapes of tall trees, wild animals, and a red-haired girl in an off-white dress playing on the beach with her brother. Placid, still, unthreatening.

There was no music. No voices. Nothing in my head at that point. Just the sound of the sea.

And now – now, even that sound is fading.

Now, for the first time in years – I believe I am at peace.

CHAPTER THIRTY

This morning, I had visitors.

It was early. The sun was still low to the ground, sending streaks and shadows across the desert and through the thinly-curtained windows. They played over my face and made patterns on the walls.

I was sitting on my work stool. My feet were up against the refrigerator, and the back of my skull was propped against the wall behind me.

I had been sitting like this for too long.

The sun was baking my naked skin. Flies had settled on my face and navel. I looked at my feet; thought, detachedly, about how long my toenails had grown, how chipped and fungal they had become over the last few days, weeks, months. They didn't look anywhere near human anymore. It seemed like quite an achievement.

The little wafts of air escaping from the refrigerator were cooling my feet softly, pleasantly. Inside that mangled, mutated box was the culmination of all my suffering and passion and emotional turmoil; the project I had been labouring over since leaving Alexander and the laboratory and going my own way, so long ago now. It had all seemed so wonderful. Such a righteous mission.

Now, all I knew was that it was there, in that refrigerator - and that I had to protect it with my life, no matter what. Even if it all came to nothing, and shrivelled and died inside that refrigerator - I had to protect it.

I repeated these instructions to myself as I reclined in the sun and burned. A little flicker of enthusiasm was still lit, somewhere deep within me. I had to keep fanning it. Logic told me that a drop of water, a bite of food - a lot of coffee - were probably all that were needed to jump-start me into becoming something similar to my former self: the confident devil's child who, days ago, had injected the final tissue samples into the remaining test tubes of solution; who'd had to keep her hands from shaking with the excitement as she put them all in a row in the refrigerator - her children - and whispered goodnight to them, before closing the door.

But I couldn't find the energy to go looking for food, water, even coffee. I would do it, I told myself. I would do it later.

And I closed my eyes.

The next thing I knew, there was a multi-coloured party going on inside my head. I could hear three hearts – two of them beating fast. A voice, a quavering female voice, was repeating the words 'stay calm'. My nostrils flared as they filled with the scent of adrenaline.

Somebody was afraid.

Using every part of my body that still had feeling in it to steady myself, I levered myself up onto my feet, and lurched and stumbled towards the door. My heart was palpitating. But the smell of sweat and adrenaline lured me onwards.

Prey...

With a hand so numb that it didn't feel like my own, I opened the door and stood in the doorway, breathing hard, mouth encrusted with dry saliva, noticing how powerful the sun could be; squinting out at the world for the first time in a long time. It was agony to do so but I forced myself to peer through the intense, white light - and look at my guests. There were two of them. Well, technically, three.

The woman spoke first. She was wearing a brown headscarf, a faded floral dress, and a warrior's expression. "Hello. My husband and I would like to speak to you for a moment. May we come in?"

I shouldn't have been able to understand her. She spoke in a language that I had never been taught to speak. But I found that I could.

I looked from the woman to her husband. A short, stocky man in khaki slacks, with a dark, wrinkled, bristly face. Young, brown eyes peered at me through folds of prematurely aged skin. He was clearly petrified, poor devil. He stared fiercely at me but couldn't keep his hands still.

Then I looked down at the baby. The woman's hands parted from across her swollen abdomen.

My eyes went to her again, held her stare. In my mind, I formed the words I wanted to say to her.

She smiled. Nodded.

I stepped back, urging them with a final look to follow. The woman reached out to the man, took his hand. They came inside.

I sat back down on my stool.

Frieda took up position in front of me and crouched down so we were face to face. Juan leaned against the refrigerator.

I snarled.

Frieda turned, glowered at Juan. Confused, he moved to lean against the wall.

Frieda turned her attention back to me and beamed. Her smile was gentle, non-threatening; yet she had an aura of maternal strength about her. She would make a powerful mother when her son was born. "Did you like the food we left for you?" *she asked.*

"Yes." *The word fell clumsily from my malformed lips. I wiped away a trail of drool.*

If Frieda felt any revulsion at this, she hid it well. "I don't know what you would have done for food otherwise," *she said.* "It isn't easy to live off this land, especially when you are not used to it. But – sorry, I am sure you must be a great deal stronger than either of us! I forget, sometimes. When you are like this, you seem so – human."

I looked down at my hands. They were cracked and red from where the solution had dried on them. Bleeding.

"It has been wonderful, listening to you work," *Frieda continued.* "You are clearly something special. When I told my husband what you are, he dismissed it. But then I made him look closer. Now he sees."

Juan frowned. Then Frieda glanced at him, and he gave a stiff nod.

"How did you know what I was doing?" *I asked.*

Frieda tapped the side of her head. "You were sending me messages," *she said.* "In here. I don't think you knew you were doing it, but they were a pleasure to receive."

"I didn't think human minds could do that."

"Not many can," *Frieda said. She smiled again – but sadly. I could confidently place an adverb with the verb now, and it surprised me. I instantly understood Frieda's expression. My brain had re-wired: now it was allowing me to see what I had never seen before.*

"People don't like what they don't understand," *Frieda continued.* "They don't like it when things don't 'fit in'. For every abnormality, there has to be a cure. In fact, if it wasn't for this wonderful man here..." *She trailed off, and gazed lovingly at the man by her side. Juan smiled back.*

If their loving pair-bond reminded me of something, I stifled the memory. This couple was too beautiful to taint with such comparisons.

"If it wasn't for him, I would still be locked up in the hospital. They said I had schizophrenia." She paused; shook her head, and gave a shrill giggle. "And... well, so what if that's all it is? I'm happy. People have no right to normalise and abuse what is different. But they do. It's human nature. There is no way of stopping them, not without forcibly changing human nature – and that would be hypocritical, wouldn't it? So we've been hiding out here for twelve months. We haven't seen another human in all that time. But now things are changing. I'm about to bring another human into the world."

She looked at the refrigerator, touched her abdomen.

"I'm five months gone." She looked back at me with big, brown, hopeful eyes. "Am I too late?" she whispered.

"Well..." I got up, walked slowly to the refrigerator. Juan moved quickly out of my way. "I was eighteen, or thereabouts, when I changed. So I suppose not."

"Which would make you how old now?" questioned Juan, something gruff about his tone. I chose not to answer.

So many more important things to do.

I opened the refrigerator door, crouched down to examine the test tubes. Each one a vessel of potential.

"You look perfectly human to me," I thought I heard Juan continue, under his breath. Or maybe it was my own mind.

I fingered the bottles. The possibilities. My children.

"Which one should we try?" I asked, turning. "I have tiger, leopard, cheetah..."

"Tiger, please," said Frieda. She smiled at Juan again, clearly acknowledging a prior conversation between the two of them. "We want him to be able to fight."

Juan's stance was defensive when my eyes went to him; arms folded, shoulders hunched. "Would you like to say something?" I asked.

"Several things. My wife tells me you were held captive for three years?"

"Yes." *Alexander Bai's fingers in my flesh. Eyes burning into me. His instruments of torture* – my hand trembled on the test tube of tiger; I willed it to be still.

"And yet you supposedly 'changed' a year after Ferdinand Mann was elected," said Juan.

"The election happened the winter before," I said.

"Yes. The thing is: Mann's only been in office for just over a year. Which makes me wonder..."

"Juan," Frieda cut him off.

It was real, *I wanted to tell him.* It was real. *But already fading, fading... Katrina's old memories disappearing into the void. I'm something else now.* "But you're still willing to take a chance on me."

Juan looked at me fiercely from across the room, and said, "I have a friend in Germany. A Mr. Randolph. He lives with his wife, and two girlfriends. They became pariahs when he started preaching that mankind should be succeeded by another race, something better." He snorted. "People! They're all for 'improving' themselves, to the point of steamrolling everything nature gave them and replacing it with drugs and machinery - but threaten them with putting something else in power, a better dominant species, and they start loading up the nuclear missiles."

"The nuclear missiles," Frieda repeated, nodding excitedly.

"People are addicted to power," said Juan. "They need to control things - that's the bottom line. And even if they have adopted these hippie ideals as their latest fad... well, what difference will it make? They still use the Monroe Pill. They're still going to destroy the world." He put his hands on the back of Frieda's chair. "You want my opinion? The truth is, I find all this very difficult to believe. But my wife has made up her mind, and more often than not, her intuitions do prove correct." Frieda put a hand on Juan's and looked at him admiringly. "Besides," he continued. "My son deserves better than humanity. Frieda tells me I could be the father of the new dominant species... If there's any chance, however miniscule, I'll take it."

"We want our baby to be able to tell friend from foe, instantly and logically - instead of picking on petty differences," said Frieda. She was dreaming now, of the future she had seen in my mind. "We want him to be able to master his intelligence, without succumbing to a lust for power. To thrive on a shameless, natural existence. Like you."

Oh, what a wonderful life that would be. What a wonderful world. Mountains and forests, sunshine and harmony. No stresses. No hypocrisy. No heartbreak.

"Okay," I said. I loaded up the syringe. "It's a single injection into the uterus. Then we'll see if it's worked. Your embryo should dissolve, and then fuse with the tiger molecules in the solution and rebuild itself as a hybrid." I stopped. The words had come out of my mouth without any conscious thought, and as I repeated them back to myself I realized - to Alexander, to the Professor, to anybody, they would sound insane. "Should," I emphasized. "I'm not making any promises."

Frieda nodded. "I understand."

I gestured to my stool for her to sit, and then I knelt before her, syringe in hand. Frieda pulled the hem of her skirt up over her abdomen. I sensed Juan shifting uncomfortably. I felt for the uterus – there. I felt the foetus's head, not with my fingers but a new sense, something stronger, more reliable. I looked up at Frieda. "Last chance to say 'no'."

She shook her head. "Not a chance." She smiled.

With effort, I managed to draw my lips back into a matching grin. "Good for you."

Down went the plunger.

Behind us, Juan began to murmur, "I'll give you the address of this man, Randolph. He would be interested to take part in your work, as would his wife and girlfriends, I'm sure. And he could introduce you to others. We're not alone, Katrina. There are thousands of us, all over the globe. And if this turns out to be the miracle we've all been searching for - well, just think of the possibilities!"

"In this book, my colleague and I have demonstrated that man is an animal with some traits which make him superior to his fellow beasts, while the lack of others makes him inferior to and envious of his mammalian cousins. However, there is one conclusion I have drawn from our data which has not been included at the request of my co-author, on the grounds that it could be considered 'unscientific' and a product of my emotional state. Yet I feel it necessary to share. In our study of the lower mammals, we have witnessed and written on fatal battles between competing families, the ostracization of ailing specimens, mothers devouring their weak or disfigured young. Since man is an animal, I cannot help but conclude that the same impulses exist in my fellow researchers: I fear that this makes our motivations to 'improve' the human condition dubious indeed. Here, it seems that I and Doctor James Bai disagree."
~ Doctor Jean-Luc Tati, *Humanity and Parahumanity* (Author's Note, Unpublished)

BIOGRAPHY

Hannah Hoare lives and writes in North-East England. Her work has appeared in *Mechanics Institute Review*, *Open Pen*, the *Grindstone Literary Anthology*, and *Infinity Wanderers Magazine*. 'Parahumanity' is her first novel. Her website is: www.hannahhoare.co.uk

Printed in Great Britain
by Amazon